TM

i

ALSO BY NANCY BAXTER

THE HEARTLAND CHRONICLES:
BOOK I   *THE MOVERS*
BOOK II   *LORDS OF THE RIVERS*
BOOK III   *THE DREAM DIVIDED*

*GALLANT FOURTEENTH: THE STORY OF AN
INDIANA CIVIL WAR REGIMENT*

For Children

*HOOSIER FARMBOY IN LINCOLN'S ARMY:
THE CIVIL WAR LETTERS OF JOHN R. MCCLURE*

THE MIAMIS!

ALL THE BRIGHT SONS OF MORNING

Nancy Niblack Baxter

The cover of this book is based on an artistic reconstruction of the high mound at Cahokia done at Cahokia Mounds Site.

Guild Press of Indiana, Inc.
6000 Sunset Lane
Indianapolis, IN 46208

Library of Congress Number 92-082744

ISBN: 1-878208-14-4

CONTENTS

Chapter 1..7

Chapter 2..25

Chapter 3..41

Chapter 4..71

Chapter 5..103

Chapter 6..119

Chapter 7..139

Chapter 8..163

Chapter 9..189

Chapter 10..223

Chapter 11..253

Chapter 12..287

Chapter 13..315

Chapter 14..345

Chapter 15..383

Chapter 16..413

Chapter 17..425

ACKNOWLEDGEMENTS

I truly appreciate the aid of Frank Ettawageshik of the tribal council of the Odawas in northern Michigan for reading and critiquing this manuscript for woodland Indian lore and custom.

I am indebted in an important way to Bill Iseminger of Cahokia Mounds Site, one of the great historical resources of the world in Collinsville, Illinois, for reading and helping with material on the mound building culture.

AND YOUNG AS-ON-DA-KI SAID,

"Mother, tell us a tale of the Old Ones, of the times before the great-grandfathers' great-grandfathers."

"Ah, would that I could," said M-Tak-wa-pi-minji, "but that knowledge is lost. We do not know where we lived before we came to these woodlands. But it is said that we lived in cities, great cities, and worshipped the sun as Lord.

> 1785   Kekionga
> Indian Settlement,
> Ft. Wayne, Indiana

To Judy D.

Chapter One

Western North America, Circa 1100 A.D.

What a day to make the bones ache and the heart chill with cold! The old ones always say that the star spirits go into their lodges and shiver just as we do on cold winter days like this. There in the dome of the heavens, deep black and cold it must be in those spirit lodges where the stars group together– Monster, who also looks like a cup, the Running Deer, the Seven Little Maidens.

One time, so the Old Ones say, the Son of the West Wind, whose steady star we love the most and which rises almost overhead, came to earth and built himself a lodge. He made up his mind to stay in his lodge for many moons. One day he looked up and there was an old man sitting by his fire, a man dressed in heavy skins, with white face hair unlike us.

"Who are you?" the Son of the West Wind asked.

"I will not say," the visitor replied, "but I am going to sit here, and you must struggle with all your will with me. I will search your spirit. If I find weakness there, or fear, I will prevail. You will faint and fall." For four long moons the Son of the West Wind lived with the man, and the lodge grew day by day colder. The old man sat stiff by the fireside, never budging. His presence seemed to feed the cold, as wind feeds fire. West Wind's son went out bravely each day from the lodge. He found oak logs and beech logs and finally bone chips and made the fire burn. Never did it go out, never did the Son of the West Wind Nanaboozhoo fail to look into the eyes of the old man.

One morning the old man seemed to be in a heap. He was growing smaller and smaller. When Son of the West Wind went outside, he found the air warmer, the green of plants showing through the white of the ground. Going back inside his lodge, he looked for the old man, but all that remained was a chunk of ice by the ashes of the fire.

A voice said, "Nanaboozhoo of the strong will and courageous heart, you have won. But I will be back. Watch for me. When plants droop and die and the honking birds flap wings overhead, you will know I, Winter, am coming to test the will of men."

Nanaboozhoo left his lodge and flew away like the wind. "Winter will come each year now," he said. "Thus the will and strength of men will be tested, and we will know who is of strong, unconquerable spirit. The greatest of all conquests will be the battle with the cold, dead world of winter."

So now it is winter here in this fine, large lodge where we live, and we are before the fire staring down the old man with the white beard. To make the hours pass into moons, we tell stories, and since the wind and snow and ice howl outside like the lost spirits of dead warriors who have fallen off the path to the stars, I will tell the story of the Old Ones. You, my children come closer to the fire. You are old yourself now, too. And you, little ones, lie down on the wood bunks, put your heads out of the fur and listen. Never have I told all the story, no, never. I wish to do so now, though it takes several campfires to complete. Why? Perhaps because I am so very old. My teeth fall out, my knees wobble when I go to hunt on the windy plains. But my heart is strong, strong as the Son of the West Wind. I have faced down many of my own winters, so many I cannot count, even with the sacred counting stick. Perhaps it is better that way; some things only the heart can count anyway.

Now, as the sleet sends arrows at the side of the shelter as if the warriors of the renegade band have come to surprise us, now, as the short day has faded into grim twilight, let us go back to another winter, long ago, away east across the river shaped like a branching tree and yes, across the Father of Waters, too. Let me take you there with me, when I, and my birthland of Lakes-Like-a-Necklace was young.

At this very time of year, you can imagine us there, on a mild day in mid-winter. Oh, it was milder always there in the months of Bear Asleep and Northern Lights. Nearer to our Father the Sun it was, I guess, and when the warriors bear him from his Sun Lodge each morning, carrying him on a litter until at end of day they sweat like in a sweat lodge, the people of Lakes-Like-a-Necklace seemed nearer to his trail.

Still, it was cold enough in that far-off place, and think of a line of The People, all wearing skins of bear and elk, walking, moving their feet to the sound of drum and rattle. The drum goes sharply, Ah, ah, ah, ah! Sharp the drum is this morning, like the cracking of a tree in a storm, because it has sacred work to do and the Great Lord Sun to alert.

Rattle, rattle go the pebble stones in the shaman's gourd, the same, sharp beat that keeps us trudging. With dignity and glowing faces, we are going to the Hill of the Sun. It is not far; our camps are along Lake-of-the-Boulders only a thousand paces or so from the five sacred hills.

Still, I have left the camps reluctantly, though I will not for the world admit it. Fourteen turnings of the sun cycle had I experienced on that day, but I am not happy with myself. And I have had the vision time in the wild, but did not come back a man. Since I will tell you true in all this tale and hold nothing back, I say that one of the things I was thinking of was the cooking pot, and not the sacred time we would all soon have.

There was dried venison and squash in the pot last night, but my mother would not warm it up this morning. "No," she said, "This is purification time. We go to greet our lord with empty bellies and open hearts. No food for you."

Picture us, then, as we trudge along the path, our skin shoes black with the muck of these lakelands, the frost shining on the bent blackbird weeds. Springs bubble through little dishplates of ice by the side of the path; the pre-dawn wind tries to pull and tug at our robes, as it rattles the bare branches.

Picture me, kicking frosty little stones, completely out of the mood to notice the star spirits retreating and the pink dawn streaking a few black clouds, lighting up the three sacred hills. No, I am angry. I am hungry and–I am thinking I would divorce my mother and father if I could.

There, there he is on the Sun Hill—my father the spirit guide, the Sun Watcher. He stands, tall as a young birch, with

10

robes of beaver, sewn with bone needle close and true. We walk from the back of the hill, down the lane of the dead, gather in a half a circle near him, a little hurriedly, because we are all supposed to be there at the correct moment.

There he stands behind the sun finger post, the tall, old post of finest cedar, stripped of bark, burnished with sacred oil. He looks far off, away from the lake, to the hill our grandfathers have stripped of trees in the distant past, that we keep cleared with fire at all times—to the second hill—the Hill of The Sun Stops. There is the fore-mark post, there on the horizon. There he is pointing. And here I am hating him, against all law of the people towards a father and especially a sacred priest, but still I do.

"Asondaki" he chants. The people answer, "Asondaki." We are calling the rising sun god in a sacred hymn and as if in answer, over the two posts of the Old Ones, through the black streaks of midwinter clouds, come the first tremulous beams of the sun.

"Yes. Come at his call, that disgusting, deceitful, abusing father of mine," I chant my own little blasphemous song in my heart.

An old woman's voice, ecstatic and joyful, cries out the welcoming hymn:

> Oh, Father Sun, you are here, ah we oh.
> Come from your chamber in the East to greet us
> Dim you are and far away
> Return to your house of summer.
> Oh, Father Sun, stay near our lodges.

A wailing goes up from each person, louder than the sound of a hundred dirges. The drums grow louder as the sun rises, borne by the invisible warriors in the skies, then goes behind a gray-pink cloud.

I think that our lord the Sun is very weak indeed, his fire looks pale and yellow-white today, on this shortest day of the year. Probably it is because my father is such a miserable Sun

Watcher. And a miserable father who first slaps and then ignores me. And most of all a miserable husband to my indifferent mother, who all but abandoned me when I was born, but whom I still love beyond all reason.

I sigh and decide to try to participate. Bad things may happen to me if I do not welcome the Sun Lord on his winter shortest day. My toes may turn blue, parts of me shrivel up. Such things have happened.

Two men advance, bearing fire in a sacred earthen vessel. Ceremonial sticks have been laid the night before. We circle the firepit, ringed with consecrated field stones. Fire-bearer (my friend Shell-god), takes fire from the fire reed, kneels before my father, who touches him on the head and breast. As my friend retreats, he walks behind the circle and nudges me. "Hey, Bear Belly," he says in the smallest of whispers. I nudge back, hoping no one has seen us. Then Shell-god advances and sets fire to the mountain of sticks and logs, which blazes to repeat the color of our lord, the Sun.

Another fire-bearer comes to sprinkle herbs on the fire.

Now my father has been joined by his own brother Bo Jo, the Grand Shaman. This shaman's name is longer, but he is called Bo Jo by all in our tribe, who love him for his good works of healing and care. There is a slight tautness of spirit between Father and Bo Jo, just as if a bow has begun to be bent but is not tight. They are brothers, but they are not brothers of the spirit. Two holy priesthood offices there were with us then, shaman from the days of oldest of old and Sun Watcher, the new kind of priest, come from the time of our grandfathers.

My uncle Bo Jo steps a small step forward, standing before the sun finger. "Each of you now, my brothers, can come forward. Kneel by the sun post and ask of all the spirits forgiveness for ritual insults. Purify yourself, and as you do, you will give strength back to our lord the Sun and he can climb higher again to give us his blessing warmth and rays. It is between you alone and the spirits."

They all came, my family from the clan of the traders, we who take pride in making far journeys to get goods, my aunt the wife of Bo Jo, kneeling and sincerely begging from the Sun spirit or whatever other spirits might be nearby forgiveness for having laughed on the day of the Swallowing-of-the-Moon ceremony, after which she bore my lame cousin. Then there are several of my cousins and distant relatives asking for strength in the hunt, purification from having got close to menstrual blood or spilled semen at the wrong times of the moon. Finally, my own mother asking for freedom from punishment (which was no doubt living with my father) for having let the muskrat cross her path on the east side of the lake just after dawn, a very great ritual insult indeed, and for which the old shaman told her she would suffer the rest of her life.

These were ritual insults brought to light under the old shaman. But now my uncle, Bo Jo the great seer, had taught us to also look within for that sense of high man and womanhood that is real purity. To ask the spirits that we may have wisdom and strength to remember the unfortunate, love and care for husband or wife with true unselfishness.

And, shivering, I could only wish it was the other celebration–the summertime one, when the marker pole points further east and north, and we chanted the Sun Lord's arrival with flute and dances, feasting and bonfires. In the summertime there would be fish and whatever the hunters have brought— perhaps if we were lucky hump of buffalo or paw of bear, the delicacies that are best of all.

And in that summertime longest day, you could really feel a sense of worship. Sitting on that hill, if you squinted your eyes, The Sun Lord seemed to take the shape of a shining cross, or a pouring gourd, running out into the lake, to warm the grass beneath our bones, bring fertility to our squash and corn and pumpkins, bringing pleasurable light by which to see the sweet vines which fill the air with their fragrance, the beautiful girls who lower their eyes as we who had just finished manhood rites boldly look at them. Adoration! Joy and exultation in the day of our Lord Sun. He brings these good things

13

for us, only for us, and his eye seems to say, "Enjoy the goodness of life, my people."

But I have strayed. That was Long Sun Day. I was really talking of Short Sun Morning, the day of crisp cold when I was fourteen summers. We had all welcomed the sun that winter day and would have our own short ceremony on this cold day, so all sat down on the hills, wrapping blankets and skins about the knees against the rising wind. I was to do my part to beg the Lord to return to us and start his eastward trek. My anger had been forgotten; I was no longer hungry. Yes, I was important, young as I was, part of a group who showed reverence in a different way. I might as well speak truth.

I was a clown. A ritual clown. How can I tell you what we did? Four of us, all young but through with the manhood rites. We wore animal heads, masks. We had tails, too and–the symbol of manhood–a small club, tied between our legs. We cavorted, laughed, sang the priest songs backwards or in squeaky voices, anything to show fun. There had been too much ritual and seriousness, and our clowning showed the people that our Lord Sun wished us to be full people with as many sides as a carved effigy figure.

We pulled people into the dancing ring and danced silly dances. We acted like we wished to fornicate with old women and even men. Then we left, to lead the people to the camp again. Our rites were over. We had saved the sun.

Sad to tell, on this one day I speak of in winter we could not save ourselves. While we had been dancing these two hours on our Sun Hill, the Dune Devils had crept into the camp from their own winter camps to the north, had come with the first rays of dawn, blasphemers that they were to dishonor the Sun Lord so, and had come and destroyed our winter stores. They had spied on us and knew where we had stored our corn supply and roots and dried meat. So it was a sad day after all, caused, my father said, perhaps by the mischievous girl spirit of the moon, jealous that we had honored her lord and not her.

14

She is a child-woman sometimes, a grandmother other times, and this day she was a bad girl.

But that was not the end, and the next day, as we tried to forget the raid, throwing the chungky javelins in the frozen field, the young men by twos throwing out a rolling stone and betting on whose javelin would go the farthest after the rolling chungky, the young girls came near us.

Morning Glory sidled over to me, tossing her head just slightly, making her ear ornaments wobble. She wore white fur, and frost was on her hair, pinned up with a wooden hair pin. She must have just brushed against a tree.

"She looks beautiful, as usual. I do not see how anyone as lovely as a lake can act so much like a mud turtle," my friend Shell-god said softly. He was quiet and thoughtful, almost like a woman sometimes.

"It was your fault, you know," Morning Glory said, looking, but not looking at me.

"What do you mean?" I asked, picking up my javelin. Did she know how I had spent the sacred hour yesterday hating my father, the priest? Dishonored the law that way? I was not really troubled by it today. I had won the contest, and the others boys gave me small seashells, valuable translucent ones brought by the traders from the Mississippi mouth. I usually won the chungky contests; especially in this cold, crisp weather my aim was good.

Shell-god drifted away with a small frown on his face. He knew the torment this girl could inflict, and he did not like torment. He was a teller of stories and a master of the lore, and he tried to avoid conflict.

Morning Glory stood stock-still, looking past me. "The ritual clowning was not well done. You did not mimic the Sun Lord's coming out of the caves of the sea correctly and left out a part of the story."

"Who is to know "

"My father is a Wisdom Teacher, you know."

"You are a girl." This one kept her nose in the air like a prancing skunk since she had gone to the menstrual lodge-when we called the sun back last time, a year ago.

"My father has taught me the stories, too. I know the sun was once a man who climbed the tree of life into the night sky when all things were dark to try to find the father of the West Wind. I know that he asked something for men to keep them warm and was rewarded by the Maker of Stars by being given eternal fire himself–a spirit forever. But you did not tell the part where he steals the fire from the firekeeper's daughters, how he lied."

I turned away from the game and spoke to her in a low voice. It did not do to let the other young men see you talking to a girl, even the daughter of the Wisdom Teacher. "Listen to me, Morning Glory. I did forget that part. But there are many lines to recall. It took me almost a year to know all the ceremonial stories "

"That is not good enough. If you leave one thing out, it offends the spirits and spoils the next few moons for all of us. They wish all the things that honor them to be perfect. So you have offended the Sun Lord "

"I think it was the Moon Maiden "

"Some spirit was offended. And the Dune Devils came and took our corn. And you did it." She was silent. For a moment I thought of how she looked last summer, when she wore the ceremonial morning glories in her hair. Morning glories, which turned to the sun. Sacred flowers, sacred young woman. With a tongue like a snake.

The other young men had drifted away; the two of us walked towards the cooking fires of the camp. "That is not all," she said in that same haughty voice. "We all know your mother disobeyed strong animal taboo when she was pregnant with you."

"I cannot deny that. But the shaman has begged the spirits for forgiveness for this impurity."

"The spirits have not forgiven. You are marked." She was tossing the words back over her shoulder, as if she could not

16

stand to be by me. My heart, which had been exultant at winning the chungky game, just fell like a rock in a stream.

"Marked?"

"You know it. You are not a man but a baby who chews too much on corn porridge. No one else here has so much " she gestured in a vague way and hurried into her own lodge. She was pointing to my stomach. I was marked. I was . . . well, I may as well say it since I am telling you all things true I was round. Heavy. Fat. The girls called me Bear Belly. The huge, round, belly of the bear before he goes into his winter cave, swollen high with fat. And since hardly anyone was fat in the village or other villages around for that matter, except perhaps a very old man, they all said I was marked.

Why was I fat? I do not know, except that I liked above all else to eat. Ever since I was toddling around just off the cradle board, I ate things. Like every child, my world was wrapped up in my mother, and she paid me little heed. She was interested only in talking to her sisters as they made mulberry fiber skirts or hoed the corn, and she often acted as if I did not exist. Perhaps it was because of the taboo trouble before my birth, but she did not seem to want me about. In those days I was not angry, of course; I was too young for that. I was only pained.

I was like the fledgling bird kicked out of the nest too soon, and I was on my own almost as soon as I could talk. It felt good to fill my belly with the mush and maple syrup, the dried, smoked deer meat, the pumpkin stew. So I went always to the cooking pots, begging for food from all over the village as I made my own way about the lodges. And I grew larger and rounder and soon everyone thought of me that way and I could not conceive of myself except as Bear Belly the village clown, the odd one in the litter, the weak little fat man.

I never knew whether my mother did not like me because the spirits punished her for violating the ritual rule, or just because I caused her so much trouble at my birth. The avoidance of muskrats was very strong in our village, stronger than forgetting to ask forgiveness of a rabbit when you shot the

17

bow at him, or eating possum meat when the Grandmother Moon is full, or the new taboo of walking on the avenue of the Sun Watcher when it is not sacred celebration time. My father had put that one in himself, and he told us that the Lord Sun had told him that the way to the sacred watching poles and horizon lines was under his control.

You could get into real trouble, get really sick if you did not abide strictly by taboos. There you would be, lying sick with the strong stomach fever right out of the sky, so it seemed, and you might not know, probably did not know, which taboos you, or your parents had violated. Well, you know about taboos. I do not need to tell you. But in our village, among the people of Lakes-Like-a-Necklace, muskrat taboo was the worst. Perhaps it was because muskrats are a vile animal, edible by us only in times of famine. All we know is the spirits deal the taboos, throwing them as boys throw round rocks in play on sandy ground. So said the shaman to my mother, when she was in early childbed labor for me and when she lay in awful pain, so unlike most of the women who squat to have their children on the floor of the lodge and bring them forth easily.

"What have you done to displease the spirits?" he growled at her. This was the old shaman, not Bo Jo. She writhed and cried and said she did not know what she had done, and truly I think she told true because she had forgotten what had happened at the pond, had perhaps pushed it out of her mind completely. But finally she said she thought it was animal taboo, and the shaman cried out, "Muskrat!" She nodded, then screamed in pain again.

But the shaman said they would await the events and deal with the spirit problem later. He called the herb woman, who came and brought periwinkle and other things to make me come and bring peace to my mother, and in the spirits' good time I made my entrance into the world of The People.

But my mother's troubles did not stop. She had birthing fever; they thought she would die of it. The shaman came back into the lodge to do the spirit travel ceremony. He was a rough old traveler, this shaman before Bo Jo. Often had he travelled up the tree of life which leads to the spirit world. He must have had bumps on his knees from spirit bark.

So my mother told me many times, as she bitterly talked of her troubles. At least it meant she was speaking to me, and that was something. She lay there, she said, in the darkness, with a son who had seen just one moon. The fire in the firepit blazed, for it was a chilly night just after the harvest.

The Shaman first explained the problem, using the lore of our people. "The spirits are wise, all wise. They send laws for all men to observe. When the earth emerged from the great sea, when Earth Mother came in a boat with all the animals and sat on the back of the turtle, when the otter dove to the bottom and got just a chunk of land to start the formation of the island of earth, then the spirits organized the laws of the world.

"Certain things we can do, " the shaman said, "We can observe the coming of the Lord Sun and Grandmother Moon, revere the beasts of the forests and know their spirits, honor the dead. Otherwise we upset the balance that the great island of earth has. The spirits are shocked, offended, and this is reflected in our own bodies. Sickness. Mental illness. Unhappiness."

My mother knew all this. She just ached and sweated and feared she would die. What would the shaman do? Would he have a dream which would reveal the particular offended muskrat spirit and the punishment or oblation she must do to get better? Would he tell her that there was also an offending object in her stomach and suck on it to remove the small pellet or whatever it was, and then produce it for all her fearful relatives to see? No, this time the shaman did the tree-climbing ceremony. In spirit he went into a trance and climbed the big tree which leads from earth to sky to find out what muskrat was offended and what ought to be done.

He sat on the floor in a corner, smoking his ceremonial pipe, his medicine bag between his knees. His assistant, my friend Shell-god's father was his guide, to keep his body safe while his spirit journeyed into the great world of spirits. Tobacco smoke wreathed about, mixing with the smoke of the fire pit. (My mother always had a dirty lodge and in the best of times our lodge was smoky. Now that she was ill it was filled with choking smoke.)

"I am passing through the long passage, the trail which has no end, past the lakes like necklaces, the small and twin ones, the little pond ones, to the large one north and east. Now to the black bog swamps. I see their grass, like a sea, brown now with coming winter. On a rise in the swamp grows the sacred tree of life which leads to the realm of the spirits. Its branches are high above the ground, higher than an oak of many generations, but one many climb in spirit if one is pure, as I am. Sacred smoke, help me climb," he puffed. "Ah, ah, there is trouble here, an angry bear does not wish me to climb, to find out this poor woman's trouble. Ah, ah." The helper, father of my friend, holds the shaman's body down as his legs thrash about, his arms flail. He is in spiritual combat with the angry powers of the spirit world.

"I have pursued him, saying my quest is just. He lets me climb, up, up, limb after limb." He is sweating with exertion. "Now, off one of the utmost branches I see a tunnel of light. Although I am afraid, I shall enter it, to save this young mother, Poplar Leaves. Someone is coming, someone. . . " He is silent. Nothing more is said. We all wait expectantly. My mother's mother mops her daughter's brow with a soft deer-skin soaked in creek water.

The shaman has dropped his pipe. No one in the winter shelter has gotten up to throw logs on the fire, so it has died and even the smoke has thinned out. It is cold; my mother shakes. The shaman sits up, rubs ashes off his ceremonial garment and speaks. "The spirit of a muskrat came to me, strongest of taboos. He is offended by Poplar Leaves." Coolly he looks at my mother, weak on her pallet.

"How does he say I have offended him?" she asks.

"Only you know that. He did not tell me," the shaman says. "Think, think. You must be exact. It must have been when you were heavy with this child," his glancing gesture involves me, in the arms of my grandmother. I have begun to snuffle and whimper, causing disruption in the sacred ceremony. The shaman stands tall, his long robe, embroidered with signs of the sun, moon and sacred animals, falling to his feet.

"Think, woman! You must free yourself of guilt. The spirits will give you power to do so."

The communicator, my friend's father, speaks. "The shaman has taken a dangerous journey into the world of the spirits. He could have been damaged himself, even lost his life, as he extends his spirit out of his body. He has done this for you. Now you, in kind, must exert yourself. Think! How exactly did you break the taboo?"

My mother breathes a sigh of recognition. "Yes," she says. "I went to the pond to wash the clothes. I see the muskrat in my mind."

The shaman draws near. His voice is like a rasping tool. "Where was he? Tell truth."

"On the left."

"I thought so. The spirit guide told me there was grave insult here. You have not fully repented, I see."

She had gone to wash garments at the pond in the mists of early morning and she had seen, oh yes, she confessed she had seen the muskrat there. She should have turned, right then and returned to the summer shelter, especially since he was on her left. But she was hurrying. My father was coming in from a journey, and there was much to do for the evening feast and dancing. And he often yelled at her if she was not prepared with what he needed.

She skirted wide, but she did not avoid the animal, and he ran and crossed her path. And so, she had broken the rule of ritual avoidance, offended the spirits who provide laws for us in the universe of order and tell us what we should do and especially what we should not do. She had pushed it out of her mind, completely. Perhaps she was a little bit of a non-

21

believer. My mother quivered on her pallet. It was all so much, the sickness and now the insult to the spirit.

"I will admit my mistake. I will ask to be forgiven. Make the spirit of the muskrat leave."

"I cannot do that. You will have to make your own peace. He seemed very angry to me when I grappled with him there in the spirit world. Perhaps I can intercede for you. Make another trip if you do not find absolution. It could take a year. It could take ten."

It took ten. At least my mother thought so. Bad things kept happening, and poor weak woman that she was, so dependent on her sisters for her thoughts, she believedthat the spirit of the muskrat was still angry and causing trouble. Her sisters told her so. Her husband was too busy becoming Sun Watcher to take the time to discuss it. And so, every time she looked at me, following her about whining and unhappy, she remembered the blight the spirit world had placed on her. She was barren ever after that, in fact her woman's bleeding came on and never stopped again, not when the Grandmother Moon smiled full or when she hid and showed only the edge of her face in a crescent. The bleeding was a real mark of disfavor that the whole tribe knew about, though the elders ruled she did not need to stay in the lodge of the monthly time; she could go out amongst us. My mother lived in pain, too, on and off for the rest of her life.

And so did I, unfortunate result of the connection with the frowning spirit world. And thus it was that when the beautiful Morning Glory scorned me and told me I had not done well in the ceremonies, the pain hit me in the same spot that my mother's scorn had wounded. The scab was broken again, and I thought that never would it heal, always would I ache, fat clown with a poor sense of manhood that I was.

And perhaps the spirit of the very malignant muskrat did seek revenge on my mother, as the shaman said. All I know is, my father once told me that the shaman charged high, very high for his services in the case. He took my father's pink-and-white-edged conch shell from the far-away lands of Always Summer.

Who am I to judge about the muskrat? They called me a doubter, with too many odd ideas and a mouth as big as a bass's, among the other things they said. I do not think I was a real doubter, though, but more of a curious cat. All of those little trips around the camp, with no mother to worry me until it was time to put me into my pallet and forget about me for the night, awoke my mind. All I know is that from the time I can remember I wanted to know things. How does the blue-bird go into the air with his wings? Why do we not do so? Why does the snowflake have thousands of gentle crystals while the hail-flake has dots of ice? When my uncle Bo Jo trained me for my quest in the wild, I asked him hundreds of questions. Why does the rattlesnake hate us and wish to give us poison in his fang while the larger blacksnake is our friend? Is water in the cloud? Is a spirit in there too? Does the spirit get wet?

Finally my uncle Bo Jo laughed and said we had enough questions for ten moons-in-the-wild. But he had answered patiently best he knew, for he was a wise and careful shaman, a real messenger of the spirits, who brought good to all. Especially me. He and the gentle Shell-god were my only friends. Bo Jo was my counselor, the reason, really I could live and grow in all those years with mockery and disregard as my daily bread from all the sides of the village. Especially so after the moon-in-the-wild, when I got scared out there alone with only an axe and a fire-flint. And, I grew cold when it rained three days, and sick and coughed so hard I came back without any vision and the village heaped scorn on me like dirt on a pile of fish offal. And my uncle only said, "Do not take it hard, my young one. You will get your real name when it is time. The spirits may have planned a special testing time for you. They will give the name." I looked at him curiously, and he patted me, and after a while, I could walk the paths again, though never in peace.

It was about this time, listening to the harsh taunts of my father when I did not complete my moon-in-the-wild, that my dull uncomprehending child's pain turned to anger–anger which became a slow, smoky fire that smothered out love and trust. I came to trust no one but Bo Jo. And he loved me, I know, as a son.

And so, as he watched me pine in the weeks after the sun ceremony, drooping, refusing to play at chungky or anything else, he came to me.

"What is the matter?" he asked, and I told him of Morning Glory and how she blamed me for the taking of the corn, so that now we all had to eat whatever miserable nuts and greens we could find under the snow with the rabbits the hunters brought back.

"Well, do not fret. Old Man Winter stays long this season. But soon the signs of spring will come. You need new sights, new tests to make you stretch your young limbs and young spirit.

"You are fourteen summers old. We are members of the trader clan and you have not as yet been on the trading voyage all men must make. It is time. Be ready to go with me to the Place of Rivers Meeting, Tippecanoe."

I told him I would like that, and when I saw Shell-god, I told him I would be going on my first man's trading trip to the fine town when spring came. Shell-god patted me on the back and said to get him a new rattle, if I found a special one amidst the stalls of the traders. And when I met Morning Glory on the trail the next day, I sniffed a little and put my nose in the air, too.

Chapter 2

And so, on a beautiful morning in early spring of that year when I was fourteen summers, as the blood root flowers were just beginning to peek through last fall's leaves and orange-breasted birds were hopping about, we took to our canoe.

The lake was as smooth as could be; the swelling yellow buds of willow trees were reflected in its waters as we pushed off from shore. We paddled through mists which rose in swirls from off the shore and the creeks which emptied into our Lake-of-the-Boulders. Many are the rivers in that fair land; you would rejoice to see so many. We were going to the Place of Rivers Meeting not very far from our home—one day's travel it was more or less in a canoe.

Here is how we went. Through the morning mist to the "Lost Lake" beyond ours, then down a narrow creek, carrying the canoe sometimes, till we reached Tippecanoe River. We went on shore and ate our dried deer meat and corn bread and watched eagles soar, majestic and serene. I remember well that day.

"Like the Bird of Thunder," I murmured. Often we ritual clowns mimicked the flying of the eagle, swooping, re-creating myths about this king of birds.

"No, the Bird of Thunder is much larger, you know that."

The sun was high; we would wait an hour to proceed so we did not sweat in the canoe. Bo Jo leaned back against a tree. "Tell me the story again," I said to him. I loved to hear Bo Jo tell the stories of the Old Ones. His words were chosen deliberately, each like a pebble in the clear water of a stream, his voice almost caressing the words, singing a song of meaning for all the people.

"Well, and in the old days you know that almost all the world was under water, a giant sea. This was before Earth Mother came in the canoe and sent the animals to make dry land for us. The Thunderbeings reigned over the world of oceans. They were giants. When they died they took wings, huge wings and became huge spirits. The thunder comes from

25

their mouths. There are only four giant ones left now—a blue one, a red one, a yellow one and a huge black one and they rule the four cardinal directions of the earth. Their children are like them, but weaker. When the thunder comes, you can hear the children of the Birds of Thunder, repeating their fathers' rolling, clapping voices, off, off all the way to the horizon." He was silent, contemplative. "They are the strongest of the voices of nature. They teach us truth and honesty—to keep our hearts single on the path of life."

There were catfish jumping in the river—they would be good to catch and cook for dinner at the camp not far from the Place of Rivers Meeting. "Tell me again what the Birds of Thunder look like."

Bo Jo looked at me narrowly, and a smile twitched at the corners of his mouth. He was indulging me, amusing his nephew because I, and all the boys in the village, had heard these stories over and over.

"They have clouds around them, no specific bodies because they are spirit but the wings—the wings have four joints. They move with the deliberation of justice and power and can blind you if you ask them to favor you with a sacred vision and you come to it impure."

This sort of talk made me impatient lately. "But how can one know, Uncle, what is impure? There are so many things."

"No. I do not mean that," my uncle said, taking out his pipe.

"Of course there are the spirit taboos. But purity is about the path of life. The Birds of Thunder point the tips of their wings at the path of life for each soul. They ask, when their voices roll off the hills, `Are you walking in union with nature or are you treading the path of riches?' They turn their backs on the path of riches and power." I changed the subject. "What will we see at the Place of Rivers Meeting?"

My uncle stood up and moved towards a nearby brook to take a drink. "Much that the Birds of Thunder might like and much that they would not like," he said in a voice that made me know there would not be more discussion on the subject.

I did not care if he spoke at all; it was such a relief to be away from the bickering and unpleasantness in the home of my father and mother.

What we did see at the Place of Rivers Meeting opened my eyes, I tell you true. Boy that I was from the tiniest of villages, now I was where many folk lived, tall and sturdy folk of our kind but different. When we beached the canoe I could see at once what a marvel their town was. It had been built where the Tippecanoe goes into the Ouabache—the long river with white stones along its shores. All about were fishing weirs to stop and catch the catfish and pike. Men were in canoes bringing them in. On shore I could see women cleaning pikefish as long as a man. Children on this warm day ran naked. A group of them were pulling mussels from the edge of the river, opening them and putting the sweet meat into a clay bowl. What a feast we would have tonight if they observed the customary sharing! From the woodlands behind the village a group of young men about my age had come in with a deer tied by the legs on a carrying stick. My mouth began to water. Tender young deer, skewered on a stick with onions and roasted over the coals—but there I was, at it again. Thinking of my stomach, I sighed. I was trying not to eat so much and think of food so much. Since the time last winter, when Morning Glory had mocked me to my face—I would show her! Because of the corn being gone, I seemed a little slimmer to myself, more like a wolf, well, maybe a fat wolf.

"Look, Uncle," I cried. "This marvelous fence! It protects better than any I have seen." I was wondering at the stockade, huge posts of oak dug three feet into the ground, placed so close to each other that an awl needle would not have been able to go between them. There were doors with thong closures, also tight and well made. And holes for firing arrows out. The Dune Devils would not attack here, or if they did they

27

would get their come-uppance, sure enough. I imagined them all, lying dead in rows before the walls of this town. It made me happy, I tell you. We had not liked having to dig for dandelions under the snow because they took our corn.

Escorted by barking dogs and cavorting children, we came into the village itself. It was not a few miserable shelters of sticks bound and covered with branches and bark like ours at the Lake-of-the-Boulders. Oh no! These were houses, real houses, five strides on all sides. Let me tell you about them, because they are so different from what you know.

The houses are of stripped trees, young walnuts because their wood is hardest, brought into the village and set in post holes dug deep. The tops were bound together, first the four corner ones, then the other ones, at the top of the house. These are tied in a bundle at the housetop with split canes of the type which grow everywhere in the riverlands there. So the whole house has the look of a round-top woven basket.

But it was not enough for the builders of the Place of River Meeting to have just houses made of wood. They made mud daub for the walls, reinforcing the mud with crushed pieces of pottery and ground-up vines for binding. The whole village would come together, in fact I saw them doing this that very day, to build the house of one of the townsmen.

The builders were almost finished, and I peeked through the door. Women in their reed skirts, men in the same, were kneeling, digging a pit, a firepit with smoke able to go out an opening they made in the roof, able to be closed when they did not wish fire or it rained. The roof they were thatching with turf and straw intermixed, and placing over all they placed mats of woven cane and cattail leaves. Each person had a summer and winter house—the summer one being a pavilion with no sides, where all slept amidst cool breezes. But I did not see how they avoided being tormented by bugs. My own village's summer lodges had thin sides, which I thought were better protection from the pesky insects. You could keep a small fire going, shut everything up, and swat what was inside into bug fry cakes.

All of these houses were in rows, oriented to the cardinal points, all neatly set out with paths between the house rows— roads they called them.

At the end of the central road was a mound like our sacred sun mound, but there was a house on it!

"Why, who inhabits that?" I asked.

"You will find out soon enough," my uncle said, shrugging his shoulders. A man had come from the house on the mound and surveyed us solemnly.

"The town chieftain will welcome us." My uncle raised his hands to show we came in peace. The old man was a giant, at least he seemed so to me, not as tall as the thunder people who carved out the canyons and riverbeds of the world before the floods, but almost two feet taller than any man I had seen, even among our kind who are always tall. His face was wizened; he was an old chieftain, that is sure. He recalled my uncle as one of the trading clan of the villages of Lakes-Like-a-Necklace. As we walked along the road, he said, "Many traders are in town today for the spring bargaining. You will find the bargains good this season."

My uncle nodded.

"The spirits of the gateposts will be pleased if you honor us with your presence tonight," the chieftain said.

"We had planned to camp beyond the walls," my uncle said, but smiling, added "We accept your offer. We do not wish to dishonor the spirits of the gatepost."

Uncle and I left the village to go to the riverbank, where traders stayed. They had their wares displayed in small shelters thatched with cane. There were furs, otter and beaver mostly, nicely tanned, ready to sew into winter garments. Buffalo skins from the animals west of the Father of Waters. They made good bed coverings on chilly nights. Obsidian tools from the south and west. Fine tools they were too, chipping and smoothing knives for making house posts, chopping axes, adzes. There was a man with chunks of black rock, so shiny they looked like the precious stones the old women talk about in the tales of the spirit gods. I stared at the two men who had laid the rocks out on a log. They wore the short skirts of the people of the Illinois region, with shawls about their shoulders caught up with bright pins. The pins were painted with the serpent god of the southern people.

They asked me a question I did not understand; my uncle, who had been taught middle-river traders' dialect, translated.

"They want to know if you like the rocks."

"They are very pretty. So black they look like the sky before the stars were born." The black chunks were too big to hold in the hand very easily, but I stroked one of them. A dark, dusky powder rubbed off.

"Where did this come from?" I wanted to know. "Truly it seems as if the black Bird of Thunder must have dropped it when he had to go up the path—" I laughed and ducked my head, realizing I might have been blaspheming. The spirits did not make trips to the woods.

The man spoke, using gestures showing me that it had come out of the ground.

"It was found under the hills," Uncle said. "When they dug to move dirt for a priest's mound, they found it in an outcropping. They believe it is magic, for it burns like wood."

"Ah, a magic fire stone," I said. Suddenly I wanted it very much.

"Would they take—two big catfish for it?"

My uncle spoke to them. They nodded their agreement, and I smiled weakly. Now I had made my bargain, where would I get the catfish? I could catch them in the weirs—well, that would be too much trouble. Besides, I did not want to leave this fascinating town for even an hour. It was the most interesting sight my fourteen-summers-old eyes had ever beheld.

Of course, I had seen some young maidens down by the water. Perhaps I could get them to give me a couple of fish. I had to have that magic fire rock; my hand burned for it, I would walk over bramble bushes, swallow pebbles, look a bear in the eye for it—what I would not do was to go out and fish the weir. That would be too much trouble.

The maidens were out in a clearing throwing a set of deerskin balls about. Two balls were tied together with a string and you had to catch both on the fly. It was their way of mocking males. I pretended not to notice and holding my head high, advanced to the largest girl. "Hey, girl, I am a stranger."

"Who cannot see that?" the girl, tall with light brown hair, answered. Her eyes were merry from the game; perspiration stood on her lip. It had turned into one of those late afternoons when the weather is warm, very warm. Old Man Winter had really melted into a blob.

"I noticed you were netting fish from the river earlier today. I would like to ask two of them of you."

The other girls gathered around. They had slightly mocking looks on their faces, as if they had just been waiting for a young man of their age to come up.

"Brave youth," the tall girl said, looking me in the eye, "why do you want these fish?"

"You do not need to know—it is the law of hospitality that I should get them."

"And so it is," said another voice from behind. I turned to see a short girl with protruding teeth. She had the balls in her hand and was swinging them around as she came up to me. "You are marked," she said. She pointed to my stomach, which happened to be growling at the moment. Some herb on the meat must not have agreed—my thought was cut off.

31

"The wind god must have got into his stomach," said Teeth-Sticking-Out. It was one thing when the pretty girls teased me, but this ugly one was too much to bear.

"What is it to you? Do the great stars care? Where are the fish?" I demanded.

The tall girl had turned and walked away, returning to throw two fish in my face. I picked them up with as much dignity as I could muster and walked away, laughter floating behind me in the grove, withering me like a hot wind. Someday I would show them, someday. The way they threw the balls—they way they jeered. There and then I made up my mind that I would be a hero someday and stop these girls' laughter in their throats. Wind-in-the-Stomach. Bear Belly. Someday, some way, I would not be laughed at.

Finally, the rock was mine and I walked about carrying it in both hands. My uncle called to me, saying it was time for us to set up our own booth. We had flints to trade—flints my trading clan had gotten by being go-between for the flint pit peoples to the east. "Finest flints" we began to call, as other men came along the avenue of trade.

From all over they came—all the way from the Stony Mountains, bringing their own sandstone tools. After we got to know them, trading our flints, they took us aside, behind an elm tree and showed us a basket with a deerskin in it. Wrapped in the skin were a few, carefully hidden necklaces made of green-blue stones that made me marvel at their beauty.

"Why, who would wear these?" I asked, my eyes wide.

"In many towns the Male Sun wears these."

"The male sun?" I did not know the term.

"The chieftain. In his sacred house he wears them over his white robe. On the high days, people kneel at his feet."

I turned aside to laugh a little at such an idea. My father was Sun Watcher. If he wore a white robe (and who could find such a thing?) my uncle would mock him, pointing the finger of scorn at him for being a "Puff Ball Head." Perhaps the Male Sun was a shaman. If my uncle, or even the old shaman, who had much power of fear over the people, had worn jewels, the band of elders would reprimand him, perhaps caused a shunning. Nobody liked a big head,with too much pride over the rest of us. We would not stand for it in the woods. Fall on our faces? It was not to be conceived of. Where were such places? New ideas began fermenting in my mind.

I walked the traders' lane and saw the other things—many fine pots the women in the village had made—with serpent lines to represent the spirit of the land which goes underground and then appears in spring bringing new life, and copper adornments and many, many pipes for tobacco.

But as we left to go to the house of the old one, the maidens came back from their play in the meadow.

"Ah, here is Wind-in-the-Stomach," said the one with her teeth sticking out. I pretended not to notice, walking with dignity, carrying our flints wrapped in deerskin like some sacred objects on a festival day.

"Perhaps he will play his stomach like a drum tonight at the corn planting celebration. It is big enough." The laughter through which I walked was as harsh as crows' calls. I held my head up higher. Before I knew it, I fell suddenly, hard. Someone had put a foot out and tripped me. It had to be Teeth-Sticking-Out. I saw her shrewd eyes out of the corner of my eye. Was there no end to my troubles with girls?

The incident that happened next made me feel glummer yet. Uncle and I returned to the home of the giant chieftain and took a pipe with him. That was indeed fine—he had a row of effigy pipes on the stone stand in the corner where he kept his medicine things. I admired the fine pipes of the best clay. Some had heads of wolves, some heads of wildcats, some animals from the people's tales of old. He offered us tobacco; we sat and watched the smoke rise to please both us and the spirits. But afterwards he had us march with him up that main road of the town to the house on the mound. Somehow it seemed odd to me to have a house on a mound. Was it for the spirits to live in? For the Sun Lord when he spent a brief time on earth when the sun stopped in the sky for a few days? A breeze wafted an odd smell to us as we approached. It was the smell of death.

The giant chief bowed to the ground as we reached the door. He touched his head and his heart to show great reverence. Well he should have. There on scaffolding in the middle of the small house were the bodies of three chieftains.

My uncle gestured to me to bow also to the ground. It was hard because the smell was making me sick. There are lots of smells in the world and camp that make one walk aside. I will not say, of course, that they are bad; they are part of nature just as perfumed blossoms are, but they do make one walk aside: the smell of the two-week-old carrion the bird is pecking at by the side of the path. The smell of the bear in heat (may you never smell it because you may not live to tell the tale). The smell of crude folk who do not bury their ordure near the camp but let it pile up near the camp, attracting flies. The smell of the skunk angered two feet from you; the crazy man who does not wash for a year. But the smell of that dead house was harder to bear than any of these for me as I lay on my haunches, my nose on the ground before the dead chieftains.

Do not clamor to know what they looked like; I will tell you. Their bodies were wizened and shrunk; the attendants of the dead had put powders on them to dry and desiccate their flesh. One, the chieftain said, was a hundred years old and was but a skeleton with a covering of cracked dry skin; another had been put to rest sixty years ago. His flesh was hanging on the rib bones like a deerskin sack hangs and his toenails protruded from his skeleton toes, yellow, cracked, odd. I could not help but think of him walking the road outside. The third dead king was the father of this chieftain. So he told us in hushed tones when my uncle asked who the great personages were, although we might have guessed, because this particular skeleton was as tall and straight as an arrow, too. But its thigh bone was smashed. I couldn't help but stare at it.

"Watcher of Eagles, my father," said the giant chieftain. "The wild rice people to the northwest were our enemies then and came and raided and they smashed my father's thigh with a club. He lay in agony and though the shaman went on a spirit journey for him, he died anyway." He sighed. "I had a copper neckpiece at that time and the shaman took it. I almost smashed his thigh in return." He looked up quickly and you could see he wanted to take back what he just said lest it desecrate the place of the dead. "We had five days of feasting while the Sun Watcher and others prepared the body. They carried it here, up the avenue—" he gestured outside. "All these honored dead have gone to join the Sun. Their spirits ride the day with him."

As we left the House of the Dead, I whispered to my uncle, "Why do they keep the bodies out so?" We had always dug small holes for our dead relatives, then mounded up dirt around them so the animals would not offend the corpses. Over all we put the stones of the field and more dirt.

"They are powerful men. The villagers are afraid their medicine will extend beyond the grave. The spirits may harm or help, as they wish. If their bodies are nearby, they can be controlled, at least."

"They are his ancestors?" I asked, gesturing over my shoulder towards the house we had just left. The chieftain walked in solemn silence before us.

My uncle nodded.

"Are the chieftains not chosen by the elders in council?" Shaking his head a little sadly, my uncle gestured for me to be quiet. Just then the girls ran by, heading for the evening feast. This time they did not even glance at me, and one bumped my shoulder and did not beg pardon. It was as if I were a groundhog. In fact, I thought with rue, that is probably how they saw me.

After the feast of catfish and venison stew, my spirits rose a little. Still, as the star of evening rose from the home of Nanaboozhoo, behind the great nests of the Birds of Thunder, I felt something burning in my stomach. It was not just the herbs of our mid-day meal gone mad, but more. The girls had brought it to my mind, but I had really felt this way for a long time, though I did not acknowledge my feeling. It was my shame crying out to me. I was not a man, but something deformed. Seeing the honored dead—the chieftains so revered as heroes that their bodies were preserved whole for all to see—that made my insignificance seem more keen. What worthy deed on all this earth had I done? I could not even stay in the woods for my manhood quest. No one would care if I died (well, perhaps Bo Jo). All looked on me with either indifference or scorn. My parents at this very minute were in the home camp either screaming at each other or not speaking, but certainly not thinking of me—never. Somehow, though, all this did not make me discouraged as it usually did; instead, it kindled my rage and ambition.

The maidens sat in the shadows as the feasting finished and the fire burned brighter. Dances began, the men circling. When they finished it was the time of sacred drumming, and music, with a flute of such artistry as I had never seen. "Oh, oh, oh–tweeedle eele, eee," it sang, in imitation of a birdsong. Then the traders of the northwest, those who had brought the wild rice grains, raised their hands to bring us to solemn attention. "Wait a moment," their deeply lined, brown palms seemed to say. "We have something fine to add to the celebration." Two of them went into the woodlands which fringed the clearing. Soon the two returned, bringing with them a great drum. It was large enough that two men had to carry its bulk, although it had fit in their canoe well enough.

The girls caught sight of me across the firelight, and although they risked being rebuked for very bad manners, they smirked behind their hands at me. This time I did not look haughty. I stared moodily into the flames. But the fire of anger and frustration burned deeply, like a firecoal in my stomach. My newly emerged manhood was at stake.

The drum was beautiful, the most wonderful drum I had ever seen. Truly these people were masters of the buffalo skin drum. They had prepared the rawhide to perfection, stretched it taut and scraped it until it was as tight and resonant as the skies when the Thunderbird babies are ready to begin their rumble chants.

36

It was dressed almost as perfectly as a woman, in woven fabric, painted with the sacred symbols, woodpeckers, human figures in the antler headdress of the shaman, serpentine, the circular whorls of our Lord the Sun. Fringes of the hair of the dead decorated it, looped and tied in several places.

The drumming began, one man drumming on each side with rawhide covered drumsticks. The sound was not deep bass but richly high. It was a drum with a voice that had just changed to manhood, like mine, not an old man's croak, like so many had. "Boom, boom–boom, boom": beats paired together. It began softly, almost thoughtfully, like a prayer chant. Then it rose, louder, with affirmation. All beats equal strength, strong, confident. "Boom, boom, boom, boom, boom." On and on it went in the spring evening, echoing off the cliffs of the rivers around us, filling our minds, pulsating in our blood streams until it joined the very rhythm of our hearts, connecting us with the spirit world, explaining the mysteries of life. "LIFE-has-mean-ing" "LOVE-the-spirits!" So the drum said, as that fire crackled and the spring darkness wrapped the village round like a soft mantle made of the skin of a fawn.

Then the beat died away and all was still. A sapling log popped loudly, sending sparks into the enchantment of the enraptured circle. One of the northern men who held the drum held up the drumstick. Odd—he was looking at me.

"This one is chosen. He is to play this drum."

I could hardly believe what I heard. I? Play the huge sacred drum? I had played the shaman's drum, learned its meaning in my training time. But those who played the ceremonial drum had to be appointed in a dream. They had to make their own drums, setting out on a quest. Seek the mighty buffalo or other tough-skinned beast for the skin–commune with the spirits until they were sanctified enough. I did not understand.

The taller of the northern men, one who looked almost black in complexion, fixed me with his eye. "I have seen this one in a dream. He is chosen of the spirits to play this drum."

I looked at my uncle, and he nodded so slightly no one but I could tell. I rose slowly and went to the drum as the two men moved aside. Every eye in the circle was on me, as I took up the drumstick, its end covered in rawhide, and leaned over the drum.

Above me, through the clearing in the trees the moon was rising, not quite full, but amazingly beautiful and I was conscious of it behind me. I began.

I do not know if it was the influence of the Grandmother of us all (who is at one and the same time the young maiden she once was) living amidst the council fires of the moon, I do not know if it was a dream or vision. All I know is after a few tentative beats, I found the rhythm I wanted, established a cadence, let it build until there were murmurs of appreciation, felt the smoke come into my head and heart. I became one with that drum. I began to chant, and the drum sounded the story, too.

I sang the song of the earliest times, when the giant Birds of Thunder ruled the earth, then flew away to rule the heavens. I sang the nether times of Second Earth, when Nanaboozhoo strode the world. I sang Nanaboozhoo's search for his father, of his talk with the moon herself, of her guidance to the west. She sent him from the farthest east, where the Great Salt Sea is, on to the west! I wailed in a holy voice the chant the Original Man's journey on the trail to the great Falls of Power. Grandeur! I sang his crossing of lakes and rivers to go to the huge Great Freshwater Lakes, west, ever west. The drum throbbed the story of the glory and majesty of the Father of Waters, of the lessons of nature about the harmony of creation. Beauty and grandeur! Together the drum and I reached a height of glory in that moonlit night, before the campfire, as I saw before me in a vision of power the buffalo who gave all wisdom and friendship to Nanaboozhoo. Enraptured, I raised my voice at the end—where the Son of the West Wind reaches the great stony mountains. Grandeur and beauty and spirit of worship! Nanaboozhoo finds his father the wind and great peace—the woods rang with my hymn of praise to the glory and mystery of all creation, in which we are one forever with nature—the children of blessing, always.

Then the drum stopped and I sat still. One at a time all arose and walked away, as the campfire smoldered a little, with the ember sticks falling apart because nobody had fed the fire. The last one to leave was the teeth-sticking-out girl. Her eyes did not meet mine. Still, from around her neck she took off a tiny garfish—amulet of great power made of copper— and gave it to me. Then she disappeared into the night.

As I was leaving, the wildrice men of the north stopped me. They did not look into my eyes but off, into the darkness of the trees. "One thing more," the tallest one said in a low voice. "Someday you are to play a drum you make yourself. So the vision spirits said."

"But where—when?" I asked.

They started walking off and the one who had the vision called back, over his shoulder, "You will know. When you have suffered enough, then you will begin to sing your song. Then you will build the drum."

Chapter Three

"Why is the strange house of death there at Place of Rivers Meeting?" I asked Bo Jo later. We were sitting in front of a campfire the next night, on the trail. The weather had changed, a rainstorm had blown in the morning, and now the sky had cleared. Above us the star grouping, Seven Little Maidens, gleamed and sputtered; Fire Tiger's light trails streaked across the sky now and then. It was cold; I wrapped a blanket around me.

"There are different ways of honoring the dead and keeping them from revenging their anger on the village. We have our ways—but there are seven kinds of death rites of our people," Bo Jo said, staring at the stars.

"Revealed as sacred law? Of the old ones?"

"Some, I think. More practiced recently and gaining popular support. Made up by Sun Watchers and their friends, I think." Bo Jo's eyes were fixed evenly on the moon. He seemed charmed by her lovely presence, drawn into the aura of her light and almost unaware that I was with him. He was silent for some minutes.

I thought about the strange, putrid-smelling death house I had seen in the town we had just departed. Did people take so much care with the dead? I had only vaguely known there were ways different from ours of burying the departed. As I have said, we simply took them to the edge of camp, took a shovel and dug a shallow pit, put in sacred things that would mean something on the trip to the land beyond the stars, and heaped up rocks. Then we put on more dirt. A little mound was left so all would know the sacred dead were present, near the campsite to bless but not close enough to harm if they were not appeased correctly. Sometimes we built a little pen around to keep animals off.

"Tell me of the different rites," I said to Bo Jo.

"Well, our simple rite was probably the first for all The People. I think it was practiced since the days before the Great Time of Ice. And even before that, when we walked across the

41

top of the world to get to this place of Nanaboozhoo's pleasure. But others I have seen in my travels have other rites.
Many build houses for the dead. There they put the bones,
honoring them by keeping them near the towns. The ancestors' bones stay there forever, in whatever cave or barrow or
other house the people have constructed.

"Another kind has the Ceremony of the Burning of the
Bones. They, like the others, build a nice summer shelter for
the dead—I think you have seen this when we went south
when you were a child."

I did seem to recall that trip and seeing the strange little
houses, with thatched roofs over them and mounds beneath.

"But unlike the ones with the barrows or caves, who leave
the body or bones there forever, these people wait until the
flesh has gone from the bones, or they think it has, then take
out the body. Then they heap tinder and kindling over it. With
sacred prayers and songs and chanting of the songs of the
dead, they set fire to the mortuary house and it falls on the
firewood pile. This burns the body to a few charred bones."

"These they inter again?" I asked.

"Yes. In a charnel house of the dead near the village.
Many, many bones are there. It saves burying space and time
and keeps the sacred ancestors' remains nearby."

"And the fourth way?"

"This I have seen done in the lands south of us, and east,
where fine fruit grows and shells abound. They peel the flesh
from off the corpse when it has rotted enough to come off
easily."

"And who does this fine job?" I asked scornfully. My
friend Shell-god always taunted me for having such a delicate
nose.

"Oh, in that land, it is an honor. The Sun Watcher tells
everyone it is a job sacred to the spirits, and all vie to get
chosen."

"Well, I suppose if the Sun Watcher says so," I offered
tentatively. In our village people did not do everything the
Sun Watcher said. I did not think they would peel skin off

corpses just because the Sun Watcher said so. But maybe—
sometimes I got confused about things like this.

"When the sun has finished bleaching the bones, they
interred them near the village, perhaps with many others." Bo
Jo stretched out, grunting a little as he settled in on the
sleeping robe.

We paused a moment to watch the Moon Princess. She
was extremely beautiful tonight, changeable in her moods.
When she rose she was almost blue-red, the color of smoky
elderberries. Perhaps it was because there was much smoke in
the air; grass fires had burnt for several days across the
prairies north of us, so they said.

Now she was higher, richly yellow and shining like the
color of mothers' milk when it first comes in the breast, so that
the whole forest was illuminated, its branches outlined, swelling with buds.

"Another kind of burying puts the bones beneath the
houses," Bo Jo said.

I understood. "Ah, the spirit of the grandfather, perhaps,
will be near to bless when times are hard for the family." Bo
Jo nodded, throwing an acorn into the fire. Then something
else occurred to me.

"Yes, but I would not want him there if the family had
offended him. Not tended him well, perhaps, in his last illness.
Or forgot to put his favorite pipes by his side."

"I wonder just how much the spirits of the dead do harm
us," Bo Jo said, his face turned towards the wood. What in the
world did he mean? Everyone knew the spirits could do all
kinds of mischief. The shamans went on their spirit journeys
to contact them and find out what they were angered at. Often
it was some part of the burying rite ill done. Bo Jo said strange
things sometimes.

"There are those, far, far south, they say, who burn the
body whole on huge pyres and save the ashes. Before they
burn the rich and powerful, the rites are three days long. There
is music and sacred dancing and processions with copper and
stone jewelry interred."

"How curious it would be to see the pyre burn," I said in awe. The sacred cities of the far south were told of in awe. Hardly anyone had seen them.

A cool breeze stirred, flaming the campfire up a bit. Bo Jo nodded to me and I brought more wood for the fire.

"And the last kind of rite?" I finally prompted.

"Some few, very rich and powerful, are buried in the sacred mounds themselves."

"They lie where the Sun Lord rises?" I asked, almost not believing. Such burying would seem like profanation.

"They believe the highest honors lie where the Sun Lord's rites are observed, where he comes to earth for the few days when he stands still in the heavens. Thus—the hill."

We were silent for many moments. It was growing colder, no doubt about it. Chilling winds stirred the trees, and cloud shreds began drifting over the moon.

Finally I asked, "Uncle, how long have our people had the worship hills? How did they come to be?"

He cleared his throat a little, as if he waited to see what he would say. "Some say they go back to the time of the giant—the Thunder Beings—but I know that is not true, for the true lore teaches us when things have come into being in the universe." He flipped at an ash which had landed on the edge of his sleep robe, then went on. "Our own village people have been about these lakelands for many moons—well, as many as there are leaves on an oak tree."

"That many?"

"Yes. And take half those leaves on the oak tree, and half of those, and then you will have the number of moons since we came into the lands of the Lakes-Like-a-Necklace and made the mounds of earth to honor the Sun Lord."

Now it darkened, as shreds of clouds covered the mother moon almost completely. "They were built," Bo Jo went on, "with baskets of earth, as we do when we bury."

"Mounds built by carrying baskets? I do not see how they could get so high."

Bo Jo raised his hand; it cast five long stick shadows on the other side of the campfire. "I do not mean they made the whole site that way, although in many places they do. But we have our own hillocks back of the lake, and some were placed in just the right places to see the sun."

"You said in my training time that the Sun Watchers marked the sun times from early days."

"Yes. Well, as long as there have been plants to tend. Squash, pumpkin and corn. I told you they needed a season-marker so we would know when to have our sacred festivals. Although we can use the leafing out times and other of nature's signals to plant and clear, the sacred times must be exact. So many days from Summer Long Day, we have the feast to Grandmother Moon. " I nodded; he went on.

"And so they watched where the sun came up, went down each day. When it came to the farthest spot in the winter, there they raised a pole to mark the sighting. When it reached the spot of longest day in the summer, there they marked it with a pole also. And many spots in between."

"To mark the calendar. The fore pole and the back pole on the hill."

"Yes. But to see best, and to have a spot for the sun celebrations, those early priests wanted the viewing spots high up, near the Lord Sun as was possible. And so they called the village together and had them bring earth in woven baskets made of reeds or white oak strips. As large as each could carry, that he brought, to the glory of the Sun Lord."

"How many baskets that must have been," I murmured. "They got so much by digging?"

"Well, for us it was not as hard as for some. Our soil is sandy and we used the digging pit, taking sand from it and carrying it to the sunwatching hills. The three sacred hills. All the village sang, all the village stamped until the dirt stood."

"And did it always stand?"

"Well, bad times came, so the legends go. Once on the sunrise hill, steep as it is, the rain drenched deep right after the

45

stamping, and almost the whole hill slid down. The sun priest must have cursed the powers of darkness then, I tell you."

That made me smile.

"Basket after basket was brought, to raise the high hill higher. And finally it was done. Still, each year, it was repaired. And always the sight posts were kept in repair, the offerings prepared correctly."

"All for the calendar—well, and to honor the Lord Sun."

"Of course. That is what I taught you in the manhood classes, is it not?" There was an odd note in his voice. The moon began to emerge from the shreds of clouds, and its brightness waxed around us.

"Yes. So you taught me," I answered.

"Well, so I did. But truth is a stone set in the ground. You cannot see all sides, and sometimes the best part is hidden down below the surface. I did not tell you all."

"So? Tell on," I said, with an expectant smile.

"You have seen the sun record disk that your father has."

"Yes—you mean the flat, burnished piece of wood that mimics the way the sun rises on the horizon day by day with notches?"

"That is the one. It is a piece of great power is it not?"

"Surely. The Sun Lord himself has blessed it. It is what the Sun Watcher uses to predict the shortest day and longest day, what tells him to warn us when to beg the Sun Lord to go no farther but return to the warm part of the sky."

"And yet, could not anyone who really watched, over a period of years, perhaps through a whole generation, create such a disk?"

"Yes, but that would not be done."

"Why not?"

"Because he who creates a sun disk calendar would be cursed. It is the right of the Sun Lord, so they say."

"So they say. But it is a totem of great power, that is sure. Some, I expect, have wanted it."

"Well, and it has power to invoke the Sun himself, to cause grain to grow, to bring us together to cause fertility—"

His face in the moonlight seemed almost stony, like the face of an effigy. "I do not mean that kind of power."

"What then?"

"Does your father not have many new pots? One of them metal? Does he not have shell jewelry from the islands of the sea? Did someone not bring him the chocolate drink traded from the far south last year? And did I not see in your lodge things of pearl and copper?"

"Well, yes. And it is true our granary is the fullest. He asks for some tribute at the time of the ceremonies, other times people seem to bring it. They ask him to beg the Sun Lord for things for them; then if good happens, they bring gratitude offerings."

He did not answer immediately, so I finally did. "Ah, I see. You mean the sun piece gives the power to get the shells and pearls and copper."

"Yes. The sun is power. For those who know how to use it."

It was a new idea for me, and I did not thoroughly like to think about the Sun Watcher—or the Sun Lord—that way. The way of the spirit was the way of our people and Bo Jo was making it sound like—gathering possessions, plain and simple.

The discussion seemed over. We banked the fire, left extra wood by its side, and lay down in our sleeping rolls. After a while, just as I was growing drowsy, Bo Jo spoke again. "Sun Watching is not hard. It just takes persistence, through some generations. Star Watching is more difficult. One must chart, through many years, the rising of certain groups of stars or bright beacons in the heavens. Some people mark the risings of the bright stars with mounds and poles."

"You are a Star Watcher."

"Yes. It has been in our clan for many lifetimes."

"Does my father know the skill?"

"No. It is passed on only to the oldest son."

47

"Such knowledge is valuable. It could be on a disk, bring things in to the possessor if what you say is true. Star watching could be power!"

"We do not wish it to be so!" Bo Jo said shortly. Then he was silent.

I shut my eyes, then opened them a few moments later. The moon was now out full again, and its light was a glaring, bright white, pouring into the clearing and making it almost as bright as day. It was the soft color of sifting snow, the stark color of wave caps on the lake, the rich color of the elderberry in full bloom, so beautiful it makes you want to catch your breath—all in one.

Bo Jo's voice emerged from the sleeping robe, deep and sepulchral. "But the real power would come to him who watched the moon."

I sighed sleepily. "Who can chart the moon's ways? She is a woman, grandmother of us all at one time, princess of the sky another. She is wily, changeable, jumping around the sky, high, low, thin like a fingernail, fat and flooding with holy light, as tonight." I thought a moment, watching her face, but unable to see its usual features because of her brightness tonight.

"And yet, some do chart her ways—or they have," Bo Jo said.

"Otherwise we would not know what moon we are in and could not measure time," I affirmed.

"We do measure time by what we call moons, but now it is the sun we really measure by. We have lost the full knowledge of the moon's movements—if we ever had them. We are as children learning "hide-the-stick" games from the ritual clowns like you when it comes to knowledge of the moon's ways."

"Thus has it been, thus will it ever be," I said, in the language of the rituals. I was getting a little tired, both in my eyes and in my mind of all this talking.

"I do not think it will ever be thus," Bo Jo said softly. "I tell you again, whoever had the knowledge of the moon's true

48

movements, not only the jumping through the sky but also the most wondrous thing of all—the hiding of the moon—this person would have the power, even over life and death."

My thoughts grew fuzzy as cottonwood seeds, the noises of the wind on the river below us blending with the sizzling and spitting of the dying fire. Had he really said that about the moon and life and death? I blocked the moon out of my eyes by shutting them tight, and I drifted off to sleep. When I awoke in the morning, I thought that all that Bo Jo had said was nothing but a dream.

Bo Jo did not mention anything profound and mysterious when we returned to camp. Quite the opposite, he was occupied with many practical matters, most of them quite dreary. For one thing, my father had decided to put away my mother, to divorce her finally, after all these years, since she could not be a wife to him. She was broken-hearted and even more distant to me than usual, as she set up a household with one of her female relatives. Bo Jo, as the eldest in my father's family, had to attend to the details of providing for her. I came into my father's lodge, knowing I had to confront him. I had avoided even going inside since the children had met Bo Jo and me at the edge of camp on our return with the news of the parting of my parents. But now I must meet him.

"You are putting away my mother," I said in an even voice. In other tribal groups, it was common to have more than one wife; in ours, one wife was the tradition, one wife to be knit to, to honor. It would not do to let him know how much I despised him for the rare act of putting away his wife, and for all the other despicable things he had done in the several years I had been in the lodge. I was a dutiful son, after all, as the Birds of Thunder have commanded. Their commands controlled my tongue. They did not control my heart, though.

"It is time," he said indifferently. He was absently arranging things at the stone stand in the corner of the lodge where he kept his medicine things. Eagle feathers, sacred god-pot for the corn meal he scattered, tobacco and sweet smelling herbs.

The trip had cleared my mind, as a rain will do the dusty heavens in mid-summer. Or perhaps it was the anger I'd felt over the girls' comments on our trip, but I felt exceptionally bold. "Is it time to throw away an unfortunate woman the way you throw away a broken ceremonial pot? Discard her because she has a flaw in her?" Bold indeed I was. My mother would not want me to speak for her, but I still loved her and could not refrain my tongue.

My father turned to me with a snarl, walked to me and smacked me so hard in the mouth that my teeth cut my lip.

"That is against the law of the Birds of Thunder," I said painfully as the blood flowed from my lips. I just could not stop.

He looked as if he might hit me again, but held back his arm just in time. Someone was at the door of the shelter, outlined against the setting sun, seeking a prayer to the spirit of the rain. My father's voice was suddenly as smooth as bear oil.

My teeth, my jaw, my heart—everything in me hurt. Whom should I seek, of course, in my pain and sorrow? As night filtered into the camp, I looked for Bo Jo. He was rocking his youngest daughter, White Wings, who happened to be my favorite (and his too, I think). This little one, fair of face and disposition for all her two years, had a fever. The cooking fire in the center of the shelter was smoky; his wife Rose-on-the-Hill saw my face and went from the shelter.

I told him I wished to make petition to the elders to leave my father's shelter and stay with him, my uncle. I no longer respected my father, I said, even though he had given me birth. I did not think of him as the wise parent I wished to emulate. Quite the contrary, with the outbursts that happened when the flap to the shelter was closed, I thought of myself as the father, he acting often like a child. I was too old to live in the house of my mother, too young to choose a bride of my own (if one would have had the Bear Belly, which was not at all likely).

He looked at me with a long look, like one who reads the streaks in the sky to know the changes in the weather. Then he nodded a brief nod. The council met and the wish was granted. I was to move in with my uncle Bo Jo.

This was not without complications. My uncle's rather young wife had the voice and disposition of a wolverine–at least sometimes. It was whenever the Moon Grandmother was getting ready to send her women's cycles, so said the old women in our village. The cycles must come rather often, so I thought, living in that house of ranting. The sun came up, my Aunt Wolverine (so I called her) rose and began ordering everyone around (meaning me and her older daughter; even she would not have ordered a man. She got her way with Bo Jo in other ways). "Go to the spring with the leather bottle. Get the water and be sure there is no mud in it this time," she would say to my cousin her daughter, who was about ten winters and who had just begun to pull her hair back from her face with a hair clip. "Pick up that birch broom and sweep the front of this house. The spirits will come swooping down and look to see if our doorstep is clean. If there is trash, they will not leave us any blessings for the day. Hurry up, you slovenly girl."

Then she would turn her attention to me, as if to make up for not berating me for all the hours of the night." Make the fire quickly; do you think we want to wait all morning for the meal?" "What do you mean by putting a fork into that pot! To test? I'll test you, fat bearson!" I would run around with the fork, speared meat still on it, laughing hysterically. And so it went. I did not really need to provoke her, to bait her like a caged raccoon to see how quickly she would snap, but it gave me something to do—when my uncle was out of the lodge, of course. What it really did was release pain and pressure, like lancing a boil.

Part of the problem was that my other cousin, my aunt's oldest child, was spoiled and pampered. He was a cripple, it is true, but he could have done some things, truly that would not have been too hard, things like clean fish and thread fishhooks and arrange the trading goods. But she would not allow this young sluggard to do anything. He wished each day to play moccasin. This he did, betting with our family servant Ghost-on-the-Lake, who had come to us from the north as an orphan and whom Bo Jo had raised.

"Get my moccasin and call Ghost," he would say, pointing out the door opening to where the hunchbacked servant was mending fish nets.

"Do it yourself, Lazy," I would tell him in a low voice, so his mother would not hear.

But his mother ran to his aid. "There, there, Lean Sparrow, do not move. I will get your game."

Then, as she left, he would smirk at me, simpering, "Get them yourself." How I hated that simpering voice.

But it wasn't only the spoiled cousin that blighted my spirits. I felt dark, like a cloud in the summer before the big rain comes. The parting of my parents had distressed my spirits and I moped about, refusing to go on hunting parties or even play the games in the square. The village elders watched me, but I could not seem to help it. Seeing Morning Glory on the paths each day, haughty and proud of her status—she was a new wife—did not help. I reverted back to my childhood in a way, hiding beneath the log bridges to frighten the children, calling myself the bad snake spirit of the bridge, ho, ho, ho.

Finally my shrewd uncle, tired of constantly upbraiding me, said he had had enough. He decided we would take a day fishing at the Lake-of-the-Boulders down the hill from the camp. It was the end of May and the trees about to spring into full bud. White cupped flowering trees bent low over the shady shoreline, lining all the lake, except for one brief land-ing my people had built to launch canoes.

Some members of the boat builders clan nodded to us as we sought a canoe. They were there, blowing on coals in a tree trunk as they sought to hollow it out for a canoe. Po-to-tak-in-i–a reed–was used to blow on the coals. They had to be careful so the coals did not burn through the hull, and they were intent on blowing and watching. They were skilled; well they should be. They were members of the boat clan and were taught from childhood the way of the lake and river. In that place we had two clan groupings: ancient sacred animal and the trade we served for the village.

"Choose a two-person canoe," my uncle instructed. I entered, being careful not to rock it too much, and set down the tackle—line made of mulberry fiber, fishhooks of sharp, notched slate and worms. It was not as quick as the weirs or nets, but it gave time for contemplation on the peaceful water of Lake-of-the-Boulders.

We glided beneath a drooping black willow tree, its thin branches trailing in the water. Then we cast the lines on sticks and waited for bass, pickerel, pike or dog-fish—whatever would strike. Nothing seemed interested, as a matter of fact. It was a rather hot, bright, morning and the surface of the lake reflected bright light as we paddled along.

I watched the heads of turtles far out in the lake, lily pads at the edge. My heart was full—of hurt, anger at the world, frustration at my own uselessness. Finally I spoke. "Is it necessary for a man to marry, Uncle?"

He pulled the line in a little, then gently swung it out again. "Most men do, but a few do not. There are the eunuchs made by nature. They seem not to like women." I knew—had seen— a couple. They were marked, so the village thought, and regarded them with the same wonder they had for the witless and for the servant Ghost-on-the-Lake, who was a hunchback from birth.

"There are those," he went on, "who dedicate themselves to a just war or holy vision search. Women are not always good for us—nor we for them, I guess. The Bird of Thunder forbids us to be near them before we go to war, or meet in important council." I knew that from the training. Stay away from women if you will need your manhood's strength. And especially stay away from them when they are taboo. "But it is good for most to marry," he concluded.

"I do not know if I wish to. It seems like a trip through pain—a slow walk through nettles higher than your shoulder."

"You have seen more pain than most in the marriage covenant. But it can work." His eyes evaded mine. He did not wish to make the conversation personal because his own marriage left something to be desired, and yet he wished to bring balm to my heart. I could feel it in his manner, see it in his eyes. He loved me. Good uncle! I loved him back. I had to. I trusted no one else in my life, except, possibly my friend Shell-god, a little, I suppose. I hadn't seen him much lately; he had been away hunting. I don't really think I trusted him, either, further than I could see him, heart-sore boy that I was.

A small sunfish jumped at the bait, but as Bo Jo pulled him in, he jumped from the line, swimming away from us, leaving little circles on the water. "A man and woman can live together, can help each other to walk the path of beauty and blessing. What they need is respect for each other, deep respect. That is all."

"But what about love? Beauty of face and form."

"That is not as important."

"To me it seems so. Morning Glory is so—"

He interrupted me. "I know. To all young men the call of the beautiful face and body is strong. And that is natural. The Maker of Stars has created men and women to come together to make the people for the world. So the coming together of bodies and spirits is important. But it is respect and unselfish care that matter." A shadow seemed to pass across his face— or was it a cloud that had come to edge over the sun. "I made the mistake of thinking that beauty in a woman was all."

My uncle had never talked to me about his past; my father had scornfully said he was a "wild whelp" when he was young. I knew that he had travelled as a part of his trader's training and life before he became a shaman, was, in fact the greatest trader of us all. But his life as a lover of women? It embarrassed me just slightly to hear him talk in that rueful voice; usually he was quietly, strongly confident.

We sat, feeling a slight wind rise. "How did you get to be a shaman, Uncle?" I finally asked. "The tale is often told in the village of how you climbed the tree of life in a cave, far away. But I do not know more."

Bo Jo smiled up at me. "Very few here know more than that. Perhaps I shall tell you. Are you old enough, strong enough, to bear the burden of a long, sad tale? Are you man enough to hear the shocking details?" I nodded eagerly. "Ah, then I shall begin."

And, under an increasingly cloudy sky, as we caught fish, put them on a string by the side of the canoe, baited and rebaited the lines, he told the tale thusly.

"Truly your father did tell you that I was a wild whelp. Though I was the first son of a wise and reverent Star Watcher and shaman loved by all the village, I rebelled against the thought of following in his footsteps. I scorned the shamanism, though I knew enough of it for all that matter. I was taught Star-Watching, but it was an old skill, not called for now. My brother, the second son, was prepared to be the Sun Watcher, the newer craft. I was just left alone, the village shrugging its shoulders at my unpredictable ways. Loud mouth, raucous laugh, indifferent practice of the traditional ways.

"They were not surprised that I did not wish to follow the shamanism; they knew that one can only be called to the spiritual way of intervention with the spirit world through a holy call and long, dangerous pilgrimage.

"Those were not for me. I found my pleasure in standing out, rebelling against the ways of the village. I made fun of the doddering ways of the old women with their herbs, I went off hunting alone, looking for (and finding) the great bear; I spent hours from sunrise to sunset sometimes gambling. It was the chungky games that I was drawn to, like smoke is drawn out the hole in the house.

"I was good at the game, inordinately good. The spirit of sport must have chosen me for his own blessing. My spear could stop the rolling chungky stone oftenest, my bet come off on top. I took most of the village's precious shell-trading necklaces, then took special possessions: buffalo robes, beautifully wrought pots, finely woven men's tunics all rested on the shelf by my bed.

"When I had overcome competition in the village and those around us in the land of Lakes-Like-a-Necklace, and because I was of the trading kinship group in the village, I travelled with my own uncles to the city and learned the ways of trade. As we do now, we sold the fine flint of the Ohio pits. We went along the Ouabache and the White, then along the Father of Waters to the cities of our people. There, in the Great City near joining of the big waters—there at Cahokia, I found the maid who would mean so much to me and who brought me pain as strong as the breaking of a limb."

I looked past him, past the serene, deep, black eyes that hid so much I had not even suspected. I had thought my uncle was always the ritual-perfect shaman I knew.

"You speak of beauty in a woman and you see Morning Glory as fair as a flower before your eyes. But she is a dim light to the woman I found there in the streets of the Great City. Eyes-of-the-Deer was a high noblewoman, first-cousin and servant to the ruler there."

I interrupted—really I should not have done it. "Tell me of Cahokia, Uncle. You will never talk of it, and none of the other villagers, not even the traders have been there to tell me."

"No. Only I have ranged south. Still, I will not tell you, because if it is your path to know of it, you will know by the sight of your own eyes. I have told you it is the City of Bright Metal and that is enough to know. Bright Metal rules there—trade is all and the power it brings. Still, I will tell you that there are many, many folk there. Among them, as a ritual cupbearer to the ruler was Eyes-of-the-Deer."

"Cupbearer?" I asked. I had told myself I would interrupt no more and I meant it, but the phrase caught me unaware.

"In the Great City there are many pleasures, many vices, many officials, many occupations. The ruler there has bracelets and rings, and there is a cup nearby into which drink has been poured and into which the ruler may dip a gifting bracelet. Someone holds it always."

I shook my head. It did not make a bit of sense, but my uncle went on anyway. "One spring day I had just come into the city, walking along as listlessly as a limping rabbit towards the trade stands, when I saw her looking at shell jewelry across the way. You have seen the way the fur of the beaver glows and shines, dark and rich when the pelt is first brought from the animal. So her hair, hung in loops about her face and tied off with more than one hair clasp, shone in the late sunlight of the day. The bright stone you found at Rivers Meeting and traded catfish for, the one you keep by your bed now, her eyes might have come out of the depths where those black shiny stones live. But there was fire there, too.

"When I asked to meet her, an elder took me to her and I nodded and smiled at her name. 'You think Eyes-of-the-Deer an odd name, do you, stranger?' she said, with a lilt in her voice. I later found out her father was the ritual hunter who brought the offering at the green corn festival, the deer which we leave at the altar on the hill for the corn god. He and his wife went to the woods in late summer to do the kill and came right upon a huge stag which thundered down off a little rise, jumping completely over them. The eyes of the stag had met those of the mother, and she delivered a baby in the winter who was marked by such beauty that they thought the soul of the stag had passed into the girl's."

Bo Jo was contemplative for a while, then went on. "I loved her; my soul was knit to hers there, then. We spent time together wandering the paths away from the village, sitting on the cliffs above the mighty river. We whispered and walked all the day and night long; we could not be out of the other's sight; she swore she would love me as long as grass grows and water flows. All I wanted to do was sit and look at the lovely face, the perfect nose, the hair that smelled sweeter than wild roses.

"But the spirits were frowning; she as a ritual cupbearer and high cousin of the ruler was promised to one of her caste. They had a system of marriage ordained by the priests—never mind. We could not be together. She was prepared for marriage to one of another kinship group—a lanky warrior who was assigned as a soldier to the stockade in one of the outer villages.

"We were together one last time on the cliffs upriver; three stars were in conjunction that week and I thought it was a sign. We must be together. 'Eyes-of-the-Deer, flee with me' I said. 'It has been done—we will throw ourselves on the mercy of my village, or one of the others, perhaps far to the east.' I knew that it would be dangerous for any village in the tribute area of Cahokia to shelter us, but there were other villages, far away. Such things were done—for love.

"Perhaps,'" she said, but her eyes were on the river. Her love is as great as mine, I thought, and my heart felt great tenderness for her.

"But the next day she came with her father. She would not see me any more. She would not even look at me with those beautiful eyes of the king of the forest. I am pledged', was all she said. Do not pursue me any more.' It could not be true, I thought. She has been forced. But when I sought her that night, among the shadows behind her house, she pushed me away. He is very rich. His father's stores are the largest in the town, second only to the ruler's. It must be. The gods wish it.'

"I cursed the day I had entered that town. That very night I left, leaving all my trading stuffs, and with my heart about to burst, went into camp by the river. But the next morning an evil spirit seized me—a very evil one indeed. Revenge! Desire to be even—with her—with the rich rival I barely knew—bit at me like a rattler's fang.

"I went to the stockaded outpost downriver. Behind giant logs, on a ledge with a spear, stood the young man I now hated with a loathing as thick and cold as a chunk of lake ice. I had a plan, smooth young beaver I was then, and angry. I went into the stockade, greeted all as a guest. That night I feasted with them all, eyeing my rival across the fire, eating new corn with them and singing the songs of tribute.

"He was a stupid man, rich though he was and son of a powerful one in the Great City. We feasted. My rival was a glutton, among his other faults. `Corn, new corn,' he slobbered more than once. He had to go to the bushes more than once as he ate ear after ear.

"I remember the feast well, and it stands clear in my mind as if I were there this minute. We sat above the great swell of that most mighty of rivers—Mississippi. Truly it was glorious to see the raft of colors on its waters, the glare and power as the giant ball slipped beyond the skyline. The chieftain of the village spoke movingly of the power of the Sun Lord.

"`The stars are lesser lords of the sky,'" he said. "`Each morning the Sun Lord conquers them and they flee to the far tents beyond the sea. No star may stay when Lord Sun is on his throne.'

"All repeated, as the sunset deepened. `No lesser lord may stay when Lord Sun is on his throne. Even the Star Lords flee.' It was a sacred tenet of our faith—that the Sun Lord ruled, and so it had proven in reality even in my small village. Truly no one cared any more about the star sighting as in ancient times; everyone wanted the sun, only the Sun Lord to worship. In my arrogance I saw myself as like the Sun Lord, sending the lesser lord who would steal my love fleeing.

"That night we sang chants to the sun and to the corn god who had sent new corn. We danced, beating the mud flats of the great river with our feet. They had drums, but no one played as powerfully as you did at the last feast on the rivers."

So he had noticed. I had not touched a drum since, but the memory of the power of that night was fresh in my mind when evening breezes stirred.

59

Bo Jo went on. "As we left to go to the thatch houses they slept in, I slapped his arm and gave him other ritual tokens of friendship. `Tomorrow,' I said, `let us go to the playing fields. Chungky for all young stalwarts strong enough to take my challenge!' He nodded eagerly. Small knowledge did he have of what he was undertaking when Lord Sun rose, sending with his power all the Star Lords scattering to the far reaches of the sea.

"Need I tell you how it went? No, you will know that I sent them all scattering with the swiftness and sureness of my chungky pole. They looked at me in surprise, then in irritation. This outsider challenges the village, they thought. Challenges our manhood. My rival, the Corn Clout, as I called him, was especially provoked at my skill.

"`Why not place a few wagers,'" I suggested slyly. They grunted affirmation and began to take out shell pieces, body adornments, and other trifles. The chungky stone was thrown, we threw our pikes after it, and mine fell where it stopped as likely as not each time. A small pile of tribute appeared near my feet as the morning, then the afternoon wore on. Oh, do not think I won it all. I was clever; I let other youths achieve also. My friend the Corn Clout was not losing all along, no, not at all. His skill was not to be laughed at, and I kept him on edge with my continual chatter, my scornful laugh at the right times.

"The stakes grew higher. Necklaces with copper pieces in them were bet. Still I threw, as straight as an arrow. A crowd, then almost the whole village formed behind us. My rival was sweating in the hot sun; beads stood on his strong, heaving chest. He was coming into his stride in the game, winning now. I was holding back, like a cat stalking prey, allowing it a little space to think it is free. He had little left to bet, and yet the stakes were high, very high indeed. There were three of us still playing, and the third youth, another very rich lord's son, bet beautiful tunics of purple cloth, traded from the City of the Mountains, far south.

"My rival was ahead in the game we were playing. `I think I should retire,' I said, shrugging my shoulders, deferring to his skill. `I am not so good as you.'

"`We will see this through,' he said. `You have taken all—my three corn stores that are mine as a chief lord's son. But there is more. You will not defeat me.' His eyes were slits. Was he determined to succeed in the eyes of the village? Was it that I had now made myself rich with the thousands of baskets of grain that were in his storage bins, now mine?

"`Well, if the stakes are high enough,' I said. `If you win now, in these last three throws, I will return the stores to you, all of them.' The crowd gasped; surely no one would give up the chance to be a rich man. I did wonder at myself a little, too. But hate is a stronger cat than even greed, and when it gripped my throat I had no relief.

"`And if I lose?' he asked in a low voice.

"My answer was low but firm. `Why then, you will be my slave.'

"He stood tall. `On with the throw,' he said.

"The first throw he won. But then my mouth became a tight line, and I breathed deeply and called on the Lord Sun to help me master this callow youth who had so deeply insulted me. `As you master the Star Lords each day, let me master this throw,' I prayed. I threw. I won. The second time the chungky stone rolled onto my spear.

"The crowd fell back, parting for their chieftain. He wore feathers and a crown. My rival said nothing, standing mute.

"`You have made your bargain, now you must go,' he said to the Corn Clout. `Let us all learn the danger of the play. It can turn us into ravenous beasts, and we promise all on the throw of a stone. Bring the slave brand.' He waved his hands. A brand was brought; I hesitated only a moment. Even then, I was not really a bad man, only driven by the demons, straight from Fire Tiger, Gitchimanitowac, I suppose. Could I brand a fellow human being over a game? I could and I did, wretch that I was then. I took the brand and burnt his leg. He did not howl, though the crowd did.

61

"The chieftain spoke again. `Go, stranger. You have violated the laws of hospitality, I say. Never come to these parts again. Go, take your slave. And may the gods wreak vengeance on you both.'

"With the curse ringing in my ears I prepared to leave. The youth's branded leg was bound up, my few things packed for the canoe. I even had the nerve to take my winnings with me—although I could not claim the rich corn stores. Those the chieftain had decreed were forfeit. Still, I was a rich man.

"I kept my knife by my side in those campouts, my slave in the front of the canoe as we travelled. Still, he did not try to escape. His spirit was spent, like a wild animal who has been faced down and who must capitulate to the stronger. He recognized his fate as decreed by the Sun Lord. My prayers, evil ones that they were, worked, so I told myself.

"Or did they? In the dark of the second night, his voice spoke out hollowly. `I know very well who you are,' he said. `No one else would have tormented me so. You cannot marry her. My brothers will see to it that if you ever again set foot in Cahokia or its territory, you will be captured and beheaded. You are now an outlaw.'

"I will make the story shorter, since it is growing longer than a possum's tail and there is more to say. I took him north and sold him to the Dune Devils. They were in their usual camps."

"The Dune Devils?" I asked, astounded.

"You can see to what depths the demons of the Great Serpent were driving me. Not only that, but I stayed and traded with them a month or two. I saw him suffer, working among the women."

"But the Dune Devils—"

"They do not treat their slaves poorly. But I must admit I did not endear myself to them. I left and went on."

He was silent for a moment, but I knew I must find out more. "Tell me—about your life as an outlaw."

"I was an outlaw from my own heart. I could not return to claim my love, for what my rival had said was true, and gradually she lost her hold on my life. Day by day, as water trickles slowly out of a cracked jug, so my pain trickled away. I took my trading goods and wandered south, avoiding Cahokia but travelling down along the Great River. I stopped and learned varieties of tongues, the habits of other cities and villages. Everywhere the Sun Lord was being worshipped, everywhere the trading sped his religion. Our flints were treasured and brought other, more specialized trading goods to me, and I was rich, richer yet.

"Finally, I came to the land where the river widens, heading to the sea. I looked at it, there, when my canoe reached it, and even though I was jaded, inured, by long months, even years of doing what I wished and living to increase my own hoard, I was awed. 'Truly,' I said, 'this is where the Star Lords go when the Sun Lord comes with his bright day. They are far away indeed, for this largest lake has no end.'

"There was a city near there, out on a spit of land, where many, many lived—not as large as Cahokia but great in a different way—no, I will not tell you how because if it is your destiny, you may know for yourself. But there I found more trade than ever, from foreign places with people who did not speak tongues anything like ours in the valley of the Great River. These were knowing men, brutal men, from the cities of Mexica, where the feathered serpent is worshipped. And from farther south of that, even. They had come to trade their gold and precious things for our robes and cloth and shells. And even for our grains, for their land is not as rich as ours. Huge canoes they had, with sheets of woven fabric they called sails. They could cross the shining sea, they said, with these sheets, which flew before the wind like moth wings. They were going to the cities of the south, the huge cities, the sacred cities, and my heart determined I must go there too.

"I made friends with one of the traders of Teotihuacan, and he allowed me to come with him in his sailing canoe. Far, far out we went away from the city on the point, high were the waters, strong the winds, but they were all with us, and finally we came to the mainland, with sparkling white sands and dry,

dry lands within. He wanted to take me to see his ruler but somehow, since he had told me of many things strange and wondrous, I decided to leave him and go south, to a land of high trees and vines and jumping and crawling animals and insects. It was the land of the Old Ones, who had all wisdom in the past but were now in tribute to his lords. They, he said, had the knowledge of the lords of the heavens and the secrets of the universe.

"I followed the path he described to me and I came after not too many days to the lands of power—of the Maya, as they are called. Their land was an old one with many high towers. I settled on a city of trade, a fine city, where a wizened old man with a lecherous disposition seized on me finally as his minister. He made me lord of the traders, and mine it was to give them leave to come into his presence or to be turned away. I even went for him to the fabled city where he owned the tribute—Let that pass. It is another story. I saw odd things, too, horrible things, done there, and my lips cannot speak of them.

"When I returned, my lord the wizened old man said he had a quest for me. It would be dangerous and difficult, and take me far into the land where the Oldest Ones had their cities, now broken down. I was to go see if I could follow an old legend, to let it lead me to the place where the sacred treasure of the Oldest Ones was buried. There was rock quartz of great beauty and sacred power, there was a perfect metal called gold, enough to fill boxes, and there was the greatest treasure of all, the greatest treasure in the world, he said. It was a jade god, as big as my forearm but clear as light and powerful, very, very powerful.

"What is jade? you may wonder. Ah, to tell you what it looks like is beyond the tongue of Michaboo himself. It is green as grass, but it also has a touch of the blue of the sky in it and it is clear, so sunlight seems to pass through it. Precious it is, of all the stones we know. And a piece as large as your hand, worked by man into the shape of a god—I said I would go. Why not? I reasoned. I was growing impatient of my endless travelling, my life devoid of love or home. I could not settle here, I could not return. Truly I was an outcast—from myself and from the gods as well as from humankind.

I prepared to go. The old man ruler told me the legend, passed from father to son of the present rulers of that city and to no one else. When the last days came for these Oldest Ones, when, finally, their fair cities and great power were destroyed, a trusted servant took the treasure and hid it far away. No one from the rulers' caste could follow—it was deadly taboo. And no one else could be trusted. But the wizened one's grandfather had had a vision. He said that a tall man from the north would come to seek the treasure. And sure enough, I had arrived and had been 'chosen' to take the great risk."

I looked at my uncle expectantly. We had pulled in our fishing lines; the afternoon was wearing on; the rock we used as anchor was slipping as the wind and waves came up.

"The ruler called me over to him one night in a house without a fire in it. `Here is the song of the hidden buried jade' he said. I will sing it to you in our tradition, because it would not have any meaning for you in the words of their tradition:

Across the trail seen from the sky
Through where there are no cities high,
To where the lords of land and water vie
Past three great cats who never cry
To the house at the foot which knows no day.
Where Star Lords never scatter.
There is found the Olmecs' hoard.

I was so intrigued with what my uncle had just said that I made him repeat it again. I said it myself, fascinated with it as a chant, fascinated with its meaning.

I could not wait to hear the rest. "What did you do once you heard the song? Had no one else followed the song? No prince of the line? How did you decipher—"

He sighed. "That I cannot tell you. I swore on the Sun Lord at the time I took the quest—and received the promise that I would get to keep an incense bag full of treasure. That is what the ruler swore. At the last minute, when he felt he could trust me to accept and fulfill the quest, the wizened one brought out a piece of deerskin. On it was a likeness—a plot of where cities of these Maya were, with cities shown by stars and dots, with wavy lines for rivers and bumps for mountains. It showed the land where this treasure was, how far, near what, but past that—the song must be my guide.

"It is enough for you to know that I followed the deerskin and the song, sought out the places on my own, for that is the way it had to be, made many mistakes, almost lost my life to the forest and its naked peoples—and came at last to `the house at the foot which knows no day.'

"In the midst of giant trees where there were rock outcroppings, at the bottom of a hill I found it—a cave—the house that knows no day. I went inside with a pine torch and fire and found strange and wonderful things. Signs painted along a narrow ledge, where the sounds of water dripped, took me towards an open chamber where I could see an ever so faint lightening of the blackness around me. I stumbled my way along, slipping all the way and then I saw it—an antechamber with a domed roof and with a very faint light above—from the outside. It illuminated—the treasure.

"Such a sight I saw in my torchlight. I bent and unclasped the metal catch of a woven box. There were necklaces and headdresses and crowns and jade pieces, shining with green splendor. There, on the top was the jade god. His lips were fat, his nose broad in the style of the lower lands, and he wore a headdress like the leader. But it was his eyes, set in some bright green stone I had never seen, that made him unforgettable. He was bent at the knees, kneeling, unclothed, and unlike the other figures of their sculpture I had seen, his male organs were shown—in full bloom." He chuckled.

"A fertility god of some sort, perhaps for rain. I did not know. They had many gods, not just the Sun Lord and his aids as we do and the Thunderbeings as we do. There was a tightly closed container with some sort of sacred oil, beautiful small pots of god incense—other things—the chest with its weight was as large as a man could carry—not more. The trusted servant of the Oldest Ones in the long-ago times might have had a slave carry the chest for most of the journey, but he could have, must have, borne it alone into the cave.

"A crystal skull, of the kind a priest could use, with a movable mouth to demand offerings from the people, was there and the torchlight lit its hollow eyes. It scared me—me, the toughened, impure man who had sold a man into slavery and fought with savages to get to this place. I put the skull down and watched the torch for a moment, casting shadows on the strange spikes and cavities made of stone, the dripping water in this 'house that knows no light.' I began to think. I would have to get out of this cave with the treasure, bear it back soon—or would I?

"My depraved instincts, my greed began to speak to me. I could simply take the wondrous things to the surface, return on the tortuous path I had come, and then turn another way, towards the north and the great cities there, trade my fabulous goods for power and riches and—and what? Return? Make a life among the strangers in the cities where these great kings ruled? Perhaps. At any rate I began to gather the treasure up. Then my father's teachings rang in my heart. 'When a man has sworn, his whole spirit is tied up in a ball. He has put his soul on the line for a time. It is suspended between heaven and earth—the tool of the spirits. If the word is broken, the soul is cracked. It may not even survive—'

"I snorted, yet it was something to think about. I had sworn, had done the arm clasp, had even given a token. My soul just might be suspended on the bow string between heaven and earth. The Sun Lord would know. He was all powerful, scatterer of his enemies, who saw all. He was watching me when I went into this cave, he would see me when I came out. He was out there—I looked up, really for the first time. And, odd to tell, oddest thing in all my life, I could see out of the hole at the top of that cave, where there was very dim light. And what I saw, I tell you true, blood of my blood and my brother's son, though I have told no one else, is the stars. I saw stars, though I could not tell you which ones. There were stars there, even though it was daylight, only a short time, really since I had left the surface. The sun was lowering in the sky, but surely He was there. So why were the stars there too? It must have been the darkness of that place, shutting out the sun so the stars could be seen. Yes, in fact that is what the verse had said, though I had forgotten to note that part.

"But the Star Lords—they were supposed to be scattered! They were beyond the sea during each day. So we had been told, so I had believed all my life, so every priest and Sun Watcher and shaman who ever lived taught us. But—it was not true. They did not know. The stars were not scattered. They lived, they stayed. The Sun Lord had not conquered them and—it followed that he was not all powerful. Sun and stars all dwelt together—there was no one Lord—I sat down, overwhelmed.

"It was all so new. I see you, mouth open, agape, not believing what I have said, but it was—is—true. If you and I were in a cave, if you could find the right cave deep enough, near to us here and go in, and if there was an opening to the top, you too could see the stars. They do not disappear. I sat stunned, all the teachings of my world tumbling about like dead leaves in a whirlwind in autumn.

"No Star Lords scattered, no Sun Lord all powerful—no Sun Lord? Why had they told us—made it up? My mind went in dangerous, unspeakable directions. I blasphemed, I tread upon the forces of the spirits, I denied in my heart. Probably, natural blasphemer that I was at this time, I had just been waiting for someone to tell me the priests' beliefs were wrong. It suited my own rottenness of spirit.

"In a mocking spirit of revelation I began to dance about, there on the slick porous rock, to sing

Oh Sun Lord come—vanquish the lord of the night
If you can

68

And you can't, then don't.

"I laughed till I screamed. I had not offended the Sun Lord when I sold the Corn Clout into slavery because there was no Sun Lord's power anyway. I rolled on the ground, hugging my knees. Suddenly a rumbling began. It sounded like the Birds of Thunder (if they even existed, I thought) but then it had a sort of clacking with it. Things began to fall from the ceiling of the cave, huge spears of rock. These, in turn caused other rocks to fall and suddenly there was a great cascade of rock behind me, around me. Dust came into my eyes and mouth; I could not see and I covered my head to keep from being hit.

"When all was still, I could not see the path back. Frantically I turned, spitting rock dust. I clawed, I threw rocks, I tried to dig. There were too many rocks. I was trapped, blasphemer that I was. I lay there on the earth, stunned, and finally, in despair, I slept. I do not know how long I slept; I only know that I awoke with a faint shaft of light on my face. The sun (I would not call him lord) had arisen anew, but the hole above seemed smaller now and now both sun and stars were gone; I watched the opening but could see nothing. During the next hour or two there was a very small light from the roof of the cave. I tried to open up the path, or create a new one before me, but the stones would not budge. The treasure sat there, untouched for some reason, but what did it matter now? I was going to die. I did not like the idea. Hour followed hour, day followed day, I guess. There was a little water in the cave, in fact a pool of it had been opened up. I could drink, but of course I could not eat. And I could not see past my face. Up, up there was the world I'd come from, but it was as far away as if it had been across that ocean I had come."

He was silent. Twilight was coming; the waves had risen and we were paddling home.

"And yet, Uncle, you are here. What happened? You are keeping me in as much suspense as if I were at a war council waiting for the vote to attack or not attack. Tell me of your escape!"

My uncle smiled mysteriously.

"I think not, now. It is time to eat, time to think. Tomorrow we will walk to the traps in the woods. See if we have caught any rabbits. Look at the sites for winter traps. Then I will tell you the rest."

And try as I would, I could not get him to continue. So I spent a sleepless night, looking at the moon and stars out a tiny crack in the cover of the shelter. And, in the way a thing you have been impressed with, a snatch of a song, the certain beat of a drum, an odd saying, will sing itself in your mind for a while, so I spent the night with my mind saying

Across the trail seen from the sky
Through where there are no cities high
To where the lords of land and water vie

The moon came up, a good, strong half moon. "That song would do well set to a drum, Old Grandmother," I said, before I finally fell asleep.

Chapter Four

It rained hard the next day, and in the shelter Bo Jo did not show the slightest sign that he had told me a story that had set me on my ear. Every now and then, during that rainy day when we could not go out, I doubted that our conversation had ever happened, doubted that those strange things had actually befallen him. Somehow, though, his tale had the ring of truth, the strong, true coloration of a stone seen at the bottom of a stream—like everything he did.

Well, I tell you true the confessional part of the story had shocked me but—I wasn't perfect myself. Not Bear Belly. The girls were not letting me forget that; even now that Morning Glory was married, as she hurried to the stream to wash the garments, she still murmured the words. Bear Belly. Not even sneering. Just accepting the name as the true one. Secretly there was some admiration in me for what Bo Jo had done— though part was terrible. I was still praying for the strength of manhood to stand up and show them all. Do something great, some great quest like he did. Most of all, I was tantalized by the picture he had drawn of cities of the south—of great temples, kings, gold, gods made of jade. It was difficult to imagine as I went about the chores of the day, putting mud daub in the cracks of the shelter where the rain dripped in, playing hide and find with the children when the rain let up for a while, helping the women and the hunchbacked servant Ghost-on-the-Lake salt the fish we had caught.

Living with Bo Jo was respite from a storm, peace after battle. What a good man he was! A neighbor came to get him, in a hurry. Someone had a raging case of the fever. He was wanted—to do a shaman trance. As he gathered his medicine things, I went to his side. He looked at me, then nodded. I might come to assist him, to do the ritual clown duties. It would be only the second time I had done the clowning for a sickness spell.

It was one of the most squalid of shelters, on the edge of the village, and inside was a bunk with a dirty fabric rag on it for

71

a bed covering. A husband stood nearby, with his back to us. Small children cried outside, being cared for by relatives of the woman.

"Please," the small voice of the woman, Crying Cloud, said. "I have a fever, pain inside." She pointed with a little embarrassment at her stomach. "It happens since the birth of my last child." Her voice was small. It was not usual for women to discuss matters of their sex. "But now it is so bad I can hardly stand it."

The place smelled. Her husband sat down in the corner, cross-legged, looking at us sullenly.

She raised her hand weakly and Bo Jo placed it in his. "Please, Shaman. All love you for the spirit you show. I have heard the song about you—`Bo Jo came from the lands of mystery to heal us all. He cures the bite of the raccoon, he sends the lung fever far from our shelters. Bo Jo walks tall with the West Wind.' You will know what is the matter. Climb the tree of creation for me and ask the spirits."

"I will," he said, and sat down by her bunk. "My nephew here will help us seek the spirits. You know that he is a ritual clown and can help me disarm their charms with his antics." I put on a wolf mask and booed around the shelter. I rattled gourd rattles, beat a small drum I carried under one arm.

I was screaming and making my noise particularly hard when I reached the sullen husband's corner. He looked as sour as a shrew. What? Did he not wish his wife well? "Rrowl," I growled inside the mask. I kicked dirt at the man with my "hind paw." Then I set aside my drum and rattle and sat down by my uncle. It would be my job to anchor him, so to speak, to the earth—to talk him in and out of the tree of creation. You know what it is; you have seen our own shamans do this. When their spirits wander, it is dangerous for them on the earth. They must return in time, must have a safe place for their physical bodies while they search the spirits on the tree for answers to the problems of their patients.

My uncle lit tobacco, blew it towards the door to make offering to the spirits. Then he was silent for a long time. "I am

72

going deep within the spirit of creation," he finally said. "To the tree whose roots reach from Turtle Island all the way to the heaven of heavens, where we all will go some day. The bark is rough, the first branch far from the ground. But I will reach it—for Crying Cloud of our people."

It was quiet in the shelter for a few moments. Only the woman, coughing at the smoke of the dying cooking fire and trying not to moan was heard. Then Bo Jo spoke, in a voice slightly higher than normal. "I—am—up. I am among beautiful branches, their leaves as shining as quartz rock. I am grasping, pulling myself—up, over larger branches, into the depths of the tree. Up, up." He grunted. Time passed. "Many are the spirits I see above me but I cannot make their names out." Next followed a sort of grumbled conversation in which my uncle seemed to be talking to someone—it seemed to me it was a large animal who would not move aside. "Elk. An elk," he finally said. "I told him I must find the spirit who would tell me why Crying Cloud is having after-childbirth pain, why she is troubled." The husband cleared his throat discontentedly in the background.

Minutes passed. There was more grumbled conversation, then, "Ah, I see. A mouse. Large mouse with mean eyes. He is coming towards me, mouth open like a rat's—" There was distress in my uncle's voice, sounds of a struggle. His body thrashed around; I held it down. He was sweating. "Yes. I have prevailed. He will tell me why he is tormenting Crying Cloud." But no answer was forthcoming. Instead, within a few minutes, my uncle opened his eyes and stared haughtily at the husband.

"This man is demanding too much of you. There have been too many children in too short a time." The man turned, looking as if he would dispute that, but the shaman's dignity silenced him. "He is not keeping himself clean, has visited other women. So the spirit said."

Then he turned to the woman, who was sitting up now. "The spirit of the rodent said that you are timid, afraid. You do not assert your true womanhood in the name of our people.

73

Did you not have a naming day, a week-in-the-wild with your aunt?" The frightened young woman clung to the rag that was her bed covering. She nodded affirmation.

"Then you know how to be strong. You must have your female relatives clean this house and tell your husband to help keep it clean. Do not be with him until he is clean, until he has done purification rites. Not only women but men must be clean before the Maker of Stars. I will give him the rites he must observe."

"But how can I get strong, tell what I need and wish and do not wish," the women said. "I have always been afraid."

"The spirit told me how to heal you," said the Shaman. "I will suck out the timidity and fear. You must push them out from your side, too, while I remove them with my strength."

He knelt by the woman and picked up her arm. Gently he began to suck it, near the wrist, then more strongly. Crying Cloud kept her arm rigid and clenched her fists. In a moment the rite was completed.

"Now, if you can live as a strong woman of The People, you can be healed. Stay clean, inside and out. Tell your husband how it will be in your bed—if he visits other women, and so forth. Let your relatives take care of the children. The fever will be better. It is decreed."

"I will send her good bed coverings of fur; then you see to it that you take care of her," he said to the husband.

We walked back, through the rain. "How does the sucking help?" I asked.

"We all must get rid of the bad things in ourselves. The broken law must be identified. Then it must be cast out. That is the way of purification. But it helps if someone can point the way."

"That is the job of the shaman," I added, understanding. Bo Jo nodded.

The rest of the afternoon we watched the little girl, his youngest child White Wings, play on the floor. She was about two at the time, and the favorite of all the household. She was beginning to talk, to put two words together, and she would clap with her little hands when anything happened that delighted her. I took her for walks each day and we pointed at things by the side of the path. She could not seem to get enough of the new experience of life since she had come from the path beyond the stars to us. When an interesting animal, a beaver, for instance, would poke his head up in one of the ponds near the lake and swim by, showing his funny teeth, she would point and cry, "More beaver!" I often laughed at her, had played with her since she was a baby, and loved her.

Finally we came upon a bluejay, senseless from having run into a tree. He was standing in the path looking dull-eyed, and it appeared his wing was hurt.

"Help birdie, help birdie," White Wings pleaded.

I went to the bird, and holding his wing with leaves so I would not leave a human scent, brought it to the shelter, where I put it in a little woven cage. I put a splint on his wing, and White Wings brought seeds and nuts to put in the cage. She clapped her hands and laughed at me. "Tan-dak-sa, Bluejay," she chanted, as if she were a shaman, healing the bird herself.

In the shelter, she put her hand on my arm. "You help the birdie, Bear Belly." Even she! But there was tenderness in her touch, and I thought that of all things, young children are the most perfect gift of the spirits to man.

Still, what I had heard from my uncle was never far from my mind. Evening came, and I slept again, hoping tomorrow would tell me why in the heavens of stars there had been two Bo Jo's—one who could sell a man into slavery, and the one who now spent his life healing body and mind.

The answer came the next day, as we walked through the woods, looking for places to set our traps this next winter—strong wooden boxes tied with hemp rope with lures for beaver and hares. We could eat stewed beaver or rabbit and use the skins the next winter when Old Man Winter held his sway. To do the trapping well, one must set a course of traps before the snow falls.

Bo Jo talked of this and that. He had a slight smile on his face, tormenting me. And I was not going to ask—not I on that day.

Finally he said, "And so, I expect I should finish the tale of my life, don't you think. How I got out of the house that knows no light?"

"With the treasure? Do you still have any of it? How I would like to see the god of jade, the incense pots, the gold jewelry."

"And so would I. But I will tell you that part of the story right now. I left the treasures behind. I had to—by command." He could see my surprise, and then went on, continuing the story as we found a few rabbits we had snared and marked spots for traps, plotting the winter's work that would be ahead.

"Four, or perhaps five days I lay, eating nothing, only drinking a little water. My spirits were broken, not by the thought of my sins, which were many, but by the thought that death was inevitable. I would face it like a warrior, son of my father, without whimpering. But the pain was intense, because I had always had a burning stomach pit, worsened when I was in situations where there might be danger or scorn of me. Only food made it better, and now there was no food.

"As the days and nights passed, without my knowing really which was which, eventually even the burning stomach ceased its clamoring and a sort of serene peace settled over me. I seemed to float above my very body itself, up to the top of the cave where I could not go. It was the light I yearned for, and my spirit, rather than my poor dim eyes, ailing from the dust, seemed to see the evening star, star of the west—the very being of Nanaboozhoo—well, since I no longer believed, quite, that these stars were beings—the home of the West Wind's son. In my vision, or whatever it was, I saw the star and basked in its light, loving it as my ancestors had always done,

76

yearning—perhaps soon I would go there, or beyond, if there was a beyond. I think I really did, finally, again see a star over the small hole at the top. Then, I watched with wonder as the star's glow seemed to grow, disengage from the sky, and come down towards me, moving in a straight line. I could see, then only sense with my spirit, the form of a great hare. I prostrated myself.

"'Mitchaboo—Nanaboozhoo in the form of a hare. I have doubted you, doubted all of you. Do you live on the star?'

"'I live everywhere and have many names. I am the Son of Man.'

"'But the Sun God?'

"'The sun and moon are under my feet. I am under Another's feet.' He was silent a moment. "'Do not ask his name. Perhaps if you are wise, you will know.'

"'But I am dying. I cannot live in the cave—' I gestured down, towards my restlessly sleeping body.

"'I know. I know all things.'

"Suddenly something occurred to me. 'Why have you come to me in the shape of the hare—the trickster—instead of as the young warrior hero we have always loved?'

"'Perhaps because I thought you would recognize me sooner.' The vision voice sounded mocking. 'Trickster,' it said. 'Did you not bring about your own fall?'

"'No—well—' I paused, took a breath. 'Yes. Of course. I have gone down many crooked paths. Harmed many of earth's people.'

"'And so?'

"'I deserve to die. It is just punishment. So, why have you come? To escort my soul to the place beyond the milky path to the heavens?'

"There was silence, and the light I had seen changed, became clearer. The hare had transformed himself into the warrior hero, tallest of all men, with broadest shoulders, strongest heart. 'Nanaboozhoo, Son of the West Wind,' I murmured. He looked down at me.

"'It is not destined that you should go down the path of the stars at this time. No, there is much work for you to do here on earth.'

"I did not answer immediately. 'I am not worthy of your mercy. I should better die. There is no impurity I have not steeped myself in. I have—'

"'I know,' the vision said sharply. 'You will pay the price for those. You are to become a shaman.'

"'I, a leader and healer of my people?'

"'Yes. But before you do, you must pay the price, climb the tree of spiritual purification and see the heart of things.'

"My weakness, shock, kept me from asking the questions I might have. The wise hero spoke, and as he did the light of the evening star suffused his being, pulsating before my awed eyes. His voice rang out: 'You will go north again, up the Great River. Then go east. Take the great inland seas. Follow them from the City of Skunk Smell, Chicaga, north, then east, through straits, past worship islands. Come finally to the river and follow its course. At last, over water and land, you will come to the Great Falls. Your journey will be long and you will suffer. But at each place you will learn. Then return to your people and teach them the inner core of life.'

The light began to fade, slowly, gently, as evening comes after a bright day. I called out, 'Wait, Son of Man. How will I live, get out of this cave of doom?'

The light continued dimming but a voice, almost too faint to hear, echoed, 'Climb. Climb, son of the stars.' Then I was back in my body.

"'Wait,' I tried to call at the roof of the cave. 'You did not tell me the name of Him who is above you.' And in my heart I heard it: 'Maker of Stars.' He whom my father had told me of, but did not know. It made sense that if the Lord Sun was not all powerful and if the stars gave homage to one above, there would be a Maker of Stars—and all else. That was the answer. Now I knew. I rose, and somehow I had the strength to stand, to look up. There was still a faint, pulsating starlight, and in it I saw what I had not seen before with my dust-dimmed, ailing

78

eyes. The earth shaking that had loosed the rocks of the cave roof had left rocks piled up—some. Between them and the narrow ledges and outcroppings there might be—could be? a way out. Climb. I did. Weak as I was, I received the strength to climb, over many hard, sharp and agonizing rocks. And after I was out, to finish this long, long, tale, I recovered myself and found my way back across the great sea and up the river and across the land. Finally, suffering all as He said I would, I learned the sacred lessons of life all along the way I went, and I changed. Each living thing spoke to me, each declared that we are all brothers, all live to serve each other.

"Finally I came to the Great Falls the ancient tales and my vision spoke of. I stood near them, felt the spume as it hit the rocks, looked up again, as I had in the cave and I knew the power, the beauty, the grandeur of the creation we have been born into. I could not cry, I could not speak, I could only gaze.

"'Truly, truly, the Maker of Stars has made an earth of meaning,' my heart said. I was changed, utterly changed. I swam in the river downriver from those greatest of all falls. Its swiftness and rocks almost killed me, but when I dragged myself on shore, I was purged, cleansed of all the horrors I had done. And I came back to serve my people."

We were on a hill, overlooking the campfires of our people. "Why have you told me this?" I asked, after a while.

"Because you are the one to whom the torch will be passed," Bo Jo said. "When changes come."

"I? Bear Belly?" I asked scornfully. And I was also the one ordained to build the giant drum, so the wild rice traders said. Certainly Michaboo, the jokester rabbit was having a good chortle out there someplace.

"With the gift of healing, Nanaboozhoo also gave the gift of prophecy. I have seen the coming of change. " That was all he said.

And the next morning, before dawn, the Dune Devil people attacked the camp and killed several of our people, including my own mother and father and my uncle's crippled son, and carried off the women and children. They marched some of us, younger and older, off to their own camps to be slaves. Change indeed.

While Bo Jo and I marched, prodded from behind by lances of the Dune warriors, my uncle registered no emotion, not even knowing that his wife Rose-on-the-Hill and his girl children were among the captives taken to another camp, far away from us. The darling White Wings was marching a dark trail, her little feet stumbling, and her joyous cries to see all the "more beavers" of life would fall upon cruel ears.

From childhood we had all known of this ruthless tribe of savages, and it had been they who had stolen the last of the winter food from us earlier in the year. They were a renegade band from a large tribe who lived almost as far away east as the Great Falls Bo Jo had seen on his vision quest. We had known their raids before, though they hadnever carried us away. Tales of their tortures were so awful they were spoken of in whispers. So I knew that great must be Bo Jo's vision power indeed that his face was so serene in the face of an unknown that was as terrifying to me as a storm in the night to a toddling child.

We plodded on, our bare legs beaten when we faltered, our old ones driven through heat until they dropped, to be left by the road. My friend Shell-god, gentle and thoughtful youth that he was, seemed to suffer much. It was the mental anguish, the idea that we were in the shame of capture, that seemed to rob him of strength. Still, I saw him command himself as a true man, and I admired and loved him as I saw it.

Over twenty died that way. One who almost died but not quite, was my uncle's servant Ghost-on-the-Lake. This small man whom the village had raised, who walked as if he had a burden on his back, came slower than the rest, and he was beaten and ridiculed by the Dune Devils. I watched him plod along, making his feet take more steps than others to keep up, and I told myself that here was valor indeed, even if it was in a servant.

We were fed on scraps thrown from the hunter's catch by the fire by mocking, painted Dune people (we dared not use the other word—even to ourselves. They understood our language just as Bo Jo understood theirs and they would have killed us instantly with their sharpened spikes or cut off our heads with the sharpest of knives if they had heard our derision.) But on the second night, as we slept in the open, bitten by horrible flies, I whispered to Bo Jo. "It was the Dune People you visited before, when you were young. Your rival—the one you sold to the Dune—people. You did not tell me what happened to—"

"Hush. He is not there. He was ransomed but—"A Dune devil came to slap his mouth, and we dared not speak again the rest of the trip.

We came into their camp, a crude village of stick huts on a huge sand hill overlooking the end of the Long Finger of the shining big sea waters—huge lakes you could not see across. There were dogs everywhere, raised in herds for food, piles of bones and garbage and animal offal near the camp as if to break the saying of the Old Ones that a squirrel will not foul his own nest.

The Dune Devils lived always in camp—they did not build homes as we in the villages and cities. Well, I do not know what they originally did in the far-away land from which they came, a land set in huge forests near the great falls Bo Jo had visited. It was in their great-grandfathers' times that these swarthy people standing in a circle in the middle of their huts, yelling gleefully at our capture, had left their people in the east.

The Dune Devils had been cast out for their offensiveness, some said—and came west as far as our lands, staying to collect copper and other western trade goods and returning every four or five years along the great way of the lakes to their people. They did not have the plots of corn or squash but lived from the hunt and wild berries—that and pillaging. All lived in fear of them, small numbers that they were, with their three or four camps. As we walked through their midst, with small stones thrown at us in derision and those Dune Devil dogs baying and snapping, I asked myself, What were they good for, spirit of the Star-Maker? If you made all for the path of brightness and blessing why did you make these hornet-mosquitoes in the world, these tormenting, ferocious, wolverine-people who were good for nothing but to cause pain?

We soon had good reason to know well enough that the Dune Devils lived to cause pain. Exhausted and tried as we were by the merciless prodding and starvation of the trail, we were to be put to the torment immediately, therein the midst of the day, before all the howling men and women, screaming, squalling children and barking dogs.

You know what the torment is; I do not need to tell you. All say that it has purpose. It is to show revenge, of course, if you have just cause of insult given. But beyond that, as all people say, it is to show who is a true man or woman, who should be saved to stand as a servant, who discarded onto the dung heap of death.

But I did not know the torment from seeing it with my own eyes. My village, small and humble as it was, and far from the great cities, had a command of peace on it.

It had been given by the Great Shaman—Bo Jo's and my father's grandfather, after the time of the Mad Fighting, when brother fought brother and many died. We were not to seek either war or the torment but to live under the wings of the White Bird of Thunder. The warriors' way was not forbidden to us; far from it; we were taught to fight well, but only if we were attacked. "The skies are happiest when they are calm; we should not seek the thunderstorms," the Great Shaman had told our people after a very powerful vision he had. We were forbidden to seek war or great power as others did, or to do the torment. I think he did it because we were so small, such tiny ants among the great cities and villages of the world of Lakes-Like-a-Necklace and the great river valleys. He told us the woods, not warfare, would teach us truth, and so it had proven.

But I had heard, truly I had heard, of the torment. Nothing could prepare me, though, for the trial of torture as the Dune People did it. Their chief man was old but as sinewy as a stag. Around his neck was a huge necklace of eagle and hawk feathers and other bits of medicine. His eyes were bright rocks; in fact, he was called Bright-Coals-in-the-River. He wore a breechclout, no skirt, and his thighs were like oakwood. "Captive men, your women and children have been taken to our other two camps amidst these dunes. You we will test." The people howled like wolves, roared like bears. Truly they loved to see the testing.

Bo Jo was quiet, his face as impassive as ever. He was pushed into a line with three others from our village; after some talking among a group of young men, it was obvious I was not to be placed with the main group of those who would stand the torment; no, I was given lower grade torments—was I being reserved for something later? Bad enough were my trials; I bit my tongue determined not to show pain. They stuck the long firespikes under three of my fingernails and while they smoldered, they tied me in my agony to a post to watch the torment of my uncle and the others—including Shell-god.

The women were to torment me. They were boiling water in a pot; it was not reassuring, I tell, you to watch them chortling and stirring over there and pointing at me, while my fingernails charred and I smelled my own flesh. But that was only the beginning, and where the sun was, or how long my own torment lasted that day, I cannot tell you.

Now as I tell you the story, it seems a blur, that we were carried on a slow tortoise's back into a forest of suffering. The group of women came to me now and then, grabbing my hands to put the burning sticks under more of the bleeding, charred nails. Then, when I was not expecting it, from behind, the younger ones poured small driblets of scalding water on my shoulders. They seemed to take pleasure watching the agony go on for several seconds. Young girls, perhaps only nine or ten summers old, surrounded me with axes, yelling at the top of their lungs, taking small swipes, just enough to break the skin.

They were sent forward or called back by an aloof young girl of about my age; naturally, it would be one of the beautiful ones, the Morning Glory of her tribe, who would be sent to be in charge of my torments. Not only would she watch me try to hold back my shouts of anguish at the pain, but she would scorn and mock me in her mind. Her derision could not be stronger than my own against myself; Bear Belly, in his usual role as jokester and hind end of the group. My pain was even greater, seeing her there.

But my pain was nothing compared to what the young men of the village were doing to my uncle and the three others. The village had fully assembled and sacrificing oblations had been made, to Nini Pinja, the evil fire tiger, and other gods and spirits. My uncle was in the middle, two others on one side, one on another. Two were the boat clan people we had met the day before, oh long time ago. A father and son who had been recently married, they had been building the canoe on the shores of Lake-of-the-Boulders. And, of course, more sadness to me, my best friend Shell-god.

First, a little at a time, their toenails were gouged out with knives. and no one cried out, though it took an hour. But in the next torment, when burning faggots were stuck into the skin, the new bridegroom moaned. They threw axes at the three of them, and when one cut off the bridegroom's private parts, the crowd yelled even louder. The young man began to bleed. He was already covered with blood from the cuts, but now it seemed as if he would bleed pots of blood. The village gathered around and watched his life blood flow as he first fainted, then slowly slipped away into the path of death. They pointed and murmured; clearly they had never seen anyone bleed so

84

fast. His father, Flying Goose, did not even look at him; he had been silent except for grunts through the whole torment. He was true man, I say. Surely the spirits blessed him, because he saw his son go to the path of the stars and beyond where he could suffer no more.

I say that because the others had to endure the axes for quite a while until all manhood was removed and their humiliation was complete. Finally my friend began to moan, to yelp, in spite of himself, and the Dune Devil men shook their heads at him, shouted he was a coward. I prayed he would faint soon too.

And what had my uncle been doing through all this horrible torment? In spite of my own pain and apprehension, I could not help but watch him. Bo Jo, Grand Shaman of the Lakes-Like-a-Necklace, like a block of wood as they tortured his body. He did not even grunt. What animated him, kept him going? I marvelled. Water was running out of my eyes as I sat unwatched as all the girls and women observed the more serious torments in the council ring. First there had been mocking cries for more punishment in the early minutes of torment, then wonder was expressed that even when all toenails were gone, and dirt and salt dumped on Bo Jo's feet to add to the pain, there was no response. Finally, as the hours wore on, there were murmurings, admiration. These I heard in snatches, as I moved out of the cloud of my own pain.

And, towards sunset, when the blood had been stanched from the wounds of his groin and he slumped, still tied to the pole, the tales of my uncle passed before my eyes, and I saw the good he had done in the twenty summers that he had been Shaman. Our village, and all the other villages of the region sang of him in their song.

> Bo Jo the shaman,
> beloved of the stars,
> Knows to call the rain, the rain from
> the Home of the Thunderbirds
> Walks in the night with peace and

Healing in his footsteps
Walks in the day all the way to the
Beautiful River to heal the madness
With the stone of great medicine.
His door opening is never covered
When he can go to heal.
Love of the stars, of Nanaboozhoo
for all the children of earth,
Warmth of the Sun Lord, Justice of
the Stars, Might of the Birds of Thunder
Love of the Evening Star, Nanaboozhoo
For all the children of earth,
Bright sons of morning
Is in his eyes.
Praise him, praise him.

My thoughts, moving in and out of pain visions, sang the song loud. I could hear drums that were not there. Bo Jo once said I would build and play the Great Drum, and now I heard it in my mind, as they say young brides can see and hear their children yet to be born in sweet night dreams.

I tried to concentrate for just one moment, to put aside the throbbing agony, to think of this uncle who loved me so much. Why were they not afraid of such a great shaman, purged in the fire of vision, one of a generation? Surely they must have heard of him, be afraid of his wrath now, that he would bring a magic curse on them—well, he did not do that, but I knew he could if he wished.

The chief Bright-Coals-in-the-River finally came up. His voice was harsh, barking, as he stared at the slumped Bo Jo. "You have done well in the torment, Shaman. Where is your power now? I ask. Where is the medicine bundle, the trip to the vision lands we hear about from all who walk the trails. Your power is gone, I say." Bo Jo opened his eyes, finally, and looked straight at the chieftain. There was no fear in the eyes.

"I know you, Shaman," the old man said. He spoke in our dialect so that all of us might not miss what he said, and it was rough, but understandable. "I have been first man here for ten years, but years before that, when I was a warrior above all else, I knew you then. You are different, but you are the same. I did not know that the shaman of great fame, the shaman of songs was you—who came to us from Cahokia many returns of the sun ago—you mocker of the justice of the spirits, player of games, seller of men. When I saw you walk into the clearing, captured—the spirits have finally delivered him into our hands, I told myself. And others—" He gestured around the circle; the older ones nodded their heads. I do not know why I had not thought of it. Of course there would be some who knew him as the trader who came to sell the young nobleman of Cahokia. He had not stayed many days, many weeks, but they remembered.

The chief, whose shoulders were slightly bent, put out a finger as gnarled as a dead oak branch. "Do you not recall the night you traded the one you called the Corn Clout for our furs? Do you not recall the first night of feasting, then the trials he underwent? We did not wish him to run away, strong slave that he was. He threatened—the lords of Cahokia would find out and come to claim him, he said–I laughed. I told him we do not ally with Cahokia—or any other of the walled cities. Our people sang the song `Even the Lords of Cahokia fear the Dune people—fear the barbed arrow, fear the raid by night.'

"After he endured the torment he became my son." Even through my haze of pain I listened to that. "That same week he came my own child had died; he came and braved the worst we had to give him. I took him for my own and loved him. I knew his story well, by the time the lords of Cahokia redeemed him with too many stores of grain to say no to, I knew what you had done to him." He laughed, and his laughter filled the glen where they were torturing, waking my friend from his unconsciousness, causing him to groan, then cry aloud.

Distracted, the chieftain ordered him cut down. "The old man, father to the dead one, we redeem. One in the tribe may claim him for servant." Someone came forward and the old boat clansman Flying Goose was cut down and given to him. Ghost-on-the-Lake, who had not been put to the torment, was given to a young couple to serve. The young man had led the scouting party to our village; brave he was, I suppose, in their eyes and deserving of a servant.

I did not pay attention to any of this, really, because I heard the next words, "Him," (my friend) we will burn tomorrow. And him" (for the first time he took public notice of me) "him of the fat breasts like a girl's"—everyone hooted—"will run the torture tunnel. Let him shake his fat legs through that."

The girls ran up again, pointing and planning their next torments. I had provoked the highest ignominy. I was not even worthy of the most ferocious torment, not even treated as a man of The People. I looked up and knew what scorn I seemed to read in the eyes of the tall, silent and lovely girl who was the girls' leader.

With cool eyes she gave orders, and with glee the girls came to me with knives and sliced my skin, this time more deeply, then cut me down and rolled me in the dirt.

But through the pain and humiliation, so deep I wished ardently for death, I heard the crow-call voice of the old chieftain, waving a stick of power at my uncle. "You, the player of games become shaman of might, you who mocked my son and made him a slave, we will have you watch the burning—then you will have the highest death of all. The death of unwinding snarls."

The cool, silent maid ordered the girls to stand me up again. I was there, naked, covered with dust, bleeding from wounds everywhere. I wiped dust from my mouth and eyes with hands that were not bound any longer. "The death of unwinding snarls?" I said to the cool maid, in a voice only she could hear.

For the first time she spoke. She did not need to, but she did. Perhaps she thought it would put a further edge on my tortures to know. I could understand a few words of the language, but mostly I saw what she meant as she moved her hands to show me. "A slit is made in the stomach. Entrails are pulled out and fastened to a tree. The tested one must run around in a circle until all the entrails are pulled out—"

I saw a bright flash before my eyes. It was my own anger, my love for my uncle, kindest and best of men—to be killed by hideous, drawn-out torture—I found enough saliva in my mouth of the desert to spit. Her face was near mine; the others were watching the chieftain. "Your own dogs have their throats slit before you eat them. To cause pain like that—are you human beings?"

"You dare to say that to me when I have power to—" the girl hissed at me. A few words. I caught the gist.

"Do you not fear the gods?" Fever was beginning to burn in my cuts and wounds. My eyes were hollow and bright as I stared right at her. She turned from me, then seemed to gain new strength. "Whip him with the willow switches till his wounds reopen," she said and haughtily marched away.

I lay at the side of my friend and my uncle that night under the stars. Hard the far away lords of the heavens looked, and cruel beyond all else to me. His body broken, his senses muddled from the loss of blood, my uncle lay silent, mumbling at times inaudibly to Nanaboozhoo, the Star Lords, the Maker of Stars. Then, about midnight he awoke. The campfires at the council ring were dying, the kaskasks—the catydids suddenly still. "My nephew, are you awake?" he asked through his bruised lips.

"I am, Uncle. They have not defeated my spirit yet."

"Nor will they," he said. He tried to move a little, gave up the effort. His arms were broken.

"Uncle, if I could take some of your pain, I would."

"You have enough for yourself. Besides, I do not feel it. There is a place beyond pain."

"Tomorrow, Uncle, you will face worse. I cannot think of it—"

He sighed and there was—was it contentment? in the effort. "Tomorrow I will not be here. The Maker of Stars has granted great mercy."

"What is it, Uncle?" I wondered, turning to look down into his face. We dared not raise too much noise; they would return and bludgeon us on the spot.

"I have lost much blood from the cutting. But I also have the flux and know from it that the burning stomach has come, as it did once before when I was in the land of the jade. It opens up the stomach,"—he chuckled a little, painfully, ruefully. "They wanted to open me, to see the inside of me. But the inside is torn open and bleeds steadily. It will pour out my life soon."

"How long?"

"Before the stars set," he said. Then his voice grew more labored. "Now there are things to say. The moment I die, that moment your quest begins in earnest."

"No, Uncle—"

"Do not act the cub anymore. You will journey far—repeat the trip of Nanaboozhoo—and of me."

"I—will—go east or west?" I whispered.

"To the four directions, like the Birds of Thunder. And within."

"But I am to be put through the tunnel of torture. I cannot survive."

There was harshness in his whisper. "You can survive. You must tell yourself to run. Not fast but ever on. Steadily. Cover your head above all else. A blow to the head will fell you."

"The girls will be there," I said softly. "Throwing axes at me, yelling `Bear Belly.'"

There was silence. Off in a clearing, dancing and rejoicing over the day's activities made the woodlands ring. My friend, Shell-god, was delirious. Would he last to be burnt?

"You have a name, do you not?"

"Yes. Of course. I was not taken to my vision quest and named Bear Belly. I am Sinking Beaver." How little that name had been used.

90

"I re-name you. Drum-of-the-Gods. For what you will do tomorrow. And afterwards, when the quest—takes you far, always the Bird of Thunder, Bird of Truth, will be your guide."

"How will I know where to go, what to do?"

"You will--know."

His voice was growing weaker. I took his hand, the hand I had loved so long, that held mine when I walked the grassy paths by the lakes as a tiny child, that steadied me while teaching me the art of bow and arrow. "One thing," he said, opening his eyes. "I did not–tell you all of my life story. In the–cave."

"Yes, Uncle?" I said, leaning towards him. They were leaving the clearing. They had left us unguarded, thinking none of us had strength to flee. Right they were, but we had the strength to talk, and now that the dancing was breaking up they would be coming to check.

"There was a token of great worth I did not—tell you of. A tablet of clay, with scratches on it, like the Sun Watcher's tablet."

"Yes?" I urged. Girls rushed by, shouting jests about our tribe. They did not see us talking in the shadows.

"It is a Moon Watcher's tablet—of great power. It tells the times the sun will be swallowed by the moon—in the future."

"Ah?" I said, surprised. We had spoken of this before. Such a thing would indeed be valuable—one of the things most powerful in all the world. "The trading folk of the southern sea lands had such a thing?"

"They had their own moon things but no, none this great. I took it in there with me, had carried it with me ever, wherever I was. It had been given in greatest secrecy by—my father and to him by the father of the Great Shaman. It went back three generations."

"This tablet of the moon. The Old Ones in our family had made it?"

He shifted his weight very slowly and his voice faded further. "No—there were travelers who came three generations ago. When we lived in campgrounds further east, near the Beautiful River—I am ready to go, I must tell you"—I leaned closer yet. "They came from across the ocean and brought the knowledge of moon swallowings from the magic of—their land. The—Blue Eyes, they were called. They lived with us, then some of the tribe went with them west— The tablet is yours."

"But there, far away—how would I—"

"It is in the cave. You already know how to get there. If you can claim it, great power, great danger—"

And that was all. He bubbled, he sighed, and was gone. Bo Jo, the good Shaman and my uncle.

When the chieftain and his warrior came, they saw the dead man on the ground. They knelt, listened for a heartbeat, cursed and spat. Then they carried away the body of my uncle to be desecrated and burned tomorrow along with that of my friend. I looked up, at the pathway of the stars. "Go to the Son of the West Wind, Uncle. Ride with him, fast, fast, across the path of the stars, and may your journey be content," I said to myself.

I will not tell you of the agony of the burning. By that time something in me had dried up, my springs of human caring, and I could not react. Stonily I watched, smelled the awful smoke of flesh, heard the yelping, hideous cries of the gentle Shell-god, the boy I had walked the trails with since babyhood, which started as agonized protests, developed into almost automatic yelps and then degenerated into half-unconscious moans until at last the spirit left the seared remains of my friend.

And then it was my turn. Time for the tunnel of testing. "Nanaboozhoo, help!" I called out. "Or whoever you are—" thinking of my uncle and his sacred doubts. "I am weary to dying already and I must take my flabby self along the torture path—old and young alike ready to strike me with stones, axes, sticks, and if I fall—HELP!"

In a blur I saw them all. In a blur I started, my hands about my head so I at least would not take a blow that would fell me there. In a blur I got a quarter of the way through a rain of blows and sharp pain, water thrown in my eyes, laughter like salt raining down on my wounds. Then I was halfway, and in some way hope dawned, small as a new sprout in Young Bear Moon that I might go the whole way. Of course that did not mean I would live–quite the contrary. Then I was three-quarters of the way and saw the end of the tunnel, where waited little children ready to throw rocks, and I felt the pain and blows would make me faint. I began to stumble. There, within sight of the end, I went to my knees and the scene began to fade as they all closed round.

Then I heard it, the sweetest words of my life, guessed at, more than understood. "The young man is brave. He has run the tunnel and deserves to live. I claim him as slave for my grandmother. He shall be adopted." I looked up through pain clouded eyes and saw—the beautiful girl. She had saved me. "Truly," I thought, "Nanaboozhoo or whoever you are—you have taken me in death to be with you in the Happiest of Hunting Grounds beyond the stars. I am dead and gone on."

But it was not so. The girl, whose name was Loon Feather, was ordering my broken body dragged to her family's shelter. For an instant I knew—just as I had been often tormented by beauty, now I had been saved by beauty. And then I did not know more for quite a while.

When I did awake there was balm on my wounds. Next to the fire, on her haunches like a dog, was an old woman, stirring a stew.

"And so, you are back to the world of Turtle's Island," she said. Again, I felt it, more than understood, because I did not know many of the words of the Dune Devils' language.

"And so I am," I answered, wondering at it a little myself. Before long I found that the old woman's husband and son were lost in the cold winter trip three years before, when snow

caught all the Dune Devils in the canoes going to their homeland before the leaves were even off the trees, and waves
tipped the great fur canoes and some fell out into the roaring,
dark waters.

"Yes, you can hunt for us," this old woman, whose name
was Thistle Child, said, pointing at hunting things on a log in
the corner of the rude shelter. "But you can also do work." She
pointed at pots and the broom, then at herself, at limbs
swollen with pain. Then she pointed at the girl and at the fur
frame. "Loon Feather must do the fur-stretching every day.
She is best of all in the village." She said it over a couple of
times, and I repeated and picked it up. One of the first things
I was given by the Bird of Thunder at gifting time at my birth
was the gift of tongues—remarkably, easily, I pick up languages.

I picked myself up to walk outside to greet the day I never
thought I would see. There, outside, in the shadow of the
shelter, was the beautiful girl. She was deftly combing the
blood and intestines off the back of a fur animal, with the
movement of one who has often done the act. There was a reek
from the animal flesh, and in spite of all the reasons I had to
hate her deeply, I could not help loving the way she looked,
sitting there, with the spring wind flitting over her, rumpling
her garments, and with hair escaping from the headband.

I pointed at my breast, shook my head, and asked her
softly, "Why did you save me?"

She thought about what I had said, tried to understand the
words. Finally I knew she had understood, but still did not
respond for such a long time that I thought she was not willing
to answer the question. I was in a briar patch of a thousand
small and large pains, and so I almost did not care.

"You rebuked me," she said, pointing at me, staring through
the smoke with large eyes. "I had the power of life and death
over you and yet you snarled at me, like a fox caught in a trap
hissing at its captors. You said I was acting evilly." That was
the gist of it.

"As you were," I thought, rather than said. But perhaps according to their own lights. I shrugged."We have a command of peace on our village. We do not do the tortures."

She did not understand. She laughed a little, then went on with her scraping, throwing the blood off the scraper into a huge fire, which heated stones to boil the hair off hides. She gestured around the camp, naming things right and left—tasks that I would do when the morrow came.

Thistle Child came out. She sent the girl, Loon Feather, to a relative's shelter; it was not seemly that she should stay there with me now at the cooking fire. And then the grandmother looked at my wounds and grumbled to herself, nodding with satisfaction, that I was well enough. I could begin the slave work when the Lord Sun rose the next day.

I did not feel at all like I could even walk well, let alone work, but work I must. Summer was bright like a briar rose, but some mornings in this northern land the winds were strong and cool and the fire must be replenished often. Then there was much wood to stock for fires we burned always to do the hides, and clothes to be taken to the stream and beaten on the rocks, and saplings to bend and tie for a new shelter.

All these I did from the first rays of the sun to its last, sinking behind the dunes of the great lake where we lived. Little by little I came to know their language, which was not hard to know. And though I went to hunt, I did not get much, because I did not know the hunting ways well, so the pot was not very full of venison, at which the old woman would whack me with a stick she carried about and call me names.

And since I was so often at work and since the food was poor in the pot, my bear belly shrank and shrank as the days passed and the weight passed from my limbs and I became lean, as my uncle had been lean, and I wished he was there to see it, though I would have died for shame to have had him see my doing the woman's work. I thought of him as the wind moaned low at night about the shelter, thought of him and mourned for him, wondered about my people at home, wondered even about his wife and his two girl children, whom he had entrusted to my care. And I thought particularly about the little maiden, White Wings, and wondered which of these tribes of the Dune Devils she was with, or even if she still lived. And my heart was as a log laden with water, heavy, sodden.

Ghost-on-the-Lake I saw often, lurching about, as he worked around the shelter he served. He did not speak to me, and I supposed that was because it would increase his pain if he made contact. The days that used to be stood between us, like a painful wen, too tender to touch.

The boat-maker Flying Goose was there, adopted also, and I spoke to him sometimes. He was a man of strong humor, who could sometimes chuckle, even here, even after what had happened to his son. They had put him to work on the canoes that would carry the furs back east, and through his work, he found life. His strength was far inside him, but I could not feel that way. Not then. I ate my pain daily, chewing and swallowing it as I ate the meat and corn of my adopted house.

One day, as I stopped off briefly at the lake to see him hollowing and burning and blowing inside a log, he told me that my uncle's wife was dead, his two girls separated. He had heard that from a messenger who came from one of the other Dune Devil camps. "White Wings," I thought, "where are you now?" Pain even worse than the torture now seemed to hang on my soul. It was that they were gone, all gone, the family, the people gone. All that I had lived for, everything I had known, had been scattered and crushed like an anthill kicked into nothing.

After I had been in the shelter for a time, I determined to wear my grief on my face; to paint the black lines of mourning for my uncle and the others who had died here in this camp by the large lake. It was a bold gesture, one that would surely anger the Dune Devils, but something in me swelled and felt as if it would burst. I felt I could not go on another day, eat another meal watching the stars through the door of this grandmother's poor shelter one more time if I did not honor my dead. The feelings grew, swelled, as I have said, not like the putrefaction of an animal in the woods, not at all, not malignantly, like a boil. No, rather like the milkweed pod, which yearns to spill itself so that new life may start.

I took charcoal from the firepits. My wounds had healed, but I opened the ones on my arms, like the mocking girls had done, with willow switches. I cut my hair short. All this I did in front of the shelter, which was near the center of the camp, near sunset one warm summer day.

Bright-Coals-in-the-River came walking by on his way to the sweat house and saw me observing my rites. "And so you have the effrontery to mourn? Here in our camps? Who do you mourn?"

My heart leapt within me. I was afraid, truly afraid, and yet the swelling need to do the rites was greater than the fear. I now spoke the language fairly well. It was not too far distant from ours.

"I honor my uncle, dead in the testing torture, my friend, Shell-god, of my youth and blood brother. And the son of the father who died when we came into camp. His father Flying Goose has not honored him."

"No. No honor was appropriate for one who whined like a puppy in the torture." It was a direct taunt, an insult to our village men's bravery. But I did not rise to take it so. I could not afford to do so; I was walking on the thinnest skim of ice on a newly frozen pond as it was.

"Today I saw that the father has been sent away." I wanted, needed news of the others in our village—my little cousins, my own mother and father—and could not ask it.

"Yes. Now that our boats are completed, the boatman has gone to serve in another village, with my sister's children. But let us not stray, Belly of the Bear, from the matter at hand. You are mourning, and none has given you permission. You mourn for a man who did our village insult. He sold the man who became my son."

I looked directly in the fire-coal eyes, which still seemed to me like Nini Pinja's—fire dragon's deeply brooding, evil ones.

97

"Surely he has paid," I said softly. Then I turned to my charcoal, making the lines across my own eyes deep and shadowed.

"And so he has," the old warrior said.

"And as far as mourning, I honor him as my uncle, as the Birds of Thunder decree—honor parents, revere uncles who give the gift of wisdom. To leave him unmourned is to do less than the rites the spirits expect."

"So much wisdom in one so young, Belly of the Bear?" His voice was strident, but he took no step towards me.

I stood up then, nodding deferentially as if to thank him for allowing me to go unmolested with my mourning rites. But when I did he could see, because I was in breechclout only, that my belly was not that of the bear (as if he had not seen that before), but was flat and taut with muscle. And that even in the few weeks I had been with them I had gained stature, so that I was as tall as he, Bright-Coals in the River, chieftain of the tribe.

The young maiden came daily to see her grandmother, and stretched her fur frames under an elm tree near the shelter. She worked silently, concentrating on the several steps of scraping, dipping in ashes and water, scraping some more, stretching on the frame and so forth that readied furs for the winter use of the tribe and to take, the choicest ones, to relatives in the tribe back home in the East. Now that I was no longer cousin to a bear, the younger girls had quit mocking me, or even noticing me.

Loon Feather did not mock. She did not speak often, either. Instead, we suffered each other's presence, I working on the shelter or fire, she on the skins, with mutual acceptance. We had been thrust into each other's presence, had gone through the awful turmoil of the torture, each hating the other, playing our own roles, and now we were part of the household of the old woman. We had toleration which comes from duty—and, I think, respect. Respect, above all, each for each.

Near the shelter of the old one I slaved for, as I have said, was the Marked One I have spoken of before, the young humpback who was the servant of our family in the country of Lakes-Like-a-Necklace. They had not, of course, put Ghost to the torture; he was considered special because he had a strong mark from the gods.

After not speaking to me in the beginning, because, I think, of his pain, he began to come about our campfires and tried to talk to me with his halting tongue. He could not speak well; it was part of the affliction. Anyway, he missed the affection he had received, almost like a child, at the campfire of Bo Jo and Rose-on-the-Hill. He wanted to talk of them, to remember, and that pained me more than his ignoring me had done before.

I had never given him a moment's thought back at Lake-of-the-Boulders; he had been taken in, taught to work some; he was about as important as the sled that carried furs from the forest. That was all. Now, though it hurt me to recall the past, I began to try to take notice of him anyway, because I thought I should, that my uncle would wish it.

At first, as I went about my daily routine, struggling to carry pots of water from the ice-cold lake, or cleaning the hunting kill I sometimes managed to snare or shoot in my bumbling way, I had scant patience for Ghost, with his short, stocky frame, his odd, bright eyes, his tongue which could not seem to stay in his mouth at all times.

But as I listened to him, I became fascinated by him, by his mannerisms, his speech. He was called Ghost-on-the-Lake because it was believed his mother was frightened by a ghost during a violent storm a few years ago, when some people, we knew not who, had gone north to fish for giant pikefish in the big lake.

"Why did you not die when the oth—ers did?" he asked, twisting his hands about as he looked up into my face. I was skinning fish, the easiest way to provide food for the table. I

99

tried not to stare as he humped about. It would not have been seemly, as I know Bo Jo would have said. "Because I was too tough to die," I answered. "Because the gods sent me their grace—because the spirit of the oak tree I sat under liked the corn and pipe I sacrificed to his brother four moons ago—who knows?" My tongue was sharp these days.

His smile was slow but sure. "Or, because your feet were strong as you ran the tor—ture tunnel? Strong—er than your heart?" He had hit on the truth and knew my secret—a heart that often failed with fear. How true the old ones were when they spoke of the Marked Ones. They said the dull-minded, the hunchbacked, the dwarfs, had secret truth—communion with the Maker of the Stars or insight from the spirits who served him. They hit on truth as a chungky pole hits the mark sometimes—by luck? Or by wit. For the first time it occurred to me that he might have an intelligent mind in his twisted body.

So he became my companion. The young woman, wife to the scout leaders, did almost all the work at the shelter he had been given to, and so he was often free. I let him help me carry my loads sometimes, to blow on the coals, to find dry grass or fur to start the fires in the damps of evening as the fall wore on. And he took to me—as a puppy takes to the child who feeds it, following me, always looking up to me, hunched as he was, doing anything he could to please me. Ghost-on-the-Lake was my adoring puppy.

But I got something from him, too, because he was the only one in the camps who cared for me, who seemed to know I even existed except as a thing—the slave of the old grandmother, like a stool or cooking stick in her shelter. In him I saw reflected the manhood I was finding in my life, discovering it new, as one unexpectedly finds a fine vista on a hill on the trail.

And still I wore the mourning. One fine, crisp late summer morning Bright-Coals-in-the-River stopped and keenly surveyed me with his sharp eyes.

"Tonight we celebrate at the council ring," he said. "You may end your mourning and come." He went his way.

100

"Bo Jo," I said, addressing his spirit. "The time prescribed is not yet done; still, I will obey him. He has power over me and I have pressed him far enough." Then I thought a moment and added one more thing, which was real truth too. "And I do want to see the celebration, perhaps see Loon Feather in her fine clothing." It does not do to tell the spirits half truths. I could go with an open, curious heart to the rites of the green corn.

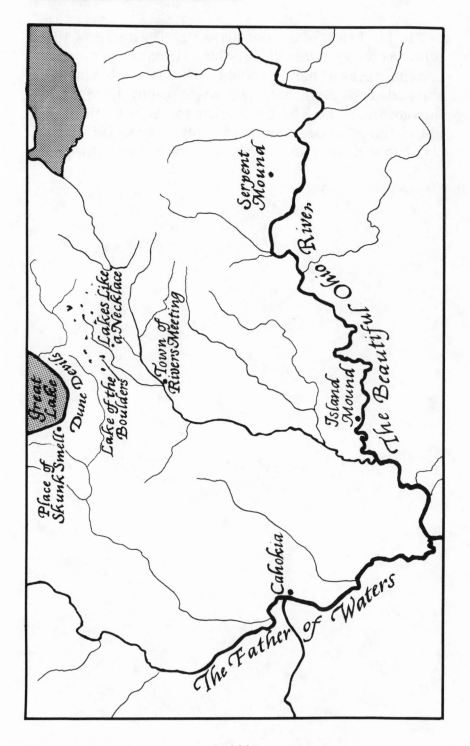

Chapter Five

As the Sun Lord sank that night, the clans assembled, and I walked alone to the campfire, wondering what their rites would be, wondering at myself that I would be celebrating with the killers of my friend and my uncle—with my tribe's hated Devils of the Dune.

I spat on the ground, trying to hate them with all my being, but it did not work. I had come to be one of them, in a way, eating their food, serving their needs. And I now knew they were not all bad. Not at all. I had come to know that their religion was a good one, a pure one, at times. The voice they listened to above was like the one my uncle had heard—a vision voice which could heal and purify, deep in nature, high on the branches of the tree of life. Why they heard it sometimes as a call to torture, while we heard it as a call to peace was something I could not explain. Perhaps there are other voices people listen to, and believe it is the gods speaking.

The campfires were blazing for Green Corn Festival. Well—it was not really our Green Corn, because they did not eat much corn, only what they stole, living on the hunt, fishing, and what the women could gather instead. I think Thistle Child had called it a War Triumph at the Time of Blackberries feast. I suppose they were rejoicing at overcoming our small camp and some others like it, I told myself sadly.

We came around the great campfire as always at a festival in the woods. All of the clan groups of the Dune Devils had a part in rejoicing for the victories in war and praising the bravery of the warriors. The warriors wore special belts tied about their waists and pouches on their backs filled with several things, I was told, always the same. You have seen similar things here in this land, but the pouches were different, very elaborate. Each thing in the pouch was carefully selected, like a medicine bag, but touching of the things of war the man had done.

Tobacco, of course, began the ceremony, filling the clearing with its pungent smell. Pipes were white clay, reserved for

103

this purpose only. When the spirits had been summoned sufficiently, the chieftain called the first group of warriors to come forward, whose purpose I did not know but supposed they were scouts. From their belts hung leather thongs with sharp stone knives, whistles which made wonderful noises like the calls of birds, and whips. They rose from special places around the fire, to which they had marched when we all came in.

These scouts began to sing a sacred song, one they had learned from the spirits, so it was said (though it was from their tribe's original homeland where the great falls roar, I suppose) and danced, in a circle, touching shoulders and moving their feet to beat the earth in ways they had been taught, slower than what we do here.

As they made the circle, the drum began. I say drum because, again, instead of the small drums I had seen the shamans and music makers use always, the warrior men of the Dune Devils had one big drum made from the trunk of a tree. It was like the one that had surprised me, that the wild rice people had brought in a canoe to the Place of Rivers Meeting. One drum again! How strange it struck me here, also.

Two women with fine voices knelt in front of it to sing, and a nephew of my old grandmother's played with the covered sticks.

"Ah, wa, weeoh," they sang. "The scouts please the spirits, we thank the spirits, we ask for more strength to conquer—" that was the gist of it.

There were more dances, one for each group being honored and bringing petition for more victories in battle. The last group, the advancers-into-battle wore special belts, knives, and whips but also bundles of grass, to show how far they camped to build their fires when they were preparing to attack the enemy, to steal his power. At the head of the advancers-into-battle was the young man whom Ghost-on-the-Lake served.

Finally the drum began to resound. The one playing it, a man with an otherwise impassive face, began to throb a thudding rhythm that grabbed one's very gut. "Boom, boom," the rawhide-covered sticks hit the resonating drum. Two of the former dancers, the best warriors in the tribe, began to bound about the circle in controlled leaps. Then someone in the shadows lit, and then threw them torches. They tossed each other the torches; bright arcs of light spun across the circle. Little ones held in their mothers' arms gasped at the beauty of trailing sparks, held their arms out towards the fire-trail. Two warriors held fire sticks in their mouths, grasping the brands with their teeth. Finally the drumming stopped. Then, there was a clapping of the hands from somewhere in the back of the circle and the two men, bowing, retired.

As the circle parted, the chieftain, Bright-Coals-in-the-River, proceeded into the council ring. He was dressed in only a breechclout. His old body, which must have seen fifty summers, was lean, and muscles rippled as he began this, the final part of the leaping fire dance. He squatted on his haunches and kicked his feet out. Then he leapt about on his haunches, all the while shouting war cries, denunciations of his enemies. He frightened me enough, I tell you.

But then he began snatching burning sticks out of the fire. With his hands he snatched beech and oak brands, holding them at first with the unburnt part, then tossing them from hand to hand until at last he was catching onto the burning ends. His shouts grew louder. Finally he began to snatch the hot rocks which ringed the fire, tossing up not one but two, then three. He was a juggler as clever as any of the shaman jugglers. Finally, his face a mask of power and anger towards enemies, in the most frightening way, and screaming ritual insults, he went to the pot which was cooking venison and snatched out a piece from the bubbling, boiling water. His arm could only have been in a moment and yet the children gasped, one cried and was quickly hushed by its mother. But then he reached his arm in full, to the very elbow, and kept it there for a slight instant. Then he emerged with the very deer bone itself held high and all the warriors in the tribe followed him, wearing the medicine materials which gave them power, their bodies marked with paint and charcoal, glistening in the firelight. They danced to that continual gut-beat of the drum, wailing their own refrain.

The chieftain came to a halt near me. He stood, arms folded in front of him, feet and legs together, to allow the breath to return to his body. Seated there with the rest on the ground, next to Loon Feather, I knew what I must do. I breathed a prayer to the spirit of my uncle, or to Nanaboozhoo or to the Maker of Stars or whoever in the world it was that controls things that I would have the awful courage it was going to take to do what my spirit knew I must do.

I stood. I faced the chieftain, who now stood moodily staring into the fire. "The drummer does not play skillfully." (Well, I did not say skillfully. In their language they had a word which meant "inspired by the gods"; that was the one I used.)

Just a shadow of surprise passed over the face of Bright-Coals-in-the River. "So—his playing is not from the gods? And you are a judge. You, the slave of an old grandmother, survivor of a tribe of weak silly girl-warriors."

I let that pass me by. I had bigger fish to cook. "I wish to play the drum. I am under a vision command." Yes, and this was the time. I knew it, feeling it in the depth of my heart as a plum feels the ripeness come to its cheeks and falls off, ready to pluck and eat.

There was a long moment. Bright-Coals-in-the-River continued staring in the fire. Oddly, I wondered if his fingers hurt. He certainly was not favoring them. Finally he turned to me, took my shoulder in his bony hand and marched me to the drum. "Play, Belly-of-the-Bear now turned to Ribs-of-the-Wolf. Play as if the gods favor you. Perhaps they do."

And so I played again, there in the camps of the enemy, who had destroyed almost everything I cared about, and this time instead of Nanaboozhoo's quest, I sang of my uncle's and all the pain he caused others and the youth he squandered and the trip he made to the odd, rank lands to the south and the strange cats and people and vines and the cave and the visit–divine and inspiring–of the Lord of the West Wind went into my drums. I played, I chanted, all listened. When I was done, the fire had sunk to flaming embers.

"I am under command to build a drum now. When I had suffered enough, I was to build the drum, the messenger said."

"And you have suffered enough?" the chieftain said.

"Only the gods know that. But my heart feels as full of suffering as that pot—" I pointed to the pot, which was now cooling. The women were handing its meat round to all who wished to eat.

"What is enough?" he said, almost absently, and as he stood looking into the dying embers of that fire I noticed his hand. He did not attempt to hide it from me; the fingers, long and supple, were held carelessly by his side. The fingers of Bright-Coals-in-the-River had blisters from tonight. And behind the blisters, scars, and behind the new scars, old, tough scars all the way up to his palms, scars that went back as far as his manhood. The gods had not protected him from pain, no, they had only allowed him to endure it. Perhaps it was better that way.

The next day, following the chief's command to my Old One, I began to build my drum.

What a time it was! Ah, as I look at you here, bright and young, I see myself across the years, in the camps of the enemy, tied to him as a dog is tied to a master who has kicked him into submission but whom he grudgingly respects. It seemed as if I were enduring, but really, I was triumphing, because I had my drum quest. I was a slave but I was free. Captive, but really chieftain.

107

For instruction in the sacred job of building the great drum, I had the relatives of my Old One. especially the nephew who had played the drums the night of the feast. And I had the lesson from the wild rice men at the Place of Rivers Meeting.

Cottonwood, that was what we needed, those who knew said. It sang, so the nephew of Thistle Child said, a song of the wind in its branches. After a time had passed, we went out a half a day's walk from the camp (he guarded me; I do not think they trusted me, though I would not have gone while I was on the vision quest) and found a big tree. Wonder! A storm had just felled it; its wood was not rotted, though the roots had been undermined on the hill where it stood.

We walked its length and selected a round, firm cross section near the base. We had axes, sharp, of best flint from the fine pits in Ohio, and we chopped and sawed as best we could, breaking two heads off our axes to get the cross section out. "Ah, aye, oh, spirit of the tree, honor us for our drum," we sang.

Then we used the fire and reed blowpipe as our village boatmakers had done, to hollow out the round. It was as wide as two men's feet end to end, and as tall as an elbow to fingertip span, and its wood was firm and good, so there would be work. Yes, there would be work to steal its core from it.

All that day, carefully, oh so carefully, we let the fire burn. Then we scraped with scraper rocks. Then we burnt some more, until the inside was hollow—almost. We had to leave a collar of wood, thin and even, on the bottom to attach the straps of leather, the carrying straps. And oh, the wood did smell pungent and good in that early fall forest, and how the air did refresh us with its breezes as we sat to rest and eat our pulled venison and maple sugar corn. And how the water did cool us as we knelt to drink from the stream. It was a time of joy as pure and bubbling as the waters over the pebbles in that stream. I did not feel guilty about that joy, that I had it over the graves of my clan; I knew my uncle would wish me joy in this.

The drum came home, strapped to my back. It had to season; meanwhile I must find the hide to make the top and bottom of this drum. We had decided on a moose. A deer hide would be too thin and small to make the two, strong, skin heads I needed for my drum.

I could not start to get the animal for my hide, though, right away. No, because as soon as I returned to camp, ran right out to meet me.

Both Loon Feather and Ghost-on-the-Lake met me, she with a strong walk, he, proceeding slowly along behind her. "The Old One is ill," Loon Feather said. "Why have you lingered so long?"

"We have been honoring the vision quest."

"Who would challenge a vision quest? Not I." Her eyes were cool, angry. "But Thistle Child has need of you. Her legs do not move without pain, the joints are swollen, and you are her slave, saved from the torture tunnel and I think—"

It was the most she had spoken to me since I had been adopted.

"I am glad to know what you think. But let me ask if you have been helping. I think, I know, she is your grandmother."

"Of course." Her eyes were like the flashes of far-off lightning. "What do you think I am, unfaithful to the spirits of my father and mother? I have been bringing water, carrying food, making fire. But there are many furs to tan before we start the long trip back, before much longer. And besides you are the servant. It was given to you of the Maker of Stars in return for your life."

"True. And so I am here."

But not for long. I stayed a day or two, long enough to outfit. The nephew of the old one was perfectly content to prepare for us to take a trip. It would have to be a quick one, as the time was coming up when summer darkened into autumn, and the people returned to visit relatives in winter campgrounds east of the lakes. He was, if truth be spoken, rather indolent of nature and loved the roving and roaming of the free life of the hunt. North, along the shores of the great lake, the moose ranged. We would go.

Thistle Child was ill, it is true. She sat by the fire, hugging her knees, which were full of pain. So many things had to be done to ready a canoe for our trip though—pack food, prepare the medicine bundle and hunting tools. Ghost-on-the-Lake helped us in his halting way, bringing dried meats, storing nuts in woven pots, finding deer brains to store for the tanning process. The couple he served had freed him, fearing perhaps, that as a marked one he was bringing them bad medicine. They had lost a child through a miscarriage while I was gone.

And during the three days we prepared, Loon Feather's eyes flashed fire and anger. We were deserting. I was a little bothered by it myself, to tell truth. I had a vision command about the drum—but then I had been saved by the spirits to serve Thistle Child. Which one to obey? Truly, through many years of life, I have found that if one wishes to honor the commands of the spirits, or better said, the Maker of Stars, it is hardest of all to know what is the true command among many which seem to float on the wind.

Off we went. Ghost-on-the-Lake stood on the shore, watching us go, and we watched as we paddled the canoe northward, we saw him become smaller until he was a tiny doll on the wide sands.

Haste lent even more excitement to our quest. We had just a moon to go north, stalk our game, and prepare the skin. Naturally we must prepare it before bringing it back; the rawhide had to be cleaned and preserved immediately after the kill, could have no salt on it or other preservatives, to serve as drum.

I could not think of what would happen when we returned—the striking of the camps, the heading out for the long migration back east. My heart was an empty pit when I thought of leaving the lands of Lakes-Like-a- Necklace.

Ten days we travelled, and then, on shore, we saw two of them, standing in the quiet waters, drinking. Moose. We pulled quickly into a small bay to observe; they retreated onto shore and up a path. Tying our gear on our backs, we followed them. If we lost these, at least we knew we were in moose country.

We tracked, not far behind, looking closely at the leavings on the trail and at the trampled earth. They were an hour or two ahead of us and we had their trail.

We sang the hunting songs. "Ah, Nanaboozhoo or Who-ever," (I sang) "help us fell the moose. One is all we need." Later, at the camp, we sang, "Ah, moose we follow, grant us peace with your spirit. We kill you for the sacred drum, drum of the vision quest. Your spirit will ring out, over the hills for all to hear. Eternal is your song, then, oh moose we kill."

Apparently the Whoever heard, because the next day we got downwind of the moose, three of them, and praying and then shooting sharp, well-wrought arrows, we brought the smallest one to earth.

How easy! We gutted and skinned him and ate the fine moose back meat over the bright fire. Right away, yet that evening, we would be able to begin the curing of the skin.

We washed the heavy, richly-haired skin in the stream, then carried it to a small side pool which had spilled over. It was important not to have running water on the skin; it must putrefy enough to loosen the hair so we could scrape it off—adding hot stones from the fire to raise the temperature and hasten the rotting—you know all this. You have seen women treat the deer and perhaps—have you?—you may have seen elk or moose. You know the steps, when the hair is loose, scraping off hair with the tool, taking pains, pulling down only a small swath of hair and removing it then moving on another hand span or so, and when the hair is gone, turning the skin over, hanging up and scraping the whole skin free of membrane and other matter.

How easy, how joyous! Working with the scraping tool made of antler of deer and cut with fine sharp notches. Singing the songs we would be singing with the drum, cooking and eating a lot of the moose meat, smoking and salting a lot more

111

for the trip home while waiting between the steps of the tanning.

How easy, joyous and pleasant, to draw with charcoal on the clean hide the size of the drum heads we planned for our cottonwood drum, making them four finger widths larger than the wooden circles themselves so they overlap, then cutting with our sharp, flint knife.

How easy, joyous, pleasant and beautiful (most of the time) returning within our time, along a coast which surely is the smile of the Great Spirit, with golden dunes clad in pine trees pushing to the skies, waters as clear as a crystal rock, to the camps. We would complete the final step, the lacing of the two heads together around the edges of the drum, when we were with the people. We hastened as we beached the canoe, carrying our prize skin pieces, refreshed from the time in the wild–how happy, pleasant, joyous it would be.

How difficult, bitter and grievous it was to walk beyond the birches into the campsite and find the people gone, the camp a shambles and the smell of death everywhere.

We turned over broken shelter poles, lifted tromped-on mats which had been the shelters' sides, kicked at the stiff bodies of dogs we had left behind alive and yelping such a short time ago. Abandoned furs sat miserably beside the kicked-out campfire inside the shelter I had lived in. The nephew of Thistle Child took up charcoal and began to mark himself and quietly sing the rite of the dead—obviously this had been a terrible ambush. But who would, who could—ambush the Dune Devils?

As shadows fell and the sun sank behind the dunes and into the lake, wolves approached. We built a huge fire, bewildered, asking ourselves questions which had no answers, when, out of the woods crept Ghost-on-the-Lake, limping even worse than ever.

"Men, warrior men, came," he said. "Just at dawn." At first light, as they were wont to come, the Dune Devils had been overcome themselves. Somehow I could not rejoice, and yet there was a sense of justice to it. "But where is"—I didn't want to ask where is Loon Feather—"where is the Old One?"

"She was hurt." His face was pained. "The b-b-bad warriors killed the men and took the women and children off. When they saw that the Old One could not walk, they—" he did the action of stabbing his side with a knife."

"And—Loon Feather?" I pointed to the shattered fur frames, the furs left in the mud.

"She was t-t-taken too. They did not want the furs." What kind of people would this be? Not want the furs?

We sat cross legged by the burned-out, desolate campfires, stunned, completing the process of painting with the charcoal. The Sun Lord was bright in his glory tonight, certainly, in the midst of our distress, as he often is, seeming to mock pitiful man. He sank amidst purple fingers as lovely as the loosestrife around the shores of Lake-of-the-Boulders. The nephew of Thistle Child spoke finally. "Where is Bright-Coals-in-the -River?"

The hunchback shrugged his shoulders. His attitude seemed to be apologetic, as if all of this was his fault. "Killed by the torture, but—fast, before they left."

So. The sky had come full circle, and the Lords of Justice had had their due. Still, this chieftain had let me mourn, let me make the drum. "Did he die with courage?"

"He did not c-c-cry out. I would have."

Yes, poor, halting cripple. The only one left in this whole camp.

A thought came to me. "What of the other camps of the Dune People?"

"They went early to—the far fall place. Started yesterday."

That night the nephew and I strung the two moose skins across the drum. We put straps on it and then—even though it was not fully seasoned, I played. I sang a song of sadness for all of the ones who had died—the dancing men who had shouted at the fire and drum that they were the bravest and best, the old chieftain who had blister upon blister that said that he was strong for his people, and for the old one, and the other weak ones slaughtered rather than taken on the trail and, yes, for all of my tribe that the Dune Devils had killed in their own time. The boatman's son, my friend and his father, my poor excuses for parents, my uncle and his wife and two of his children. It was the funeral song for two entire villages of living people now dead.

I boomed the drum and loved its sound and thought it was the finest drum every made and worth all the work and pain of being in this camp just to have it. Then, when it was quiet, I stared at the evening star. "Nanaboozhoo," I thought, "why have the powers of the sky made so much pain? Is there nothing, nobody left for me?"

And, suddenly, as bright as a star in my mind, came the face of White Wings, my loved small cousin. And then I knew.

"We must follow the departing camps of those of your people who are left," I said to the nephew. "I know you will wish to be with them."

He nodded, indecisive man that he was. Then I asked him, as the last of his aunt's family, to free me. He clasped my arm in friendship and the deed was done. "Ghost," I called out to the hunchback hovering behind us. "Let us get ready to move out at first light. You are coming with us. Perhaps you will go east with the Dune people's tribe."

"I wish to serve you, Bear Belly," Ghost said with a little fear in his voice. "I am of the—people of Lakes-Like-a-Necklace. And you are g-g-good to me." It was the known against the unknown.

"Very well, get my pack ready. You will carry the drum." That settled that thorny question of how this big drum would get around. We would sledge it as far as we could, canoe it when possible and carry it by the straps on our backs when all else failed. Morning could not come too soon for me, here in the camps of the dead of both the tribes of my life so far.

When we came upon White Wings and her camp of Dune Devil people, they were moving rapidly along the trail north to the point of the lake where they would meet and take to canoes. We arrived almost too late. They were on the beach, loading the huge voyage canoes, covering them with poles and shelter fabric for the sick ones and babies, rolling up the windsails, stashing all the needs under furs and bed covers. They were in a hurry; who knew when the intruders might return and strike dismay into the hearts of the remaining bands? The scouting warriors were out that day along the shore and on the trail, I tell you.

The nephew spoke quietly to the old men of the band; I could hear them arguing about White Wings. Finally one shouted out, "Let him take her, I say. She is a little bitch dog and will never be tamed well. Her blood is bad."

Her mother, my aunt, and my other girl cousin had long since died in the camp of this band. There, with a stringy bean of a woman was little White Wings. "Come run to Bear Belly, Little White Wings," I called out joyously. "Hug the last of your people." I could hardly wait to feel her little arms around my neck.

They carried her forward, put her up to me. She reached out and bit me, screaming in anger. Bit my face, like a fox.

I tried to laugh, but really, I was too hurt. After all the pain, all the times the vision of this small child, last of my family with me, had sustained my bad nights and now—she kicked my belly.

"What is the matter?" I asked her.

"You not Bear Belly," she said. "You thin."

So. It was the change in me that had scared her. Or was it? She continued kicking and screaming, pounding on the ground when I told her we would be traveling together.

We bade farewell, I to the nephew who had found clan kin among the band, the child to the old string-bean woman who had cared for her.

115

"She is like a raccoon held in camp," the woman said. "Her eyes leap at you with hatred. I could not get her to do one thing I asked, though I beat and gave sweets both."

But more beatings than sweets, I thought. "Still, we will fix you up, White Wings," I told myself, gathering her few things together. "The wounded bird must get out of the storm to heal its wing." And I thought for a fleeting instant of the walks we had taken in our home forest and of the time we found the wounded bird, when all was peace and contentment, and my heart pained me.

"Ghost, you will be nurse to her," I commanded. He nodded, his mouth open. I had seen him before, taking care of the small ones in the camp at Lake-of-the-Boulders, and the Dune Devils' camp too. He was patient and full of love. White Wings went to him, and strangely, put her hand in his. The clans got into the canoes and headed hurriedly out.

We started up the trail to—where? Oh, I have not told you? Did I forget? To Cahokia, of course. It was the city of Cahokia that brought sudden death to the camps of the Dune Devils, in revenge for former insults and to show their dominance of every camp in the river valley system watered by the Father of Waters. In truth the Dune Devil song sung by the warriors at the fire dance was not true:

> *Even Cahokia trembles*
> *At the dawn raid of the Dune Devils.*

We were going to the Place of Skunk Smells Chicaga, by trail (not by water; I was not skillful enough and I had a two-year-old wild child), and from there by river canoe down to near where the Ohio meets Father of Waters.

To that glorious, golden, forbidden city, with as many souls in its precincts as pebbles on this very beach, seas of cornfields around it, and with as much power as one of the very stars in the sky.

Why was I going? Well, to tell true, I wanted to know what had happened to the vicious, lovable old Dune Devil captives,

116

especially one who had delicate hands and plaited hair. I yearned for her, thought of her all the time, much as she hated me. And I wanted to take the drum and see what they would make of it—boom away on it in the heart of the greatest city where the Sun Lord shone. Most of all I was just turned fifteen now, and it sounded like sport. I was curious, and I have told you that above all else in my being, curiosity was the liveliest trait. Well, it couldn't be any more dangerous than a lot of things I had done lately. Seen in higher terms, I was accepting, readily the pilgrimage that my uncle had foreseen—a trip to manhood, a quest for maturity.

Well, to think of it, my journey did not really seem to remind me much of Nanaboozhoo's—bouncing over the trail with a drum on a sledge and a hunchback and a two-year-old screaming wolverine of a child strapped into a sort of chair on my back.

My uncle had gone through far-away jungles, braved unknown torrents, and finally found the rushing waterfall of all waterfalls pouring out its secrets of the world and all beyond. I had to keep myself awake and alert enough to capture some miserable food for my two poor dependents. Ah well, it was the quest given to me. Cahokia, be awake! Send out the guards! Mighty Bear Belly comes.

Chapter Six

Cahokia! City of splendor, high on the riverbank of the Father of Waters, with the tallest of temples and burial mounds visible for miles downriver, with hundreds of small villages of huts clustered like piles of nuts around a tree in fall. And beneath and beyond, all the golden food fields to support 20,000 souls—city of power and riches! When a moon and a half had fled again, my little group approached.

It was a warm morning, almost summer-like when we arrived—ah, I thought, the climate is warmer here, nearer the Sun Lord's face. All around the many insects of fall hummed. Bright blue sky, trees showing touches of red, and below the towers and huts of the city was the wide creek which led to the river, a dirt-brown, spacious path into the rest of the world, a gate from which we had come.

I was coming as a trader, with my travelling group. Young as I was, I had been trained in the trading clan ways, and Ghost and I and White Wings had taken the time to go to the camps at Lake-of-the-Boulders, those desolate, sad places of many graves, and taken the flints of my clan from the hidden storage pits in the woods. I would have trading goods when we entered the city.

We walked now across a flat of large and small trade and war canoes, some pushing out, some coming in, some idle. We were approaching a huge log-stockade, with doors open wide on the bright day. From the earth a good smell arose, different from that I had known in the dunes of the Large Lake—composed of fallen sycamore leaves, richly decaying, browning grass, huge cotton-woods breathing and sending their sweet breath to the heavens for the Sun Lord to savor.

When we had nearly reached the gates, White Wings began one of her tantrums. I had come to recognize the symptoms because I had seen them these last days on our trip. They began when we were on the trail. Sometimes I had to let her walk the long miles along the Large Lake. Ghost could not carry her on his poor back, and sometimes mine grew chafed, raw from the chair and her kicking legs. So I let her walk, and when I did she often

119

protested—with a mouth that looked like a quivering wave on the lake, clenched fists, ashen face that became almost blue. Then she would go limp and howl and kick.

Then, when we did take to the canoe and went on shore at nights, she found other causes for the screaming fits, like being asked to eat or go to sleep or be quiet or just, lately, for no cause at all that I could discover. Sometimes the tantrums happened in the night and she would flop all over the ground. What was it? I would ask, perplexed, what was tormenting her, but she only shook her head and wept, finally, tears that fell like raindrops splattering on the parched ground in the hot months of corn.

Now, as we approached the great, swung-back log gate of the city, she sank to the ground, still held by Ghost's arm. She would not get up. "Not going in, not going in," she chanted. Perhaps she was frightened by the noise that came from the walled city—the swell of talking and children calling and dogs yipping and love flutes tootling and hucksters crying out. She had never heard anything like it, and in her troubled mind it meant more danger. She knew nothing else to do but crumple up and cry.

After asking, commanding and finally begging, I picked her up in my arms and carried her through the gates, past the eyes of watching sentries in towers at the corners of the stockade.

We strolled along the main street of the town, then, drinking in every sight with our eyes as if it were maple water. There was so much to see—youths in the chungky playing fields that Uncle had told me of—Uncle. My heart leapt to think of him, my love for him was as bright as a copper ear ornament, though I had not polished it for a while. He had walked these streets, played on the field, won, gambled, dissipated. Passing the chungky field, we came to the tall mounds which stood, impressing all who saw. On the tallest, a full ninety feet high, was the temple of the Sun Lord. Steps, so many steps, carefully laid into the hill with chopped log reinforcements, led to the temple, and beside it, the house of the ruler. Uncle had never told me about the ruler; I realized I did not know the story of exactly how the Cahokians were ruled. Other mounds were before our eyes, and in back of us, many other streets—what could be their purpose? I would find out later. Then on, past people bustling about, carrying stores of corn and pumpkin on strings, past women with huge jars, past men coming into the village with deer, past merchants in stalls, like the ones we had seen in the Place of Rivers Meeting, near our own home—so much to see.

I tried to maintain dignity, to walk like the son of the Sun Watcher that I was, nephew of the Grand Shaman. I would need to see the ruler—or his men—soon, to report that I wished to stay here, seek refuge, show my flints, learn their ways, perhaps serve as a merchant to them also.

I pressed back my hair, which was long and rather unruly, smoothed my ragged clothing, lifted my chin. Still, if truth is told, as it must be, the fact remains that I was entering town as a scraggly youth, not too clean, with a squalling brat of a child under my arm and a crippled helper behind me. I was a hero only in my own illusions.

"Wah, wah, wah." On the yelling went, Ghost shrugging his oddly deformed shoulder in back of me, people staring. A man, young for sure but still a man, caring for a small child? There was surprise, even contempt in some eyes. This was the work of the women.

We came to a spring, a marvelous thing with bubbling abundance that had been caught and held in a basin of rocks and clay—women were coming to it with their water jars and dipping deep to fill them. I was panting with the heat of this unusual warm day and I thought giving White Wings some water might divert her.

We sat on a wooden bench beside the spring. I saw a half-broken pottery jug which had been carelessly left on the lip of the spring and dipped it, offering it to White Wings. She pushed at it, breaking the jug and spilling the water all over me. In frustration I raised my hand to smack her, then found it caught behind me. A woman's firm hand was on mine.

"You do not wish to strike the little one. She has come a long way, I think, and is in a strange world." I turned to see calm eyes and the lightly wrinkled face of a woman of about forty summers. She had spoken in a tongue that was not at all like the Dune Devils, and yet, I could understand most of what she said. The tongue was close, but not exactly like the tongue of Lakes-Like-a-Necklace.

"She is my cousin, the only one left of our family, and I am her caretaker, a poor one at that," I said.

"You are young for such a burden."

"She is not a burden. My uncle, her father, was my life." She let go of my arm. Oddly enough, White Wings had quit squalling. Still, I thought I should offer explanation.

"It is just that she tries me so much. I am not a woman. I do not see how the art of taking care of children is done. But there is no one else."

The woman smiled at me, tilting her head to one side a little. Once she had been a beautiful maiden, and even now her serene spirit shone through her eyes. She knelt to White Wings and took her up in her arms. Instead of fighting her, White Wings relaxed, sighed and shut her eyes.

"She has the burning buttocks," she said, looking under her little dress. "Have her needs in going to the woods not been cared for?"

Ghost turned and walked away. He was embarrassed to be talking about such matters with a woman, and so was I. "Well, we did the best we could in the canoe. But sometimes she—wet herself, and I could not rightly clean her. Even if I knew how to do that with a female child."

"Well, it makes walking hard for her. She has a bad rash, and it chafes her to walk." Delicately she was arranging the child's legs across her own. "I have some salve in my shelter. It is good for burning buttocks."

And soon we were following her, down a side street, past the stalls of jewelers and pot vendors to her dark, cool shelter. We ducked down; it was built into the side of the ground, its posts firmly planted in the deep earth. A thick roof of grass, held down by tightly woven sticks, kept the hot sun off the nice little house.

In one corner was a piece of furniture made of rocks. I had never seen one quite like it. In my father, the Sun Watcher's house, there had been a medicine chest in the corner; it, too, was made of rocks and on it he kept his turkey feather charms, his white pipes, and the other things only he could touch and which had great medicine power. But this was not for medicine; it was large and held many things of this house. It was good, I thought, that all was so neat; nothing was on the floor except the cot beds and the firepit. Even the pots this woman cooked with were stored in the rock chest in the corner.

"Have you no family? No man or children?" I asked her.

"No. My husband died in a raid last year. To the north. There are many such raids these days. Cahokia's warriors seem always on the march."

I thought of the Dune Devils. The Cahokia town was ranging far afield, and I wondered why.

"Here is the ointment. It is made of the soothing roots which grow near the creek in back of the town. My mother knew all herbs." She clucked a little to White Wings, and with some reluctance, but not too much, the child went to her. She turned her back on us, and soon had put soothing balm on the child's hind quarters. Then she went to the water pots, took out a piece of woven cloth and dipped it and washed White Wings, all over.

"You have come from far?" she asked, finally, raising her eyes to us.

Ghost came out from behind me. "We lived with the Dune people. Bad tribe came—from here. Killed the people, pulled the chief apart with trees." The woman's face was stricken. "Well, war is war, as the old ones say," Ghost finished.

"We have come to live here. I thought there would be help for the child. Two men alone cannot care for her long," I said.

"No." She gestured for us to sit down. Outside, over a wonderful tripod the likes of which I had never seen, a pot of stewed turkey was simmering.

"You could stay with me. I have no relatives. The town cares for me since my husband was a fallen warrior. We could be a family."

I nodded eagerly. "But, Mother, you have not even told us your name." I told her all of ours.

"Walks-Up-the-Steps is what I am called." I stared at her, wondering what the vision had been that had called the name forth. "I am allowed to walk up the hill, the tall one. I am of the ruling clan."

"Can you, then, take us into your home?" I wondered. I was from a sort of ruling clan—well, that stretched it a bit. We did not have ruling classes in the land of Lakes-Like-a-Necklace. It was frowned on where all must struggle equally to live each day.

"I can do as I wish—as long as I do not affront the ruler. We shall go to see the ruler tomorrow about you. What can you do to be useful?"

I said I hoped to be a trader. As I spoke I felt the power of the enormous city and what I had undertaken, and I felt very young to be presenting myself as trader. I told her I was a ritual clown— she said Cahokia did use them at festival or ritual burial times, but she did not know if a stranger would be allowed to participate. I said I could lead parties to the great flint pits in Ohio. All of that might be useful, she thought. Then, with inspiration, I almost yelled out, "My drum. I have a marvelous drum. It came from a vision—it plays the songs of the very gods themselves."

I sent Ghost out to get it and when he returned, she marvelled. "Ah, a drum as large as this is—there will be some use for this and it will bring you notice and power here." Then she turned to the dinner pot outside, and we sat before the firepit, watching an early dusk creep in through the open door. White Wings was asleep before the food could even arrive and we slept that night on the cots, under fine robes of bears and buffalo. Still, I lay a long time, listening to the sounds of barking and baying and coughing and fine love flutes playing and men and women arguing and all the other night-time sounds in a town so large that it would never really sleep, no matter how dark the night.

I arose early; the first rays of dawn were coming through the door of the house, and I slept on a cot right in the path of what would be the sun when it rose. It had been planned that way; people wished to see the Lord they worshipped as he first appeared. Here, as at Rivers Meeting houses were built to the four cardinal points. Priests came and consecrated each house when it was built so the Sun Lord would bless it each day as he shone.

Well, as the sky grew pink, then orange and red preparing for the rising of the Sun Lord, one could understand how these people worshipped him as god above all others. The results of the joyous shining of his face were everywhere in humble as well as great ways in this city. His symbol was blazoned on everything, painted and carved on stone, wood and cloth. And later in the day I saw the sun's marks were tattooed on the men's backs and arms.

But the richness of his providing was really seen in the store of food crops. Around the house of Walks-Up-the-Steps was a fine granary on stilts. In it stores of corn, maple sugar, dried nuts, spices were gathered and hung on rafters; even pulled meats were stored with a door to keep out raccoons and squirrels.

In the yard was a great corn-grinding stone, with a good grinding pestle to make the work easier. Hung between a tree and the house were strings of dried squash, pumpkin, gourd dippers, and wooden stirring spoons with holes in them for cooking.

I watched as the village awoke, lighting cooking fires, walking to the river creek to wash, sweeping the fronts of the houses with rush brooms, shooing dogs away and cleaning up after their night ordure. These were a clean people, clearly. Last night Walks-Up-the-Steps told me that the good spirits would not come to her house if they found trash about, and so she swept it not once but many times a day.

There was noise in the streets already, men and women milling about. I watched as a man with a small headdress and a necklace of power about his neck organized these aimless people into ranks. They seemed to be a military marching force, but they had no weapons, only hafted hoes and wooden rakes. Several old women carried baskets; I think I had seen one of these at the other city Uncle and I had visited; it was a flint box with the implements to make fire stored within.

"Where do you go?" I asked one man, adding "I am a stranger."

"We march to the far fields, stranger," the old man answered me. "We harvested a moon-and-a-half ago. Today is the day of the burning off of the fields. The standing corn stalks will be stacked and then the remaining ones burnt off to help next year's crops grow."

"And it takes so many?" I asked. At our homestead village each family took care of its own cornfields.

"So many. So many it takes to feed the thousands here. We work together, and the ruler tells us how. To the ruler, too, belongs all the corn and we have none unless the ruler so allots it."

"Ah," I said, understanding. All was done in common here at Cahokia. A wonderful way! All working together, under the ruler who was in turn ruled by the Sun Lord.

I walked the streets just before sunrise, free for a time of the care of White Wings, since Walks-Up-the-Steps had wanted to care for her through many of the days to come, it seemed. I came to the ring of the SunWatcher, just south of the great Temple Mound. What a place he had to see the Lord each day! How the people of Lakes-Like-a-Necklace would have marvelled. There, in a huge open ring were poles placed for key times of the year. As I walked towards the ring, coming from the temple toward the north, the town SunWatcher also walked towards the ring and, as I stood, nearby, proceeded to its center. There he watched as the sun came up on this perfectly clear day; he seemed to bellow, or sing, a song much as my father did to herald the coming of the royal master.

Then, from up on the hill of the highest mound, came the answering sound of howls. Yips, like a dog's, not like anything we heard in our country. A man with a load of reeds on his back was near me; I spoke to him.

"What is the yipping like dogs?" I wondered. He stared at me sternly.

"Be careful, youth, that you do not run afoul of our customs. Our great ruler's family on the top of the sacred mound is greeting the coming of the Sun. It takes much noise to reach his sacred precincts."

Well, that was true enough. Sun Lord was up there a good ways. At my small village, we had to bang on logs. Perhaps I ought to bring the big drum out and cart it up to the top of the hill, I smiled, a little irreverently. Well enough the Sun Lord could hear its resounding booms!

The man I spoke to was going down the road, towards the reed basket makers' street, where, I supposed, they would take the reeds he brought and make all kinds of the containers they used for storing things. The reed basket makers' street was next to the reed mat makers' lane; so many different occupations did they have at Cahokia! Only a few of the higher traders were within the walls; the more common ones were in cluster villages outside.

As he passed me, my stern friend admonished, "Better turn and bend towards the ground, young one. The procession will soon be coming to the sun circle."

"Why do you not stay to watch it?" I called out to his back.

"If you are humble and wish to stay out of trouble, it is best not to be noticed in this great city," he called back. I wondered if I should take his advice, but since I did not think of myself at the moment as particularly humble, I turned and did, indeed see a procession coming towards me, towards the Sun Ring.

At its head was an old man with a huge staff in his hand and a round woven headdress, his body tattooed and his face oiled to make him look as if he shone like the sun itself. Behind him, two by two, were men dressed in various rich clothing, each pair alike. The first two were dressed in fine fabric tunics with shoulder robes of minks whose little heads hung down over their furry stomachs. The men's faces were tattooed with circle designs.

Behind them were several rows of younger men with long staffs or military pikes, also tattooed but wearing white rabbit robes over woven tunics. They wore feather headdresses and huge ear spools made in circular sun designs. Finely crafted leather sandals were on their feet and their hair was piled up on the tops of their heads, held fast with shell-decorated hair clips.

At the end of the procession, deferred to by all along the street, was a man of slightly taller height than the rest, with a huge headdress made of the gray and yellow feathers of eagles, but also from feathers of rare, brightly colored birds whose nesting places I had never seen—feathers bright as the Lord Sun himself. His

127

woven robes flowed; he wore a shirt of shells sewn onto fabric. Before him walked two heralds blowing on beautiful ocean shells, all mottled pink and white. "Ahwoo,ahwoo," they called to announce the arrival of this royal personage.

I had bowed to the ground, as I saw all the others around me do. Still, I could see his eye fall on me, wearing my odd country deerskin breechclout and leggings and cape of skin.

On the processional moved, the shell horn blowing. On they went to the circle of the Sun, where the group paraded, sang a hymn and fell to the ground prostrate before a nobility higher than they were. When they returned, one of the heralds stopped before me. "The prince wishes to know who you are, young stranger, and who has given you the right to be among his people. You are dressed in clothing of the north. Are you a trader?"

"I am from the trading clans of—" for some reason I did not wish to say Lakes-Like-a-Necklace. Was it that they did not really exist? Surely all the villages around my own in that area so dotted with lakes had been carried away to slavery along with the Dune Devils. Many were probably right here. Or was I reluctant to state my home because my uncle had a sour connection here in this very city so many years ago? Anyway, I said "from the travelling fur trappers of the Dune People. "Well, it was not far from the truth. Definitely not far, recently. "I am staying with Walks-Up-the-Steps in her ever honorable dwelling." Didn't that sound good? I thought so.

He smiled a very small smile, as if appreciating that I was a rather bumptious, fifteen-year-old youth trying to gain city ways.

"What is your name, noble exalted one?" I asked.

"I am not especially exalted, though noble enough. I am Fire-on-the-Plains, and I am training for a high court position, and acting as herald. And that is enough for you to know."

He turned and walked sedately to the tall, well-bedecked prince at the rear of the procession. They spoke a few words. Everyone was bending their noses to their knees, since the processional had stopped. I was glad to be standing; it was rather uncomfortable to remain prostrate in the dust. "You are commanded to come to the common meeting house hill when He Is Halfway Home. The noblewoman is to come with you."

"Goodbye, exalted Fire-on-the-Plains," I ventured, to his back, and oddly enough, he did look over his shoulder at me, with that same, half amused smile.

On the Great Ones went, shuffling along their way to the large mounds, and the more common folk with me rose from their haunches and began the trading, food gathering and preparing, child rearing and gossip about the Great Ones that constituted their day.

White Wings and Ghost were eating a very good hominy porridge when I returned. Walks-Up-the-Steps was bustling about, pouring maple syrup on their hominy, humming a little tune that sounded like a soft love flute refrain.

"The child is hungry. You have not fed her properly," Walks-Up-the-Steps said finally to me.

"Well, I do not know what little maidens should have to eat. I never noticed in the camps of my childhood. It has been so long and I did not intend to be the nursemaid of a baby." I sighed and flopped down by the fire. All the troubles of the past few months, put aside by the diversions in this town for a while, seemed to return to me, and my old feelings of despair and uncertainty about myself returned. I was in a strange place, strange indeed, far, far from anyone who loved me—except, perhaps this small girl who was eagerly eating good hominy and syrup now with a wooden spoon.

Walks-Up-the-Steps looked at me with keen eyes. "You are but a youth yourself," she said. "Will you tell me how on Turtle's Back Island you came to have the charge of a child so young? How you are travelling with this marked one?" She smiled over at Ghost, who was playing with a firebrand in the coals, content with his life at the moment.

And so I sat, and as the morning wore on, I told my story—from the beginning, of the time when I lived, almost an orphan in the quiet villages of Lakes-Like-a-Necklace, to the trips my uncle made with me to teach me the ways of the trading clan, to the raids of the Dune Devils and the scattering of my family and my uncle's death by the torture trial to the building of my drum.

And then she began showing me the differences in tongues between ours and the speech of Cahokia, and since I pick up words from new languages as easy as a bird finds cherries on a full tree, soon I knew many new words from their tongue.

The Sun Lord was indeed high when I had finished my tale and Ghost and White Wings had gone out long since to chase dogs and find games to play in the city's streets.

"And so, loving your uncle so, you have taken on the child, last of the line of the Grand Shaman." That is what I had called him when I told her of Uncle. Naturally, I had not mentioned the Cahokia connection. Best to let that dead dog lie and recall Uncle in his transformed shape, great man of the spirit and flesh.

"Yes, though I do not know what that will bring. Nor why I have come to the city of the ones who destroyed the only life I had." Nephew of the Thistle Child was surely well on the way to the camps of the east waters to winter. But Loon Feather, where, where are you? "To the conquerors belong the tribute, and perhaps I am part of that. I know I am ready to serve, and surely there is refuge for the three unfortunate ones here. A city so great as this must have a great heart, too."

"So it should have, and so it still sometimes does," Walks-Up-the-Steps said in cool tones. "At any rate your skills as flint trader and even clown and drummer may be of use. The ruler will tell us. We go to the meeting place when Our Lord Is Halfway home, I believe you said."

"So the herald told me," I answered. Then, after a long moment, I added, "What do you think the ruler will think of me?"

"That I do not know," she answered with a slowly warming smile, looking into my eyes. "But I know what I think of you. That you are a kind, courageous heart as big as your drum, Drum-of-the-Gods."

She had honored me with the name given me by my uncle, and which I had told of in the story, though I had not previously used it. Everyone, including the Dune Devils, had called me Bear Belly. Ah, she was warming to me, respecting me, this noblewoman of the big city. I smiled a little myself, and all the old Bear Belly doubts that had come to plague me again, went back to their hiding places in the shadows.

"I am Drum-of-the-Gods," I said, proudly, savoring the sound of the name. "And soon I hope I can let you see why I am now called that."

I took White Wings and Ghost down the lanes to the villages of craftsmen of the nobler guilds. We arrived first at the stalls of the shell crafters. Interesting they were, I thought, too. Here sat a whole lane of craftsmen in front of their shelters making all sorts of jewelry from shells of the Father of Waters and other places. It was smelly enough, certainly, for here they pried open large and small double shells from the river and popped their mussel insides into pots for the women to cook. Then they boiled them in large pots which had hot stones placed in them, so they would be cleansed for working. Some were flaking off small pieces to decorate buildings with, others, young men with sharp eyes, were using a sharp flint bowstring drill to make holes in the shells so they could be strung into necklaces or sewn onto the clothing of the noble clans. White Wings held up one of the shells, peering at it in the sunlight, making it catch the morning sun in several different ways. Then she put the shell down and danced about in a circle. "Cahokia, Cahokia," she chanted, clapping her hands. I picked her up and brushed her cheek and, for the first time since we were reunited, she snuggled against me affectionately in the old way.

The young man who was using the bow-drill so skillfully came to her and knelt to her height. "Small one, you are adorable," he said. "Please accept something from me. Your—cousin—?" he looked up at me and I nodded "can keep it for you for your future. I found it today, and the spirits must mean for you to have it."

He put in her hand a beautiful, rather large pearl. I had never seen one so beautiful; in fact, I think I had only seen one or two pearls in all my lifetime. I let her roll it around in her hand, keeping careful watch, then put it in my own hand and turned to look into the honest face of the craftsman. He was a young man a few years older than I.

"Friend," I said, "do you find many of these in the Father of Waters?"

"Now and then we do. Many smaller, a few larger. The shellfish are plentiful." I was doing pretty well with the differences in words. He had used a word I did not know for shellfish, but I could tell what it meant. I made a mental note of it.

"Do the double shells from Father of Waters comprise all the raw materials of the fine shellwork on this lane?"

"Most. But some come from the south—from the Point Settlement on the Great Sea South. And a few—" he gestured across the lane from him, to where an older woman was carefully cutting with a flint knife—"a few are of the Great Horn Shell with the colors of sunset, from the islands of the far south."

"Could I—buy—these precious pearls and horn shells?"

Already I was thinking of my status as a trader. I had only a small stock, and could not as yet think of how I could obtain more trading goods.

"Ah, no, friend," the youth answered, returning to his drill and shell work. "The precious shells belong only to the ruler and the ruling clans. They take them all. We work for them."

"Does everyone, then, in Cahokia, work for the ruler?" I asked.

He glanced around with just the slightest bit of unease. "We all work for the lords as they work for the Sun Lord. And the ruler is the greatest lord of all, child of the Sun Himself. The ruler collects the riches the Sun Lord gives, garners it for all of us, and gives it out."

"May you keep none of your own squash and corn?"

"There are communal fields, in which we work four days a week. Then there are the fields individuals may have the rest of the time, but even there they must pledge, and deliver, half the harvest to the ruler."

I lowered my voice. "So much goes—above?" I gestured towards the temple mound.

His voice was low, but firm. "There are 20,000 souls here to feed. Many are too young, or too infirm, to fend for themselves. There is opportunity for those who wish to work for their own families to prosper here. The corn will grow."

"And if it does not?"

He turned towards the Sun Lord, now past He Is Halfway Home by some short time. He touched his forehead, then saluted the sun with dignity. "Sun Lord provides the corn. We strive to please him with the ceremonies and sacrifices—if he were displeased and the corn did not grow—" he shrugged. "There would be no Cahokia. Cahokia is built on corn—and the worship of the Sun Lord who sends it."

Walks-Up-the-Steps had appeared by my side in the lane. Nodding to the young man, who told us his name was Winter Bird, she kneeled beside White Wings. "Keep her for us, take her to the shelter," she told Ghost. "We go to meet the ruler."

The common meeting shelter was built on a mound not far from Temple Mound. Thousands of reed baskets of dirt had been carried by men, women, and children and dumped, to pile up higher and higher, as in our own village. Of course at Lake-of-the-Boulders, we had started with a hill—and carried a few hundred miserable loads. But what a marvel this was! Thirty feet high, levelled off and now the site of a huge house where many of the elders of Cahokia met and advised the ruler. When he asked.

Up the steps we went. I felt honored, even a little fearful. After all, what real business did I have here—I would have to justify myself. I began to practice my speech, reviewed my own meager accomplishments, tried to think of how to make them appear more significant—we were there. Around the top were planted garden plants and small, ornamental trees surrounding a huge, low-roofed lodge.

"The ruler is inside already," murmured Walks-Up-the-Steps. She was noticing two guards placed outside with spears visible in their strong hands. Bowing with her head towards them, she advanced towards the door.

Just outside the door, she began conversing with somebody. Soon my new friend, the herald, appeared, although not seeming

133

to notice me, and spoke a few words with Walks-up-the-Steps. In a moment another face peeked out into the late afternoon sunlight. Ah, it was the Great One, the ruler, as I had seen him early at He Is Rising hour worshipping at the log sun circle. I began to bow and advance to the door.

When I got there, the herald and spear men standing stolidly, Walks-Up-the-Steps deferred to me and I went through. The Great One I had seen was no longer near the door; I saw him, dimly, at the back of the council hall, with a few others. We were in a huge room with no chambers. There were no light openings except for the huge door, and conscious that Walks-Up-the-Steps was following behind me, I advanced. The Great One of the parade stepped forward. "So he comes to see us," I whispered to the darkness back of me. "I know him from this morning, the Great Ruler of Cahokia."

Her answer came at me out of the darkness with an intensity I had not expected. "No, foolish one. That is not the ruler. That is the prince; the ruler is behind him. Bow down now!"

I did so, almost to the ground and in this odd attitude finally approached great stools at the back of the hall. Figures began to take shape in front of them. True enough, there was the man, looking without emotion at me, that I had seen this morning, and he stepped back and bowed himself to the person beside him. I saw, advancing towards me, the ruler of Cahokia, a fat woman dressed in a sack garment covered with shell discs and small pearls.

"Behold, the Female Sun," the voice of the prince resonated through the hall.

Of course I had not been prepared for it—that the ruler would be a woman—the Female Sun, as they called her. As if the Sun could be female—but there she was, with her crown like the sun's corona all around her tightly wound hair. She carried in her chubby hand the rod of power—a copper rod with a circular sun design on its end.

And what a pang for me, that she was fat. Fat. All my old irresolute feelings returned, then, at the very moment I needed to be the brave drum of the gods I was supposed to be and I felt more like a newborn cub, licking my fur and wondering what the world would be.

"My cousin, daughter of our Fair Lord on High," Walks-Up-the-Steps was beginning.

"Hush, cousin," the Female Sun answered. "Let me see for myself this wonder of a boy all the town is talking of." She came towards me; I was beginning to see a little better and could distinguish her features; beautiful enough she was, or had been at one time, with a small, chiseled-in-stone nose and large eyes. Her breasts were covered, unlike those of the women outside. One did not gaze on the paps of one who gave suck to the descendents of the Sun Lord.

She stared at me for a long moment. Not a word was said in the great hall. "Tell me his story, oh my noble cousin," said the Female Sun. Her voice was rich and resonant, something I as a drum player was particularly conscious of. Then, before her cousin began, she said "No, let him tell me himself. Where have you come from?"

"Oh, Great One, from the north, from the country of the Dune Dev—People. Your—most valiant soldiers destroyed the village and took most of the people away it is said to slavery in the outpost villages or killed them, and—I remained."

"And yet," she said shrewdly, "your features do not resemble the people of the dunes—the ones who come from far away near the Great Falls. They are darker, smaller. You are taller than most of us here."

"Well, I was taken as one of their slaves from a nearby village near the Tippecanoe River." No point in telling her anything else. The truth is nearly always enough.

"And, I hear you have a small child with you, like some sort of wet nurse. How does a young man schooled in the arts of war,

135

descendent so they say of a Sun Watcher, take a child about to our city?"

I wondered what to say. She was assaulting my manhood. I could say I had just brought her to the women here for care. Only had kept her for some few weeks. But I had been since my first naming day under a command from the Bird of Thunder to tell only truth. Something like loyalty rose in me, though, then, and to deny my small cousin seemed like denying the uncle I so admired and loved.

"The mark of a man is not his indifference to the weak and needy but his care of them, no matter what others may say," I told her proudly. "The ties of kin are stronger than the sneers of other young warriors. I shall take care of my cousin until she marries, for I am all she has, and we are the last of a proud family."

Her eyes studied me for a long moment, then she smiled, a radiant joyous smile. It was the smile of a mother, and her next move confirmed that she was looking at me with eyes of both ruler and woman.

"Come, let me see that face in the light. Come outside." Quickly we all exited and when we had gone through the door, she set down the rod of power and came to me. She took my face in her hands, as if she herself were a female relative of mine. Oddly, though she had spoken of the short height of those at Cahokia, she was as tall as I was.

After a moment of study, she nodded, and we moved to benches set under cooling trees. Servants brought us maple water to drink and wonderful little cakes made of sugar and corn fried crisp.

"I wish asylum here for myself and my small cousin and servant," I said, looking at her seriously. And then I told her of my training as a trader, of the travels and special knowledge of my clan.

"The flint pits of the Beautiful River, you say?" she asked.

"Yes. I can get the best flints there and I know the ways of the wily ones who live there, although in real truth I have not as yet been to them myself. Still, I was initiated into the secrets in the sweat lodges and special rites of my clan manhood ceremonies."

"West and south we go often, not so much east," the Female Sun said. "We can use more excellent flint."

I took out the small hoard of flints I had taken from the pit, and handed them to her, and she marvelled at their quality.

"Perhaps I will send you, as a trial, to see if we can trust you."

"Well, yes but—well, I have no trading goods. These few flints I leave with you." I bowed.

"So, young Drum-of-the-Gods, as they call you—you come to us as a trader with no trade goods?" Her eyes, within the round, smooth face, were laughing.

I opened up my palm, let the pearl go to the center, where it glistened, catching the light. "You have many of these," I asked "in the royal treasury?"

"And so I do."

"If I can take some of them, I can return fine flints to your flint knappers, many of which can become again part of your own holdings."

I could feel Walks-Up-the-Steps tugging at my leggings. I must have been going too far. Well, but the words had already been said.

It was at this time that the prince came forward. "These pearls you speak of, brash stranger, cannot be used in the way you suggest. In fact, no part of the royal treasury can ever be taken from the coffers." His voice was cold. He did not like me. Perhaps I had known it the first time I saw him. He had a closed face, like a cat, and bad teeth from too many maple candies.

But his mother's voice was firm. She had made up her mind. "I believe we can risk a few pearls in the hopes of better flint. You may start when the moon comes round to full again. In the meantime, you are to stay and learn the ways of Cahokia. Your tongue has the rude sound of the forest." She beckoned that I should kneel before her. Raising her hand, she gave blessing.

"May the Sun Lord give you full effulgence of his blessings. May his warm face shine on yours." Her voice grew low, so the others could not hear. "You remind me of someone I knew so long ago, loved in the time when the world was new. It is as if you have come to haunt me." The last few words were said in wonder and pain. I looked up, into her eyes, and knew then who she was—had been. I was again reminded that it was a woman I spoke to, as well as a ruler.

And so, I had come to the city of my destiny, which was also the city of my loved uncle. I was walking the streets he had walked, past the chungky field where he had proven his strength and ability. And the woman I had just left, the Female Sun, connected me without understanding with the love of her youth; she was, in fact, the woman he had told me of, that he had sacrificed all for, even, almost his soul. She had grown infinite in power, while he had fallen. Or was it the other way around?

But it was odd that she should have connected me with my uncle. No word could possibly have reached her—I was intending to hide it. I went to the stream which flowed near the Temple Mound, found a pool which collected over rocks, where the women washed their clothing. I looked in, and I saw the reason. My own face, now lean, matured through pain and suffering lately, was almost the face of my uncle. Not only had I returned to the city where he met his fate first, not only was I walking in his footsteps, but now I had his face. Truly the past was circling round, casting strange, foreboding shadows, like the ones I had seen in the Sun Circle only this morning.

Chapter 7

As the leaves left the trees, and the first, cold winds of Burning Prairie Month began to blow the acorn cups and dead grass about, I said goodbye to Cahokia and took the Trail of Buffalos east. I had decided this was the best way for me to go; there would be some game to eat and the track was well known, going all the way to the Beautiful River a good ways east. I had asked for, and was allowed, a companion, and I named Winter Bird, the young shell craftsman. White Wings and Ghost stood waving us goodbye as we headed east and a bit south to pick up the Trail of Buffalos.

From thence we travelled, well supplied by me with backpacks full of dried meats, parched corn, maple sugar, pulled venison and so forth—all the things we people of the woods know well how to use. We had a routine trip, journeying along that wide and fair path through the prairie lands. There were no buffalos; it was said they had gone west.

I must admit that Winter Bird, good company though he was, was not a very adept trail partner. The first night out I gave him hunter's rights to bag one of the large jackrabbits which bounded about our path. It was then I realized he was not well prepared with weapons of the trail.

"Where is your bow?" I wanted to know. "The small, tightly strung squirrel and quail bow."

"Well, I do have a bow." He took out a handsome warrior's great bow, well strung, but of a slightly old-fashioned kind. "My grandfather gave this one to me. Will it do to get the game?"

"What did they teach you on your manhood moon-in-the-wild?" I asked sharply, but still with a wide smile on my face. This young man was getting to be a good friend.

"I did not—our customs are different. There is training by the sun priest, apprenticeship in the crafts, isolation before religious ceremonies. We do not practice time in the wild. In the city such things are forgotten because they are not needed."

"Ahh, so that is it. You do not really know trail skills." I should have guessed it. I had to show him the way to get his leggings firmly on, the way to sort the needles and extra deerskin for the several pairs of moccasins we would need.

"We do not need trail skills, do we, at Cahokia? Perhaps we have lost them," he said, shrugging. "I was born in the city, as were my father and grandfather before me. We have hunter clans, trapper clan groups. They specialize."

"Well, then, I suppose you do not need these skills of the trail. And I do not claim to be the prince of hunters myself. My skills lack perfection. Still," I said, with a rather mocking twist to my smile, "they do serve well when one gets hungry." I showed him my short bow with bright, sharp arrows and we knelt in the grass. Soon a fat jackrabbit came by, chasing one of his maiden friends, and I shot him, in the raptures of his love, poor thing.

"Shall I prepare him for the fire?" I asked Winter Bird, holding up the rabbit, twisting the arrow to remove the barbed point.

"I can skin—but I would prefer to make the fire and gather herbs. I am an excellent cook," he said. All was soon done, and as we sat in the cold darkness, I spoke to him of Cahokia, a subject that was never far from my conscious thought at any hour these days.

"You are not of the noble lines," I said.

"No. But I am one of the marrying lines."

"The what?"

"Several secondary lines, commoners, are breeders for the royal line." My eyes looked at him questioningly. "Well," he went on, "from ancient times we all knew the royal lines, descendants of the Sun Lord, were too few to make the stock strong. And there were many abberants—"

"You mean retarded children?"

"Yes, and though we all know that these special marked ones of the spirits should be held in great respect and have many lessons to teach us, they do not make good rulers."

"I should think not."

"So the laws of marriage are carefully regulated. The direct descendents of the great Sun Lord marry with the breeding lines of fine artisans, like me, the priests marry with the military nobility, the secondary cousin nobles choose mates from the traders and building guilds."

"And the workers? The ordinary farmers?"

"They choose mates from among themselves. It does not matter in that case, anyway."

"Except to them, I suppose," I said, softly.

"Yes, of course." Winter Bird was beginning to clean up the campfire, to sweep clean the area where we would sleep. He was a very particular person.

After a little while, when we were in our sleeping robes, he said, "Were you surprised to see a Female Sun?"

"Yes. But Walks-Up-the-Steps told me the story. The last Great Sun, on his deathbed, said that he had a vision that his beautiful cousin, Eyes-of-the-Deer, should succeed him. The Sun itself had ordered it. So the priests confirmed it with prayer fasts and vigils to the Sun Lord, and she was chosen.

"Her reign began the day after the pit interment."

"Of her cousin?"

"Of course. He died on the night of the Return of the Sun Feast and because of the special omen, even greater festivities were held than usual." He was silent, remembering. "I was a child, but I shall never forget them."

The smoke from the fire was pungent, the embers glowing bravely against the black of the forest. I thought briefly of the campfires with Uncle and with the nephew of old Thistle Child near the Great Lake.

"Sixteen of his companions were sacrificed, along with the handmaids who took care of the sixteen for the five days from death to funeral."

"Handmaids?"

"Yes. Their every wish was gratified by the handmaids, and then they all died together in the pit."

"How?" I had an idea, but I wanted to hear it from him.

"Strangled. With special cords of the sacrament consecrated by the priests. They are woven by the handmaids themselves months in advance of the death of the ruler."

141

"But how do they know? Who gives instructions like these?"

"Well, the Lord of the Funeral Death, of course. Months, even years in advance of the death of the Great One, because of the extreme significance, and because the Great One and those who go with him, go to be with the Sun Lord, all must be in perfect ritual order. The ones who will accompany, who will serve, who will carry the bier, who will dance, who will sing and who will die for the Lord are chosen."

"Did you say months in advance? That must make the lives of the ones chosen to, as you say, die for the Lord, blighted from then on?"

His voice, clear with conviction, rang across the clearing. "Why should it? It is the greatest honor the world has to offer to die for the ruler—the child of the Sun Lord. People have been known to fight over it, to beg at the court, to bribe with fine gifts."

"Oh, well, of a certainty," I said, not knowing anything to say. We all loved to serve the Sun Lord in my small village, but nobody would have been overjoyed to have been told to die for him in the funeral pit. I doubt if they would even have done it, might have, sacrilegiously for sure, turned on the man handling the "special cords of the sacrament." My father had grumbled that one could not get our villagers to do much they did not want to do.

"Independent people who have to fend for themselves to put meat in the pot day to day won't take orders, even from the gods," my uncle had said. "They will go to endless trouble to suit the shaman, to get themselves healed or helped, because that is for themselves. But tribal worship only goes so far out in the woods."

On we travelled, through groves of trees where the last leaves clung to them like tattered garments, with sharpening winds biting at our backs, and I hurried Winter Bird on because the season for which he was named was coming on. Across the flat plains we went, burnt off prairies where the hunters for generations had made great circles of men and women and had caused the fires to burn before them, driving all sorts of animals into the center so they could kill them and preserve them for the winter. And so they could cleanse the land, and cause fine, lush grass and nourishing plants to grow for all of us on Turtle Island, animals and folk alike.

Then, across the Ouabache, which I knew, and through the places of marshes the elders who taught me had spoken of, with swamps stretching on along the White River bottoms, with strange, almost frightening forests of dead weeds as tall as a man, past stamped-down ground at the river crossings where the great buffalo beasts thundered across in their stupidity, pushing each other, sometimes trompling if they took a notion of fright and started running.

Up, up a little, where the trail widened and separated, through flocks of birds still going to the warm climes, so many, so many, they darkened the day, and then, with strange, knobby little hills in sight, on a particularly clear day when the Sun Lord hung bright orange at He is Setting. we saw it. In a meadow, the Great Sign.

Standing, we saw a shape tall as the wall of a shelter, larger by half again than the grandfather of all buffalos, gray, hairy, with a long, long nose reaching to the ground and strange narrow horns coming out from beneath the snout.

We fell on our knees to do reverence to the powers which had created such a beast. "What is it?" Winter Bird breathed. I was glad he seemed to have seen it too! I had wondered if I was seeing it in a vision dream. If it were so, it was for both of us.

"Great Snake Snout." I whispered. "My uncle spoke of it from the time of the old ones. There were many, in the days of the Birds of Thunder. They were hunted, and only the mightiest of hunters could bring them down."

The beast was eating at bushes with its huge, elevated head. Using its snake snout curled up into a little curve, it pulled leaves off the bushes and thrust them into its mouth.

"I thought these beasts had disappeared," I murmured, "like the giants who walked the earth and the other creatures of the tales of the Old Ones."

"No mate is here, and this one seems very big and old. No man has ever spoken of one in my city, though strange bones, long and curved as those beneath his chin, have been seen when digging was done. Perhaps this is the last one on Turtle Island."

143

"Perhaps, and if that is so, sad indeed is his fate, poor beast without a friend. Or," I added, "it may be a vision. Yes, it could be a vision." We watched the animal calmly eating vast quantities of leaves. He seemed to be a peaceful beast. Finally we rose from our knees and, doing obeisance to the last rays of the Sun Lord's departure, we ventured on down the trail.

"What does the Great Sign mean, do you think?" Winter Bird asked me.

"I do not know. Let us seek the Sign Tellers as soon as possible to interpret. A sign as portentous as this must not be ignored, and we must do it quickly, while the spoor of the spirits is still fresh on earth."

We came to the Beautiful River, obtained a canoe and directions from the people who were settled there.

"You can go to the fine flint pits of the north. But as reverent people, you should not miss a pilgrimage to the Mound of the Great Serpent. It is the most marvelous of all the sights built by man in this land of the Beautiful River."

"Will there be hospitality there? Perhaps a fine medicine man or shaman who can interpret signs from the spirits?"

They nodded and one woman, who seemed to be a spokesperson for the rest said, "Near the Mound of the Great Serpent there are no great cities any more. It is from an early time. But there are villages with many wise men indeed. From the time of the ancients, the spots there have been sacred to the worship of Gitchimanitowac."

We gave them a medium-sized but perfect pearl for the canoe and began to paddle upstream to camp along the shore. At the spot upriver that they had told us of, we took the trail north, now frosty and easy to follow. Winter Bird was coughing; he had not brought warm enough garments, poor girl-on-the-trail that he was.

For a few hours we followed the trail away from the river, and then we went up an incline. There, on that frosty, bright day, with

Winter Bird coughing harder than ever, we saw the sight the folk had spoken of, the Mound of the Great Serpent.

How shall I describe it to you? It was a sight to bring the eyes out of the head indeed. There, spread about before us, was an earthwork built by hands but planned for the spirits.

It WAS the great serpent himself, spread out across the land, bumps in his snake-like self built with dirt. Finally he opened up into a great womb-like oval.

"In the sky he must have been pleased with this tribute," Winter Bird said in his hoarse voice.

"Perhaps," I said in a low voice. I had always been afraid of the serpent, did not like to hear him talked of. He was evil, great evil. My tribe of carefree sun worshippers did not include him in their rites, feeling the bad luck he brought when invoked was not worth it.

We descended to a small village near the serpent mound, arriving after dark. We were welcomed and taken into the round lodge of the elder of the village, and seated before his lodge fire. A bright, good one it was, with quails toasting on a spit which the lodge woman turned. We sat, Winter Bird wrapped in a blanket they provided him, hacking away and spitting discreetly into his hand instead of the fire, I warming my cold feet and legs and watching the old man.

When I say old, you should not envision a grandfather. You must see a great-great grandfather, who was close to one hundred summers, older than all you have ever seen on earth. His hair was white. Many years indeed it takes for a grandfather's hair to at last turn from the color of charcoal to white, and few among us does that happen to, so you know indeed he was old. On his hands the veins stood up like blue mountains, the nails shrunken in from their edges. Wrinkles so deep White Wings could have put her thumb in them coursed his cheeks.

But he sat tall. Tall, taller than most I have ever seen. Somehow my own people came into my mind, the elders and my own uncle. But this spirit man was taller than any of my people—he was close to seven feet tall.

We nodded and grunted, mostly, as we ate the quail and good bread and dried peaches. His wife, who was twenty summers younger than he, it seemed, was a masterful cook. I had heard that the people of the Ohio were the finest cooks on Turtle Island, that they knew the use of herbs better than any, and now I saw it was true.

The Old Dream-Singer, as he was called, asked a few guttural questions, which we answered, and then, as the shadows flickered about, said, in a clear voice to me, "You are one of us."

"What is your meaning?" I said, surprised.

"You do not see your resemblance to those in this village?" I nodded. "You are big, too, and your head is flat, not like that of your friend's."

Winter Bird was dozing in the corner.

"Well, yes. Those of the trading clan, and the Sun and Star Watchers—they wear boards on their heads as children. Do you do so?"

"Yes. Some of the villages around here who do not come from our clans call us the broad-heads. We have wide faces, while theirs are narrow."

"But how—how could I, and the people I come from, look like those all these hundreds of miles away?"

"I do not know. But I am the keeper of the tradition. And tradition says when we all came into the valley of the beautiful Ohio from afar, we were the tall ones with the broad heads, and the people already here, the Ancients, were shorter, stocky, with narrow faces."

"Long, long ago?"

"Not so long as you might think, inquisitive boy that you are. In the time of the great-great grandfathers great-great grandfathers, great-great grandfathers."

"And did these broad-heads build the Serpent Mound?"

"Not so. It was built by the narrow faces who were here before us. This serpent they worshiped. And they used to do their star watches, with the bumps pointed at the Great Star Lords. They predicted with it."

"And you and your villages do not worship the serpent?"

"No, although I respect him enough to want to hold him at bay."

"And how do you do that?" I wondered. It would be very good indeed to know how to hold the Evil One at bay.

"By appealing to the good spirits and the Creator of Stars who made them to fill up all the space with their goodness so there is no room for anything else to abide. And by trying to perfect my spirit enough to withstand the wiles of the serpent god."

I smiled, cracking a few nuts from a woven basket that the woman had set before me. "And have you succeeded, Old Dreamer?"

He chuckled, clearing his throat. "I do not know. But my spirit is as hard as rawhide. I do not think the serpent spirit or any other mischief maker can get through very easily these days."

I put the nutmeats in the palm of my hand and rolled them around. Then I tossed the shells in the fire, where they blazed up briefly. "But you have not told me, reverend Grandfather, why I should look like the broadheads you call your people."

"After the time of those many grandfathers back, hundreds of summers ago, when we came into the lands of the Mound of the Great Serpent and scattered or married with their people, we began to multiply. There was not hunting ground or field ground enough for us, for we taught these people to use the corn and squash, so say the old legends. We began to send out villages like a pumpkin plant sends out runners. North, to the Great Lake, even, some went. And west, through the river valleys, to the sites which had been used for star watching and reverence to the Sun Lord for eons. Perhaps they came to your spot—where did you say it was?"

"Land of Lakes-Like-a-Necklace, Old One. It is near the Tippecanoe and Ouabache Rivers, amidst great forests."

"Yes, I think so—wait. I will go into the dream trance. I feel the spirits moving now, here, in this place with you as visitor."

"May I aid? I am ritual clown."

"Then you know how I climb the tree of life. Yes, I will visit the dream world and see the answer to why you are a broad-head."

147

So he smoked a clay pipe, blew tobacco smoke for the spirits and climbed the tree that night as the winds began to howl outside and my sick friend slept fitfully in the corner of the lodge. I held onto the old man's body when it thrashed around once or twice, grappling with the truths of the spirit world, and then he opened his eyes.

"It was as I thought. A beaver came and told me much, in great friendship. You are a part of our clans. Your people were sent as settlement villages to the west, and not heard of much. In a distant age, when time was new around here, we were all one. Welcome, my son." He gave me the armclasp, with his old, thin arm and we held each other for a brief moment. Then he said he was worn out with all the excitement, that he did not often climb the tree of life any more and it was time for him to go to bed, and then he rolled over and was snoring with the blink of an eye.

The next day Winter Bird was much worse; he was having trouble getting his breath.

"It is the lung fever," the old woman said. The old man nodded, solemnly.

"We should call the torchers or suckers," he said.

And so while Winter Bird sat, wrapped in blankets, looking flushed of face and hot-eyed and struggling to breathe in the corner of the lodge, the torch-flinger shaman came and yelled and chanted his chants and sucked the poor invalid's chest and then tossed torches high and danced about. I looked at him with suspicious eyes. He does not have his feet in the spirit world, I thought. Instead, his mind is on his gift, the present he will receive when he is done with the torching. He is a false shaman—I guessed I should know, having seen the shaman of the spirit, my uncle—so many times.

The cries of the shaman grew louder; Winter Bird moaned several times and seemed to sink. Then a voice came out of the darkness. "Stop. Pay the shaman off. The spirits are not listening tonight. He has done his job—pay him off." It was the Old Dream-Singer's woman. How firm her voice sounded. She had surprised me.

"Give him one of the fine pearls you carry," she whispered to me. I reached into my leather backpack and pulled out White Wing's pearl which showed pinkly translucent in the firelight and handed it to him. Withdrawing, and nodding in gratitude, the shaman backed out of the shelter.

When he was gone, and with no sound in the lodge but the feeble hacks of my friend in the corner, the old woman spoke. "These shamans now know nothing but the importance they hold at the council fires and the women they can get from parents who are afraid of their ire. It is well not to cross them—" she nodded at the pearls in my backpack, "but this sick one needs something else."

The old man looked up at her with clouded eyes. "You mean—the herb treatment."

"Yes. We need to take the sick one to the sweat tent and put in the healing herbs for lung sickness."

"I am too tired, by far to do the sweat things," the Old Dream-Singer protested.

"I know," she said sharply to her husband. "Our new young clansman will help me. I will watch all night with him." Her voice was now coming from the corner of the lodge, where she was looking at Winter Bird with concern. "If we do not act quickly, he will not last out the night. As it is, we do not know. But there is a chance."

I scurried about like a squirrel, following the old women's behests, bringing fresh stones, setting and lighting the fire in the sweat lodge not far from her door, closing the chinks so the heat would stay in. Then she and I took Winter Bird, now like a limp baby, into the lodge and removed all his clothes. Quickly, before he should chill deeply, we brought in the hot stones and I sprinkled the water on them exactly as Old Dream-Singer's wife told me, in tiny droplets. Then she came in and brought in the healing herbs and put them on the stones. The steam came up in clouds, pungent, aromatic.

"Well, at least my friend will die among sweet smelling odors," I told myself.

All night long the old woman and I sat watching by the steam lodge. I kept the fire going, the stones heating, and the old woman replenished the herbs.

At last as the Dawn Star rose, looking cold and far away in the winter sky, we heard a real coughing fit, deep and from-the-pit-of-the-stomach coughing. Then Winter Bird appeared at the door of the sweat house wrapped in his blanket. His face was beaded in huge droplets of sweat but his eyes seemed clear. He went rapidly past the fire to the edge of the woods where he vomited, and vomited again.

The old woman went to him. "Go to the lodge and make up the fire with bright oak wood," she said to me. "Wrap him carefully in breechclout and bed covering and put him near the fire. He is past the crisis now. I think the spirits do not want him yet."

The old woman said that one recovering from the lung fever could not travel in the cold air for a while. I would need to travel on to the flint pits by myself and stop by on the way back. By that time he might be ready to take the trail home. I prepared my pack again, and at the midnight hour sat by the fire. Old Dream-Singer had not gone to sleep, but was smoking a pipe of sacred tobacco. He was communing with the spirits again.

Finally, when I thought he was finished, I spoke into the darkness. "I had meant to ask you about something. A sign. A great one indeed. I thought your wisdom might recognize what was meant by its portent."

"Speak on."

"On the way here, by some odd hills, we saw a strange, huge beast. It had long, gray hair and a long snout. `Great Snake Snout' my people call it, but it is known only in legend."

"Yes. In our legends too. You say you saw it. Was it a vision?"

"I do not know. Perhaps it was, though it seemed real. But I knew, felt it as a very great sign."

He was silent for a moment or two. "The last time a Snake Snout was seen, it forecast the coming."

150

"Coming?"

"The coming of the Blue Eyes." I looked at him, his eyes closed, the pipe on his knee now. Something flicked at the back of my thought.

"Yes. It is a tale to tell in the dark of the night in the month of Burning Prairie, as this." I settled down to listen. "Some years ago, five generations after the time we broad-heads came into these lands of the narrow-faces and melded with their people and adopted their customs of the dead rites, and they took ours of the building of the mounds, came the great sign. A warrior near the river but on the other side, in the land of the dark and bloody ground, saw one of the Snake Snouts. Two, in fact, standing in a clearing near the cave that is called Wide Mouth of the Gods. Struck in awe, he wondered what it meant, for they had not been seen in the flesh for generations.

"Time passed, but the sign was remembered from father to son. Then, finally, when I was a child, word came from the eastern lands that the gods had landed in their heaven canoes, which had brought them to the land of Nanaboozhoo. They were coming across the land, down the river, it was said, and all were in awe before them."

"The Blue Eyes." I remembered now. My uncle had mentioned the Blue Eyes. He had said—what was it? I tried to recall while I listened.

"Yes, these were fine gods indeed—white of skin, blue of eye, with hair like the Sun Lord himself. And tall—as tall as were we broad-heads."

"And they came here."

"It took many summers. But finally their canoe did land and they came to see the Serpent Mound, as all river travelers do. I saw them, lived with them myself for a time, as a young warrior. Others, visitors from all parts, came to see these wonderful beings who stayed in our shelters."

Winter Bird's breathing was smooth from the corner of the tent, and his fever was down. He had been sipping broth all day, well ministered unto by the hands of the old woman.

151

Old Dream-Singer went on. "They were wondrous to behold. They had fine knives, but not of flint. No, of metal harder than copper, able to cut—and to kill. But when I saw them close hand, observed them for a day or two I knew the truth. They were not gods. No, not at all. They got in fights. And they brewed the juice of the wild grape and went out of their heads in nightmare vision. It was awful to behold how they did fight."

"How many of them were there?"

"Some two dozen. They had wives from the tribes of the southeast with them, for they had landed along the coast of the Great Sea."

"And did they miracles?"

"They had wondrous pots with them, and things to make fire fast and jewels around their necks, amulets I guess, in the shape of the cross. Their tongue was odd and they looked lofty and knew many things. "

"Ahh, almost as gods."

"Yes, but they were not happy. They had lost their people and could not tell how to get back. They were from across the Great Sea, from a land of many and wondrous tribes, who knew all wisdom. They knew things of the sky gods well, but that is enough. The fire burns low. I am sleepy." He turned over in his furs and snorted and passed gas. It was warm and I too was sleepy.

Still, I had recalled what my uncle had told me. The Blue Eyes. The odd ones with odd knowledge. The Old Ones of our very clan had seen them too. It was here, he said, in the land of the beautiful Ohio. Perhaps on a visit to lost relatives, perhaps because they had heard of the wondrous god-beings.

My folk had known the Blue Eyes, and the Blue Eyes had known the key to wonderful sky lore. They were able, with an odd device of stone that they had, to tell when the moon would hide her face. They could, in fact, do what no one in all this land that I knew of could do—they could tell when she would do this horrible and portentous thing. Such a device had passed into our clan's hands and, through years of Sky Watching, our wise ones had known how to use it, though they had always feared its power too much to use or teach to others. Hidden lore it was, because, as Uncle had said, whoever could predict such great events would be Power Lord indeed, over all. Yes, even over such a one as the Female Sun, I thought. The Blue Eyes—something occurred to me.

"Did they die here? Are they buried in special mounds, with honors and metal trophies fit for special messengers of the spirits?"

"No. They left us in this Ohio country. They wished to rule their own lands, take their women, have children, since they could not return across the Great Sea. They went west," his voice was trailing off. "West, with the Sun. To the Father of Waters, and beyond. I do not know where they are. Now speak to me no more. I must sleep, because soon I sleep the sleep of forever in the halls of the stars."

West. The Blue Eyes had gone on. And, if our traditions were right, they left behind the wondrous device, which had come to my people in the land of Lakes-Like-a-Necklace and had come to my uncle. And he had taken it south, far south, and left it, when he had his great religious experience, in a cave. The Star Device of Power, resting now, in a cave somewhere far away.

But there was more, and as I tumbled into sleep I had just one more thought. Somewhere, out there, beyond the Father of Waters, was a tribe or clan with my blood. Mine, and my clan's, mixed with that of the Blue Eyes. Because my uncle had said, had clearly mentioned that members of our tribe had gone with the Blue Eyes. Had gone with them—now I knew it was to the west. They had the children of our women and our brave young men with them.

So the Great Snake Snout, reality or vision dream, had been a fine sign indeed. But of what? When it had come before it had meant great change. Perhaps I would have time to ask the Old Dream-Singer about this when I returned. Certainly I would not get anything more from him to- night, except snores and bad, close-lodge odors. I slept fitfully and woke with first light to go on my journey.

The fire burns low this night, and I need to make this part of the story short. The flint pits were—the flint pits. There were people who were traders, as my uncle had said, and they knew our clan by sight, and wanted to know what I would trade. And I showed them a small pearl, and since they were backwater people and did not see the beautiful pearls of the Father of Waters all the time, they thought they were fine and wished to trade, and so I had my wish and got another fine flint store indeed. In a hurry I returned; the ground was hardening.

But I was doomed to disappointment if I thought I would take my friend home with me down the beautiful Ohio or on across the Trail of Buffalos. He was fitter, but still pale and bent over half of each day with the stitches—his chest hurt hard and he prayed not to cough.

"He will rest through the winter here with us. He is already beginning to amuse Old Dream-Singer with his tales of the Great City. Preposterous!" she chuckled. "So many people. I think he exaggerates as good story tellers sometimes do. Why, where would all the privy holes be for all the people to go to? So far up the trail they would be a day's walk. And for this old one here that would be impossible, so many times a night he gets up." She chuckled to herself.

Two nights only could I spare, and the second one I asked what it was I wanted to know so much. "What do you think this second sighting of the Great Snake Snout means?" I whispered in the darkness after the other two had gone to sleep. The Old Dream-Singer slept only fitfully, tired though his old bones always were, and I could hear him breathing and sighing next to me.

"I have asked the spirits," said Old Dreamer, "and they have spoken, quietly inside my mind, to confirm what I already sensed of your sign. Change, great change it means. Perhaps not now, but in the time of your grandchildren's grandchildren. The Blue Eyes will come once more to our shores."

"You said they were men. But so very skillful, with such bright, hard new tools and knowledge. I should like to see them."

"No, you would not," he said, sadly. "They bring the seeds of our destruction with them when they come this time."

"How can they get here?"

"The Blue Eyes will come again in the fast, strong canoes they have, bigger than any I have seen, with fair sails like they say our people of the south have too, to travel to the sacred towers of the Maya." And as the Dune Devils had. I had seen them. How else could they travel the Great Lake to go home?

"The Maya," he mumbled. Was that what they called the people of the South, who had the jade and tall shrines, where Bo Jo had lived and stored the treasure? Maya. I had not heard the name. But the Blue Eyes were smarter even than they.

"How will they destroy us?" I snorted a little disrespectfully. I could see how they could destroy the folk here, small villages, and even ones like the bands in Lakes-Like-a-Necklace country. But I did not see how it could go farther than that. "Cahokia?" I demanded. "A small group of wandering Blue Eyes can take down the city of 20,000 worshippers of the Sun Lord? With armed warriors as many as pigeons in the fall and stores of corn to surpass the gardens of eternity?"

"Ah," he said in a cracking voice. "You should see the pots they brought. They can sit right in the coals for hours, cook the stew meat to perfection, never crack, never need to be remade by the potter."

"Old Dream-Singer, what can you mean about stew pots?" I demanded in the same doubting voice. Perhaps because it was dark, and he was so very old, that I dared to be so disrespectful. Still, I did not understand it at all.

"It is not the stew pot, young loud-at-the-mouth, but the idea behind it. We do not have that idea, nor would they share. They said they had an axe of it, too, but it had been lost on the trip. An axe of that hard metal, instead of stone, could cut down a whole forest in a week instead of two cottonwoods. And a knife of it, how wonderful their knives were! Whoever had those in battle would— well, he could cut quickly and to the heart, do you not think?"

155

I was silent. There was truth to what he was saying. If, indeed, there were such a metal it would be truly a metal of power, like the device of the moon predicting.

"But who can cast down the great places of worship? The Sun Lord will protect the tall mounds and towers where he is worshipped." If he is there, said the small, doubting voice which had been in the back of my mind ever since Bo Jo had told me his tale of the Maker of the Stars.

"The Blue Eyes carry their gods or spirits with them. They do not need temples made of hands. They say their god is everywhere, listening to their needs." So, really, had Bo Jo felt.

We were both silent a moment. Then the old one coughed, spat and cleared his throat. "Yet it is not the Blue Eyes and their pots which will bring down a tribe or a people if they are to go."

"Who then?" I wanted to know.

"It is in the cities themselves—the fine, spread out, rich centers of wisdom and worship that your friend is telling me of that the seeds of the downfall lie."

"How can that be?" I asked bewildered.

"I cannot tell you. Watch for yourself and sometime you will see what the Great Sign means. Each must finally interpret his own sign, for wisdom comes individually."

Then he was asleep, and I lay awake for an hour pondering what such a thing could mean. Still, when I slept I dreamt not of Snake Snouts or Blue Eyes but of beautiful maidens, of Morning Glory and the girls at the Place of Rivers Meeting and Loon Feather, and I desired all of them with a strong desire that I seemed to feel a lot lately, and all of them were scorning and reviling me, as they always did, so that I awoke, finally, sweating, with tears of shame streaming down my face, and the feeling I used to know when I could not find my mother and I went to eat to take the pain of missing her away.

I hurried, well did I hurry on that trip back to Cahokia, and the spirits of the Birds of Thunder were at my back and sent me flying. I had left the canoe at the Beautiful River, and the downriver currents took me swiftly past its gray-white cliffs and clumped, bare-armed trees. Then, though I failed to recognize my stopping point at the Trail of Buffalos and had to turn about and paddle upstream, I did get there and headed back west on it.

Without the encumbrance of my poor trail mate, who was resting in comfort before the bright fire of Old Dream-Singer and his wife, I could camp quickly, and be up early and off at the first rays of the light. I used the small bow and found that necessity made my arrows go true and the animals understand my need and come to me.

With heart in throat I came to the odd, knob hills where we had seen the Snake Snout sign, but the clearing where he had stood was empty, though a few deer came poking their noses into it just as I passed through.

There were few folk on the trail, and those I met were families traveling with sledges and small ones on the cradle board, heading to visit their own to spend winter camp, or men returning with game who had no need to trouble me, or be troubled in return.

The camps were cold at night! Truly I tell you it is so, and yet when I made leantos and kept the fires going, I could survive. And, across the dismal, barren swampland, one day mucky with sudden rain, on another frozen solid, I went, and then across the prairie passages, which had been burnt off in some spots even after we had passed and stood blackened and ugly and smelling of pungent smoke.

And finally, of course, I came back to Cahokia, saw its huge temple and burial hills rise against the sky and was flooded with a sense of security at the strength and permanence it spoke. "Ah, Old Dream-Singer, you are silly and feeble now. The years are too much for you, for nothing can shake what this mighty city is." And I felt good to be back at what was now my home.

Many were the spots I had to cover, the things I had to explain, since I had been gone two moons, and I was like a squirrel darting about to store nuts when the days go short. First, though, I owed obeisance to the Female Sun, of course and must visit her to report on the success of my mission.

She was in the Sun Palace, next to the temple on the highest hill, and I knew I had access, for so she had told me before I departed. Up, up, I climbed on, up the many steps, past guards on duty with pike spears with flint points. On the terrace near the top was the herald, Fire-on-the-Plains, polishing copper ornaments with sand and marl. "Well, it is the young man who would be noble," he said, smiling. "Did you find out how to use your tongue correctly enough on your quest so that you do not sound like a waste collector?"

"Yes, my tongue is noble now," I said, "although I was always noble."

"Noble of heart, I think," he said. I did like this young man, who had such good perceptions. I asked him about those at the top of the hill. He thought a moment before answering, and then his answer was casual enough.

"The sun rises, the sun sets. The river flows on. The prince entertains his friends and harlots. The steward orders food tidbits and the Female Sun eats them. The corn grows, the armies march. Thus has it ever been." He put his rubbing cloths down and held up a copper necklace—one of the prince's—to the sunlight to see if it gleamed sufficiently.

"And how do you know all this goes on?"

"My grandfather was ruler, the Sun in his time, and all happened in the same way then." He lowered his voice, "Except for the harlots and the armies. They are refinements of the present day and age." He turned away then as if to pursue his business, and I climbed the last few steps, to the very top, where I had never been, where both royal residence and temple were.

Truly, it was a mountaintop of power. All around were tablets painted and carved with the sacred signs: the sun, the serpent, the hawk, the eye of the universe. And there, the temple. I had not seen into it—it was said to be a sacred shrine with relics not to be seen by any except the Highest and Greatest, of which, of course I was not. Those to whom I had spoken about the nature of the relics would not, could not speak of them. To do so was profanity. I went to my knees before the closed door of the temple.

Then, best of all dwellings in Cahokia, the supreme palace of the Female Sun. Its caned roof swept low, to within three feet of the ground, and its roof rose high. Its door was carved with the sun and within it, the eye, and the paint was bright orange.

I stood outside while a minister lord announced my presence. Soon I was invited into an antechamber, where she received. Her personal rooms were beyond, out of sight of the common herd.

Female Sun sat on a huge oak bench. Her garments made her body look as if it were swathed in a turban, and again I was reminded that her face had been, still was, one of the fairest in all the land. She was the Sun's true daughter I told myself, refusing to even listen to the odd nagging voice in the back of my mind that wondered how he got a daughter if he didn't have a wife.

She beckoned me to stand before her chair. "And so, you have traversed river and land to get the trading goods we sent you for."

"Yes," I said, digging into my leather pouch. "I have five of these, loaded with the best flint I have ever seen. They were hard to carry, and I had to sledge them, but—"

"Yes. You have done well," she said, inspecting the grain of the slabs. "There can be more when you lead another trip for us next spring. We will send bearers then to help you."

"Well, if they wish to go. Each man must listen to the spirits' commands in his own way, and I would not want to subject any man to a long journey for me."

"It does not matter what they wish. They are slaves, all of them."

She saw me raise my eyebrows. I said nothing, and then I heard the voice of her son from the shadows. "Does it not occur to you that everyone in this city is the slave of the Female Sun? It is true. You, too, must operate at her will. After all, she controls the strongest force in the world, does she not?"

I bowed again, but did not answer. I saw her dismiss the prince with a wave of her hand. She beckoned me to come and sit down on a small bench beside her throne.

"Now, Drum-of-the-Gods, I do not wish to have you think of me as power ruler."

"How else shall I think of you, oh, Female Sun?" I wanted to know. All of this made me a little uncomfortable.

"As a mother. I am Mother to all my people." I agreed.

"Besides, she went on, "You and I have a special bond." She reached over and patted the knee of my rather soiled legging. "I have thought often of you since you left on the trail, and of the past, and of a man I knew so long ago and loved."

Well, so she did know after all about Uncle. She was speaking truth right out, I thought. I would need to speak to her honestly too.

"I have thought often too about the past. With my hurried departure I did not get to ask the question which has troubled me, knowing my uncle's tortured story here in this city. What happened to the man he wronged? Who was sold as a slave to the Dune Devils—ah, People. Their chief told me he had been freed."

"Yes, but do you not know?" She looked at me brightly, smiling a wistful smile, her head cocked on the side of her huge neck. She looked like a little girl.

"Know?"

"How could you? It is forbidden under heavy penalty to discuss the private matters of the Sun Rulers. The noble-man who was sold as slave returned to—claim me as his bride. When the Great Sun died, he called for me to rule and my husband ruled with me, until he died, his constitution worn out from the year in the harsh northlands as a slave. But not before—" she gestured toward the door—"my son was born."

"So," I breathed, understanding. "The prince is the son of the man my uncle wronged." The stupid one. Whose son now hated me, somehow.

"Does the prince know who I am?" I asked.

"Yes. I share all with him, as he may succeed me to the Sun Throne if our Lord so decrees. But you are protected by my sacred decree as long as you are in Cahokia." Her voice was almost a whisper. "I never stopped adoring him, longing for sight of him, and now—you have come." She came to me and raised me with her own hands.

As the afternoon sunlight waned on that bright, crisp winter day, the Female Sun and I talked, of the pearls I had taken, of Winter Bird left among the Serpent Mound people, of the mound itself, of which she wanted to hear all details, though she must have known of it before. Finally, when all talking was done, she leaned close to me. Cooking smells drifted in through the doorway as servants prepared the evening feast for their ruler, but no servant was in the house.

"You are a strong young man and have done well. The opening of the trade east is something my ministers and I have talked of. You shall be the agent, come spring, of a new trading connection that will serve us well. I shall reward you—then and now—beyond your dreams."

Well, I thought, I can stand that, I believe. So far life has done little rewarding to me. Closer she came, until I could see the slight lines in the smooth skin of her face. There in the darkness, she seemed quite beautiful as a woman, as well as powerful as a queen.

"I have been long without a consort. I am as other women, holy though I am, I yearn to feel male strength, male power." She put her hand on my knee. "It is our custom for experienced women, particularly noblewomen, to take consorts from among young men. It allows us to teach them the lessons of love aright. And who better, for you with the face of a young prince, the instructions of a queen?"

I was thunder-struck, I must say. When I had thought of these matters, and of course I had, increasingly more every day, being the strongly growing young hunter I was, I had seen myself with—Morning Glory or Loon Feather or the other young maids of my dreams. I had never even dreamed of being with this queen woman, because she was a goddess spirit on high. She did not know me.. But now—the Female Sun's hand was going higher on my leg. She put her carefully washed and pomaded hand behind my neck and drew my lips towards hers, breathing spiced breath. It was not what I had in mind, not at all, but—

"You are his image, the man I loved so desperately so long ago. I never had the yearned-for caresses we had promised each other. I was his virgin, and yet he did not take me. Now you will be mine and we will know the joys of love together. I will teach you all there is to know."

The thought crossed my mind that I did not have the power to resist. To deny the lusts of the Female Sun would be instant death, surely. And besides—I would soon be sixteen summers and the waters of the creek run high and fast, uncontrollably, at that time of life.

It was not at all what I had in mind. Yet, there had been signs of change, and this surely was one of them. In two or three minutes my life was changed again—it had been foretold by the Old Dream-Singer, hadn't it? Who was I to deny the will of the spirits? I allowed myself to sink into the flood and ride its crest for a while.

Chapter Eight

Modesty wants to keep me from telling you what it was like being the young consort of the Female Sun and her pupil in matters of the heart. Still, the fire has burned low, as I said, and yet still you listen to this part of the tale. The young ones have all gone to bed and will not be shocked, and so, I will detail some of the happenings of those times in the palace at Cahokia.

During the day I lived normally with Walks-Up-the-Steps, Ghost and White Wings, pursuing my life as a trader and noble-man of leisure (for such had the Great Sun designated me, drawing on my heritage as son of the Sun Watcher and noble family in my home village).

At night, though—that was a different matter. The Female Sun (who wished me to call her in private Soft Fur, a name she had been called as a child and which seemed to fit the situation) had me come only when dark sent its soft fingers around the town, and enter by the back side of the hill, where food was carried up and household matters conducted. There were niche steps there, facing the river, harder to go up, of course, than the ceremonial ones, but nevertheless accessible to anyone who had a purpose.

Winded a bit I would arrive at the top and find my way to the back door of the palace, unnoticed, I suppose by command, by guards and servants. Waiting in the back, barred room of the palace would be the ruler, now a frenzy of a woman, swathed in the finest garments to decrease, I suppose, the impact of her large body size. She was eagerly ready to take me to the luxurious, large royal bed and, on its fur, to show me some new lesson in the large lore of love she had amassed for herself.

Well, she had long been without a consort, but she had not been without lovers. Skillful ones she had known, skillful lover she had become. What she knew, and taught to me during those hours of darkness, was a real study in the higher trail lessons of love making. We started with basic lessons, because, of course, all was new to me and I had troubles with being too eager and quick to demonstrate my skills.

163

But she taught me the value of caution and step-by-step stalking as one heads the prey towards the height of the moment of conquering, and the use of restraint, just as one does in hunting. And she showed me the value of surprise, and the heightened pleasure one receives from teasing games one plays in a hunt of this sort. And, of course, of the shades of meaning in the final complete conquering moment, the possession of the other's being, the surrender of the soul, and ultimately, the power of possession, as the lover reaches the height and climax of love just as the hunter reaches the climax in the kill.

Am I being too strong to compare those sultry nights in the closed room, when we experimented with the shades of feeling and pleasure over and over, when I thought I would die of excruciating pleasure and burst with feeling—to compare them to the rigors and threats of the hunt?

Sometimes, when our bodies dripped sweat before that small but hot fire, and the moaning of my partner filled the room as we came together in new or old ways until finally even my fifteen-year-old powers were exhausted, I thought of the death of the animals I had stalked, their blood poured out, their panting efforts to breathe at the end. And I felt guilt. It was the guilt of my true warrior training at the hand of my uncle, who had taught that one withheld himself, rather than satiating himself in love, to gain power and spiritual strength. That the Maker of the Stars wishes us to subdue lust, rather than cultivate it like some sort of exotic flower.

And yet, here the voice of the gods, the Female Sun, commanded me to indulge, and indulge again. And, in those dissipated nights I knew two truths. The first one was that all was different here in the city from the life in the forest. And the second one was that lust and death are close. Very close, at times, indeed.

One of the great joys of my life, again, was being with White Wings. She had not wanted to come to me when I first returned from the flint trip, but by the next day, at the urging of that good woman Walks-Up-the-Steps, she came over as I sat eating on the floor of the shelter and put her arms around my neck. She remembered the old days! She cared! I set my dish down and went to my pack to take out a necklace made of bright beads, which I had traded for in the Ohio camps.

We wandered the streets again, as we had before I left for Ohio and discovered the spilling-over pursuits and interests of the great city.

On cold days we stayed within the shelter of the stockade, down the muddy byways behind the main streets. We went, often of course, to the lane of the shell drillers, the jewelry people, Winter Bird's clan. His father had come to greet me the first day after my return.

"Tell me of my son," he begged. Eagerly he clasped my hand, and I watched the long artisan's fingers, the carefully pared nails. His hair was a black shock and his stature stocky. I stood two handspans above him, growing as I was each month. I was aware of what the Old Dream- Singer had told me of the mixing of two peoples in these river valleys in the time of long gone great-grandfathers.

I knew it in another way. On the hill, sometimes, and occasionally in other places in the city I would see people of my own stature, the tall broad-heads. It was said they had been captured in the raids around Lakes-Like-a-Necklace after I left, and now they were serving as slaves to those at the top of the hill. Once I saw a cousin, son of one of my mother's sisters who lived at the Twin Lakes near us, but I did not even nod my head. We were in a different life now.

I was glad to be able to tell Winter Bird's father about the fate of his son. "Winter Bird is alive, I trust, by the good fortune of the spirits, and getting well after nearly going to the great spirit path." His eyes flicked fear, but as I told him of the goodness of the people near Serpent Mound, and of the Great Sign, he melted and smiled, with an almost toothless smile. So many here had sawed off teeth. It came, they said, from eating so much of the coarsely ground corn.

"Stay with us the morning," he said, and I sent White Wings off to play with the young cousins who seemed to be everywhere around the outside fires, chasing puppies, throwing balls of deerskin, running to a jump line to see who could hurl himself the farthest into a sand pit from a standing position.

The young girls of the shell crafters' lane had finished their morning's work and were building a house for a corncob baby out of sticks. Fascinated, White Wings watched, then, as they welcomed her, brought sticks of just the right size for the shelter. It was a square Cahokia house with a long reed roof.

After a while, I left the side of my friend's father and came to lie on the ground by them. "Let me show you another house for the babies," I said. "A forest house." I gathered a few twigs from the woodpile and began to build a shelter of the Lakes-Like-a Necklace. Something welled up in me like a spring of water as I began to stick the little beech twigs in the ground, then bind them with a small grapevine in the middle at the top. The girls watched a while, murmuring among themselves about the differences between the baby house I was building and their own models. Then they forgot me and I worked on, creating a home of my beloved village, putting fabric scraps over the outside of the circle of branches tied at the top, sweeping a little area around it, as the women of my village did each morning in the bright summertime by the shimmering lake.

My mind afar off, I started to feel the presence of Winter Bird's father. He was kneeling beside me. "You are no artisan," said Hail Like Rocks, for such was his name, looking at the uneven job, "but you put feeling into the job."

"It is my home. A house like those in my own village in the far-off woods. I do long for it sometimes, and I did not know it until I built this—" I gestured towards the little house.

"You are an odd young nobleman," he said, but his gaze was not disapproving.

"I do not think of myself as a nobleman, although I have been so named." The whole dark, hidden world of my nights came into my thought, and a flash of disgust passed through me.

"Where does your home village exist?" he asked.

"Only in my dreams. It was wiped from the face of the earth by the raiders who captured me. I wonder if whole villages exist, mothers, babies, dogs, old aunts, somewhere out there, with the Maker of the Stars." I told Hail Like Rocks my story with broad strokes, like a skin painter, leaving out details I did not think needed knowing.

As I finished my story, I looked beside me to see White Wings. She had left the screaming, running young maidens and stood staring at the house. She pointed at it. "Mama," she said. "Daddy," she cried. Inconsolably she began to cry and cried so hard, with large tears falling all over her leggings, that she would not be comforted. Finally, I had to take her home.

"Come again tomorrow," I heard Hail Like Rocks call after me, and, occupied with my own worries over the last of my clan, I waved back at him that I would.

I held White Wings by the fire as the shadows of evening danced. Walks-Up-the-Steps left us alone and cooked the meal outside; Ghost sat like the spirit he was named after in the corner. There we sat, by the fire, White Wings and I, as the shadows of evening danced. She sobbed, her little shoulders heaving up and down, but this time it was without anger. Sadness had replaced all the wrath she had felt towards me and the world, the sadness of loss and remembrance of something that has been taken, like the brown leaves of autumn, to come no more.

"Mama," she said. "Daddy." Her voice was choked. "The lodge. Bad men come. Yell. Took us. Far, and bad stones on my feet."

"I know, White Wings. They were bad men; bad women."

"Bad woman. Bad woman. Mama gone." I stroked her hair, now so neatly combed and pinned. She cried harder until she could cry no more. Then she turned and touched my cheek with the back of her little hand. "You walk with me then. Took my hand where birds sang. Fix the birdie sore leg." There was a kind of accepting in her voice of all the bad spirits had sent. She slumped against my shoulder. "Fix the birdie sore leg, Bear Belly" she murmured trustingly and touched my cheek again.

My arms and leggings were wet with her tears, as I lay her on a rabbit skin bed covering.

"She did not even know what it was she missed, because she had shoved it all away in her baby way, underneath a blanket of pain," Walks-Up-the-Steps said. "It is hard to return to the land of remembrance," she went on, serving us plates of squirrel stew. "But one cannot live in the cemetery of forgetfulness forever. It makes one, even a little one, clean to face the truth."

I grunted affirmation without adding anything.

As we finished the evening meal and Walks-Up-the-Steps went outside to wash the trenchers in a water bucket, Ghost crept up to ask me what I wanted done with the ceremonial moose drum. For, he said, the winter was hard upon us and the drum sat outside, behind the house.

Irritatedly I brushed him aside. I did not want to think of the drum now. "Put it wherever you want for the winter—well, wherever the drum head will be protected," I grumbled. I had no time for Ghost, not now or any night lately. I was ignoring this good, child-like man who had chosen to serve me through love and need. I avoided the pain in his eyes as I left the shelter.

I changed into the tunic of a Cahokia nobleman, donned the shell and copper necklace. I tossed the tear-stained leggings into the corner and with an ill tempered snort went to my meeting with the goddess of the sun—and secret love on winter nights.

The morrow again found me at the dwelling place of Hail Like Rocks, the shell crafter—this time with White Wings left behind.

He and his wife sat near a fire on this rather mild looking winter day working with a circular stone stamping tool and a tiny spinning hempen bow stringed drill. They were making hundreds of shell ornaments with holes in them to sew onto the clothes of the Female Sun and her noble family of assistant suns.

"So many?" I asked, watching the weak sun cast the beautiful colors of sunset on the shining shell fragments.

"It takes many shells to make a tunic glitter for the prince so that he shines like a bassfish," Hail Like Rocks' wife said. She was a handsome woman named No Corn, ten summers younger than her husband, with an odd, short stub of a thumb and a sense of humor sharp as a thorn.

I was curious. "How long—how many days each winter will you do this?" I asked.

"Every day," her husband nodded solemnly. "It takes every day we have to supply the needs of the royal Suns."

"And—your reward?"

The wife, No Corn, said, "Not enough by half. Three garners of corn, special store of spice. And privileges through marriage. We are of the marriers, you know."

"Yes. Winter Bird told me." We all were silent, thinking of him, their son and my friend, out by the Beautiful River at a stranger's campfire. Would that he were well and we would see him when the streams ran free in spring.

There were many things, they said, to be made of shells and they showed them to me. Necklaces, bracelets, shell decorations for ceremonial clay pipes, amulets. Fasteners to hold the clothing together with a hole on the other side of the jacket, ear spools. These they crafted from the river mussels, mostly from the Father of Waters, although the traders did bring shells of different iridescences from waters further east, almost to the Great Sea.

The greatest honor for the shell crafters came when they shaped and polished the great horn shells of the southern ocean, even the far islands of Atlantis, the shell larger than a man's hand which reflected the hues of He Is Setting.

"They show the Sun Lord in his greatest glory," said Hail Like Rocks proudly.

"The Sun Lord—" I said, bowing my head towards his weak eminence in the sky.

"Everything is done for him."

"Yes, I suppose," I said absently. The Sun Lord and I were not very good friends these days. That was because I wasn't sure he existed—well, as a god anyway. Sometimes I thought if he really was an omnipotent being who went at night to a big hall beyond everything, I would be struck down for blasphemy, but it hadn't happened yet. Maybe that was because I did like him, whatever he was, nice yellow, friendly blob up there in the sky. It was what people made out of him that I didn't much care for, rude forest youth that I was. I shifted about uncomfortably. Sometimes I had these disturbing thoughts, but mostly I put them aside. The Sun Lord must rule! How could a people so glorious make any mistakes about all that? Cahokia! Splendid! Who could not think it the greatest force in the world? I sopped up its interests and pursuits during the day, explored the innermost parts of royal life during the evening—who could want more?

A group of soldiers headed past us on one of the main roads to the north of our little lane. "There they go to the glory of the Sun Lord," No Corn said rather ruefully. She did not look up from counting the shell ornaments and dropping them into a clay pot.

"Where is it they are going?" I wanted to know.

"To get tribute from a people south of the bend of the Father of Waters," she said. Her voice was even, almost a monotone. I did not know what that implied.

"So? The tribute is—copper perhaps? Fine jewelry?"

"Yes, and corn. Many shares of corn."

"Have they not paid it?"

"Apparently not, or not paid enough to suit the Female Sun. Or, more justly, the prince." She said it with a sort of low snarl and her husband looked up at her with a warning glance.

"That is a thing that should not be said, woman," he said.

"Of course," she sighed.

After a while I could not resist asking, "But it is winter. Are there enough stores of corn to pay the tribute and feed the people too?"

"There will have to be," said her husband. "It was arranged last summer when we conquered the lands and made them tributary to the Sun Lord."

"And if they do not have the stores?"

"Then the soldiers will teach them to know obedience to our Lord and his child on earth. They will learn humility. The soldiers will be the instrument of their instruction. Their men will bend in obeisance and the eternal laws of justice will be set right. So the town herald said at the He Is Setting chant time yesterday."

"Fire-on-the-Plains announced that?" I asked. I had not seen him for a long time, because I came at night, and he left the hill after He Is Setting.

"He announced it, but he doesn't believe it. Fire-on-the-Plains is a good man," No Corn said, and when her husband raised his hand in admonition, she ignored him.

"What the herald means," his wife said in a very low voice," is that the men will be killed or brought back in slavery, the corn taken, the women and children scattered to go to their relatives, if they can find them before they starve, and the village burned in retribution."

"Woman, be quiet, I tell you. That is the thing that should not be said. You know the eyes of the Sun are everywhere."

With her little stub of a thumb, No Corn was busily counting the shell ornaments. She would mark their number on the pot for delivery up the royal back stairs. The back stairs. Last night had been more unusual than ever. There had been two virgins and both of us—well, I would not let my thought stray. No Corn was looking at me.

"It is for the corn, isn't it?" I said, meeting her eyes. "Everything is for the corn."

Later, as we stood in back of the house after a meal at He Is Halfway Home she whispered to me. "I was not always called by this name—No Corn. It was a second naming. When I was eight there was a terrible year when the crops failed everywhere. Many starved and the ruler grew very harsh. The public garners were closed. I was very bold and did not understand, I suppose. My mother was ill, thin, starving. I went to the garner and crept in for a small pot of corn to grind. I was caught—" she held up her thumb.

I opened my mouth in surprise. A child?

"His laws are sure but just," she said, with an ironic smile.

"After that it was determined that Cahokia could never again be without corn. No matter how much land we must take in tribute, how many families we must dispossess." Her husband came quickly to her side.

"You must not be found talking in this way," he said sternly to us, then turned to me. "You are my son's friend but I must have you promise you will speak of lighter things when you visit us." I nodded. I certainly did not wish to lose their friendship or bring them pain.

But as I returned to the lane, in a voice I could scarcely hear, No Corn told me, "If you wish to hear the things that should not be said, you should find my other son. He lives outside the walls, in the lane of the river-clay potters. Go, find him."

I do not believe I have given the impression that all of this splendor and life in the city was crunched together within those stockade walls. True, a good deal of what happened and who lived there was grouped behind those tall logs and palisades. There the most noble of the artisans, the shell crafters, for instance, lived and worked. But beyond the walls through the usually open door there were a series of circular villages spreading out from the wall, for a long way. These also had their sights, smells, dogs barking, children playing with toys, food cooking and so forth, and one bright day that winter not too long after I had visited with Hail Like Rocks and his wife No Corn, we ventured out, White Wings in her little fur rabbit skin coat and hood that Walks-Up-the-Steps had made her, and I.

The village of the river-clay potters, No Corn had said. It happened I knew which of these settlements that might be, had heard it discussed among women at the town spring. We had to go a long way down the path outside the stockade, past two or three other settlements, the basket makers' village, the mat-makers' village, through groves of trees and finally nearer than the rest to the river—logical it was because the potters needed river clay. Through a grove of ash trees we passed, a few shaking leaves clinging to the bare branches clashing in the wind. Hoar-frost made the bent, dead grass bright, and White Wings stopped and stooped every now and then to look at the crystals of frost in the sunlight.

The first time she did it I smiled and stooped too, pointing out the starry shapes and melting globules of water by their sides. Within a few paces she wanted to stop again and do the same thing, so I shrugged and let her look for several minutes. It was as if she thought we had no place to go, and, I suppose, as far as she was concerned we didn't.

When she did it a third time, I waited somewhat impatiently. The fourth time, further down the road I watched her dawdle a moment or two and then started to say, sharply "Look you, White Wings. I cannot wait here while—"

I checked myself. Poor little thing. Mother and father gone, suffered terribly from the hands of cruel people. And at her age. I did not have to have my way. It was only human to give her some freedom. Then she saw a squirrel bounding into a clump of trees and ran after him. I called to her, called over again, but was chagrined to see her disappear into the trees, paying no attention at all to my commands to return. I ran after her and thought I would give her a good talking to for disobedience but remembered her pitiful state and just pulled her along, screeching and dragging her feet. "See squirrel, see squirrel," she yelled and would not listen as I told her that the animal was long since gone.

We were through the ashen path and at the village of the pottery makers. There were their houses, more carelessly made, perhaps, than those inside the stockade itself, but then they were of a lower class. Beyond were dug-out pits where they fired the pots and jars they made. Further on was a large pile of heaped-up, broken shells used for tempering and a big shallow pit of clay dug from the river, which they must tend in all weathers if they wished to have the clay ready to fire. In summer dry times, their men—for they were women, all of the pottery makers—their men must pour water on the clay and stir it. Now, when the earth was cold, they must build fires nearby, deep in the ground around the clay pit, to keep the clay from freezing.

Wearing their warm garments, women sat in front of their houses. Some were finishing large water jars, putting rough cloth made of thin reeds against an already-made, smoothed pot to make an interesting criss-cross pattern.

Further down the lane, a grandmother and what seemed to be her grandchild were beginning a new bowl, flattening a bottom piece and then beginning the building of the sides.

"What you do?" White Wings asked, pointing to the handfuls of clay which the young girl of about ten was pulling out of the pile with a stone chopper.

The girl looked up and smiled. "I am going to pull the clay. It has already had crushed shells put in so it won't crumble or explode. Want to see?"

White Wings nodded solemnly, her small eyes shining out of the hood of the white rabbit coat. The girl gave White Wings a small bit of the clay and they marched to where the grandmother sat waiting in front of the dwelling across the lane. I drifted over, behind them.

The young girl began rolling the clay out, into a long shape between the palms of her hands.

"Snake, snake!" White Wings said delightedly, and began to roll her own long coil.

The grandmother reached over and skillfully took the girl's coil and with a few careful rolls and twists made it even. Then she began placing it around the flat cake of a bowl bottom she had formed. Around, around her hands went. When she had made one full loop, she began building on it with a second, always judging the space right, always connecting the loops without overlapping.

"Me try," White Wings said, coming up by the grandmother.

The old woman looked up at me expectantly, wondering, I suppose who we were.

174

"I am a visitor spending the winter at Cahokia. I am of the trading clans of the north. This is my little niece. I am looking for the son of Hail Like Rocks, a youth they say is here."

"He is two houses down," the older woman said. "Recently married to one of our potter's clan. He supervises the deliveries of the finest pots to the Royal Sun, up the back stairs—"

Why was it they always said that. I could never quite get comfortable. Back stairs–it was always thrown in my face–but that was silly. No one knew what I did at night. Besides, what could be wrong? This was Cahokia! Marvel of the earth. And the Female Sun was the most marvelous wonder of all.

"And he does other things—dig the clay for All Joy, his wife. She is with child."

But when I thanked her and turned to go find the young man I had come to see, White Wings fell on the ground and began to kick her heels. "Stay here, make pots," she insisted shrilly. I felt hot anger at her again. Was this the child who had put her arms about my neck and softly cooed about the birdie sore leg? She kicked harder the more I pulled her arm. Little spawn of the firetiger in the sky, demon—but there. I must not call her that. Poor child, I must remember.

"It will be fine to leave her here with me. Perhaps I can help her make a little pot," the kind woman said. When she smiled, she showed only two teeth, on the bottom of her mouth. I had thought she spoke oddly, as if she did not want to open her mouth.

"Thank you. She is not always so," I said helplessly. But if truth be told, I was glad to get away from her, much as I loved her. It tried my patience being always patient. How did the women stand it?

The minute I left, the yelping stopped. When I turned around, White Wings was calmly holding up a length of roped clay, looking at it as if it were alive, forgetting all about me and the tantrum. Little— No. Cousin dear. Remember her sadness, I told myself.

The house I walked towards was small, newly put up, I thought. The thatching on the roof was golden and unstained by frequent rain, the door covering unspotted fabric. Wed within the year the folk inside were, so the old woman had told me. A head popped out of the fabric covering.

"You are the brother of Winter Bird?" I asked, looking at someone with the same bright, serious eyes, the same black thatch of hair, yet lean, and small.

"I am," he said, eyeing me with curiosity. His glance was as sharp as the edge of a flint knife.

"I am his friend and bring news of him." He nodded, a small smile tugging at the corners of his mouth. We went inside, where a beautiful woman lay on the cot at the back. A small fire burned, smoke trying to escape out the hole in the top of the roof.

"My wife is feeling poorly today," he said. "The old women say her time is near and there are problems with the birth." Outside I had seen two of them, conferring and poking about in an herb pot.

"I shall return another day. You are busy with family—"

"No," he interrupted, "I wish to talk to you. But first, go to the cot and speak to All Joy. She has not gone out much in this last week or two and loves to hear of the ways of the world." He smiled tenderly when he said it and glanced at her; she waved a hand to me in welcome and I went to her side. We spoke of her brother-in-law, who seemed to be a special favorite of hers. She was fascinated by the mention of our trip and begged to hear more of the details, and watching her intent interest, her nods of affirmation, her little laughs of delight, I found myself telling her of the sign of the Great Snake Snout, the visit to the Mound of the Serpent, the Old Dream-Singer and his wife and all the details of the trip east to the flint pits.

I know not how but—she was one of those rare people—he was too—that you meet a few times on the trail of life, and you feel as if you have known them since cradleboard times. Your whole heart and soul is opened and you have found a trailmate for your spirit.

An hour passed as we spoke and she listened solemnly and nodded sadly at the sad parts of my story, and laughed at my trying to be father-uncle to a child of almost three summers. Mention of her made me remember—stupid bear belly that I was—White Wings, and guiltily I ran out to see if she had fallen in the river or scalded herself in a cooking pot. But no, she was still employed, this time eating dried apples and maple sugar and soup with the woman and girl. The woman, with her toothless smile, said White Wings was a pleasant child and caused no trouble. I looked at her in wonder. Pleasant child? Well, she could be, that was for certain. I returned to the small, newly marrieds' shelter.

All Joy was sleeping quietly now as the afternoon wore on. I ducked out of the shelter once more to breathe fresh air; clouds were rapidly filling up the sky, throwing the shelter into shadow. A cold wind was blowing; definitely there was a change in the weather coming. Hawk Eye, for that was my new friend's name, went out to get more wood.

"Not much now," he muttered, putting some sputtery softwood on the fire.

"Well," I said, growing bold with him because of the closeness I felt, "why are you using inferior wood? Softwood is good for starting fires, but you need oak and maple, good and dry."

"It is hard to find wood lately," he said.

I looked at him in surprise.

"Well, many people live in these parts and the woods have been cut down for the cornfields." I supposed that was true. I had not really thought about it. "And I do not know well the kinds of wood for burning anyway."

"You do not know the trees? The ways of fires?"

"Well—I grew up within the walls, as part of the marrying clans. There were woodgatherers, servants, slaves, I guess from the conquests, who brought our wood. I never gave it a second thought until I moved out and had to do my own work—" His eyes grew serious and he turned away from me. "Truly, I do not know the woods. Like most, except the hunting clans, I fear it, I guess, so I pay someone for wood, one of the firegatherers of the pottery kilns, with one of All Joy's fine pots and gather nearby what I can if I have to—and hope for an early spring."

"I shall get wood for you, as much as I can carry in a few loads," I said on impulse. Out I went, into an increasingly strong wind, into the ash groves nearby. Red winter birds, blue tandaksas or jays, flitted by in the way they do when they sense change is coming and the need to find shelter. The sky was dark indeed for the middle of the afternoon.

And, it was true that there was not much good wood. This forest was a new one, replacing an old primeval one. The remains of the old one were there—gaping holes in the ground which were rotted out stumps, bumps and stumps still remaining of huge old forest trees which had been cut with stone axes and burnt through—why? To create stockades and houses for this town two hundred years ago or more. Still, if you walked far enough, there was still good burning wood from fallen trees and I wrenched and twisted and stomped it off and came back with a huge armload.

Then I went off again, for whatever it was the Birds of Thunder had in mind for us was coming, and I thought I should soon gather up White Wings and go back within the wall to the shelter of Walks-Up-the-Steps. But wood first, for the husband who was tending a beloved wife infirmed by childbirth—I went quickly, gathered what I could again and walked back through hail and wind.

I put the wood under the wood leanto. "Come in—you cannot go back. You must stay with us," I heard the voice of Hawk Eye over the rising wind.

"My cousin—I must tend to her." I stumbled back through the pelting, icy deluge and came to the door-closing of the woman and girl. "White Wings. We are staying in this village this afternoon, probably the night. The storm. Come—" I heard a wail within.

"Let her be with us," an old voice called. "She is happy here with my granddaughter. There is a good fur pallet for her and a good venison stew. Huge pot. Plenty for all. Take some for the lovers who soon expect a third." I could smell the stew's succulent smell through the door closure, and I nodded eagerly. Surely All Joy would not feel like cooking.

"Thank you," I called, and returned through the increasing storm, bearing a hearty pot of the stew. When I reached the door. Hawk Eye's worried look told me that he wished to close down the door opening pelt, and I helped him secure it with pegs and weight rocks. I was busy in the next few minutes. Hail was sputtering through the opening at the top of the shelter but it did not put out the fine fire I built for them. The wood was fairly dry; I had got it back before the hail wet it through. The fire was clean and bright, and encouraged conversation.

"You do not like the woods," I said to Hawk Eye, as I sat down on my haunches.

"I do not know the woods. As a child I loved to walk among the flowers in the spring, to hear the birds or to be pulled on a small child's sledge over the snow. But growing up in the city—how much we centered our concerns on life here; how little we went outside, at least my clan."

"You were of the marrying kinship group, the shellcrafters clan."

"Yes, I grew up knowing that skill, but I did not like it. No, it was too quiet a pursuit, required too much patience. I am short on that."

"I, too, " I said, thinking of White Wings.

"Not I," said a voice from the side of the room. All Joy was awake. We sat back so she could look at the fire and enter the conversation. I poured the grandmother's fine stew into a pot, added hot stones to warm it, and we ate beside the fire.

"My wife knows the ways of the woods," Hawk Eye told me. "Her clan out here, the pottery makers, have to keep fires going and walk the rivershores for clay. They are part of the Maker of Stars' kingdom each day."

It was an odd phrase. Most out here said Sun Lord, but I let it pass. "The only nature I have known has been as a soldier," Hawk Eye went on. "I was one of the captains of expeditions for two summers."

I was surprised, both by his declaration and by the tone of his voice, which was dull and full of loathing.

"And yet you are not now? The expeditions still go, but you are here?"

"Yes. Some are all-time soldiers. It is their clan. Others, captains, must come from the kinship clans who support the Female

Sun. I, as part of the marrying group, was chosen as an expedition captain. We ranged west last summer, then north, looking for new tribute villages and spoils for Cahokia."

"North?" I asked, feeling a little tongue of apprehension licking like a flame at my thought.

"Yes, up through the lands of lakes and rivers north and east of the Illinois River."

"And—"

"And even unto the dunes. There were several parties of us."

My apprehension grew and I set down my plate. "You—ranged—to the Tippecanoe?"

"Yes. So the natives called that river which joins Ouabache. We went about small villages, claiming sovereignty for Cahokia, taking tribute and slaves, pillaging." His voice was dull. He evidently did not find it very satisfying to be a "tribute expedition captain." But I still wondered, worried.

"Did you go to the Lake-of-the-Boulders? The largest inland lake there? Surrounded by high hills where the sun is worshipped with the vision poles?" There had been rumors of the Great City's scouts about. A village not far from us on the Twin Lakes had been "added to the empire." Could it be that my new friend, the best I'd found in these foreign territories, had been the instrument of some of my family's destruction?

"No, that was the work of the scout group." I nodded in relief. "We went farther north yet, to the dunes on the Great Lake. Did not really begin our tribute attacks until fall. There we found some odd villages of the People of the East—the Fall People. They did not wish to talk of tribute and subjection, so—we destroyed them."

The Dune Devils! The Old One and the other families of the village of my torture. My feelings were oddly mixed on hearing this—I was satisfied, deep in my heart that retribution had been done, but then I had felt this before, nothing new. What surprised me was the twinge of sympathy for the people killed, people I'd lived with for months, relatives of Thistle Child's nephew I'd learned to like.

"I must go out," All Joy said, looking distressed.

"The healers have ordered you strictly to bed."

"I may get up to go down the path. And I must. I must feel human at some times."

We undid the holding stakes and weights on the door closure and she went, almost gliding, out the opening and into the storm. Her husband looked after her with anxious eyes.

"What—what is the problem?" I asked, concern and curiosity overcoming embarrassment. Men did not ask men such things, but then I was from a family of Shamans who dealt in the ailments of the body.

"She—bleeds now, too early. They want her on her back and are administering restraining herbs so the little one will delay until it is its due time." He still watched the door. "And so it does not kill her in coming. The early bleeding can be dangerous, so they say."

"Your love is profound."

"As wide as the skies. She is one of the spirits' great children. A perfect vessel cast by the Potter of All. Not only does she have the beauty of a pool reflecting birch trees, she has the heart and soul of the spirit of the pool. I could not envision a day without her, from the first time I cast eyes on her while I marched through this village as captain, in the army. We stopped to drink here on a hot day."

"And the healing herb women are good ones?" I asked. He nodded. I inquired about shamanistic healing and he said they did not often do it in Cahokia. The priests had banned the shamans, preferring to hold the rites, the powers in all things pertaining to ritual themselves, leaving the herb women to take up the slack in the rope.

"And yet, shamanistic healing does heal," I said. I told him of my family, of my uncle's powers when he was in his Greatness of Spirit days. "The power of invoking is great," I said solemnly, staring into the coals before I put more oak wood on them. "Prayer to the powers of the world does change things. I have often seen it."

All Joy stood in the door, radiantly smiling. Snow was in her shining black hair and she was shivering under her covering blanket. "It is well," she said. "I know I am better. And out there, in the storm, I felt the power of the spirits of the storm."

"Birds of Thunder," I said, nodding.

"So my grandmother used to believe, but I do not know if I would call them that. There is power in the storm, I know that."

"Yes," I said. "And wisdom, coming from the source of all creation to us, if we just listen. It feeds us in the storm as in the quiet time, perhaps more. What did it tell you?"

"That all would be well. A voice I could almost hear said to me through the howling wind, "Baby's heart, mother's heart. Now one, then separate. When all hearts beat as one, you will find healing."

"Odd," murmured her husband.

"I do believe that all life is sacred and that we are cared for," All Joy went on. "When I make my pots and vessels, I try to show forth the beauty of the Lord Sun and the Spirit of All. My belief is strong." Her eyes were shining. She went to her small cot and began to wash herself with water she had brought in one of her own fine vessels. We turned our backs and spoke, quietly by the fire. Outside the snow was flying sideways. Why is it when there is a storm you think of those you love who are not under the roof? Wonder about their welfare, think the worst.

Oddly, I thought of the red winter birds I'd seen. Where had they found shelter? I knew that White Wings was safe on her bunny pallet in the potter woman's shelter. And back at Cahokia— I was not there. The thought stabbed me with an odd, cold remorse.

I would be missed, oh yes, Soft Fur would miss me in her bed tonight. She would expect that I would show my obeisance and devotion to her, coming through the terrible elements, up that steepest of all hills to be with her. And that I did not would be taken amiss—she was full and spilling over with affection and reward to those who suited her needs and wishes, but to those who might affront her—I did not want to think of it. Yet, in a way I did not care. Outside this simple shelter there was some-thing else. There was an odd kind of freedom out here, in the midst of this storm with these honest, fair people. I was speaking again of the things I cared of, opening my heart. Confined as I was by the storm, I felt free for the first time in many weeks.

I found I was exhausted and fell asleep there by the fire. Someone covered me with a bed robe, and I slept like a baby.

The next morning Old Man Winter had established his domain, his throne on the earth, as Bo Jo had described so long ago. The trees drooped almost to the ground from the load of ice that had followed the hail. They were lovely beyond description in the glinting sunlight which reflected off their branches. I emerged from the house of my friends and walked the streets, my deerskin shoes making tracks in the snow as deep as a man's foot. All of the people of this tiny potter's village were abroad, walking about, kicking the snow, laughing at each other, pulling the children on sledges that glided over the snow. All wore furs.

All Joy stood looking at the snow, her smile as wide as her beautiful face. "Thus do the spirits of pleasant fellowship bless our meeting," she said, "with the beauty of the snow. It is rare."

"It does not often fall here?" I said.

"No, not deeply in this mild place. Not even once each winter, and when it does we all are children again." White Wings hurried by, running and sliding on icy spots with the other children.

"I think it is time for you to tell more of your story," All Joy said and, after talking to the Potter Woman, who was happy to have White Wings another morning, I followed my friends inside their home.

All Joy was fixing corn and molasses for a meal and even said she felt like cleaning dishes. But as she returned from throwing the dirty water out, her face was white. "It has begun again. I think I have done too much." She lay on the bed and Hawk Eye called the herb women.

They came. "She has flaunted the spirits," they said admonishingly. Clucking to themselves like quail, they administered hot herb potions and soon color returned to All Joy's cheeks.

183

"Let her sleep, and she is to do no more dishes until the little one is here," said the chief herb woman, a handsome, middle-aged, thin woman with hair pulled back in a bun, who was wearing a beautifully decorated skirt.

"And you, Grandmother," Hawk Eye said to the old herb woman. "You have been good to me, but I must ask how it is at your shelter. How is the servant working out?"

"She is a good girl and I am turning her into a real potter," the woman said. "If only my back would allow me do the potting again."

"She has the joint sickness," Hawk Eye said after she left, "and the herb women cannot cure it."

"One of their own. Now if they called the shaman—" I smiled at my friend.

All Joy slept and Hawk Eye and I talked again, this time outside the shelter.

"I heard you speaking of this child you take with you. It is so unusual to see such a thing I think it is a mark of the spirits and you are one of their chosen," Hawk Eye said, watching the still-playing children.

"It was my calling and I accepted it," I said. But then I told him the rest of my story, my early life in the village of my home near Boulder Lake, the Sun Watchers, my uncle in his earlier days. "My relatives, my mother's people, were at the camp of the Twin Lakes, where your scouts conquered."

"Ah, I am sorry."

"Yes. But there is more. My uncle and I were taken captive by the Dune Devils during a raid they made, about the time of the Twin Lakes attack. We were taken to the Great Lake, to the dune camp of the Dune Devils. There my uncle Bo Jo was put to the torture and killed."

"By the Dune Devils? Your uncle, the Grand Shaman? What irreverence!"

"It was their way to test a man's mettle. But I was their prisoner, finally protected by them. And though I had hated them, I came to respect them and was attached to the old one, Thistle

Child, who was my mistress. Then, while I was gone on a hunting trip, a raiding party came down."

"It was the village of your captivity that my company attacked!" he said with vehemence. The sun, approaching He Is Halfway Home, was beginning to melt the snow. Long spears of ice on the branches were dripping.

I was silent, not looking at him. There was so much pain in the world; I felt it like a lump of ice encasing my heart. Would that it could melt, drip away in the heat of the sun and leave only love among brothers and sisters under his light.

"It was over that raid that I left the army," Hawk Eye said in a low voice. I looked at him, surprised.

"Yes. The Dune People were full of spirit, wild and untamed. Their old ones spat on us when we spoke to the band chief of tribute and loyalty to Cahokia."

"Bright-Coals-in-the-River! What did he say?" I was intrigued, pained, too. I had respected the old chief at the last.

"He spat too. The General-in-Chief ordered the chief split apart."

"The two saplings? That should not be done for the brave spirited."

"I know, but the General-in-Chief does not know ancient customs. Torture he knows as a familiar face; honor is a stranger to him. That is why I left the army."

"Yes?"

"I argued that we had violated custom in killing these tribesmen for defending their own ways, that they were brave. He ignored me and killed them. Then I argued that we not violate the young slaves we were taking back to Cahokia; he at least agreed to that. But then he ordered us to dump the old ones' bodies in the woods. I argued again, saying we should at least put their bones to rest, that their spirits would harm us at the least. He ordered me to drag the bodies to the woods; I refused. Then he ordered us out that night and had me arrested for insubordination.

"When we returned home there was a meeting before the Female Sun. There was to be a hearing to see if I must be released from the army in disgrace, and since I was of the high marrying lines, it must be done only by the Female Sun herself. I told the truth, told how the General-in-Chief had violated the codes of behavior of a warrior, even a city one. She listened and then ordered me quietly released, without disgrace. She was protecting the General-in-Chief from the charge of killing the old ones needlessly."

"Protecting the general?" I was a little puzzled.

"Why shouldn't she? He was, is, her son."

I had trouble believing him. "The prince was the General-in-Chief on the raids to the north?"

"Yes, allowed too young to assume control of a force of army men. Although," he lowered his voice even further, "if the prince were to live to be one hundred summers he would never learn the manhood and character needed to be able to lead men."

I could not disagree with that; still, I was not yet in a mood to let him know my "royal connections." I was not at all sure that he would be impressed that I was male dog to the Female Sun's bitch-in-heat.

Finally, though, we approached the subject I had come out to this village in the first place to discuss. Hawk Eye's mother had told me that he had the courage to speak of The Things That Are Not Said, and I found myself, ever since I had come to Cahokia insatiably curious about what made the great city what it was. If there were things that were not to be said, my own perverse forest self wanted to know what they were, would not be satisfied until I knew them.

Especially since they concerned a woman I was spending half my life with these days.

"I told you I went to your parents to tell them of your brother's whereabouts and wellbeing."

"Yes, and I thank you for that. Winter Bird is not a thinker. He is a well-schooled actor in the great dance of life, who wishes to be always costumed correctly, following the steps correctly, not missing a beat so those around him will think all is well with him."

"That is how I have found him, but there are many times I admire those qualities in life."

"Certainly. I meant to throw no stones at my own kin."

186

I cleared my throat. "When I was with your mother, I asked many questions about Cahokia. Your father was uneasy when we veered into certain forbidden subjects."

He smiled a small smile. "My father is even more correct than my brother."

I suggested we go inside. All Joy was sleeping peacefully, the herbs doing their work. We put logs on the fire and continued our talk. "I wish to know why all here so obediently obey the ruler. Why they worship the Female Sun herself."

He looked at me, then snorted like a deer who has caught the scent of humans.

"Because it is the way in the city," he said and turned his head away from me.

"Why is it that no one may speak of the court, why people are afraid to speak the very truth? In my country—"

"This is not the forest. Things are different in the city from the forest." It was about the third time I had heard that, and I was beginning to wonder about its wisdom.

"So you will not talk to me about the court, what is behind the power on the hill?" I asked insistently.

His voice was almost inaudible. Even in his own home he feared, as his father feared. "I will not talk to you—not yet. But perhaps, if you wait long enough, there will be answers to your questions. Truth is an egg which has to hatch, but when that first crack occurs which signifies the hatching, only the spirits know. Wait and watch. In the meantime, keep this." He put a small pottery token in my hand, a miniature amulet. On it was the sun, with an eye in the middle, sacred sign of all the people from coast to coast on Turtle's Island. Nothing of treason in this. Or was there? I put it in my travelling pack, to be taken back and put in my medicine pouch.

The thawing had continued, and within the hour I decided it would be possible to return over a path cleared of snow, though still muddy.

I said goodbye to my friends, promising to see them soon, and prepared to leave.

"Dear friend, come a moment to my bed," All Joy commanded. She put out her hand and I took it. "I have a favor to ask. Go to the herb woman, you know the one you met this morning, and tell her I am feeling better. I need some more of the sleeping tea, though. She is at the very end of the lane, last house in the village." I left, her radiant smile following me like a blessing.

Soon I would go and pick up White Wings, but I was happy to deliver the message for my new friend. I turned the opposite direction from the way we had come in; I had not been this way before. There were only a few more houses; the end of the village was just beyond the last, herb woman's house. Someone was outside, pushing away the last of the snow with a birch broom. Beyond her was a frame for stretching animal skins—she turned. On a day of surprises there was another. I was face to face with Loon Feather. Her beauty was undiminished, although she was now the slave of the herb woman, carried back captive by the very hunting party Hawk Eye had commanded.

The greatest surprise of all occurred then. After a moment of shock at seeing me there, in the village outside Cahokia, she fell on her knees and gave me the nod of tribute and took my hand.

"I am so glad to see you, cousin of mine," she said, and then raised herself up and gave me the relative's kiss of welcome.

Chapter Nine

The snow retreated in a day or two, as All Joy had said it would, and White Wings and I went back again more than once in the next three weeks to the village of river clay potters. Only during the daytimes, of course; evenings were reserved for royal duties. These I had taken up again without trouble, if a little warily, I must admit. After a few tense moments and even a few queenly tears, Soft Fur had accepted my vague explanations that, taking a walk to exercise my inactive body, I had been caught in the storm outside the walls and had to stay in the home of a common person I did not know.

Did I tell her only half the truth? Not open my heart? I found that I hardly ever did that these days, and it troubled me, since I was a special devotee of the Bird of Thunder, who had commanded truth. The Female Sun's power, divine in its origins, was too great for me to bother her with day-to-day mortal truths. Said another way, I did not trust her. In this case I strongly sensed that I should put my finger on my lips concerning the village of Hawk Eye and the potters; those who Say the Things That Are Not Said out there must be saying it about somebody; and that somebody might be, probably was, a Female Sun.

But as I have told you, during the daytimes I bounded with joy to the village of river-clay potters. It was blackberry winter, now, a time of real thawing and fair weather following the cold, and I used the time to gather much wood in far-off forests on sledges with Hawk Eye.

All Joy welcomed her bright, clean fires; she moved very little now and her stomach was large. The child was coming closer to term now, the old women said, and so its life was safe, but they worried still about the bleeding. There was early separation of its womb-sac, so the old women said—I overheard them. I cared for these two a good deal now.

White Wings played hide-behind-the-trees with the potter woman's granddaughter and made mud cakes in the lanes and behind the shelters, as water leached from beneath the leaves and—joy! The first green tips of the skunk cabbages began to poke

189

through the beech tree leaves piled up in wet, forlorn drifts from the winds of the storm.

One afternoon Hawk Eye and I repaired the roof of their shelter, climbing the height with a thong-bound wooden ladder. My friend was kneeling on the matted roof; I handed him strips of river-bottom cane. Across the caning he was re-plaiting and filling in, Hawk Eye said to me in a quiet voice, "Perhaps you will stay through evening. There will be friends in tonight. You have asked who around here says The Things That Are Not Said."

My heart leapt. That insatiable curiosity, my desire to know all things about Cahokia the Marvelous spurred me on. "But I cannot come at night. I think I have told you after He Is Setting I am—occupied."

He was silent for a moment, cutting the ends of three pieces of cane with a stone knife to plug a hole. "Yes, I know you are busy. On the bed furs of the Great One at the top of Temple Mound."

I almost fell off the ladder, so surprised I was. "You know?"

"It is my business to know these things."

"Do others?"

"Only a few. No one else can afford to know or care. It is dangerous these days to think of anything except what makes the day go forward—and what pleases the pleasure seekers at the top of the hill."

"But—you are my friend. You must think less of me knowing that at nights I serve—her lust."

He said nothing, just fixed the cane to the roof with thin, strong grapevine, so I went on, "Well, and my own lust. I must be honest."

"You are very young. A buck in rut, as you, with all your forest lore would say." He smiled, and there was forgiveness in his smile. "Besides, if I know the circumstances, it would have been unthinkable to say nay to such a one."

I nodded. "Still, I am not proud of it. It does no honor to my clan or to myself. In my land, such things are unthinkable."

"A lot that is unthinkable is done these days in Cahokia. Besides, we all do what we must do."

"Do you—could you trust me, knowing what you know?"

He stopped working and looked up, directly into my eyes.

"My wife has told me tales from her grandmother of the Bird of Thunder."

"Yes?"

"You are pledged to him, she says."

"Yes. The bird of truth. I cannot betray; it was in my vows at the time of my first naming." I did not mention that I did not tell some things to the High Ones. I do not think the Bird of Thunder would have chided me for that.

"You are my friend, and truth will ever be the bond of our friendship. I now trust you with my life." He crawled over, gave me the arm slap I did not often see here in Cahokia. I was pleased, refreshed and pleased as if I had a long, cool drink that this man whom I respected trusted me—with his life. Much as I loved him though I did not, I know not why, put out my soul to him at that moment. We returned to our work, I handing him canes, he plaiting in the warming rays of the sun.

"Could not—whoever it is who are your friends—meet to do their talking during the late afternoon?"

"The day has eyes," he said. I remembered the amulet and wondered at its real meaning. I wore it on a thong inside my shirt, taking it off, of course, when I left the village of these river-clay potters.

"Still," I said slowly, "it is blackberry winter. It would not hurt river-clay potters to go to the river and see how its waters rise with the recent rain and snow."

He stopped his plaiting and looked at me. "And so, you have a head that is as active as your loins, it seems." He smiled and I continued to hand him the cane stalks.

After our meal, Hawk Eye left for a few moments. I spoke quietly to All Joy as she lay on her couch.

"I hear that you know that servant of the herb grandmother," she said, smiling. "Loon Feather is her name, is it not?"

"Yes. She has said she knows me?"

"Yes. She has told the herb woman that you are her relative."

"I was adopted by the old one whom she lived with as granddaughter. Thus I was her cousin—so they called me in that village."

"What will you do for her?"

"I do not know. But I will see her today again, to determine if she fares well enough at the hands of the herb woman."

"Of that you can be sure," All Joy said sharply. "We do not harm servants out here in this village as they do—" she fell silent, then finally smiled again. "Hawk Eye returns."

The strong face of my friend looked in at the door flap. He looked around behind him, then came in. "Leave soon and go to the river by the far path, the one we took to get the beech wood. Stay by the large, hollow log. Conceal yourself."

I nodded, but before I left, I went to take All Joy's hand once more. "Your time will soon come."

She lowered her eyes. It was not seemly to answer a man about this matter. "I am a ritual clown, right hand to the shaman. I sense you will be blessed by the spirits in your time of need."

"My faith is strong in the goodness of the spirits—of the Sun Lord."

"I have found that the path of goodness and truth gives us strength."

"So my grandmother said." She looked at me with her strong, dark eyes. "Still, I am afraid."

"We are not alone. Your prophecy, the one you had in the storm said you would prevail."

"Yes, when many become one."

"I would help you, serve you in any way I can," I said, and she dismissed me with a touch and smile.

I walked the lane, White Wings dancing by my side; I had retrieved her from her friends who made pots. We came to the last shelter, the herb woman's home. Loon Feather was not outside with her furs; I went to the door opening and peered inside.

She knelt, grinding corn in the corner. It was a neat home, with bunches of pungent herbs hanging from the poles. White Wings entered and went to the corner, curiosity in her eyes.

Loon Feather did not rise, but looked up with a smile of greeting. "This is your friend?" White Wings said, pointing.

"My cousin, I have told you, small one."

"Well, since I am your cousin, she my cousin too," White Wings insisted. Loon Feather rose and took her hand. For a while we spoke of the city, of her trip, and our long trip here, of her people, now in camp at the edge of the eastern lake, people she would probably never see again.

"You are my people now," she said and gazed at me. The eyes are the mirror of the heart, so the ancient wisdom says, and in her eyes, mirroring her inner self I read pain and resignation and—trust in me. I was all she had, all, all in the world, from the old time, which for her had been wiped from the face of the earth as grease paint is wiped from the warrior's cheek after the battle. I knew that feeling too, and it changed one. And yet I did not understand the trust. I trusted no one, no one on earth now. My childhood had taught me that, I suppose.

So why did she trust me? Because there was no one else. She had worked with me, despised me often, was angered with me for the death of her loved one and now had come to regard me in need as all she had. Like the abandoned bird fed by the generosity of the child it has feared—yet through necessity must learn to love to live, so Loon Feather had come to me.

Yet as I looked I thought not, I will help you, my cousin, but "I love you, beautiful body and spirit." Yes, in spite of myself, I betrayed the one who trusted me as a brother by yearning for her.

But there was something more. At that moment I knew the truth, special ward of the Bird of Thunder that I was. I knew that I must stop going to the top of the hill, to the warm, smothering arms of the Daughter of the Sun. What I had told All Joy was right; there is strength in good action, weakness in bad. Her warmth was the putrid and decaying heat of the swamp, and it was rotting me, and I knew it not until I looked into the eyes of

193

purity and freshness that gazed at me so sweetly there in the dusky corner of that winter shelter.

"I will take White Wings with me," I thought, in an odd mood as I left the shelter of the herb woman to go to the secret meeting. There were good reasons for the decision. I did not feel I could impose on these villagers, leave her more with the potter and her granddaughter, and I wanted her to see the woods, now that spring was just beginning to awaken it. It was the first time we had gone deeply into a real forest, like the one at Lakes-Like-a-Necklace, and I did not want her to forget the beauty of the paths through forest trees, to forget her homeland, her people. Anyway, what did it matter? I was in a truthful mood, so why should not the ones who say the Things That Are Not Said see me as I was, keeper of a child, yet almost a man? Let them know who they were trusting.

And so I would go to the men's secret society taking a child with me. As usual, at an important, serious moment in my life all was a mockery again and, like the ritual clown that I was, I must mimic the serious and live a jest. So most men would have said; yet now I was not sure. I was trying to answer to my heart these days, whose messages are deeper even than those of the tribe's.

The small one stopped all along the trail to watch animals emerging into the warmth of the day, feel the pleasantness of the air, listen to early birds flinging their hearts to the sky.

Then, as we went deeper, I took her hand, and I could feel her drawing close to me as the trees grew thicker, the vines looping over their branches, the thick, clinging plants pulling some of the trees down. We were now far away from camp and close to the river, and we had arrived at the large, hollow beech tree.

We stood, and she seemed to have listened to my admonitions that she must be quiet, like the good forest child that she was. NO NOISE! We stood, thus, hand in hand, and at last men appeared, rising like spirits of the dead out of that gloomy land of swamp trees.

Six of them there were, some I had seen at the upper end of this small village, and two from the shell crafters' lane inside the walls. They looked curiously at me, standing with a child. Hawk Eye came last, gesturing us all to sit on a little mossy knoll near the hollow tree.

"We are not observed. Let us smoke a pipe," he said, and took out a beautiful clay effigy pipe curiously wrought in the shape of a bobcat's head. He took tobacco from a pouch tamped it, lighted the pipe and took a puff. Then he passed it about. White Wings sat beside me, leaning on my arm. Clearly, she was awed, as the smoke drifted above the heads of those in the circle.

"All who sit in this circle are sworn to silence," said Hawk Eye.

"As a cat comes and watches, listens and then goes on light feet without a sound, so shall the things said here be taken away in silence." All nodded and looked at me. I took the pipe from the man next to me, nodded and puffed it.

Finally one of the two from the lane of shell crafters spoke.

"You have stood guarantor of this man's honesty and silence in spite of the fact that we do not know him," the man said to Hawk Eye. "But he has brought a child to the hidden place of our meeting?"

"The child is the spirits' charge to him, and they are the last of their clan. Let her serve as symbol of what Cahokia has done to villages about these river valleys. All who loved her were destroyed to serve the need of the town."

Heads nodded in affirmation.

"Let the two observe, then, since you stand as pledge for them," another said. "Tell what has happened on the hill, Eyes-of-the-Night."

A young man from the shellcrafter's village, from the street of No Corn and Hail Like Rocks was the one he spoke to. This young man looked off towards the city, with its mounds standing out through the bare-branched trees.

"The expedition east has proven successful. Scouts have returned to say that three towns along the Beautiful River give the Great City tribute, three that did not acknowledge Cahokia before."

Grunts and nods of affirmation.

"Two submitted without struggle, but the third, a large one with its own mounds, behind an island in the river, fought to the death. Their young ruler finally bowed his head to the ground rather than have his women and children killed and taken as slaves. He is coming to Cahokia to accept the rites of the Sun Lord here and acknowledge Female Sun as his ruler."

"They do not already acknowledge the Sun Lord?" asked another, who was Hawk Eye's next-door neighbor.

"No, the winged serpent," Eyes-of-the-Night went on. "But it has been decreed that all must worship the Sun Lord above all gods."

"Anything else from the Temple Mound?" Hawk Eye asked, putting down the pipe.

"The prince has stopped leading the expeditions." As I listened to Eyes-of-the-Night, I recalled that I had seen this young man several times in the city. Where was it? Ah yes, it was at the back stairs of Temple Mound. He often climbed up the steps at the delivery time of the suppliers. He must be bringing the shell decorations to the royal family, and thus, using his "eyes-of-the-night" to sense what was going on. And so he had known of me, surely. And had accepted. But how did he get his information? There must be someone in there, a servant close to the throne perhaps, or a kinsman who told him what he knew. Dangerous job, that!

"The army must give thanks to the Sun Lord above for the prince's being relieved of duty," chuckled the older of the men from the shell crafters' village. "And the winter stores?"

"They are replenished with the raids to the east, but low. There will be corn, but the ration will fall from the public garner."

"There will be grumbling."

"Not if what I know is true," said the other shell crafter.

"There is to be an execution of a traitor who spoke against the prince. He was second priest of the wooden star circle." Hawk Eye was suddenly alert. "There was no trial before the council. He had been found plotting. Had the nerve, or was it courage, to say the stars have found the prince corrupt and not capable of rule."

"Foolish man," said Hawk Eye. "True man. But it shows us all the danger we are in should one of us break this circle. Now tell, Eyes-of-the-Night, is that all from the realm of the Great Ones who shine on high?"

White Wings had leaned against me and gone to sleep; I was enjoying myself hugely. I knew nothing of all this, although I was at the hill most nights. Obviously there were servants willing to talk. Was it for corn or for valuables?

"Nothing but the usual," Eyes-of-the-Night said, shrugging.

"The Female Sun has her young rutting bucks up the hill each day and night." I was startled by the choice of words but beyond that—bucks? More than one. It is true I had not been there every night lately. I grew nervous and licked my lips. Hawk Eye's face was impassive.

"Unknown they are, and uncared about." So they did not know about me after all!

"The prince has begun the same custom."

"With virgins?"

"He is setting up a convent of young virgins to serve the Sun Lord at religious ceremonies and serve him when he desires. Young sisters are being taken, perfect female children."

"More pain to our people," Hawk Eye said. More reports were given: on the amount of the winter store in the garners, on the exact size of the army. Then, meeting in the center of the circle they had formed, they gave their arms to each other. I was pleased to see they included me, chagrined at my connection to the throne. In some way Hawk Eye might be planning to use me, to use my connection. Did the others know? Were they just not speaking?

As we hastened back through the woods, each taking our separate ways to the settlements through gathering twilight, I had to ask Hawk Eye, "Why do you meet thusly? Why take even a slight risk in these days of strong and brutal rule?"

Hawk Eye sighed. "For no other reason than to speak the truth. Those of us in the circle are men who cannot live with lies, though others may. Perhaps we, too, are marked to serve your Bird of Thunder."

"It is not an easy devotion."

"No, but if truth does not have a witness, it may die. And who would wish to live in a world where there is not anywhere truth?"

I smiled a little and nodded. "And my part?"

"I do not know as yet, but that will become clear. I think you will play a role, an important one, when the Sun Lord decides."

Or whoever, I thought. Carrying my small, sleepy cousin, I parted at the road and returned to the city within the walls, Cahokia the Great. Just before I entered the stockade, I slipped my amulet from around my neck and put it in my deerskin shoe.

I was feeling very uncomfortable as I climbed the back hill that night. Seeing Loon Feather, realizing I loved her purely, joining with the circle of those who say The Things That Are Not Said— all of the events of the day had convinced me that I would not be a slave to anyone's lust any more—not my own, not even the that of the Daughter of the Sun.

But how to break off and still keep my head—or whatever it was they cut off in these executions of theirs. I thought of one plan—I could say my parts were red and sore and I worried about the Foul Part Disease and spreading it to my queen—that might work. Actually, I was worried. Foul Part Disease was abroad in the camps and cities of the south, so they said, and the way the Female Sun had taken lovers, she might herself have given it to me. But I thought not.

But as I came in, the steward met me. I had spoken to him briefly before, a haughty cousin, surely a tool of the prince's, not at all casual and friendly like Fire-on-the-Plains, my other contact on the hill.

He was taller than I, odd for this race of short, broad people and he never looked in one's eyes when he spoke. He was of one of the eight marrying kinship groups which brought new vitality into the royal lines when it was time to take official mates.

"The Female Sun asks that I tell you she is not receiving tonight." A joke, I thought. Receiving, as if she were having sass-afras tea served to guests in the golden afternoon in the throne room.

"She is ill." His eyes looked above my head, as if I were a dog.

"Tell the Female Sun I am sorry she is troubled by the spirits. I will pray to them to stop their torment and return her to her fullest health."

He looked at me curiously. Perhaps—probably—it was an odd thing to say in a city where the priests did the praying.

"She does not need prayers. She is the Female Sun and has a direct track to the god of us all."

Perhaps I was put out of my head by all the truth I had imbibed that day, but I felt like saying what I thought. "I am of the Star Watchers' clan, son of the Sun Watcher myself. All of us may pray the powers of the world and heavens for help."

"You are bold. Perhaps too bold," the steward said coldly, and turned away from me, and I thought at that moment that I had made an enemy I did not need at court. Still, it was good to return to the shelter of Walks-Up-the-Steps and have a calm, decent evening in which my body did not leave my soul and walk among the spirits of dark lust.

The Female Sun remained closeted for the next week or two, and I was, thankfully, at home. Ghost was there, of course, now part of Walks-Up-the-Steps' family himself, and I spent some time paying him attention, something I had not done in the last weeks.

"I am man here," he said to me pridefully one night as we sat tending the fire. "I hunt now for the pot."

"Good. You have brought in venison?"

"Well, no, the—hunting clans provide that for us. But I have got rabbits and ducks, many ducks. Some did not fly to the south.

I went with three from the hunting clans and they taught me to sh-sh-shoot straight as the ducks came in to land."

I nodded, impressed. Duck was good to eat, and I had wondered who had brought it in when I saw it roasted on a spit. I had not even had time or interest enough to find that out.

"There are many type ducks here," Ghost went on, nodding knowingly. "I am learning of them all and making their spirits my friends. There are the blue belly ones, the dull green ones, the ones painted blue, black and green like men in war paint. One calls them to come in when they f-f-fly over the riverbank. I am learning to make the duck call." Holding his hand over his mouth in a fist, he honked like a duck. I smiled, but not enough to make him think I was making fun of him. More than anything else, Ghost hated to be mocked.

White Wings had gone to sleep in the corner, wrapped in her little rabbit skin blankets, but Walks-Up-the-Steps was still bustling about in and out of the shelter, cleaning up the eating things.

"It is good to have you home," she said. She had often lain awake until I returned home from my evening 'hunting trips' up the hill and I had to avoid her troubled eyes, something I did not like.

"I think I can say I will be more often in the shelter of evenings," I told her. She nodded, pleased.

"Ghost-on-the-Lake often tells us fine stories these winter evenings," Walks-Up-the-Steps said.

"To White Wings? Is he telling tales of the dead? I do not know if I want her frightened with the old tales. She might—"

"Ah, these stories are good for children. Thus has it ever been, the old ones telling spirit tales around the winter shelter. How will she learn there is death if someone does not tell her?"

"She has already learned about death by seeing it before her eyes. That is her trouble," I said sternly.

"But she does not know how the spirit goes on after the body dies, migrates, lives. That is important to know."

"I suppose so. All right, Ghost, tell us one of your tales, then."

He settled himself a little, putting his short legs under him. His hunched back cast a mountain-shaped shadow on the wall of the shelter, now large, now small, as the fire flared up and receded in its central pit. I will tell this in my own way, because his speech is hard to mimic.

"I heard this at the town where Ouabache and Tippecanoe join," he said. "There people take the rites of the dead more seriously than most. They have contact often with the wild rice people, and these do the dead rites in detail. They believe that we must honor the dead bones above all else. It is in the bone that the dead person's spirit is tied to earth. The flesh is nothing to them. So they put the body in the death shelter, wait only a short time for it to rot in the shelter or in the caves of the dead. When the flesh is soft, they bring in the nail-scrapers. These are old men who let their nails grow long as talons on a hawk. They harden their nails, too, with fire ashes and oils. They scrape the flesh completely off the bones and throw it in the fire. Thus, the bones are left. These they bury in the small mounds."

"Well, I have heard of this," I said. "It is different from our burials at Lake of the Boulders, where we put the dead in a small grave and heap it with stones."

"Yes. These want to know the bones, to keep them in a place they can visit. For they have a great Feast of the Dead each year in the fall. They take out the bones, or go to visit them if they are nearby, and take food to the dead and talk to them."

"Go on with your story," I said.

"In such a village where the dead are visited, there was a young man named Sky Warrior. He had gone on a war party far away, well, at least two days' journey to the Greatest of all Lakes. There the party had attacked an enemy tribe for a slight done to the tribe. Sky Warrior himself killed three of the enemy, but one brave young man, very young, he did not kill. While his enemy was wounded, lying on the ground, Sky Warrior stole his enemy's fighting spirit and pride. This he did by taking the brave's medicine bag and scattering it about into a stream. In it were the enemy's tokens of medicine—part of an antler, hair of the first man he killed, an eagle feather. All sacred, all giving him strength in war.

"Sky Warrior, the young man from the village of the dead, thought his enemy was unconscious, that he did not see the deed of the scattering of the things in the stream. But the young enemy had only shut his eyes, and he was infuriated. `He has taken part of my soul,' he said to himself and hated Sky Warrior.

"The war party returned from the Greatest of all Lakes and Sky Warrior settled down to life in the band. Still, back up north in the camps of the enemy, his personal enemy was mad over the loss of the medicine bag. 'He took that right before my eyes while I was weak. I will go to the camps of the south and take the coup of my enemy," he said.

"'It would not be right in the eyes of the spirits to kill him for such an offense, but I will take his medicine bag and do some damage to it. Take his pride the way he has taken mine.'"

"'My son, do not risk the anger of the spirits of the medicine bag,'" his old father said. "'Your enemy has disregarded the spirits, but you shouldn't make the same mistake. Spirits roused— 'But the enemy youth would not listen. He made plans to go to the southern village and get revenge.

"Two days the enemy youth went south, and then finally came to the right village. He hid in the woods, watching. Sky Warrior finally came near his enemy's hiding place, with a young girl. Sky Warrior was playing the flute to her; she was his love. Still, the heart of the brave of the northern camp was hardened; he would take his revenge no matter what.

"He followed his enemy back to camp and in the shadows of the night watched him enter his family's shelter. There, there would be the medicine bag! He decided to lurk in the woods and watch for the shelter to be left alone.

"The next day, a bright and clear one, the family went to the woods to pick late berries, and Sky Warrior went with them to hunt. Now was the time, the enemy youth of the northern camps thought. 'I will enter the shelter unseen and take the medicine bag.'

"Up he crept, and went into the shelter. There, in the corner on an upturned log which served as bench he found the medicine bag made of deerskin, decorated with feathers. He looked inside: special things sacred to Sky Warrior were there, a bear's tooth and other things. He headed for the door opening to take the bag outside and dump it in a lake nearby, when—right at the door he met the young girl he had seen with Sky Warrior. Not knowing the family had gone to the woods, she had come to find her love."

The fire was dying with this long story. I went to the woodpile outside. I could hear the guard marching to watch the huge door opening. It was near He Is Halfway Through the Night.

Ghost had not even stopped his story while I was gone, but continued it to the wide-eyed attention of Walks-Up-the-Steps. "—suddenly returned. The two young men fought as the young girl stood by helplessly. The knife the northern camp brave carried was buried in Sky Warrior who fell dead as his love watched in horror.

"The northern enemy escaped with the medicine bag, and now his fate was in the hands of the spirits. He was killed by an angry bear as he crossed a stream going home, and his spirit escaped to the great path of the spirits.

"But the young man who had started it all—Sky Warrior, who had been killed by the other—was held accountable by the spirits. As he tried to go to the path of spirits, a spirit of an eagle came to him. `You disregarded the spirits of the medicine bag and now great evil has come. You will wander the earth until someone who loves you goes to the Northern camps and replaces the things in the sacred bag, the pieces of the antler, the shreds of hair, the pebbles from the road of first kill.' Then he flew away.

"And so, the spirit of Sky Warrior remained with the body. In fact, it did not begin to rot. When the death-scrapers came with their long fingernails to remove the flesh from the body, they found that the Sky Warrior looked as he did the day he died. They were angry, because death scrapers relish getting to scrape flesh from bones—"

Ghost eagerly held up his hands and made the fingers into talons.

"They sought the advice of the shaman, who—"

But at that moment there was a ruckus in the streets outside. A guard from the stockade watchpost stuck his head in the door opening, pushing the covering aside.

"Someone calls for you outside the wall. We would not let him in. He says it is life and death. You must come help—let me see what was her name? All Joy, his wife. You must be shaman as she is fighting the spirit world for her life now at the time of birth." He looked at me curiously. Such things struck him as quaint, old-fashioned and crude, I suppose.

I stood up and then stood still for a moment. The sentry had gone on. "Quick, Ghost, you must come. We must make haste outside the walls. And get the drum. Quickly! Every moment counts."

The surprised Ghost did as he was told, and carrying the drum and sticks as fast as we could, we hastened to the great opening. The sentry nodded that we could pass through, and this we did with the fleet feet of deer (well, as fast as we could go with the drum between us).

There was Hawk Eye, impatiently waiting at the edge of the houses. "She has just begun the labor. The bleeding has begun too. The old women fear by the time the babe is born, she will have spilt all her life's blood."

It was easy to go through the silence, up the paths through sleeping villages with no bounding children or pack-laden men to hinder us. Hawk Eye asked no questions about the drum and even helped us carry it to relieve us as we gasped and panted our way down the trail.

The women were clustered about All Joy's bed, and she looked pale and wan but brave, lying there. "The babe should be born before He Is Rising, but the mother must have strength to deliver it and blood to live on," said Loon Feather's herb woman.

It is true that I had never acted as shaman, that I had not been called to that sacred post. But the drum I had built was a Drum of Power, and as I had played it, I had connected with the spirits. Then too, I had often watched my uncle as he served as healer. As I watched All Joy suffer, something snapped to attention in me, like a branch when you step on it. I seemed to know what to do, how to take charge of the situation. "Have you given the birth-hastening herbs?" I asked sharply of the old herb woman.

"No, we are trying to retard the birth, so the bleeding does not come fiercely."

I stepped to the bed so they could see the authority in my face. I was son of a Sun Watcher, nephew of the Grand Shaman. "Give the birth-inducing herbs. And put your hands on her stomach when the pains come, to speed the birth."

"But—"

"Do as I say. And you, Hawk Eye," to my frantic friend outside the door opening. "Go rouse the men and women of the village. They must help. We will do the shaman ceremony of the drum. The one I know reaches the spirits. All must come to the center of the village. I saw the remains of a fire there in the council ring. Show Ghost where the wood is; he must build it up high at once."

Everyone scurried around like chipmunks, following my instructions. I could see a smile on All Joy's face; she reached out a hand to me and I squeezed it. "I have told you They cared. Now I will show you," I said. It was true, and it was the bottom rock in all I was. I did not know who They were, but I knew They cared. That belief never left me.

And so, we sat there in the middle of the river-clay potters' village, with all the people in the center around the now-leaping fire: the old potter woman and her granddaughter, the herb woman and her assistant aunties, and my beautiful Loon Feather, who sat down next to me, and even the three members of the circle of Those Who Say The Things That Are Not Said formed a ring, each holding the hands of his neighbors.

I asked one of the three circle members I pretended I did not know, to light the ceremonial pipe he had brought and smoke tobacco for the spirits. This he did, wafting the smoke about all our heads.

And after that was done, I played on my drum for them, for Loon Feather, who now looked at me adoringly, but especially for Whoever It Is Who Listens. "I know you are there and that you care," I chanted. "Listen now for our sister All Joy, whose life is in your hands."

I sang the song of the stars of winter, and of Nanaboozhoo their lord, of how he went out in a wintertide over a frozen river to get fire for his people—of his long, long, walk, of how he took a rabbit's shape to fool the Keeper of the Fire. My voice rose and the drumbeat echoed across the clearing and all the way to the river, I suppose. I chanted and beat out the story of how Nanaboozhoo found the daughters of the Keeper of the Fire, how he made them pity him until he got near enough to steal a torch of fire, how they pursued him angrily but how he escaped and made the long, long trip to bring his people fire.

"Oh, greatest Son of the West Wind, loving us. You sacrificed for us all. You and your father love us so. Now make your daughter whole." All the love I knew I poured into the song, and the people sang and chanted after me at the right places. Our song rose and rose, I know, as a hymn of praise to the goodness of the universe. It was a different shaman song than any I had ever heard, a song of deep love from the powers that made us to us all, and it was all my own, and I had faith in it and in the beating, resonating drum, with the skin of one who came from the created world of the deep forest.

And so I was not surprised when Hawk Eye came to us, soon after the last beats of the huge drum had stilled to tell us that his child, a boy, had been born, and that All Joy was resting comfortably and the shelter was having ritual purification. I dismissed the people and they went, nodding and murmuring to their homes.

"We have not had the shaman chant since I was a young girl," said the herb woman. "We lived in the woods, before we came to Cahokia. Your drum is a great medicine drum. We do not use drums in exactly this way in the city. Perhaps the priest should learn of it."

"If he used it, it would not work," I said simply and went to find Ghost and return home. But before I did, Hawk Eye caught my arm. "I am in your great debt. In anything, anything you ask, you are truly my sworn brother. Remember that." And I loved him, and my heart went out in gratitude for the saving of All Joy. Still, my heart did not go out to him in trust, even then.

As Ghost and I neared the gate, bearing the drum, I felt as tired as Old Man Winter himself at this time of year. Still, I was curious. "What happened to the ghost of the young man, Sky Warrior, who tinkered with the medicine bag? Did someone go and appease the Great Eagle?"

"His brother tried to go and do the quest," Ghost panted.

"But when he got to the northern camps, "(huff)" he could not find the things in the stream. The hair was long gone, the antler bits" (puff) "scattered. Couldn't tell which pebbles were which."

We yelled to wake up the sentry for permission to pass through.

"So—"I said as we went up the street towards Walks-Up-the-Steps' shelter.

"So, Sky Warrior's ghost still walks the earth, unfree, and his body is whole as the day he died. He made the flesh strippers very mad by eluding them."

"And so do I hope to elude them for many a day."

Ghost nodded solemnly; we dropped the drum behind the shelter and collapsed inside on our beds.

And so the spring passed, with visits to the villages of both the shell crafters and the river-clay potters, playing with White Wings on idle days, stocking my store of goods for the summer trading—beautiful shells to take again to the flint pits.

Winter Bird came in from his visit with the Serpent Mound people, bearing the greetings of the Old Dream-Singer and his wife. They had nursed him back to health and he had studied their ways. He was glad to see us all and we had a feast of welcome at the feast of the new corn in the village of the shell crafters, where we ate much venison and turkey and new corn pudding, made with maple sugar and duck eggs Ghost gathered.

At about that same time, I was much relieved to be free of my royal responsibilities. The Female Sun had summoned me just after the naming feast of Hawk Eye's little son. She told me she would continue to notice and favor me, but that our evenings were over. She was feeling the effects of the long winter and had not fully recovered from her illness yet. I bowed low and said I was ever at her service. She came to me, and kissed me as a son.

And so, though my loins ached sometimes for the freedom and luxury I had found with her, I could turn my efforts to the wooing of Loon Feather. Often I would go, by myself now, to the river-clay potters' village, to talk to her, to speak of old times and new, for she was happy here at Cahokia, as I was.

Cahokia! I can see you yet, ablaze with summer, while I blazed with exuberant youth! Your streets full of processions each morning to welcome the Sun Lord. Not even the prince's disdainful glances as they chanced to fall on me as he passed by bearing the standard in his hand, could sour my mood. I remember the chungky contests in the great game field, where bets were made. I can still see the fights begun, and fights forestalled as the long, chungky poles were thrown, following the round, rolling stone which made its way down the course, stopping wherever it wished in spite of all the shouting the young men did to make it land where they had tossed their poles.

I took my turn at the game, too, and developed a pretty fair hand at it. But the knowledge of my uncle's folly in those days gone by made me leery of too much involvement in the game, and I let others be the shining stars of the playing field.

And, oh! the ceremonies at the time of His Longest Day in Our Skies! The homage paid by elaborately-robed priests in the Circle of the Stars, as their fingers pointed over the rising post just at the moment He appeared! The feasting, lasting for two days, the dancing with elegantly attired dancers. Our primitive feasts looked very poor by comparison, and I began to long less for my former home. I donned the mask of the ritual clown again, and enjoyed my leering jokes as I pointed at those in the crowd and talked of their love affairs and misdeeds during the year. They laughed and jeered back (though never mentioning the Female

Sun of course) letting me know that now I was truly accepted as a member of the city.

Although my nights were free now, I did not often visit with the circle of those who say The Things That Are Not Said. Some way they seemed like sour grapes in a vat of good crushed sweet juice. How could you really criticize Cahokia? Complain of its conquests and taxes? A state that could organize such magnificent entertainments and pursuits for so many people? The members of the circle seemed like carping shrews in the northern places, who snarled and were always of bad temper.

I did visit the circle once, after seeing Hawk Eye and All Joy and the new little one. It was on a moonless night, as our small torches illuminated the lowlands beside the river, and I heard the dark-faced ones who shared secrets of truth deliver the information in low voices. The tribute portions of grain and incense and shells for each family was raised to pay for the corn conquests. Sons of even the middle-range families were to be taken into the armies of conquest. The conquests would begin earlier, in the summer, to be sure corn was in the garners by late fall.

And the royal family, and now the priests, were as luxury-ridden as ever. The prince took it unto himself to manage the temple rites, and had built a fine, new convent house on the hill. In it were maidens from first families. They were pledged for life to serving the Sun Lord and retaining their chastity—except when the prince, direct descendent of the Lord himself, required their participation in his own private mating rites—dedicated to fertility for the land, of course.

One of the virgins sneaked away one night in early summer to meet her former lover. I did not need the Circle to tell me what happened; we all knew. She was caught by the woman in charge of the pledged maidens and was killed, awfully, by having her hands, then her feet, and finally her head chopped off in front of all the people. The prince himself had conducted the execution; it

209

seemed to give him pleasure to watch the poor girl's excruciating pain and horror. The penalties for disobeying the commands of the Sun Lord were strong indeed.

But I did not credit much of the talk of the Circle, told so solemnly, or even of the few snippets of conversation I heard in the village of the shell crafters and river-clay potters. It always stopped when I approached, anyway, as if to remind me that I was still and finally an outsider, no matter how many friends I had out here. I put away my amulet in the small medicine bag I had on the stone shelf in the corner of Walks-Up-the-Steps' shelter.

"Teach me how to play the love flute," I said to Hawk Eye when I was out in the village towards the end of the summer. He smiled, took out his old love flute. "Here, make the flute from the best ash. It should be no larger than your middle finger, and of seasoned wood. Bore the holes here, this way, and blow, so gently, tootling to your love as a bird sings, calling her to you yearningly, with your passion and skill. You will need to practice, since the last love you had called you instead and was always there." There was the lilt of joking mockery in his voice. He knew the Female Sun was not my lover anymore; he knew, really everything about me, this friend of mine.

And so I learned to make, then to play the love flute, and I tootled it to my love Loon Feather, and she responded to it, and came to my arms. We pledged each other, chastely, that we would be man and wife before another summer had passed, after she had served out a reasonable time for the herb woman. Hawk Eye and I would ask the herb woman to release Loon Feather from her serving obligation, and she would not refuse us. Twice more when the herb woman had asked, I had played my drum at times of grave illness, and once again I had saved the patient from the trip to the Land of the Stars. The other time the woman had died, but she was old, and the village said that I had eased her passage along the path to the other world anyway. Still, it would not be easy for the herb woman to part with Loon Feather; she was the helper of her old age, purchased from the army by law for a good store of expertly made pots.

The joy of my life, lighting it as the Sun Lord did in the sky, was the growth of White Wings. As the time came when we had been at Cahokia for three seasons neared, we could see how she had blossomed, opening her little face and heart to the love around her. She was, now truly, dearest niece to Walks-Up-the-Steps, and Ghost was her uncle, but I was the parent, both mother and father, really, for her.

Sometimes at night I would find her lying next to me, whimpering in her sleep, dreaming the dreams of a fearful child, living again with the Dune Devils at their worst, slapped across the mouth by the horrid woman she had lived with. I would waken her gently, kiss her hair, and she would lie all the rest of the night with a hand touching my bed roll. I felt love for her rolling out of me, enveloping her small form, and I knew why parents will go through fire and submit themselves to arrows to shield the little ones they love. This type of love is stronger than any bond on earth, even beyond that of husband and wife, and the powers of the earth and heaven had given it to me, to cherish and tend like a sacred fire. I wondered why, but I accepted.

At the end of the summer, when the grass had browned and fallen flat, I took a notion to go hunting. It was the beginning of the season of the deer rutting, and I sent invitations to both Winter Bird and Hawk Eye, telling them that I, a hunting eagle, would divulge the secrets of the trail to soft city fowls if they would join me—I would teach them rattling for the deer. Oddly enough, to my thought, they sent answers that they would join me.

And so, out we went to the woods north of Cahokia, farther up along the Father of Waters. We took the trail packs and ate not the rich sweetmeats and corn cakes of the city, but the dried venison and berries of the woodland folk. I did make one concession to the city food, carrying dried maple-sugar-parched corn in bags; I could not leave the city in one leap, you know. The tame bear cub who has been nursed up behind the town huts will, after all, keep coming to them even from the wild.

"My brother wishes to get away from the cries of the small one in his summer shelter," Winter Bird laughed, as Hawk Eye took eagerly to the path which led north.

"Night Drum has a loud voice, and I do not mind being out of its range for a while," Hawk Eye called back, striding out ahead of us. When we drew up near him, he murmured, "Perhaps I could teach him the skills of the trail. Or, better yet—you would be his—what did our ancestors call it—his teaching uncle?" he asked me.

I glanced at Winter Bird; he nodded his passing on to me of the job which might in older times have been given to him. "I am better now since I have gone twice along the Trail of Buffalos. But I do not yet really know a ground squirrel from a small muskrat." Later we made our fire, ate our meal, and sat watching the smoke ascend, smelling the good smell of the fire.

"The hunting clans know secrets we do not see," Winter Bird said finally. "When the forest surrounds you, it takes you up in a clasp that makes you feel it as Mother."

"Every small thing has meaning out here," I said. "The moss that grows on the tree, tracks, dry or fresh, the cast-off antlers of the deer."

"In the city those antler are useful—for the priests to wear on their heads in the ritual dances."

"Out here they serve another purpose. Let me show you—"

I brought out two sets of young deer antlers, shed a year or so ago not far from Cahokia. I brought them together and they click-clicked, like the rattle of the shaman in a sun dance.

"They make more noise than I could have thought," Hawk Eye said thoughtfully.

"Yes. Just now the young deer are war-like, looking to battle those of their kind for the best young does. When they hear the rattle of antlers in a clearing, they come seeking trouble. Instead, they find the arrow of the hunter."

Both the brothers nodded, and I read excitement in their looks. Finally we made brief plans for the morrow. We lay before the fire in the mild evening, unbothered by the mosquitoes at that time of the year, and talked. For the first time Winter Bird told his brother in detail of his trip across the trail to the Beautiful River and of his stay with the Old Dream-Singer.

"I liked it for a change," he said. "When you get into the city, see only the sights and hear only the sounds there, talk only of the festivals and wars and priest doings, that becomes your world. But out there—" he gestured into the woods—"out there is more of the world."

"I have heard the world described often in the tales of my trading clan," I added, "and it stretches beyond even the Beautiful River. Beyond the flint pits of the north, beyond the far Falls where Loon Feather's people have their ancestral home." Trading was on my mind. I had made another trip to the flint town, had taken Ghost and another servant with me, returning with many bags full of fine flint, rough and in arrowheads and pike tips.

"So? I have heard of cities, greater even than Cahokia, to the south," Hawk Eye said.

"Yes. So my uncle Bo Jo said, and he had travelled there. They are down the Father of Waters, far, far, to its mouth, and then west across the Bright Sea for several turnings of the Sun Lord."

"Are they like Cahokia?"

"Their cities there are like the towns of prairie dogs on the sandy meadow—so numerous you cannot count. All of their coast is like one city—village after village after tower after temple. So my uncle Bo Jo said. Cornfields beyond where the eye can see, and no forest between. So my uncle Bo Jo said."

They were silent, contemplating.

"There must be great wisdom there," Winter Bird said. "The wisdom of the city." His tone was reverent.

213

His brother grunted. "And great rottenness, too. The rotten-ness of living refuse pits." His brother looked up quickly. Hawk Eye had said The Thing That Is Not Said. Winter Bird's pleasure away from the city was only skin deep. Even out here he was frightened of the shadow of the prince. The people were restless when we left, fearful of war attacks of retaliation from some of the larger cities Cahokia held in tribute, bending under the increased taxing leavied to support the sacred people on the high hill.

I looked off into the trees, where a few fireflies were dancing, turning on and off their torches, where the sound of an owl and the murmuring of the running water broke the dusky quiet. Peace came to me like a river vapor. "There is wisdom in the city, it is true," I said. "But real wisdom is in the forest. It is the wisdom of the springs of life itself."

"Then you would do away with cities?" Winter Bird asked, a little surprised.

"No," I laughed. "For I like honey cakes and chungky matches and grand parades as well as the next man. But I would have us all go to the woods and not forget the ways of the sacred forest spirits, the mysteries of the lakes, the truth of the hills."

We let Winter Bird gather wood for the sleeping fire. When he was out of sight, Hawk Eye said, "His eyes are full of smoke. He cannot see the pain of the people of the city, as they bend beneath their loads. On their backs they carry the rich and powerful."

"Yes, of course, they carry them up the hill. Especially the Female Sun. Soft Fur cannot walk even to the next temple house. It takes four men to carry her royal litter."

"I do not mean that, though it is true. I mean their lives are bent to serve the royal family's whims. The people are burdened to send tribute to the top, to a bunch of foolish children who do not care about their people."

I was silent a moment. "Hawk Eye, why do not the people do something if they are oppressed? Your group meets, speaks The Things That Are Not Said. Could not some other of the noble families rule? In the forest it is decided by who is best—"

He interrupted me. "This is the Daughter of the Sun! The child of the god, placed before us to bring us his light. If she does not

214

always know her Father's will—does less than he wishes, so be it. To worship her is to worship him."

I had known the answer.

"Still," he said in a very small voice. "Truth is truth. We will keep on speaking truth." He rolled over towards the fire as Winter Bird added more logs to the fire, then stacked others very neatly with his long, artisan's fingers.

"Such a thing has never been done," Hawk Eye said, his voice thin, as if it had come like a spirit from a long way away. "No, not anywhere. Such a people would be instantly destroyed, I am sure."

Winter Bird lay down, covered himself with an extra blanket against a chill, rising wind. He did not know what we were talking of, and he did not wish to know.

"No, never," Hawk Eye murmured. "Fire would come down from heaven and the entire city, all traces, wiped from earth's face. Surely." Soon the only sound in the clearing was the cheerful, yet somehow mournful chirping of the kaskaskas in the clearing.

The next day, early as the dawn, we awoke and went to a meadow clearing where we had seen deer at sport the day before. I knelt in the morning mist, tossed tobacco and herbs to the four cardinal points, rose and addressed the powers of the forest.

"What are you doing?" Winter Bird asked when I was done.

"Praying that we may not offend the young deer spirits. That the forest will yield its sustenance to us, because we come in peace. Drawing the spirits of the deer to this clearing." I raised my voice to sing the hunting song Bo Jo had taught me. When I looked at the faces of the two brothers, I thought I caught a flash of embarrassment. Still, they were eager for the fray.

Winter Bird and I clashed the antlers together, making a noise loud enough to raise the dead across the river. Quickly, each taking a set of antlers, we retreated behind trees, then clashed the antlers against the smooth bark of beech trees. Hawk Eye, a sure and true shot from the Female Sun's army until he raised his voice and got expelled, held a quiver of hunting arrows.

Soon, soon, two young bucks appeared, their antlers just blooming like twigs in spring.

215

"They think there are females here, with bucks fighting over them. The noise has drawn them," Winter Bird breathed in admiration.

"Shh. Their sight is poor, but they hear and smell. And curses of the cave! We are upwind. Leave it to Bear Belly."

Sure enough, one of the two pricked up his ears and raised his head. Had he caught our scent? "Quickly, Hawk Eye, draw your bow! We will have only four breaths to do this."

Snort! The hated, disgusting scent of human kind in his nostrils, panic in his glance, the buck prepared to bolt. But—the sure and true arrow of the former captain of the guard entered his chest. The buck crumpled to his knees, rolled over. In triumph we went to him, they watching his last breath, I talking to his spirit. At last we gutted him and tied his feet to a carrying pole to bring the feast for many people home.

Singing the song of hunting joy I taught them, with laughter and pleasure in their eyes, Hawk Eye and Winter Bird came with me into the street of their parents in the shell crafters' village. They bounded to the door of the house in which No Corn and Hail Like Rocks lived. But, at the door, a surprise, a sad one, awaited us. The sounds of crying came out from inside, and women's shadowy forms could be seen clustered around my friends' mother.

She emerged for a second, beckoned to them to set the deer down, looked around like a scout on the trail and then gestured us inside, into a circle of dark, winter-clad older women.

"Hail Like Rocks is gone," the mother said sadly. "The soldiers came to take him away. He is a prisoner."

"Why?" Winter Bird demanded.

"They say—we are trouble makers." She used a word in their dialect I did not know; Winter Bird quickly translated it. "But I am the one with the sharp tongue, the questions about life behind the walls."

Her sons could not deny it and looked at her sternly; she began to sob again. "It is the man who must be responsible for the woman. So often he begged me to hold my tongue, but I could not. The spies are everywhere, even down here." A shadow crossed Hawk Eye's face. I knew he was wondering if all was well in the small house down the river-clay potters' lane.

"Prisoner you say?" Winter Bird asked. The old women slowly began to exit; his mother waved them off with thanks for their condolences.

"Yes. He will not return home but will guard the Dead Chieftains' House."

A look of pain crossed Hawk Eye's face. I looked at him questioningly. "The Dead Chieftains' House. It is a place where old men go—to die," he whispered. "All the pestilences known to man are there, among the bones and worms. And the punished ones must sit inside in the winter, or freeze. They catch the fevers, and die soon."

"Can nothing be done?" I wanted to know.

"What would it be? We have no relatives in the highest kinship group. We are not the sons of the Sun." No Corn's voice was laden with anger, scorn.

My voice was a whisper when I finally spoke again. "I will go to the Female Sun and ask to have Hail Like Rocks removed from the Dead Chieftains' House," I said.

All three of the voices clamored at me. I could not think of doing so. It would involve me—make me a guilty one as well.

"Friend," said Hawk Eye, "you are a gift of the spirits in your goodness. But when you arouse the ear which is at the top of the hill, it may begin to listen deeply. And we"—(his voice grew softer, more pleading)—"Hawk Eye, All Joy and the little one, all of us, will be in danger."

I nodded, saying I would think about it and decide. I clasped my friends' arms and bade them farewell rather abruptly. Something had been building in me like a swelling mushroom after rain, and it did not stop pounding and growing even as I had listened in shock to the sad news at my friends' house. I walked briskly from the shell crafters' village through two other small villages. I was on my way to the river-clay potters' settlement—and my dear love. Soon I was in her arms. Her large eyes brimmed with tears of joy, her voice called me endearing names I blush to say, "Precious ground squirrel, Brave warrior of the woods," and, more teasingly as she caressed me, "Wolf Cub on the loose," and "Stag of my heart."

I played the flute I had left with All Joy, and we stayed in each other's arms for an hour as darkness fell.

"Can we not be married sooner? It is so easy to ask for your hand. Old Herb Woman will not stand in the way. She knows we are pledged—" I asked, aflame with love for her.

"My dear one, I gave my word when I came that I would serve her for a year and eight moons. That time will be up when spring comes again. I have my honor." And then we sat and talked a bit more. I asked of the spies, if they had been about the river-clay potters' village, because I was still thinking of my friends who Say The Things That Are Not Said, and anxiety for them chewed at my heart in the midst of my joy. Yes, Loon Feather said, there had been spies from the court, but they had only wandered about, asking a few questions. She had given the two who stopped in their lane a drink of water from a gourd, and they seemed pleasant enough.

Then we spoke of the home we would have together. It would be as near to Walks-Up-the-Steps' as possible, because we would have White Wings with us, and Walks-Up-the-Steps could not be far separated from her. Loon Feather lay her head on my knee, and I dreamed of our campfire and hearth, suffused in love and kindness after many troubles.

When I left her it was with a pang of sadness. I could not stand parting, even for a day. Then, too, my dear friend's father was snatched from their midst, and though I had promised to help, I did not know if I could really secure his freedom. I was not even sure they wished me to, though I had read in their eyes the desire that I try, even though they were afraid it would affect them. It was all so odd; in the villages of the woods, a clan's warriors so insulted would simply take weapons and steal back their father on a raid. Here all were afraid of the great power of the rulers. Sad. Then the pang passed and I was filled with joy—for I was returning to the child who had watched me go away two days ago, her little hand waving until I was out of sight. And father and mother in one that I had now become, I leapt to return to her, too. A sudden feeling of well being filled my breast. I would secure Hail Like Rocks' release, return him to his family. My little cousin would join Loon Feather in due time and me in our new shelter—happy, all happy. My happiness was as serene and secure as the bright blue sky on this early fall day. And when I caught first sight of the shelter where my little cousin waited to jump into my arms, my heart leapt, confirming my joy at returning to Cahokia.

It is said that when the Birds of Thunder met to decide how they would run the world for the Maker of the Stars and his son, they said, "It is not right that man should have too much joy at one time. For, he will think that joy is all of life and will not recognize that sorrow teaches wisdom. It is not good that man's joy should bubble all over, like the foam on the maple sugar pot. No, best we tamp it down, let it settle, with the salt of sorrow."

And so it was with me, for at the time I loved the most, exulted the most in my free manhood and those I cared for, at that time was sorrow so great sent to me that I thought I could not live another day.

When I entered Walks-Up-the-Steps' house, she was kneeling silently before the dying cooking fire of the evening meal. Ghost was outside, asleep in the summer shelter; White Wings was asleep, early it seemed, in her rabbit skins with her baby clutched in her arms.

"Why do you weep?" I asked, kneeling by the fire. Walks-Up-the-Steps' face was so dirty, her hair so unkempt, that it was obvious that she had wept long.

"Shh—do not speak of it. It is wrong to say I sorrow in this matter." I grasped her arm, looked into her face.

"Tell me. I command you," I said.

"It is—the Female Sun. She is ill," she whispered.

"I know that. Everyone does. And so?" I said in a rather cold voice. It seemed stupid that she would be crying because that soft, senseless, whorish woman at the top of the hill was ill.

"The doctors have said she has a growth—in her womb." She hesitated, and yet I had hold of her arm, was staring at her streaked face.

"It will not go away, as it is the bad sort, they think. In a year, possibly two, she will die."

The odd thought crossed my mind that here it was again—I was talking about women's wombs. Perhaps it was because of the way I had been born—causing my mother such birthing troubles.

"Well, it is sad," I said, wondering why this distant cousin of the Female Sun's should be so disturbed about the cycles of her life ending. Then an idea came to me. "I suppose you are troubled because the prince will succeed her. That is a calamity, I suppose." Brutal, incompetent lecher, I thought, voicing in my own mind The Thing That Is Not Said. But, as my friends had said in the forest, Truth is truth. Right is right.

"Of course. But we are not to be concerned about the temples on the hill. It is the Sun Lord's command is it not? Let his children rule in his name. No—it is not that."

White Wings stirred in her sleep; I went and pulled the rabbit skin blanket up around her. She turned onto her back, pulling her arm across her sweet cheek. A few wisps of hair were damp on her forehead and I pulled them back. Then I returned to the fire and the weeping woman.

"No," she said, hesitantly, then, as words came in a flood—
"They are planning her funeral already, in the sacred ways of the Sun Lord. The Lord of the Funeral Death, the priests—have been seeking objects to go to the grave with her—the sacrificial servants to bear her train to the skies with her father the Sun." She now had my full attention.

"The priests have been out with spies, and twelve maidens have been chosen. They have gone all through the villages—and here, in the city, speaking to young and old to find the perfect ones." The flood crested.

"Your promised one, the Loon Feather"—my heart leapt out of my chest— "and—the small one—"she gestured to the innocent child who sighed contentedly in her sleep—"have been selected."

I could not open my mouth. My heart was a stone at the bottom of a waterfall with icy spume pouring over it.

"No," I finally said. "No."

"We must all be glad. Many people wished their children to be chosen for this honor, to bear messages from our people to the Great Sun Lord in his House of Love in the heavens. To live there, with other sacrificed servants forever in his courts."

"No," I said. It was all the eloquent protest I could think of, Bear Belly that I was.

"I do not know why I am sad—they will not suffer," she went on in that same pained, imploring voice. "The priest in his robes came to tell me of the great honor—the rest will know soon. They give them a fine feast, the best of all delicacies, keep them in the temple all night. Then, the next morning, the older ones will copulate with the prince in front of us all and then the prince will strangle them and carry them behind the funeral bier." But I did not let her finish. I bolted from that place and stood stock still in the streets. The rock had been dislodged from the base of the waterfall.

"Bird-of-Thunder-Son-of-the-West-Wind, Maker-of-the Stars. I know you are there," my inner voice screamed. "I feel you under my heart, ready to catch it as it falls off the cliff. Tell me what to do, for do something I must. If the Sun Lord is your servant, and if he as god wants this, then I am going to be guilty of deepest blasphemy. But I will not take this as his servant, nosing along the dirt street as the rest of them will.

"Truth is truth, and killing two young girls pure as the first hoarfrost is not good. Never! Tell me what to do. "

I moved from the middle of the street, as I heard the footsteps of the night guard, and I sat by the grain garner of the house through that long night. Slowly, as water creeps through moss in a cool stream, ideas trickled into my mind, and I knew what I would do. Then I slept a little, a rock for my pillow.

221

I awoke to the sounds of flutes and rattles and drums. The procession was heading for the Sun-Watching Circle. Pink streaks and bear-fat colored clouds announced the coming of the Lord. I went to the well to draw a drink, wiped my mouth, and walked towards one of the lesser mounds. I climbed it, and stared at the Lord Sun as he awoke.

"I am sending you the belt of war," I said, staring straight into his face, the color of orange fall berries.

"We shall see. Truth is truth, after all." My voice was stone cold, but I was sweating. To confront a god in this way! Truly, it WAS never done, and probably for good reason. I backed down off the hill, hoping I had not been seen, but I cast one last look back over my shoulder at the great disk rising to the east, filtering through trees and sending streaks over all the hills of Cahokia. "This is either the last, or the first day of my life," I said and walked up the road to the Temple Mound and towards my destiny.

Chapter 10

When I reached the top of the hill by the back stairs, I attracted attention. The royal party had just returned from the He Is Rising ceremony, and the prince himself was entering his own residence. He obviously caught sight of me from the corner of his eye; I saw a hand move in a royal way, gesturing in my direction. Soon the Female Sun's steward stood by my side as I walked towards her palace.

"Why have you climbed the hill in the daytime and unsummoned, trader?" this old man said in a cool voice.

"I have come to pay my respects to the Female Sun, having heard of her disability."

"She is not receiving." I believed I had heard him say that before, in other circumstances. It still sounded odd.

"She will see a concerned friend who wishes to bring her greetings and comfort, I think," I said. His eyes met mine in an unruffled stare, and he went ahead.

I reached the door and waited; soon he came out and nodded that I might go in. There, in the dusky corner of the huge room, on her thronely chair, sat the Female Sun—Eyes-of-the-Deer—Soft Fur. My stone heart began to palpitate as if it were afraid. I commanded it to be quiet and invoked all the powers of the universe from Maker of the Stars to Nanaboozhoo himself. I was not taking any chances. I did not invoke the Sun Lord, no, not him. I shot arrows at him mentally.

Female Sun looked worn, tired. She had lost weight, and her face was not as wide, and there were wrinkles around her eyes and mouth. Still, to my relief, she welcomed me graciously, with a smile.

"Drum-of-the-Gods, I have not seen you in many risings of the Lord."

"No. I have been trading in Ohio; I sent you a full bag of the flints I brought."

"Yes, I recall them. Fine ones. And I was also aware you kept quite a few more bags for yourself." Her smile grew broader. I did not know what to say, but began anyway.

223

"I have heard of your—indisposition. The priests have not given your people much hope."

Her eyes clouded, but she did not allow herself any further demonstration of emotion. "It is my destiny to go to my father the Sun when he decrees. They say no more than two years in such cases."

I was struck with the need to be closer to this woman, to look into her eyes. After all, we had been much to each other once, and if truth is told, I retained a degree of affection for her, like one might have for an aunt who has cared for him. "Can you not come down and sit by me on this bench? No one is near—I would like to hold your hand." I do not know why I said it—I just know I felt the need to talk to her as man talks to woman.

And, just as strangely, she came down, with some effort.

"Are you feeling pain?" I asked, taking the small hand in mine.

"Sometimes. But nothing like it may be—so they say." Her voice was listless. "Whatever it is, I will bear it with dignity. I am the daughter of the Lord."

I was silent a moment, wanting to say what I had to say exactly right. "Not all ailments we have are sent by the Sun Lord as destiny."

"No."

"How can you know that this one is?"

"Whether it is or no, it is fatal. The doctors observe tumors like this in women now and then, and it is almost always the same. Death. They have looked at the symptoms."

"But if there was a cure—"

"None here know it."

"That does not mean that one does not exist."

Her eyes had a flicker of hope in them. She took away her hand. "Where? What do you mean?"

"There are great cities to the south of us, far down the Father of Waters and beyond."

"So we have heard. And some of the traders in my father's time went there, but it is a perilous journey and long. They have fine gold and cities like this, and greater, beyond counting. But what—"

"There are great priests there, full of knowledge. Great medicine, doctors. They may know the cure."

She turned her face away from mine. "What good would that do? We cannot go there. None of us has ever gone so far."

"One has," I said, and turned her face with my hand back towards mine. Truly I was bold there in her own throne room! But the Bird of Thunder seemed to sit on my shoulder that day, and his truth gave me strength. "My uncle, whom you loved—"

"More than any on this earth—" she said fervently.

"—After his troubles here in this city left and travelled far. He found himself in a great city of the far South, where he stayed and learned their lore before he returned. It is great indeed."

She looked at me wonderingly.

"I do not know the way to cure this illness. I have seen the shaman's art, but it is not my special gift to climb the tree of life and see each illness, so I cannot help you there." I did not tell her that I had a medicine drum that could heal, because in my heart I knew that such a drum could not work on one so sinful.

"I could travel to the cities of the South—I would try. I do not know if I can find the way they cure this illness, but I would try."

She turned to me and put her arms around my neck, kissed my cheek. "You are a true friend. I do not know if—it should be the will of the Sun Lord, then I would be defying Him."

"Well, then, you will die anyway. But perhaps he wishes you to try to get well. Perhaps opening up the contacts to the lands of the South may do his will, bring him glory. May I try to find the cure in the South?"

"Go, all that way, take a year or more, just to cure me?" Her little face was screwed up in wonder.

"There is more for you if I go. I cannot guarantee that I will find the way to cure you, but I can find a great treasure for your house for time to come. I know of a jade statue and more—beyond price. They will make the prince's rule firm and strong."

"Ahh," she breathed. I had hit on the mark. Even she realized how despised and scorned her son was among the people of the city he would have to rule at her death.

225

"My uncle had a great stone held in secret by our family for years. It is a tablet of great power, because it can foretell rightly when the hiding times of the moon's face are."

"So? The priests say that cannot be done. "

"And yet this clay tablet does it. It comes from far, far away. I know where it is and will get it for you." The Bird of Thunder seemed to sneer behind my shoulder, "Why are you going to give such a stone of power, your family's treasure, to these porcupine rumps?" I told the Bird of Thunder to be still for now; I had not put it in their hands yet, only promised.

"And you will do this only for love of the Great Lord Sun and his Daughter and Son-to-be?" Soft Fur asked in a small voice.

"Well—we have been much to each other, as I said. But—no." (Be with me Bird of Thunder. I need you. Truth to someone who can have my head—or other things instantly chopped off.)

I knelt before her, looked into her eyes. "My small cousin and my other cousin"—I did not say my intended one "are to be part of the great Sun funeral planned when you go to your Father."

"I did not know that. The priests have planned all. But of course it is foreordained and pure ones must be chosen." Her voice seemed a little distant.

"I do not wish them to have that honor." There. It was said. The thing that cannot be said for certain.

"But all the high families wish it, will even bribe for it. Many were disappointed that their children could not go with me to the land behind the river."

"Then they will be glad for a new chance."

"I must endure the fate but not your cousins? I be dead, they alive?" Her voice was astonished and a little harsh.

"I wish all of you to be alive. I am selfish that way."

She was silent for a moment, considering the odd thing I had suggested, trying to decide if it were insanity, treason or merely the odd quirk of someone from the woods. She decided on the latter, but even so, her voice was fringed with just a hint of exalted pride. "I do not know if I have the power to change such a thing."

The Bird of Thunder bade me hold nothing back. "Soft Fur, you have had the power to change many things, but you have not used it. You can do as you wish."

"The prince will not like it." She was whimpering like a little girl. I suspect it was all too much for her, having to maintain that she was glad to be joining her Father soon, enduring the pain, thinking of what that jackal prick her son was going to do with the Throne of the Sun once he got it.

"Do not tell him until I return. Make the change then—if you are alive." I took her hand again. "Now agree, swearing most sacredly by the Sun Lord. You will free them from death if I return with what I have promised." She said nothing.

"I will hurry away, taking the trading goods in a canoe that I will need there in the far south, for I hear above all else they cherish good flints."

Finally, in the dusk of that room, smelling of river bottom mold and perfumed incense, I saw her nod, ever so slightly.

"And—there is one slight thing more. A matter of justice. A man has been sentenced to death by pestilence in the Dead Chieftains' House. It is an unjust sentence, imposed by the prince. If you could see your way clear to reconsider and make him the waste collector or some such thing before I go. His family needs him, and they should be innocent in your eyes, too. I ask much now, but it is because I promise much to you and the prince."

Was she listening? Had I gone too far? Tears stood in her eyes. I did not, never did know if it was because I might bring her hope for her own hopeless body or if I might bring her hope for her hopeless son, but whatever it was she was moved to let me go and to release Hail Like Rocks. She would keep her promise, I knew it—if.

If I could get down the Father of Waters safely. If I could cross the great water, as few did. If—the people in the South did not kill and cook me, as it was said they often did. If I could find the land and the treasure–return –and she had not died.

I kissed her feet, bolted out of the throne room and headed for the back side of the hill. On the way out, I passed the stone-eyed steward, standing by the door. How much had he heard? Did it really matter?

Then, oddly enough, I saw Fire-on-the-Plains, the herald who regarded me with amusement. I had not seen him for many weeks.

"And so, Drum-of-the-Gods, you have been out attracting and shooting a deer, so it is said. And inside you are shooting a deer, too, perhaps?" It was a bold statement, and yet not said in malice. He seemed to know a good deal but said little. I did not think he would harm me or my plan.

I only glanced at him, then bolted down the steps.

"Thank you, Bird of Thunder, Nanaboozhoo, Maker of Stars—whoever. The ifs in this situation are a huge medicine bag to be carrying down this trail, but I will pack them and go. Father of Waters, bear us gently! Stars of the Southern sky, I come to see you." I looked above me, right into the face of the sun, and though I was blinded for a moment, I did not flinch until, deliberately and with haughty mein, I turned my back. Then I pulled the amulet out of my shoe, put it around my neck and headed to the house to say goodbye.

I would not even allow the sun to set on my quest. I explained to Walks-Up-the-Steps that I would be gone on a trip for a full circle of the Sun Lord, begged her to care for White Wings. "If you should hear—things that unsettle you about me—know that I am gone for a good purpose and trust me," I told her. She shook her head, not understanding, but promising to care as a mother for the small one. It would do us all small good should the final quandary come; Walks-Up-the-Steps was reared in this city as a part of a royal kinship clan; she would know no other course in life but to deliver the child she loved to the funeral procession. She would braid my loved cousin's hair and oil her skin for her trip beyond the horizon. Tears would not be appropriate in such a setting; she would even squelch her thoughts of grief. Such is the service of the Sun Lord in the city.

I bade Ghost prepare for the trail. He was coming with me; I had determined I needed him. He was a slower traveling companion than others I might have chosen; but not by much, and I could trust him above all others. Besides, we would be traveling by water anyway, and he was good in a canoe. I had him carefully cover the ceremonial drum to store it and then go to the river for the largest canoe he could find.

Things for travel were always ready for me; I was, after all a trader. My fine flints were in sturdy leather packets which could be carried; dried venison and parched corn were in pots in the storage granary; soon I had them packed in soft deerskin bags. I bustled about, packing my few belongings into a backpack, garbing myself in leather clothing from head to foot, finding extra deerskin for leather shoes, getting the best arrows I had perfected for the recent hunt.

I must not hurry away without getting word to my dearest one in the village of the river-clay potters and my friends—messages vague enough not to involve them. So I must take the time to rush to the village, find them for a word of parting.

Loon Feather was standing by her door, holding a water jar under her arm as she had come from the spring. She was stately and beautiful, with her hair pulled back in a clip in the style of the Dune Devils. I took her hand. "I find—I must make a sudden journey of many moons, go far away. A trading trip."

She looked at me with arched eyebrows, started to ask. I put my finger on her lips. "Soon you will hear news that will alarm you. We may not discuss it. Do you understand?" She nodded. She was aware as anyone in the poorer clans of Cahokia that there were things which could not be spoken, hardly thought.

"When you do, you will know that your love has gone far away for those he loves. Your trust must be as great as the wife of Nanaboozhoo when he makes his trip around the field of stars and she does not see him for many nights. Trust our love."

Her eyes were filled with questions, but I would not allow them. She nodded and raised on her tiptoes to kiss me. Her eyes were troubled when I left, but not nearly as troubled as they would be when she heard she was to be a sacrifice. There would be no honor in that for her; only terror. It was one thing to test a man or woman's bravery in battle or hardship or trial; the nature of our earth is that we must learn to live with its hardships. But it is another thing to be senselessly slaughtered to preserve the pomp and power of rich noblemen. We who were brought up in the woods did not believe in throwing people to the gods in the name of death or life. Would that my few words, conveying my love and small hope, would be strong enough to see her through this year to come!

Hawk Eye was not at his shelter, and so I had to deliver my message to All Joy, who sat feeding the child on her bunk. Her eyes were also full of wonder at my haste, my obviously excited spirits.

"Tell him—tell him I go for a long journey of necessity—to trade, if you will, among people none of us have ever seen. But as I go, my eyes will be wide open." I do not know why, but I pulled out the amulet, with the all-seeing eye on it, and walked over to show it to her, so she could make no mistake.

"We will see what justice is in cities far away and greater than this." She nodded, with that serene wisdom that I so valued in her. "And tell him—tell my friend, but no one else I pray you—that truth is a deer that will not be rattled, but must be sought in the deep forest by him who is willing to go a long way to find it. Still, if I return, I will tell him what the deer of truth has told me."

A small smile played about her lips. She took my hand.

"We have had word. Hail Like Rocks is back in his home. Thank you, thank you."

"And," I closed lamely, because I could think of nothing else to say, "I will bring something fine for the small one."

It was almost the time of the evening ritual before He Is Setting when I returned. Ghost had secured and packed the canoe; White Wings was standing sucking a piece of maple sugar, looking apprehensive at all the movement of things out of the house. How children sense things without being told! Walks-Up-the-Steps took her in her arms, trying to distract her with a corncob baby, and when I turned from them, it was almost directly into the path of the steward of the royal house. My heart leapt with sudden fear. Was I being detained? Had Soft Fur revoked her promise?

He came very close and gestured haughtily that we should step into the shadows by the granary to speak.

"You are commanded to come tomorrow after the Sun Greeting to an audience with the prince. Rumors have come to him."

I could hardly get out my answer. "And yet—I am allowed to go on a trading mission by the Female Sun herself, starting in just a few moments."

"Well, then, I suppose you will have to decide which royal decree to obey," he said in that same tone like ice on the river. "And yet," he said in a voice that was considerably lower in tone, "she may be willing to explain to her son herself tomorrow, for she has sent these to you to take on your way." He opened a bag of softest leather, beaded with the royal sun crest. In it were sewn ten exquisite obsidian knife blades—the best I had even seen, by far. And ten huge pearls, the finest in the royal treasury.

I took the packet, not knowing what to say.

I wondered that this steward who had always seemed to hate me was delivering the gift the Female Sun wished me to have, was showing it to me with urgency now. Did he know all? It could mean my life even yet. "You are of her secret council?" I had to ask. "She tells you all?"

"Yes, but I do not tell her all. Nor do you."

Before I could stop him he reached in the open slot of my leather shirt and pulled out the amulet. I could not even draw back before he had dropped it and opened his own shirt. In the glint of He Is Setting I could see a finely worked copper version of the same all-seeing eye on a lanyard. Then I saw it no more, and he had turned on his heel. He, of all the most trusted, betrayed most up on the hill. He was the informant.

Burnt into my memory even unto this day is the sight of White Wings, standing in the arms of Walks-Up-the-Steps, screaming and reaching for me. The rays of the setting sun glared on her face, the sound of the huge pink shell horn blaring its departing message to Him, a message that would soon call White Wings to join him, if I did not succeed. And as Ghost walked ahead of me, I turned once or twice to see her, gradually growing smaller, wailing, her arms reaching pleading with me not to leave her alone again. The picture of that child with the declining sun in back of her tattooed itself inside my brain forever, for love and strong anxiety and the agony of separation are stronger dyes than even charcoal and blood to make an impression permanent.

I will make the story of my journey short. The Father of Waters is a marvel unlike any others, and no one who has travelled its length will ever forget it. Ghost and I rose before the sun and did not stay our journey until all light was gone, camping in the dusky darkness as thousands of kaskaskas screamed in the cane breaks and swampy forests by the shores.

There is a feeling on that river that is not like any other. So full and flowing is it, even at that time of early fall, that you are carried like a leaf down it without any control of your own, so that you feel as if you are bourne on the breast of Earth Mother herself. Let me see what things I can vividly remember of the trip, so you can live it with me.

I can still see us there, on whatever highlands we could climb up by the river to camp, with our campfire winking out of the deep woods. We cooked fish I had caught, we fried corn cakes on hot stones, sometimes we shot game, but not often, because there was not time.

232

Almost a moon it took us as we travelled between cliffs or flats on either side, travelling around islands, sometimes going up wrong channels, but always finding our way back. Ghost seemed to have an extra sense about which was the right channel.

Often we felt as if there was no one else on earth but us. Animals hooted and yelped, and birds flew over and cried out in huge flocks, and I called to mind that I had forgotten in the luxury of the city what the deep, vibrant beauty of earth was like. The woods has a wisdom that then, and now, pierces my heart–the wisdom of the birth land.

We passed the settlements of man, and sometimes we stopped, because we needed to trade for food. Warily we approached, with the trader's outstretched banner on a stick, staying outside of the stockades, never sure of our reception. Sometimes we could decipher the tongues they spoke, sometimes not, and we spoke with hand signals. The further south we got, the more difficult it became to understand the tongues. I was quick, however, and mastered a few words in each place and found that many applied everywhere on the southern stretch of the Father of Waters. There was one tongue over all its southern length.

I stayed a day or two in some places that were particularly friendly, to pick up pieces of the language because I knew I would need them. The excellent flints I carried in a basket, smoothly displayed between layers of finest fawnskin, smoothed our way. True it is, I told Ghost, as they say, the trader with fine goods knows no enemies.

"None except robbers," he said. I touched the fine bow slung across my shoulder. I displayed it at all times, like a turkey cock struts his feathers. Well, they did not know I was once a Bear Belly after all, that I had trouble hitting a huge moose at one time and now could bag only rather slow rabbits or frozen deer. But that was better than many in these indolent towns; so I did have the advantage, I suppose.

We traded flints and some small pearls, which I kept in the pockets of my suit along with the precious pearl and obsidian packet, for fine pieces of crystal, but mostly for food. Generous they were often, inviting us to their feasts in the town squares, inviting us to their ball games. We ate the corn grains swollen with wood ashes overnight and then washed; we ate odd grains cooked into porridges with fishes; we ate turtles and snails with spices. We ate them all; what will you not eat when you are hungry?

I remember always the sense of hurry, the presence of that river like a breathing god before us, finally behind us, mists rising, current pushing, panting, "Go, go, the days pass, her illness comes on apace." And fear, never far from me, bold, un-manlike, make-ashamed, coward fear of 1,000 varieties. Would I never be free of it? When a snake suddenly slithered in my path in the bottom-lands, when a group of heads appeared over a cliff as we were climbing a rise towards a village, when some chieftain looked menacingly at us on first introduction, my mind saw every fall, bone-break, torture, death that there has ever been. I remember that trip as a season of fear, but also of persistence.

But most of all from that trip down the majestic Grand-father of all rivers, I remember Ghost-on-the-Lake, my hunchback servant. Shall I say friend? Yes, for he came to be just that. I do not know why I had never really known him in the years that he had been about. I suppose I was busy seeing other things. He had been half a person to me—a dependent of the village, a passive co-captive of the Dune Devils, a companion in troubles of course, then a servant of what was left of his original masters, White Wings and I. Mostly he was like a bed or a corn grinder—existing for my convenience.

But there, in those long nights under the stars, smelling new, swampy smells, hearing unfamiliar "too-wees" of the yellow and green colored birds and the "bir-rups" of huge frogs, we shared the fearsome newness of it all. Both of us were handicapped by fear; he freely expressed his; I could not for manhood's sake. We hovered together and propped each other up like those who droop inside the sweat tent, and we became friends.

I saw him as I should have seen him long ago—son of the Maker of Stars and therefore brother to me, humpbacked and stammering as he was. And a marked and unusual man at that.

I noticed it first seven days out, when we camped on a moonless, starless night. He did religious rites by the fire, tossing tobacco, praying. "We must beg help of the spirits" he said. "Tomorrow we will be met by bad canoes."

"How do you know that?" I had asked, without paying much attention at that time. Who could care about the ramblings of a crippled servant?

"I saw it in the rain." Then, as I snorted, he became quiet. "I-I am a Knowing One. Blessed by the Spirit of the Seeing Eye." He cleared his throat and I settled down for a tale. What a gift of rattling off at the mouth this hunchback had! Once he was well into any of his tales, one forgot he was speaking as though he had hickory nuts under his tongue. I will try to tell you this one as near to Ghost's tongue as I can come.

"When my mother was e-e-expecting me, she was affrighted on the lake." Well, I knew that. Not much of a story there.

"In a canoe—rough—forest one at that. My father had taken her to fish in northern camps and they went out the river all the way to its—mouth, to where it emptied into the G-G-Great Lake. She begged him not to go; waves were—high. But the pikefish were striking, and on he went." Well, this was different. No one in our camps had ever heard the details.

"But suddenly black clouds came. The wind blew as if it would t-t-turn itself inside out. One paddle was lost overboard, but still my f-f-father managed to pull his way back to river mouth, taking water over the sides.

"Just before they reached the river, a form appeared and took shape like a cloud" (he said clow-ood) "and hung over them and roared. The storm grew worse and the canoe began to swamp. My father began to bail but fell out of the canoe. My p-p-poor mother, heavy with child could not help and my father sank beneath the waves. Then, strange to say, the storm stopped and the woman brought the canoe into the river and up on sh-sh-shore.

"Was this punishment for F-F-Father's evil?" Ghost looked at me with his bright, black eyes, then answered his own question. "He was a man of—rage and had killed his wife's relatives in a fight over a suit of armor. Was it that? Or had they a-a-angered the god of the place by not doing him—honor? She never knew. Some way she got home. But her fright and the ghost's ire had marked me, the child soon b-b-born."

In spite of myself his story had caught my attention. I stopped cleaning my cooking pot and waited for the rest.

"But though the ghost took, he also g-g-gave."

"Yes?"

"After a few years all close relatives died, and I came to kin in your tribe, who also d-d-died, leaving me to the m-m-mercy of the village, and a servant. But soon, even—as a child I kn-kn-knew I had the sight. I could see things. The ghost is with me sometimes, telling me things."

"Ah, I see," I said not really seeing. "And this ghost told you there would be enemy canoes tomorrow. But tell me—you see in the rain?"

"It only tells me things in the rain or in storms. But it speaks t-t-true. It does not lie. Bad canoes tomorrow."

Well, and thus it was. The next day, around a bend, near an island at the time of He Is Halfway Home, canoes with black prows came towards us.

"They are singing a war song," I murmured. "But they have no need to do us harm—" I guess they did not like our looks. A flock of arrows flew our way. But we were prepared. Just in case there was a shred of truth to what Ghost had said, that very morning I had stowed the trading goods far astern. It was easy to instantly lie low, on top of each other. The arrows passed over our heads and soon the "bad canoes" were out of our range.

"I told you," Ghost said. "Storm ghost spirits are not wrong."

Twice more he received the storm sight. Downriver, in a land of high bluffs in a cold squall one evening, he saw in his mind a city with a cruel sun ruler—a city on the east shore set high on a bluff. "We will pass by now. They eat people," he said.

Then came the night I have just said, when we camped beside that wide, wide river. I thought we must be near its mouth—thunder rumbled, rain spattered and we hid in a drippy lean-to. We ate our cold food, then pulled our covers about us to trying to get a little comfort. I kept stuffing gray hanging moss into the cracks of the lean-to.

"The ghost is here," my humpbacked friend said in a low voice and then was silent for some time. Finally he spoke.

"I saw a huge lake—waves as high as a house. Stretched so far none could see the other s-s-side, on and on across the whole world of Turtle's Island."

"The sea. Father of Waters, so they say, empties into it." I thought it was not far.

"It called to us with a voice, and you and I went on it in a huge canoe. Finally after many trials we c-c-came to a sand strip of land at last. There on the beach was a huge serpent, writhing. It was ill—m-m-many folk had stomped on it. You could see their footprints right on the s-s-skin."

"Yes?"

"B-b-but it was still alive. It rose up, its head hissing. An odd smile was on its face. It swallowed the canoe."

"And?"

"T-that was all. Why don't we turn back? Or go live among some of the f-f-friendly people."

I smiled a little. "No, Ghost. Whatever it was, we will live through it. After all, we made it to the new land in your vision. And the snake *WAS* smiling."

He nodded, not comforted.

The next morning we did indeed reach the end of the river, as it emptied in a wide, wide swath into the Great Sea. We stood looking and I thought, "You are wide and as bright blue as copper rocks. The sun shines on you so as to blind whoever looks. Perhaps that is just as well; you and your dangers stretch on, and it is best we should not know them all lest our hearts fail (particularly one already failing Bear Belly heart). "But I do not think you are much worse than the Great Lake." So I said to shore up my sinking courage, for it was stretching thin, especially with Ghost's vision.

Near the emptying spot was a large trading town, with the banners of many trading peoples. Some were going east and south, to the land of the reptiles-who-smile, some were getting ready to go north along the trail to our lands. Some had more distant goals in mind—even the Stony Mountains to the west.

We were made welcome by all. We camped near a group of men whose type I had never seen, and who made me wonder. The people of Cahokia were shorter than those of us from Lakes-Like-a-Necklace; the old Dream-Singer had said my people's stock was tall and most people around us were slighter built. But these folk in the sea camp were small indeed; very dark skinned were they, as if burnt by hot suns through many generations, and as short as our taller children. They had a beauty of face and form, though, that made me wonder. "They seem like statues of the gods," I said.

Although I had come to understand the tongue of the lower river a bit as we came along it enough to make myself understood and understand a little, and indeed it was not completely different from that of Cahokia, I could not make out a word of what these short folk said.

One spoke to me, a white-haired man with a young wife who watched his every move adoringly. He was dressed in an odd, full cape with fur on it and a beautiful breechclout tied with a long, fringed tassel. He tried two or three tongues, then hit on the southern river speech that I knew fairly well by now.

"Giant boy! You with the hunchback!" Here he bowed low to us both, catching up dirt and putting it to his forehead. I was caught by surprise and returned his bow, without the dirt, though. It must have been the custom of the times here for traders to honor each other so. "Giant boy—where have you come from? Your skin is light but your hair is long."

True enough that was. Many of the dark-skinned, small ones in this camp had short, cropped hair, like a toddling child's, although this trader's was caught up under a headdress shaped like one of the bright blue and yellow bird's.

"I have come far from far north of this Great Sea, from the city of Cahokia near to where the Father of Waters grows great by increase of the Ohio." When I did not know the words I gestured, or asked the name of the word, for instance, the name of the sea, in the southern dialect.

"Have I heard of this Cahokia?" he asked his wife. "I think perhaps so, but that is far from our trading routes. We cross the Great Sea in search of fine goods. What do you have?"

I motioned to Ghost to bring forward the flints; both the short trader and his wife came forward to inspect. "I have not seen such flints in many a summer," the old man murmured. The wife said nothing, but motioned the husband back into some of the odd trees with spiky leaves that stood about on these shores.

He returned. "What would you take for twenty-five of those?" He held up fingers to show the number. "What do you have that I want?" I asked with a smile.

"Well—"he pointed to his display, which on this fine day was spread out, like many others, on the sands of the rise above the beach. "Fine bright blue beads, brown curling shells, cotton cloth of most noble weaving." With each trade item he pointed to, he named the name and I repeated it until I thought I knew it. I marvelled particularly at the cloth he called cotton, which was soft and had been dyed and was more beautiful than any of the coarse fabrics I knew.

I looked at it all, and fine it was indeed. "I will think," I said. Again, largely in gestures, I told him what I really needed was passage—the way to the great cities of the south.

"What one do you wish?" the man said.

"Well, I do not know its name, but it has many towers, fine and broad and made of stones."

Both the man and his wife laughed.

"Why do you mock me?" I wanted to know.

"Excuse us, giant boy," he said, bowing again. "There are hundreds of cities like that across this sea, in the land of the Mayas." His hands were working fast to show me hundreds.

"Hundreds?" My heart fell. My uncle had never told me the name of the city where he had traded, only that it was a great one. Wait—he had said, "On the trading routes of the east."

"Well, that does narrow it. Still, there are twelve cities on the seacoast."

"And all have great towers of stone?"

"Yes, though some are greater than others. Do you know anything else of the place you seek?" He had to say this two or three times; finally I understood. It did not help.

This was the time I had awaited, when I would be called on to bring forth all the information I remembered about the city of the south. Curse my bean brain! It could not remember very much specific about what Uncle had said when he described his life in those far-away cities.

"Only that there was an old, wizened ruler."

"Hmm."

"Lecherous in disposition and greedy."

"Well, that could be several I have known in my years."

"I guess I shall have to go and find it. Make the crossing." As I waved my arms across the bright blue waves, topped with foam and taller than this man, crashing in on the sand, I knew what I had been dreading of all things most, why fears had grown in my heart even beyond their usual height. The Great Sea, no ending in sight, with monsters strange and terrible in its depths. Here dwelt demon gods ready to raise their huge arms and tip the small, fragile canoe, to pull one down to choking death on the murky floor, where flesh and bone would whiten in endless water, with none of the six burial customs observed. Oh, hapless end!

My face did not show my pain, and the man went on, repeating when I needed him to. "We cross a few times each year in trade and make such a journey soon. Would you care to make passage with us?"

"How do you—go? I do not have a clear idea where the eastern coast cities of the Maya lie."

"On a piece of land which curls around like the crook of an arm." He put up his flexed, dark-brown arm, ringed with bracelets, and I tried to imagine this odd piece of land which curved around.

"How do you know this? You would have to be up in the air to see this shape—" as the Serpent Mound was seen–or by someone standing on a high hill.

"We who take to the sea get a feel for many things, including the shapes of coastal lands," he said.

"Are you Maya?" I asked.

"I am originally from a people near to the Maya. My wife is pure Mayan. There are many Mayans in trade, many at this place. They are the ones of short stature." I looked about at them, walking in the trading village, possibly hundreds of them. The trader went on. "For years I have made this passage across the sea. When we start from here, we sail along the coast to the southwest, (he gestured off along the land) and then make the jump across open ocean." (Here my heart heaved.)

"When will you go?"

"I am awaiting others who wish to make the crossing, who come from the islands east of us and then—we leave." He turned to his wife, whose name turned out to be Ibix, spoke a few words I did not understand, then said,

"We may wait only a moon, for great storms come late in the season." I contracted for the journey there and then.

Ghost had not understood a thing that either of us said, but stood stoutly by my side. Traders of all nations approached us, and the short ones with cropped hair or hair pulled under headdresses, like my new friend, bowed low and touched dirt to their foreheads. It was a little odd, and I didn't quite know how to account for it. "How courteous these Maya people are," I said to Ghost. "They bow as if we were highest nobility."

"I best bring the flints to shelter," Ghost said in a low voice. "It is well to t-t-trust nobody in a strange place."

There were rude huts constructed to house the traders, and we took one and chased a variety of hopping things out, then spent the night slapping and biting. I could not see what was biting us.

"Sand fleas!" Ibix said the next morning. "And this is not even the worst season for them." The problem with them was that the bite did not end when the little creature had finished putting his tight little jaws on you. The bite itched, and red spots appeared where it had bit, and it burned and itched more till you thought you would go mad. I determined to ignore it, in the best tradition of the woodland folk.

I set up shop that morning on one of the lanes by the sea, in front of the town which stretched back many, many streets. This must have been the place Uncle spoke of when he told me his story that day long ago. Traders came from all the cardinal points wishing my wares, but I was not easy to trade with. I took only the finest pearls and gold and copper, strapping them in the deerskins on my body beneath my leather shirt. I needed to keep my best flints, and of course my obsidian for the greatest trades of all when I arrived at the Maya—in the end I would be trading for the lives of those I loved.

Day followed day while Captain Ten, for such the traders called him, completed his arrangements and waited for the weather he wished for our trip. I spent the days painstakingly trying to learn the language of the eastern coast of the Mayan lands, though it turned out there were several. I wanted only the tongue of the royal rulers of the seacoast towns, for such I would be dealing with. I know I tired and tried Ibix, asking her to practice the tongue with me.

I enjoyed the time I spent with Ibix. She was a shrewd woman who seemed to handle many of the details of her husband's trade. She had a round face which would have been attractive except that she had crossed eyes. "Many in my land have eyes that wander so," she said once, a little sadly. "It does not hurt the vision but it mars the looks."

She took the time to tell me words and actions and then complete expressions in the tongue of the horn-shaped land. Let me tell you what I learned over the month we were with these people in that trading town, and later too, for strange and wonderful is the knowledge of the places of the south.

The entire land south and west of the Father of Waters, they said, is a land with many different kinds of places—huge areas with only dry sands with sticker plants, and high mountains and swamps with odd monsters in them. Almost all were hot, and wonder of wonders, Old Man Winter hardly ever came, except in the highest mountains.

In one part, on a jutting-out seacoast horn of land in the southeast, as Captain Ten had told us, lived the great Maya people. These were part of the group my people called "the Great Cities of the South." My uncle had visited the Maya; I remembered the name. As her husband had said, Ibix was herself of the Maya. She had, however, married one of "The Strangers," a group of roving traders who came into Mayan lands from the outside. They both spoke many tongues, and each day Ibix was willing to teach us whatever we wanted to know, until finally she took herself away to tend to the business at hand. Ghost shared some of our lessons, but mostly he stayed silent, confining himself to the simple household chores, eating fine foods we were able to trade for.

Ibix taught him to fix the drink all the Maya and other southern people here shared—the chocolate. Beans they treasured and especially valued in the trading were ground fine with special grinding stones and pestals. Then they were mixed with heated water in a pot. After the pot boiled, they frothed the drink with a special tool of copper, very valuable, until it bubbled. Then they drank deep, and delicious it was, smooth and sweet when they added a special sweet they had, made from the juice of local, thick canes or honey.

"What is the difference between the Maya and the other people of the Great Cities of the South? I asked the captain.

"Many peoples are south of your lands. They are the descendants, or maybe the conquerors, of the Oldest Ones to be there. Mayas of the horn-shaped lands have cities that are the oldest, the most revered of all, their towers the most beautiful, their lore about stars and gods the deepest.

"The Maya were greater once than now. They are distracted by warfare within and without. Still, they are great enough and their gold and treasures are fine to behold. They call my people 'the foreigners,' but we call ourselves Mexicas, and we have come among them, making some of their lands our new home. We come from the highlands to the north of Maya and we range far, worship different, war-like gods and have fabulous cities too. We have brought new gods and new fighting and trading ways to the Maya; my clans make and sail canoes for the trade, and we know much of the world."

Smiling, I slapped his arm, saying "Brother!" I had told him of my family's trips in trade, and a good deal about Cahokia now. Of course I had not told him my real mission; no ears would hear that but the ones who could help me.

When the moon had made its round again and floated new in the sky, Ghost and I stood by the seashore, watching the sea canoe being loaded. Six of us would go, the captain and Ibix, two traders from the very far south, and Ghost and me. What a ship it was. Can I make you see it, I wonder?

Take the tallest tree you know here and make it twice as thick and taller yet and you would have a cypress tree. These folk shape it with clever tools, not needing fire as we had at Lake-of-the-Boulders, until it will hold twenty men if need be, and many goods besides.

Still, thinking of the size of the cresting water which came towards it, I was more than overjoyed to see the clever addition these "foreigners" had made to the long canoe; on the side, held fast by short, lashed poles, was another canoe just as long but narrower, filled with goods could also be stored in it. The second canoe gave balance when the waves came and winds blew. A sail made of strong cotton could be hoisted by ropes and poles to catch the wind. "Very good, very strong, indeed, Bear Belly?" I asked myself staunchly and answered, weakly, "So it appears."

The great day came, the people again bowing their goodbyes to Ghost and me again in the most reverent manner, Ibix guarding the food and water stores, the captain watching the winds, and the six of us off from that shore on a bright, fair day. All certainly looked auspicious. Thank you, Whoever you are! The quest proceeds. And into my odd bean brain, perversely, flashes the picture of White Wings being dressed for a funeral, her cheeks solemnly painted with red and black—a message from the land of "perhaps," sent to spur me on. Even so, it marred the taking off.

We paddled, dipping up and down through choppy waters until we could raise the sail. Slowly the land receded until it became just a line of soft gray-green. Then the Great Sea South became all. "Seven suns it will take," the captain said, raising the sail. "Pray that the wind holds from the northeast, as the weather portents show."

Hold it did, and we bounded along with the sail, watching shining fish jump and seem to fly from wave to wave. And huge, odd fish which looked more like animals came near us and smiled. I do not lie, they smiled on us and brought us good fortune, I know.

We laughed and sang snatches of sea songs that the captain knew and Ibix gave us fruit and dried, spiced meat and bread. We ate well, and I wondered why I had ever feared.

We stopped at He Is Setting that night and went ashore to replenish water jugs. "We will not camp on the beach here, for there are hostile folk," the captain said, so we slept offshore, fitfully, with a rock and rope keeping us secure in one spot.

Then on, at He Is Rising and along the coast for this second passage of the sun, coming close enough to watch smoke rising from clumps of woods, eating and living close to each other. It was good that we were able to get off that second night and camp, for we were getting as close confined as those who must stay inside and bicker in the shelter when winter binds all fast for days.

The third sun! Still we plowed on, camping again on shore at night. And then up again. I was tired of the rocking, and my eyes seeming to burn with the constant sun. My skin was salty and parched from brine coming over the edge of the canoe. And my doeskin shoes were rotting; some new type of shoe would be needed; that was for certain. The "foreigners" and others of the south wore strapped wooden shoes, and I cursed myself for not getting better shod at the trading town. Feet are the most—well, second most—important part of a man and every care should be taken of them.

Ghost had retreated into a kind of sleep state. All day long he dozed, until called on to help pack and unpack at the camps. Sometimes I woke him to drill on words of the Maya language. I wanted him to be able to understand what was being said, even though he was just a servant. Even granted the suppostion that we would not be killed or enslaved, we would need to work our way

carefully into the confidence of the towered town which the spirits
brought us to. It would take time, and care. As I told myself this,
the picture chain of "perhaps" added another link, and I saw both
Loon Feather and White Wings being carried on litters behind the
corpse of the Female Sun. Loon Feather was trying to look brave
like the daughter of the Dune Devils that she was, and almost
succeeding. White Wings was enjoying herself, playing with the
special toys that had been presented to her—not knowing, poor
thing. I forced my mind away from the scene.

We spoke at length that day, I think it was, to the two
travellers from the far south. One had had a broken nose as a
young man. He was serious and quiet, always scanning the
horizon; the other was a jokester. Magically he made pieces of
dried apples come out from behind our ears. Or, he made a jest of
the fishing we were doing, putting his line in the water, tugging
and pulling and grunting and then pulling in—some possession
of one of us which he had secretly put out on the line.

I asked this one about his home. Ah, he said, if you wish to see
towered cities, the Mayans are fine, but really you must come to
the tall mountains in the far south. There, he said, amidst mountain heights so tall they take your breath are citadels to the gods
which are raised into the clouds. There, a great god-king named
the Golden Ruler has come to rule. He has ordained garden
terraces with fine, new plants on them, terraced fields in that high
clime, golden fountains and throne rooms and riches beyond
dreaming. All around his cities are districts of people with common corn supplies, physicians who bring good health, fine water
supplies and many game contests to amuse. And priests who can
tell the passing of the sun through his whole trip, a year, they call
it, by a huge stone.

"And do they know the moon?" I asked, my uncle's stone in
my thought.

"To tell its moods and passages?"

"The priests have some stones of the moon, it is said," the silent
southerner said. "But we of the common clans do not know of
them and we have not seen them used in the rites."

"Such a stone of the hiding times of the moon would be wondrous indeed," said Ibix.

I had developed a fine friendship with this unusual woman, wife to the captain. It was she, I found with astonishment, who told the star passages we would be needing, read the southern constellations and kept our sights on the way when we were out of sight of land. She had come from a family of Mayan Star Watchers too, and her wisdom was great, greater than my family's by far.

We needed her lore, for on the fourth day out, we said goodbye to the thin line of shore beside us and made our jump into the deep. Our course was plotted, by sun sight during the day, but really by the stars at night. The heavens were alive, I tell you in that long canoe at night far from the sight of land. In our clime, of course, StarWatchers know that the star-spirits move in two directions. One could not fix on a star and expect it to lead to a certain spot. But here the stars seem to move one way only. On a certain island, as I have seen by these coasts, if you could know what of the star groups or single stars stood straight up above the island, you could steer home to that island by that star.

Thus Ibix watched the star groupings, and the strong spirit stars that never winked, and strong single winkers. She knew in her head thousands of facts about their risings and settings and placement in her sky.

I asked the captain how that had come about, and he said that in her shelter her older brother was receiving the lore; she, his twin, was nearby and unnoticed. For seven years the aged ones in the clan transmitted ancient wisdom of star steering to the boy twin; year after year in her dark corner, fascinated, the girl twin, too, memorized it. Then the older brother was killed on a sacrifice raid, so the captain said.

The captain had the good fortune to marry a walking star guide, and it had made them comfortably well off in the world's goods.

Since it was almost calm for the first time for us that night and clear as a crystal stone, we could see the dome of the stars bright, bright. Ah, my uncle had seen some of these same groups himself

247

in that mysterious cave to which I would go—sometime, sometime soon. If, if, I did not get boiled and eaten, lost or stung by one of the strange pinching beasts Ibix had told me of, bitten by a poison snake, lost in the deep, stagnant vine forests. The ifs of the situation clattered down on my head like big, ugly green walnuts from a tree. Always I had lived with ifs which grew into giant fears.

"And how do you watch the stars in the mountain cities of gold far south?" I asked the silent trader with the broken nose that night.

He nodded courteously and said, "In the land of the Golden Ruler, our kings and priests build our cities to reflect the meaning of the universe. The heavens, with their star beings and moon mother, are above." I nodded at him; it sounded similar to our lore.

"Below," he went on, "are the powers of darkness and the place where souls go. They eat flies and have no marriage or coupling, but otherwise this world is as ours." Well, that was certainly different. Flies!

The other man, the one who told jokes often, took up the story. "The city, with its temples and hills, is the umbilical cord of the world. It joins the heavens and the earth and the netherword. Its streets are plotted towards the cardinal points, the observation of shortest and longest sun day on the horizon and the rising of the day star and other large stars. You can see these risings from certain well designed doorways, from the tops of the buildings, from sightings of posts placed on hills."

"In the cities of the Maya, too," said the captain.

"The priests watch day and night, as their ancestors have for as many years as there are stars," the far southerner with the broken nose said. "They have charts and count the days of each year, marking it by the rising of stars and sun and moon. So they can tell the farmer folk when to plant and when to harvest."

"That was a large part of what the Sun and Star Watchers did where I came from," I said.

They both nodded politely. "Perhaps once, and it is convenient to start certain festivals by the priests' calculations and observations. But now—it is done to keep the caquique in power."

"Caquique?" I had heard the word in the traders' city. I think it was a word from the southern lands of the Father of Waters. I did not know precisely what it meant.

"The ruling family. The prince on the throne of the gods." Ah, I saw. They had Soft Fur down here too.

"How does that help?"

"Where are you from stranger? Do your kings not use the priests to keep them in power? Make the people grant obeisance because the gods of rain and thunder and even the sun speak through these priests to these kings?" I had to say they did.

"Well, and so it is here. The star beings, the sun and moon gods, and all the other thousand gods we know of, all work through the ruler. He plans temples to honor them, sets the buildings in his cities to watch their glory, tells the people to take time off from their own farming to carry stone for buildings. He orders women and children to walk through the countryside to see these gods, visit their shrines, set up stones to them, and the men to march and conquer in their names and make a monument to the conquering. It all works to give praise to the human ruler and the gods he represents."

"A thousand gods you say?"

"Well, more or less."

"And you say the people build these buildings? Tall as a mountain and made of stone?" Well, it should not be hard to believe. At Boulder Lake my ancestors had carried baskets of dirt to make a hill to see the Sun Lord get up on His Shortest Day.

"Yes, and the god roads in my land go off for miles. Every few risings of the sun all the folks are required to walk these roads to the shrine of worship or monument assigned to them by their district. It is a sight to see these roads, and some families mark them with colored stones. Our land is a spider's web of roads to the gods."

The jokester's voice was quiet in the night, but I could see a bitter smile on his face. It was the same look I saw on the faces of the society at Cahokia which was ready to say The Things That Are Not Said. "The more they break their backs to carry the stones, the higher the towers go. The higher the towers go, with fine inscriptions praising the ruler, the more the gods are impressed. The more the gods are impressed, the stronger grows the Golden Ruler. And the stronger the ruler grows, the more the other rich families in the land—or the ruler in the next town—wishes him dead or out."

"Ah, so it is that way in your land, too?"

But he was not finished. "The more the rich rivals wish the ruler dead, the more he must show his power, and so he calls the farmers and—tells them to break their back to build more towers."

All laughed, even the captain. "They are followers of the Southern Golden Ruler but they might be talking of the Mayan rulers," he said, moving to set the sail to catch a breeze just beginning to freshen.

That night the wind rose and by morning the sea was coming at us, not full in the face, but crosswise. "Wind change—I hadn't expected it," the captain murmured. "No telling how long it will blow this way, but it will shift—if we don't take on too much water." That, of course, was the problem. The sail took us forward like a cloud flying, but the waves crossed our prow and water sloshed in.

"Man the bailing pots," Ibix shouted. We took the water pots and all of us, the two far southerners, Ibix and Ghost and I bailed furiously, trying to keep the ship from swamping us. Night came on and still the wind blew. As stars blinked out in the West Arc, the hum began between the rigging ropes. It rose to a loud whistle that increased to a scream as the last Guiding Star vanished. Now, only the bashing of the waves across the bow gave a sense of direction for Ibix at the steering oar. That oar began to wave as if made of willow rather than Tall Oak. Quiet, or what seemed like quiet, was experienced only at the bottom of waves before the boat was slammed nearly over into the ever increasing waves and churning waters.

The canoe took on a course of her own, driven by wind and wave back towards the Rising Sun place. The baling pots were increasingly engaged in fighting back the ever rising water inside the boat only to be overcome regularly by the relentless power of wave and wind.

"Oh, Sun Lord," screamed the followers of the Golden Ruler.

"Ek Chuah," the Mayan captain shouted through the wind.

"Birds of Thunder, Ghost of the Lake, wherever you are, save us!" Ghost pleaded.

Captain Ten arose to try to shift the sail once more. Suddenly rain began full in our faces, and he fell off the canoe into a huge wave. Ibix tried to turn the canoe, but since we were in danger of instant swamping, righted it again. She held onto the sail, wailing into the night. I scanned the dark rain behind the canoe, but there was no sign of life.

Confusion followed, and all continued to call on their gods. But I, so often floundering in the midst of seven kinds of fears, in that time when fear was the only sensible feeling, grew cold and calm.

"I cannot move the sail and guide the canoe," Ibix cried. "I know only the navigation and am afraid—"

"We too are afraid."

"Will no one take the sail and steer?"—"Prepare to die—" confused cries sounded all around me. "Ek Chuah, Sun Lord, Bird of Thunder—."

A voice which sounded strangely like my uncle's boomed inside my brain. "These gods are useless and it is stupid to cry to them. Whoever the Maker of Stars is, he does not come down and scoop canoes up. God strengthens the arm of him who moves his own hand first."

"But I am nothing but a worthless Bear Belly," a weak little voice answered and then the booming voice said, "About that—and all things in this life—you can choose. Choose now to either die like a snake on his nose or like a man face the storm and death."

I knew it was right. I swung Ibix out of the way rudely and grasped the sail. Then I began giving orders to the others about what to throw overboard, how to bail and where to sit.

From that moment on I was many things, but I can tell you this true: I was never a fat and insignificant Bear Belly again.

Chapter 11

We came to the Land of the Great Cities of the South on the seventh day, as poor Captain Ten had told us we would. A fair, even breeze from the northeast brought us landward, with me steering and guiding the sail and a mournful Ibix giving the directions.

We arrived at an island, seeing from a long way out its towers, which were not tall but shone brightly in the hot sun. We took on water here, from a spring which bubbled in a deep round pit of yellow-white stone.

"This is the island of Exchel, the goddess of the moon and rainbow," Ibix said. "You can see her likeness there on the stone pillar." Sticking out of the ground near the spring was a pillar as tall as Ibix, and on it the likeness of a woman, sour-faced and hag-like, wearing many beads and a snake for a hat.

"She looks like she has indigestion," I said.

"Shame! To speak of the gods so," Ibix said, and turned to make an obeisance sign to the pillar. "She is only distracted—busy helping mothers in childbirth and controlling the sea."

Walking back to the beach, we saw only the edge of a teeming city which existed for worship and trade here on this island. Men of different dress, wearing exotic headdresses and bearers carrying wares of every sort from fruit to ornaments and salt crowded the roads. Along the sides there were shelters and booths and tents. Jugglers tossed fire into the air for amusement of others, and strange-looking trained animals lumbered about, responding to commands. By the side of a road were a few farmsteads, and in the yard of one I saw a woman letting a deer suck from her breasts, and other deer in a pen, and tall shelters with net over the openings for doves.

These were being blessed and sold by a merchant-looking priest with wild hair who stood in front of the woman's pens. "These are for those who wish animals to sacrifice," said Ibix. "The devout are willing to spend much to get their hearts' desires."

But there were also priestly looking merchants with equally wild hair sitting squat-legged by the side of the road shouting something that must have been, "Get your images of the gods here," for there were hundreds of god images in front of them on cotton sheets. And diviners screamed about "three kinds of incense for a fair price" under booths with cotton awnings to protect them from the sun.

But many traders had no touch of religion about them, but had come from the far reaches of the southern lands to make arrangements for new goods. Beautifully dressed in embroidered loincloths and capes, with fine jewelry all over their necks and arms, they shouted at each other and looked at strange pieces of bark that had bird tracks on them and counted out beads and cacao beans. These bark pieces were records, not spoken, but put down on the bark. "There is a type of wisdom here," Ibix said without smiling. "They have been everywhere and are very shrewd."

We put the jugs full of water on board and bade goodbye to the trading city. Over a hundred canoes were in that harbor, and we looked at them closely as we left. These were far more huge than ours, with sixteen men rowing on each side of the canoe, and passengers sitting in the middle, trying to cover themselves from the salt spray in these chopping waters. One or two of the long boats had little houses in the middle, with women and some children crawling all about.

"Some are trading ships that ply north and south, all along the coast and stop over here. Others take pilgrims each fair day to the shrine of Exchel. Each Mayan must make a pilgrimage once in his or her life."

"I think we are more comfortable in our boat," said one of the followers of the Golden Ruler. "They have no balance and keep tilting."

Then, sailing on for almost another day, we beheld a sight of awe: a huge temple building set on a cliff, with other buildings stretching on along the shore for a greater distance than even Cahokia, seen from the river.

"It is Zama," said Ibix and returned to brooding silence in the rear of the canoe. No help here—she was still too distressed by the loss of her husband, as well she might be.

"I shall go on shore, but not here, further on, so as not to alarm the city until I have scouted," I announced.

"They will have seen us and will surely send out a scouting party themselves, and I want to test their intentions."

"Hello, welcome, we are traders come in peace." I practiced the words in the new language I was learning. "Plom" was the word for merchant. I was not expecting a hostile welcome; Ibix had told me that the elaborately dressed, rich merchants we had seen with the bark books were typical of an entire class in the south, and thus had it been since ancient times. The Oldest Ones had built the wide roads for trade almost a thousand years ago; the grandfathers had kept them up so all could buy and sell. Among the Maya traders were honored almost above all else, given special stone houses, beautiful robes. Often they were fat and were called the "ones of possessions." Leave it to me to choose the fat person's trade.

I drew up my shoulders. Then I took out the largest bag of flints from the goods stored in the other long canoe. These would show our intent and draw immediate welcome for us.

"All stay here in the shallows. I will go to greet these native peoples." I told them with rather lofty authority.

Ibix shook her head. "Best to wait while the observers in that watch tower you saw have time to report to the ruler. He will have to consult the priests, offer the proper prayers and oblations, Name and arm a party. They will help us land the canoe in the narrow beach strip and—"

"Arm a party? No need for arms here. I come with the finest of flints and other goods. A `plom' knows no enemies." I looked at the flints in their leather over-the-shoulder case, patted the beautiful hidden pearls and other treasure I had strapped to my body.

Ghost pulled on my shirt. "The vision I had—danger!"

"I would have been afraid for that only a few days ago. But now—I know no fear. Drum-of-the-Gods comes!" The truth was I was absolutely bursting with pent-up energy. The rest were exhausted from the storm and dried out from having salt on their skins for so long, but for some reason I didn't feel that way. My sixteen-summers-old body and spirit craved action. Bring it on! Bear Belly no more, I can conquer! At least it will get me out of this god-cursed canoe with these lifeless elders.

Fearlessly the Drum went marching forward onto the unknown beach. Bare feet touched sand, then the sharp rocks of broken shells on the beach. Eyes sought the thickly wooded shoreline; ah! the rustle of leaves. The welcoming committee has come already—no. These people coming out—of—the—sticky, foul-smelling underbrush—have no clothing on except for serpent headdresses, and are in fierce warpaint. They carry sharp spears. They are rushing out—goodbye all.

So my thoughts went. True it was that my own pride and recklessness, inflated like a buffalo bladder, had led me into a trap. I had brought my trader's banner on a stick; ridiculously I waved it and shouted the few words I thought would apply. "Peace. I come in peace. See the 'pan'—flag? I plom, plom goods." Still they came on.

I was grabbed by grimacing men with headfeathers and masks of the feathered serpent. They yelled at me, pinning my arms in back of my shoulders. Someone else was coming out of the bushes; an older man robed in a crude fibrous garment covered with—reddish brown stains. His hair was long and clotted with—well, it was blood, and he carried a charcoal brazier made of clay.

He grabbed the leather pouches with the fine flints, looked at them with interest and set them on the ground. Then, without really looking at me, he sat down the coal brazier and began to toss herbs in it. From around his neck he took a long, woven and stuffed likeness of a serpent, which he sat next to the brazier.

He bowed and shouted at the idol (for that was what it seemed to be) and showed it an obsidian knife, sharp and excellent and larger than a man's hand. I groaned inside myself; I was beginning to get the idea. I was to be the offering to this snake, and that knife was going to cut my—what? Well, it could not be anything good.

There was at that moment a general shouting in the canoe, which was about forty strides offshore. My brave companions were protesting, really risking their own lives—or were they telling each other to paddle and get out of there. Anyway, thanks to that noise, there was an interruption in the snake sacrificing and the priest dispatched a party to the canoe. I could not see what was going on there because my back was turned, and I dare not move as one of the naked men puffed incense smoke in my face and others spat on my toes.

Commotion continued, however, and splashing out there and also near to us made me know someone was coming on shore. The priest, the men binding me, all of the savages around me suddenly left off what they were doing and went to their knees. Yelling something that sounded like "Perahotan," they prostrated themselves in the sand. I turned to see, to my astonishment Ghost, advancing out of the water and onto the beach, his hand waving in the air. Fool that he was, he had come to save or more likely to join me in death, but what was this? It was Ghost they were bowing to. Truly throwing themselves into the sand, for some reason, in front of my hunchbacked servant. Suddenly I knew that all this time in the south the folk must have been bowing to him when we stood together and they prostrated themselves. But *why* in the name of the great Bird of Thunder's tail?

Tribesman were advancing on shore, carrying our cargo, food, flints—all in their arms. They had emptied the canoe and were bringing it too—for themselves, ofcourse. Just behind them were the two followers of the Golden Ruler and Ibix, all wet, with her hair stringing down looking like a spirit of the deep. All were panting and near collapse. The naked savages who emerged from the water, too, put down their spears and sank to the ground.

The priest knelt at the feet of Ghost and lifted his hands in supplication.

Ghost did not even seem to notice these things, or if he did, they did not stop his single-minded denunciation of me. Servant or not, he had something he wanted to say to the blow-hard youth who had risked all of our lives.

He raised his hands and said, in a voice without a trace of hesitancy, "I told you the Lake Ghost's prophecy. He said a serpent would come out on the beach and swallow our canoe. Are you a stupid-head, anyway?" His voice rang over the beach, and

I shrugged. The savages began to moan, raising their arms like the priest in supplication.

"Atzala, Perahotan," they intoned. Ibix had crept up next to me.

"They—they must think he is Perahotan, the hunchbacked god. There is a prophecy that he will come in a canoe loaded with treasure. It is one of the myths of the simple country people."

Good fortune and many thanks, Whoever. "They think you are a god, one that is foretold," I said to Ghost out of the side of my mouth. "Tell them to free your friends. Best not suggest they give back the things—" They were already being carried up a trail into the woods.

Ghost stood like a stone statue, trying to understand. "I say they think you are a *GOD*. Act like one!" I ordered.

But before Ghost could act at all, the natives surrounded him, putting the weeds the priest carried on his head, then picking him up on their shoulders. The rest of us were ushered up the path in triumph—to where?

"To the city of Zama," Ibix murmured. Well, at least we weren't being roasted on the end of the cannibalistic toasting lances.

All around us thick, thick woods lined the path of our passage. Wild, bright yellow-and-red birds with long feathers started in front of us. Insects and butterflies swarmed everywhere. The path was water-logged. It had been made by bending down heavy grass and cane, and you could not see four feet into the cane breaks and clusters of trees and plants that grew without even a space of a handspan on either side of us. Behind the underbrush, though, were some of the tallest trees I had ever seen, cypress trees, tall as the sky, of the type from which our canoe had been made.

Soon, walking about thirty strides back from the beach, we began to see plots cut out of the undergrowth, with houses covered by thatched roofs and small fields cut back from the forest. The family plots increased in size; we climbed a little at a time until finally we entered an area of fields. The walled city was in sight, its white towers glistening in the sun.

The tribesman continued to carry Ghost on their shoulders, but as we neared the city, in file, his voice roared out. "I would walk into the town," he said. They sensed, more than understood, the meaning of his words and he humped along with dignity at the head of the parade.

The city spread out for many measures of land beyond the walled part, with many huts and fields clustered about it in a circular pattern. But the real city, where the people of note, I presumed, lived and conducted their affairs and worship and lives, was in three sections. On either side, like the wings of a bird, were smaller walled parts of the city. Public buildings of one or two stories, large and small, and many residence houses were in these "wings" of the city. The central city was behind a wall six feet tall, with a rampart on its top—a guard walk. Its central tower, which we had seen from the sea, was a marvel which rose higher than the mound at Cahokia, built layer on layer with window holes and pillars and a central plaza in front of it. Grouped around it in orderly fashion were the other buildings, some forty of them. Zama was a city which made a statement in stone to whoever saw it: "We are important." "Our ruling family is worth noting; beware of confrontation."

A drum beat started on the top of the wall, and warriors appeared, checking to see if we were hostile or friendly to the city. Each one had on an elaborate headdress: dragons, reptiles who smile, cats glared down at us. After some conversation with Ibix, the warrior captain, a man with a decorated loin cloth and boots of a jaguar cat, so Ibix said, opened the gate.

We entered Zama by means of the west wall, through a passage so narrow I could not have slipped through it in my days of fatness.

The walls! Will you believe me when I say they were three feet thick! Neatly put together, rock on rock and stuck together with lime rock paste, they ran all around the central part of the city. Never had I seen anything like it!

The naked country people accompanied us as far as the walls, and then with whoops and commotion departed, leaving us in the company of the captain of the guard and the soldiers, who had seen us approaching from the sea some while back. I think they did not send the people to get us but—well, it saved them the effort of going down to the beach where we landed.

Up a street we were ushered, all people bowing to their knees before Ghost. A priest stood at the steps of the huge temple we had seen from the sea, but he did not invite us to go up to the top. Apparently the tall hill served the same functions as the temple mount in Cahokia did—the nobility and priests and ruler only could observe religious and ceremonial functions up there, but few others could.

The priests did not bow, but gravely deferred to us. Ibix began to speak, followed by the Golden Ruler's travelers, telling in rather angry tones the story of our trip, the loss of Captain Ten and our seizure by the beach savages. At least I suppose that is what they were saying; I caught some words I could understand.

All the while the people, bowing to the ground, were murmuring and pointing at the light-skinned hunchback who had come leading a procession into town. "Perahotan, Perahotan," they murmured with awe.

Finally the priest pointed to Ghost, bowing his head and addressing him with some sort of invocation. Ghost looked sideways at me, wondering what to do. "Nod your head, slowly," I said in our language.

Ibix returned to stand by my side. Just at that moment the heavens opened, and rain began to fall straight down. It had done that once or twice out in the canoe, huge drops falling without any slant at all. The crowd went aside to stand under huge trees just off the road; the priests and functionaries retired under some tall stone supports in a temple there at the foot of the hill. Ghost and I, Ibix and the southern travellers just stood there, glad to be getting a warm shower to wash the salt water off our cracking skins.

As suddenly as it started, the rain stopped, and people came out, picking their way over puddles, to bow again before us. Ibix spoke to me, while the priests and old men of the town were reassembling. "This is not my home town, but it is near enough for them to know my family name. I will ask for shelter for us for a while. They will decide if they wish you to trade—whatever you have left."

"Only what is on my body," I said, sadly. So much had been taken away by the wild men, my beautiful flints, carried all the way from the Beautiful River. Well, as Uncle had used to say, "It's only flint."

"Who are these men behind the priest?" I asked Ibix. There was a group of ten men with almost clean white cotton jackets and short skirts. Their very elaborate loin cloths were centered by a piece of cotton which reached below their knees. Most were old; a couple were in their middle years and the one who had acted as captain of the guard, who now stood with a hurling spear in his hand, was only a few years older than I. The hair on all of these noblemen was long, not short as the common people's, and it was tied up with ribbons and tucked into headdresses.

"These are the batab—they are in charge of the eight districts of the town. No doubt the guard called them in from the outskirts of the town. The many homes outside the walls all are ruled by noble family heads, who report to the ruler."

"And where is he?"

"I do not know him, so I cannot tell you where he might be. But we are perhaps not important enough for him to welcome us," Ibix answered.

The priest was again addressing Ghost. He delivered a reverential, but cautious-sounding speech in which the word Perahotan was often heard.

"He wants to know what you wish," Ibix said.

"Tell him food. Even divine beings need—fried flat corn cakes. Stew. Roasted meats. Fruits. Quickly." I snapped my fingers. Ghost repeated the requests and Ibex translated for the priests and assembled lords of the districts. Commands were given, and I could hear a clatter and soon begin to smell meat smells drifting down from a house about halfway up the way towards the guardhouse on the sea. My mouth began to water. I might not have been a Bear Belly anymore, either in body or spirit, but my stomach was only sixteen summers old, and it had many needs right then.

We stood, feeling a little odd, for no one seemed inclined to move. The people still stared and pointed, the priests conferred with the lords of the districts. Ibix had been called over; she was telling them that three of us, I and the two far southern traders wished to set up as trading plom with the city marketplace. As for the one the people called Perahotan, she could not presume to speak for him.

As the council was deliberating, I looked around the town, at the white, sun-bleached buildings, the tall, stone-set steps which led up to the magnificent temple and fortress structure at the top of the hill. The city was so clean! I had never seen anything like it. A street sweeper, who wore a feather mask which almost covered his face, too, was busily picking up a few fruit rinds and the bird feathers and leaves that had been knocked down by the storm. Not a twig eluded him! What methodical people these must be. And how organized and dedicated to ritual, that even the street sweeper would wear a headdress.

The batab captain of the guard with the smiling reptile helmet returned and spoke to us. This was the last day of a special five-day feast time—the feast of Xul, the god of the Sixth Month.

The people, rich and poor, had come in to be purged of their impurities and have their god images blessed. True enough, there were great banners on the top of the temple and clowns tumbling about. A huge ritual fire stood in the center of the plaza.

Perahotan and his friends would be guests of honor at this final feast; in the meantime, we could drink water and refresh ourselves in the flowing well at the bottom of a stone cistern, the place they bathed and drew water. I rubbed my hands. Bath and then food! Thank you Whoever you are out here—let's see—I glanced at the temples, and as we walked to the cenote, as they called their sunken wells—well, there were enough of these gods, and all dancing and glowering. I would make their acquaintance later.

It was exactly He Is Setting when the feast began. All of us, the far-southern traders, Ibix, Ghost and I were ushered in honor to the central plaza, where we sat on large rocks around a huge firepit and ate our fill. In my case this took quite a while. Afterwards, we were shown special dances, in which men with long, plumed headdresses leapt to the drums, imitating the bright, colored birds. The drum they used was a marvel indeed. It was called a tunkel, someone said, and was beaten with sticks which had the most amazing resonance. I craned my neck to see the drumsticks. There was a soft, pliable substance around the end of the sticks—not doeskin.

"Rubber. Ooze from a tree. It will bounce," Ibix told us. She whispered that she wished as soon as possible to ex- cuse herself to go to the women's sleeping quarters. She was thoroughly done for. I begged her to stay just a little longer.

I listened to the beat of the tunkel, watched the dancers leaping over the fires. So! Large drums were not unknown to these civilized people, were indeed valued. My thoughts strayed for a brief moment to the woods, near the herd of moose, where I and the nephew of the Dune Devils had made the queen of all drums. The vision drum! Ah, and that nephew was related to my Loon Feather, so that was another reason the drum was sacred to gods and men.

Ghost seemed to be enjoying his role as the head of the feast, being given the select pieces of turkey and deer, the top guavas (as they called them) and juicy yellow fruits with many seeds on the pottery tray brought over by a lovely servant girl.

I could not help but notice the beauty of the women, pledged though I was back at Cahokia. The heads of the noble clanswomen, like the heads of the men, were flattened severely, but it only seemed to heighten the elegance of their features. Many had huge eyes like does, and beautiful hair, plaited and wrapped around the head, adorned with ribbons and bird feathers. These people spent enough time on their appearance! The men carried obsidian mirrors with them, tied to their headdresses, and looked into them to be sure all the hairs were in place. And the women did not smell, as ours did in the villages of the woods. I could sniff, instead,

263

perfumed scents of the body, as I later found out, an orange-colored unguent they had anointed their upper bodies with.

The huge ritual fire, built in the middle of the plaza as the shadows deepened, blazed high. Finally it was indicated that we should stand to face the priests and district chieftains in front of it. Incense balls were sprinkled; the priests bowed towards the four directions.

Something was obviously expected of us. "Give our thanks," I said to Ibix. "Tell them we wish to remain to return service for their gracious hospitality by opening new trade channels to the north and south."

"No," she whispered, "you must deliver these words yourself. And before you do, touch the earth with stiff arms. Then put some dirt on your forehead and stand erect again. That is the custom here." I did so, though my muscles were mightily stiff from the bouncing in the canoe. I stumbled through the phrases I knew.

Words were exchanged between Ibix and the priest. Then, at a signal, the people crowded in, ready to eat of a special feast that had been prepared for them too. They took pieces of food in their hands; behind them the street sweeper picked up orange rinds and small bones they dropped and put them in a large pot he carried.

Then all heads turned towards Ghost. The priest was again addressing him. "He says that there is more than one hunchback in the world," said Ibix. "Even though his skin is light and he looks like the dwarf on the walls"—here she gestured towards the stone temple in back of us, with a carving of a hunchback dancing beside a god tumbling to earth—"these priests want a sign. They say their ruler will want to be sure this is a messenger from the gods and you are true people."

"And where is their ruler?" I asked.

She spoke for a moment to the young spear-bearing district lord and said to us, "The lord regrets that the Ruler of the city is not here to meet you. His name is Smoke Fox-god Three. He is away on business to another city.

The people began to chant again, "Perahotan, Perahotan," Ghost looked stonily out at them.

Then, after another few words, Ibix spoke the priest's words. "Tell the one the people call Perahotan to produce a sign from the heavens."

But Ghost did not need me to tell him anything. Astonishingly, he stepped forward. "Attend me, oh people. Your R-R-Ruler Smoke Fox-god Three is here among us. He has not gone to another city. He is here in d-d-disguise, observing us." This strange thing he said in our language. Then, using the language of the city, he said, "Your ruler is right here. Smoke Fox-god is" —he pointed at the street sweeper.

I thought Ghost had finally lost his mind. Ibix and my friends the other traders shook their heads in puzzlement—but the people cheered uproariously. It was true! In some way they knew it—had known all along—the ruler's custom to find out about strangers.

The street sweeper came forward and stood looking divinely dignified while the young lord and a priest took off his feather mask and wrapped about him the cloak of power, made of thousands of parrot feathers, re-affixed the huge headdress that marked him as a prince, and gave him a scepter with the head of a dragon on each end.

Still, his face was not unpleasant. I watched him, and, in an unguarded moment, I thought I saw him studying me too. Then he was gone, saying he would interview us on the morrow.

We were escorted to the lodgings reserved for noble guests. These, too, were in one of the fine mansions made of stone near the central plaza. Over twenty separate lodgings had been made with walls between each and courtyards curving towards the sea in this fine building, and there were beautifully-woven hanging beds (one of the most popular kinds used in this climate), fine cotton bed coverings and a table with fruit and sweets and chocolate placed for each of us.

It was well after He Is Halfway Through the Night and the torches of the town lit the noblemen and common people to their houses. A troop of merry-makers was carrying the banners from the temple to the home of the lord who had sponsored the feast of Xul. The lights of all the torches, winding down the hills into the districts which surrounded the town, looked like the flickering of fireflies, and for a moment I thought of long evenings in the summer at home, when we children played cousin-clan games, catching the fireflies in our fists in the middle of the trees by the beautiful lake. Then, the "perhaps" pageant flashed its scene: White Wings now at the foot of the temple mound, her litter being lowered to the ground, my lovely Loon Feather taking her by the hand as they approached the steps.. "Begone," I said to the picture in my mind, and as I turned about I caught the smell of incredibly sweet flowers drifting on the night air.

Ghost had come out of his dwelling room and was standing looking at the stars. "What in the world made you say that about the ruler?" I asked.

"The rain. I saw him through the rain. And his face came to me."

"But you spoke it in their language? How could you do that?"

Ghost looked up at me with dignity and a little anger.

"You think I am a s-s-stupid head? I can learn words as well as you."

"Well, and so you can," I said, looking at him with new respect through the dim light in the courtyard. "And that is good, because you will have to be anything but a stupid head if you are going to play the part of a god."

Are you falling asleep? Several nights we have been telling this story, and on this night it grows late. Well, wake up, because I must tell you about the marvel of the royal residence. It was the second best building in that town—set on its own small hill near the north wall of the city. It was grand indeed, with the support stands—they called them pillars—built of sand and lime and water all mixed together with small stone, all across its front. There was a lower level where children and women lived in luxury and comfort and above a business throne room for the Ruler alone.

The throne itself was a reclining jaguar cat carved, beautifully, from stone with its back flattened out for the Ruler to sit on. In another corner of the room were likenesses of several of their many gods on sculptured pillars, stands for servants who stood by always with the chocolate and all sorts of other refreshments, cages for the royal pets—spotted jaguars and a sort of raccoon with a long snout, and chests for riches and tribute when it arrived. To the left of the door opening, which was never closed with a wooden door at any time, stood a desk for a scribe drawing records of life at the court.

This will be hardest of all for you to understand, because you have seen nothing like it. Our northern people decorate pots with symbols of our sacred or feared animals and sometimes the spirits, but these folk in the South can tell their language with a stick, drawing pictures which stand for the words themselves. Thus, if they wish to send a message, they can send the little pictures and people know what they mean.

There are two ways of making the words. The first way is a direct representation of the thing. For instance, if the ruler Smoke Fox-god Three wishes to tell of his conquests or his lineage, he has the scribe put it into pictures with a stick. These pictures, which can show him receiving his stick of power from his father or a god, show him wearing a cat hat and killing a cat on a hunt, show him conquering enemies in far-off cities, these can be put on one of their pillars by carving on their walls by painting. These writing pictures can also go onto little pieces of hard bark sewed together so they fold out. Every time one of their nobles wishes to see the lineage of Smoke Fox-god, he can open up the little folded packet of bark and see the pictures which tell the story. Is that not wonderful?

But the second way of doing this remembering with the scribe stick is symbolic. Just as we say that the great eye on the amulet is the all-seeing eye of the Sun as God of justice, so they have a hundred, no, a thousand different symbols. Some are symbols of gods, actions, sacred animals. These are rendered in the most admirable and complicated ways, with circles and eyes inside the circles, and curling serpent curves and dots and lines to represent numbers—they all know exactly what they mean by all these wavy, intricate lines.

But sometimes the line pictures are symbols of words themselves! So they can say the word "fish" with a picture, and everyone who sees the fish can take it for either a fish or for the first sound of that word. Put two of these sound words together and you may even have a new word in the scribe writing, one that doesn't have anything to do with the picture.

But what I saw in that throne room that was most wonderful of all was the series of pictures on the back wall. In brightest colors these showed the history of the rulers of this city. There they were, with their wonderful feathered head-dresses and spotted cat skirts and war clubs, with enemies at their feet, and priests offering sacrifice and incense burning and royal animals—all on the back wall as large as life and almost as real. Just as I was studying all in this wonderful room, there was the sound of a drum and rattle and flute, and the ruler's attendents came in.

The musicians stood outside beating their drums and making their "attention" sounds and the others filed past them. A fan bearer headed the procession with a huge feather fan to rid the place of insects, and another servant, a mat-bearer, carried a royal stand for the Ruler to place his feet on. Then came the priest chanting and scattering the incense of the gods on the brazier fire in the corner. At last, came the Ruler I had seen last night, but now cleaned and combed, with ear spools in place and headdress flopping.

I went to my knees; he gestured me further down—to my nose.

He began trying to talk to me in the language of the place, but I found that I could understand only every third word.

"Can we have the woman Ibix?" I asked the priest, and finally he understood and had her summoned. She was ready to return to her family in a city down the coast and begin her formal mourning for her husband, but she was willing to stay this last morning to help me.

He dealt first of all with the rest of my party. The two far southerners were to leave at He Is Halfway Home. They would make their way down the coast in a trading canoe with some traders from this city, and they could introduce themselves and their line of trading goods to all.

The honorable Perahotan would be allowed the best room in the guest mansion in preparation for whatever honors the ruler should later decide. As for me—there was some heated and lengthy discussion between Ibix and the Ruler. I gathered that he did not particularly like me. The gist of the conversation was that it was stupid and senseless to come to a place to trade and not know the spoken tongue smoothly. It showed I would be a miserable trader. I was to stay and learn, really learn, the language—as hard as I could—for three weeks. A teacher would be provided. If at the end of that time, I knew it, I would be retained as a slave. If not, I would be sacrificed the next time they needed a message delivered to one of the gods. Did I understand? He looked at me impassively.

I rose from my nose and nodded vigorously.

Never did teacher provide such an incentive to student for learning.

At the end of my time, taught by the absolutely ancient scribe I had seen in the corner, who, luckily, was willing to try to save me, I could speak well enough to converse, and I was summoned before the Ruler to speak to him in my own voice. In my own apartment before I went, I looked at myself sternly in the obsidian mirror.

"You are not a bear belly any more. You are courageous, the man who shouted scorn at the storm, who took control of the sail on the canoe—" I told myself. My legs were weak, though, and my stomach was in knots. It was not only the notion that I might soon be the message bearer to one of these reptile-faced, serpent-haired, glowering gods on the pillars. It was also that my gut was wrenching, had been for the last two weeks. The odd foods which I had been more or less ravenously devouring were sending me to the woods about once every five minutes.

There he was, though, on the jaguar throne in the corner of the room. He was alone, the usual guards and ancient scribe and priest being out somewhere. Seeing him there, with all his power and pomp did not make me cower. I bowed, but I rose up to my full height, which was rather impressive in this land of small men.

I do not know whether it was the three weeks of learning the language like a whirlwind so that I couldn't think of another thing during the day or even when I slept, or whether it was the gut-wrenching that made me feel out of sorts, but the truth was I was more irritated than anything else. Underneath the mask of a jaguar cat he wore on his forehead, his face showed him to be about my age. He even had youth bumps on his cheeks. Pimples. I looked at him there and wished I had him in the camps of old Bright-Coals-in-the-River of the Dune Devils, on a stake. Let old Firecoals grab his man's stones for a while and twist. And then— but no. I must report.

"I am here, oh Great One, to speak to you. I will try my best, but I beg your patience." I had practiced that speech a lot.

"Well. So you wish to stay here."

"Yes. I have brought you this necklace with the greetings of the ruler of the north. She offers you her greeting and—"

He took the fine copper necklace Soft Fur had sent and placed it around his neck, then said, rather icily, "She?"

"Yes. The Female Sun of Cahokia City."

"I have not heard of it. But ruled by a woman—it cannot be more than a wart on the tit of the Earth Mother." At least that's what I think he said; he did gesture to bring the message home.

I said nothing, simply looked at the fine necklace. "I had other things, but the savages took them," I said as he unclasped it and laid it on his treasure chest.

"We do not have savages here. It is improper to call our native people savage."

"I am profoundly sorry, Great One. They had no clothes, ran out with spears, stole my things and were going to kill and eat me, so—"

"Silence! You are impertinent. How many summers do you have?"

"Sixteen." There was silence. "And, oh Great One, is it impertinent to ask how many you have seen?"

"It is impertinent. Your answer should be one thing to all questions. 'Whatever your wish, I stand ready to fulfill it, oh Lord of the city.' Did you learn that with the scribe?"

I repeated the statement, and felt sure no scorn at all had crept into my voice.

He was silent for a while, staring at me, then said, "What is your name?"

"Since my last naming I am called, 'Drum-of-the-Gods.'"

"I will call you tunkel, since your words resound like a thumping drum."

"Tunkel, tunkel," I smiled, trying to be pleased.

"Your hunchback is not Perahotan."

"No. If you were misled, it was because the savages–native peoples–ran out and worshipped him. We never intended they should think him divine."

"We may have a purpose for him, and I will not disabuse the people about his status as a god. I must say, though, that it takes a good deal to maintain a god here on earth. He has been eating all the honey cakes and fried fish the women can fix."

"Well, and I hope he has not had the same trouble I have had with them. I request, beg, plead to be excused for a moment—" I dashed from the room and to the outbuilding, returning as soon as I could, white-faced.

"How dare you leave my presence without permission?"

I fell again to my face, then remembered to pick up dust and put it on my forehead. "Whatever your wish, I stand ready to fulfill it, oh Lord of the city. But I cannot fulfill anything, when my bowels are as water, and I did not think—"

"Silence! How dare you discuss your bowels in my royal presence? I should call the guards." But instead of doing that, he

271

stopped and stared at me again. Then he began to laugh. He laughed at me, slapped his knee, laughed some more. Then I began to laugh.

"You will be a strange but refreshing slave. Something like a dip in the cenote. I have not done it since I was young, since it would cause undue commotion among the people who would be drawing water. Some eighteen years now." So, he was willing to answer my question.

"Whatever your wish, I stand ready to fulfill it, Oh Lord of the city. Do you wish me to carry you on a litter to the cenote for a dip? You could wear your feather mask again and go in the form of the street sweeper."

And then I smiled directly into his eyes. He looked at me, wondering. Perhaps my smile seemed to say what I felt: "You had better kill me now if you want someone to eat dirt. I am the son of a SunWatcher and the nephew of the Grand Shaman. My knees and voice may do you obeisance, but my heart bends for no man on this earth. And I will see about your gods."

That evening, just before He is Setting, Smoke-Fox-god (he had told me to drop the "Three" which was ceremonial) allowed me to observe the nightly Divestment of Power ceremony. One of these happened each morning and each evening, with the noble batab giving to him the carved power sticks they had received that morning to supervise each of the regions around the city.

Last to enter the room was Imi Ex Loc, the tall, calm young man who had spoken to us when we entered the village. His shoulder cape was decorated with flowers and trees in gold-colored thread; his sandals and long, elaborate loincloth were capped with the black fur of some creature.

The scepter stick he received from Smoke-Fox god was thicker than those of the other nobles, made of some very hard, very dark wood, carved with a square design I took to be a family crest. It did not have the two animal heads at either end; that was reserved for the top rulers.

"This tall slave is of a noble family in the far northlands of the Longest River North," the Ruler announced. "He shows some intelligence, and I have decided to make him tupil to manage my household for a while. It will amuse me and we may learn the customs of the north from him."

The nobles nodded assent, and one lord, who always smiled with his mouth open, came forward and clapped me on the back. All seemed accepting except Imi Ex Loc, who only stared ahead.

"The steward of the royal house will teach him to handle numbers and read," the Ruler went on. "His teacher in matters of lore will be Imi Ex Loc, my cousin, who knows well the lore of the Maya." Finally the smooth lord nodded, giving assent. I wished I felt as accepting of the situation as he; I did not like the rivalry I felt among all these lords.

"One thing more. He says that the hunchback does not claim to be Perahotan. This marked one does seem to have miraculous powers, however, and can read the signs from heaven. All our tradition teaches such hunchbacked ones are marked for special favor from the gods, and so we shall treat him with regard and special favor. But you are not to think of him as a god."

I was glad the Ruler said that; best to get that straight with the commanding nobles. But whatever the common people thought, he could not, and did not seem to be trying to command.

Then, as commander of the army, he went to watch the changing of the guard for night watch on the walls, with the thick-bodied captain of the guard and his troops. I did not attend that ceremony, but watched torches being lit along the walls and saw Honacan, the captain being borne in majesty on a litter home to the special stone house the state maintained for him, almost like a god.

Smoke Fox-god Three did take a liking to me, there was no doubt about that. He insisted that I move into the house with him while I was fulfilling the duties of the "tupil," or steward for a while. The old tupil, a man of middle years and knock-knees, head of one of the noble families, seemed not to feel displaced by the upstart visitor. He offered to surrender the precious household writing stored in the bark books.

"Please help me, Ah Chok," I pleaded. "It has been hard enough for me to learn to speak a little. I cannot write yet. If you will just show me—please, won't you, stay here to help?"

He nodded graciously, and took me out to the storage room for the Ruler's house, where stone shelves were built to hold pots of honey, spices in jars, bags of precious chocolate, corn by the bagful.

"These are the necessities for the Ruler's household. He has no dependents—except for you, now—so you are ordering for his own needs, and the special feasts that he plans for our batab and outside visitors."

"Has he been married?"

The steward seemed offended. "He will not marry until he is twenty. And he has had no children as yet."

Of course not, I thought, since—well, maybe their custom is different. It would be unthinkable to have illegitimate children in the woods, but here there was, as at Cahokia, a nunnery of beauteous virgins.

I asked to look at one of the bark books he carried and pointed at the writing out of curiosity.

"Here," he said, showing me, "this is the sign for rabbits, here the sign for honey, this for fowls and these are the kinds of fish he prefers." He explained the sign pictures, which did make sense.

"I do not know if I can ever use the sign pictures. They are so foreign to what I know."

"You do not need to know the complicated ones." Here he pulled out a long, folded book of the writings. My eyes blurred as he showed me the tiny squares, dots, curly lines and glaring faces which made up line after line. "This the priests use. They have given it to me to repair."

"What is it about?"

"It tells of our time, from the earliest birth of the gods thousands of summers ago, and shows the priest when it is propitious to do important things."

"How many daily passages of the sun for a full circle around the sky?"

"Well, it is not a full circle for us. Twenty suns or kins, is the sacred moon cycle, the month, called in our language a uinal. Eighteen of these moon cycles is one tun, or year. We do not do anything without consulting the priests' books. Time is figured in what is called a katun—twenty tun or summers. A katun is our main sacred cycle. Some of the katun cycles are bad and they recur—other times would be good to make a trading trip or get married, for instance. In the books is also the history of gods, festivals and rituals, and they help the priests bring good fortune to us. The star, sun, and moon gods and their trips at the specific moment are also part of the consideration."

"But your steward's book is about meat and drink and bread."

"Yes. Man does not live by holy books alone."

"A good saying. Now tell me how many I order each sun, from whom and so forth."

He did, all that morning, finishing his instructions by telling me that all was delivered through the gates by porters who bore the loads of goods on their backs.

"Who are these porters?" I wanted to know.

"Slaves, captured in our conquests, or sentenced by the judges to serve out punishment—for stealing, murder and so forth."

"And they can carry so much corn and cotton cloth on their backs?"

"With a strap around their heads. After much experience, some can carry a man. But if the loads are too heavy, they pull them down the path with large ropes."

"Perhaps that is the way they brought the stones for these buildings and monuments?"

"They rolled them with logs—" he stopped and looked at me impatiently. "You ask too many questions. The scribe who taught you the language told me that. I must say you are picking it up quickly. But I have other things to do. It is time for the great lord to begin your tutoring in matters of state and religion."

I wanted to know what the other things he had to do were, but I had a good idea anyway. I had been nosing around like a dog who wishes to scout a rival's territory. These batab, all eight of them, took the priests around to tell the farmers when the calendar book said it was time to plant corn, when to harvest it. This was their sixth month; in four more they would plant corn. The batab helped to allocate the land to each farmer on the basis of the size of his family. There was a plot for each child or older person in the family, with enough to allow him to let a field lie fallow. It was not really very different from the system at Cahokia, just much larger and more organized.

Then the batab collected tribute—the chief collector being the lord who smiled all the time—and probably were hated as thoroughly as the lords at Cahokia. They came when every winter was new and collected the assigned tax gifts, to pay both Smoke Fox-god and his lord, the great chieftain of the land at the city of Chichen Itza. So said Ah Chok, the steward. I thought of corn in baskets, cotton cloth woven on hand looms by the women of the houses, pottery—

Here my thoughts stopped, at the word pottery, and the unpredictable "perhaps" pageant spun itself out again for a moment. Now Loon Feather, turning to gaze one last time at her friends from the Village of river-clay potters, walked with proper reverence sideways up the steps of Cahokia's temple hill, holding the small one by the hand. The crowd below was stone still as the prince came out of the temple—

"Lord Imi Ex Loc is here." The steward Ah Chok bowed out. I could see a figure in the doorway, and went to get my lesson in lore of the city.

"I shall explain the gods to you," he said, in a cool voice. "The hunchback may come also."

"His name is—Ghost." But I used the name for "spirit" in their tongue, to connect him with the gods. Why was I so perverse all the time? I was probably getting my strength back a bit; this was the first day in two weeks my stomach was settled.

We stopped off at the noble visitors' palace and picked up Ghost, who was eating a piece of the soft, strong-smelling yellow fruit with the many odd seeds he had come to love. He silently trailed after us. I watched Imi Ex Loc as we walked to the Temple of the Descending God, across the street from the palace. If he found herding two foreigners around a demeaning experience, he did not show it. No one would mistake him for a Mayan farmer, even if he did not have the sharply sloping forehead all the rich men cultivated. His face was as handsome as a woman's, and his skin was oiled, even perfumed with a smell I was told came from the bean of an orchid—vanilla it was called, and they used it in cooking, too. I was intensely curious about him, because Smoke Fox-god seemed to feel anxiety about this batab, to be tense when his name was mentioned. Surely they were rivals for power in some way.

"For the first time you will climb the steps to the high temple hill," he said. "No one may come here but priests, the ruler and those of noble birth. It is a singular honor that you may come. We go to the east side of the temple where a small opening leads to a cave-like door set inside the walls. Move sideways up the steps; they are narrow. In that way you will not face the god who stands guard in the inner temple."

After stepping sideways along the narrow steps, pulling one foot after another, we finally stood before a pillared temple of two parts, one of which was a sort of porch and the other a worship area.

There were three entrances, formed of pillars in the shape of snakes, tails over the doors and heads at the bottom. Inside the worship room was a standing figure, a man-god with a face like a lizard's.

"There before us is our mighty god, Lord of All creation, Itzamna." Even outside of the temple, where we stayed quite a long time, we had to bow to the ground.

In the corner was another representation of the god, with serpent helmet on. His arms and legs were outspread, and he seemed to be upside down.

"He looks like he is falling," said Ghost.

"A god can never really fall, especially the one god," Ex Loc said sharply. "Itzamna has many faces, many jobs, just as each Mayan does. And he is Lord of the Day, and Sun Lord."

Sun Lord again. I thought I had left him behind.

"As the sun, naturally he does sink in the west, but it is only to rise in more glory."

"Of course." We entered the gloomy interior, Ghost hobbling along behind. In the corner was a real woman, beautiful in a light blue cotton garment, with coiling serpent earpieces. She stood beside a brazier in which incense was burning. Ex Loc showed Ghost and me how to do obeisance to the god on one knee, with arms folded across the chest and fingers of the right hand pointing upward. Then we left to go down a back stairs.

"There is no need to go down the sea stairs sideways," said Ex Loc. "You do not face the god here."

"The women are beautiful," Ghost said with a little longing. My poor friend! Women were completely unattainable to him back home, of course. Even the servants would not go near a hunchback.

"The pledged virgins tend the sacred fires. They live in the nunnery, giving themselves to a life of sacrifice and chastity— except for ritual coupling."

We had reached the bottom of the staircase, and I looked up at the grandeur of the temple against a bright blue sky. I was struck by its beauty, its balanced order. But Ghost was continuing the discussion about the women. "Who do they c-c-couple with?" he asked.

"The high priest and the Ruler only," Ex Loc answered. "Our lord does not couple as yet, since he has not reached the age of majority."

I thought of the prince back at Cahokia, probably coupling by now morning, noon and night with the nuns he had put in his nunnery.

We crossed the street and reached another temple, near the cenote. It was a shrine to Exchel, the goddess of the moon and rainbow who was worshipped on the first island we had visited. Inside was another lovely girl, this one almost a child.

"Are they not astonishing?" the prince asked me, his words drawn out like a string of honey.

"Yes, I suppose so. It was my friend who spoke of them. I had not noticed." It was a lie. Quite the opposite really. Today, for the first time, I had begun to be troubled about women. It seemed as if every twenty breaths or so, truly, I thought of women's forms, of the softness of their skins, of private areas—even of the nights on the furs up the hill at Cahokia. On the whole trip, up till now, I had been a strong man of the woodland tradition—well, more truthfully I had been busy, distracted and exhausted by a trip down a long river and a journey across the sea. But now, with leisure—but I was determined in this matter. I was pledged, and I had taken a vow of purity when I renounced Soft Fur and fell in love with Loon Feather. I needed all the help with the powers—Whoever—I could get, and I was not going to spoil it with decadent dallying. I had had enough of that. My spirit was determined—but my body didn't understand what that meant. It kept crying out.

"There are temples to many of the gods. We are a devout people," said Ex Loc. We walked around, up streets and hills to the temples of Yum Cimil, the death deity, who was ugly and disturbing, with a skull for a head, and a bloated, rotting body with bare ribs. He wore bells on the collar around his neck, and Ex Loc told me that some cities threw sacrifice victims into the death pools with bells so this death god would hear their approach.

The building at the far north, on the rise above the sea, was reached by a stone stairway. Ex Loc insisted that our tour must include this particular shrine.

"This god you must learn to adore most of all," Ex Loc said, with a slightly scornful smile. "Ek Chuah is the merchant deity. He helps the fat ones who trade in merchandise." In his shrine, again supplied with a virgin and incense brazier, was an effigy of a rotund god with a large, drooping underlip sitting on a stand.

"He is painted black," I said.

"Black like a trader's heart."

I ignored that. "What does the sign picture mean?"

279

"It is the sign of the north star, which must guide the merchant on his voyages. "Only one more," Ex Loc told us.

"G-g-good," said Ghost. "I want to return to the rooms. They are bringing the corn drink and fruit soon into the garden, and I am t-t-tiring."

A crowd of common people in the city to bring in their tribute had begun to follow us about. They had sat down their cloth and wooden benches and bows and arrows—whatever they had made for the king-god—on the ground and were hovering about Ghost. Again, we could hear the word "Perahotan," being said, reverently it seemed to me.

Now, on the street which led to the temple hill, we stood before another magnificent temple—finer than even Itzamna's. I had walked by it several times now in the training weeks I just finished, but I knew nothing about its meaning. An inner sanctuary held the worship shrine, but it was the colored pictures on the wall, painted right over the plastering cement, that fascinated me.

"Two gods are worshipped here," Ex Loc said, "and they are not jealous of the other, for they are brothers, and their other brother is Itzamna the Great One. The god Chac, the god of rain, is shown here." He pointed to a painting of a man-god, with many square and circle designs around him, with the face of a reptile and a long snout and fangs. Another reptile god stood near him.

Ex Loc pointed to a painted figure on a jaguar throne, "Bolon Tzacab, the special patron deity of the ruling house. It is here that the ruler Smoke Fox-god Three worships."

"But look—this decorated plaster picture strip is different from the others. It has what seem to be men portrayed."

"Yes. This is a history of the line of Smoke Fox-god, which happens to be mine, also." Oh? A cousin of the Ruler.

Out of the corner of my eye I could see Ghost drifting up the street towards the refreshments and coolness of the visitors' mansion. I walked closer to the story-telling strip.

"How—what is this?" I traced the drawing with my finger. "It seems as if there are two human men, joined with a snake—or is it the cord in the womb?"

Ex Loc seemed reluctant to answer. His eyes grew distant, as if considering.

"First you see the founder of the line in recent times, Imi Oxlahun. He sits on the jaguar throne, a great and respected leader. So the symbols say. Next to him are pictures of his reign—there are the conquered in a neighboring city. You see them naked, cowering." Yes. There was a head on the ground, and some of the captives were kneeling, begging for mercy. "But then—in the next square—directly beside the scene of Imi Oxlahun you see the two men entwined," he went on."

"Who are they?"

"The legal wife of Imi Oxlahun bore him twins. One as like to another as the morning and evening stars."

I turned from the paintings to look at him. "What happened then? The gods have decreed here that—the son will rule, have they not?"

"Yes, and of course there were two." He pointed at a square of picture-writing. "This says that the god Bolon Tzacab took up the scepter of justice and decided that the oldest should rule. And since Smoke I had leapt from the womb some ten breaths before his brother Smoke II, he it was that was chosen to rule. It was the god's choice, so says the symbol writing."

I ran my finger over the symbol he was pointing to. "This seems new, almost soft. And this drawing, painted, of the two men with the womb cord. Are they new?"

Ex Loc turned from the paintings. "They were done during the last moon. Others were erased and these put in."

I tried to come around to face him. Questions filled my mind like nuts in a basket. "But—couldn't the young men have ruled together? Was it fair to say a few breaths of time would make the difference when both were born on the same day? What if the younger were the better ruler?"

Ex Loc finally faced me. His face was as cold as the death god's likeness I had seen on the temple earlier. "The god so decreed. So says the symbol drawing." His finger tapped it decisively.

"Who put the new drawing and symbol writing up?" I persisted.

281

Ex Loc began walking away from the temple. "That is not for me to answer. Let us return to your rooms."

We did not get all the way back to the palace. In the street before it, a crowd of serving people, porters, and others of the commoners who had business in Zama had surrounded Ghost and hoisted him to their shoulders. "Perahotan to the nunnery," they were chanting. I tried to shoulder my way through the crowd, but Ex Loc put a restraining hand on my arm.

"Let them have their way. It is best not to incite them."

But I asked a woman with a baby on her back—a nursemaid, I suppose, "What do they want to do with the hunchback?"

"Why, to take him to his women slaves," she answered, laughing. "Perahotan in the stories and on the walls is shown followed by adoring females. And since he is a god, he can have his pick of the sacred virgins."

"My friend will be afraid," I said to Ex Loc. "He will not know what to do."

We moved closer. "I do not wish to doubt your opinion," Ex Loc said. Ghost, now walking on his ownpower, was going through the nunnery door. A young girl had taken him by the hand. He had his arm around her waist. "But it seems as though he knows exactly what to do."

Others of the virgins were on the porch; a female overseer was pushing them through the entranceway. I was close enough to see their unmistakable beauty of face and form. They had, clearly, been given the finest robes, the most precious earspools, and necklaces of gold.

Ex Loc was at my ear. "Do you not wish one of these beauties for an evening? I am sure the Ruler can arrange for you to have a discreet meeting. The rule could be bent."

My heart was in my throat; all my pulses beat a drum beat of desire. "No—no. I do not wish a woman," I said.

We walked on a way, now that the crowd was dispersing, to the palace. Again the noble lord leaned close to my ear.

"Perhaps you go another way in your desires—you are a handsome young man I like very much, and the gods give us an example." Before I knew what was happening, he put before my eyes a small bark book with scenes of—well, gods with gods, men with men and other, more bestial things. My mouth fell open; to see such things in pictures! These books could be used for good or ill, it seemed.

Instinct and years as a ritual clown made me feel my way to a right answer for this advance, which repulsed me. We were in front of the palace. I turned to him, as dificult as it was, and took his hand as if in respect and friendship. "No, I am under a vow, that is all. I thank you for your good services today." Then I was gone.

That afternoon before I went over accounts and goods orders with Smoke Fox-god, I told him of our visit to the shrines. "But when I asked him who had erased the old lineage pictures and put in the twin princes, he said it was not his to answer. So whose is it to tell me this, I humbly beg."

"No one's. You—Tunkel— you are still as impertinent as on the first day I decided to spare your life. I have told you there is only one thing really for you to say—"

"Whatever is your wish, I stand ready to fulfill it, oh Lord of the city," I finished for him. "And I believe you had something to tell me about the gardens."

He was wrapping tobacco into a fat stick, ready to smoke. Here they did not merely smoke to honor the gods, they smoked for pleasure. "Yes. The gardeners come daily. There are two of them for the royal gardens, more for the noblemen's villas. Please send a messenger telling Hoxek Yum the gardener, in the District of Five Deer, to bring slips of avocado for the new orchard. The priest has consulted the oracle men and books and says planting is propitious."

I had not been dismissed, so I sat watching the Short Day Sun sink in strips of coral, then go purple and gray. He said nothing, and pungent rings of smoke circled heavenward to mingle with the wisps of clouds.

"Do you not have the cigars at home?" he asked in a somewhat dreamy voice.

"To honor the gods we take tobacco in ceremonial pipes and blow the smoke towards them."

"No, I mean to forget. The tobacco is strong, it sends you to the underworld." He chuckled, a bit ominously. "Or, you can get fermented honey drink that makes your head spin, or the mushrooms which send you farther away yet, into the minds of the gods."

I stood up, hands folded across my chest in the serving position. "Sometimes I would like to forget. But what I really need to do is remember."

He waved me away with an indulgent laugh, as if he did not care to know what I meant. If fact, odd though it was, during all that time since we were first there, he never wished to know anything about me other than that I was a trader from the north, from the shores of the Longest River North. He asked me nothing of family, friends, or my home. He had been so long used to people tending to his needs, centering attention around him, that he was hardly aware that other people existed, except to serve him.

For two months we stayed in this pattern. Ghost returned from his overnight visit to the nunnery, staying in his little lodgings being catered to as a special personage by servants. I spent every moment learning the interesting job of steward to the Ruler's House—and learning about the Ruler, too. We were often together, and as my skill with the language grew, I began to know him, and I suppose, to like him. Above all else, I saw he was lonely. As a stag stands on a hill, king of all the forest, admired by all but close to none, so was the ruler of Zama. His parents were gone; his mother when he was a small child and his father a few years ago. Not many relatives remained in the royal line of Smoke

I and he had been put on the throne early by the will of the people, so it was said, when he should have been in the House of Young Men, going to hunt and learning to soldier and take trips and go to festivals and view the noble young women of other cities. And so I, the same age as he and unafraid, became a companion of sorts, because as always, and under the Bird of Thunder's command, I spoke the truth, and not the fawning flattery of his followers.

One day I began bowing out of the throne room.

"And—oh yes, Mouth-As-Big-As-a-Drum"—he was mocking me, and that irritated me—"we need some fish to stock the small cenote. They eat up the mosquito babies that tend to grow there. Let us get pretty ones—"

"And where do I get those, Lord of the city?"

"We will go to Xel Ha tomorrow. You will accompany me to amuse me with your quaint ways. Take large pots, and we will bring back some prize examples for the royal pools."

"Xel Ha?"

"A royal relaxation villa is there on the sea, by a bay which is also the outlet of a river. Quite beautiful, really, with many brightly-colored ocean fish to see—and eat also." He had discovered my weakness for fine foods, never fully overcome. Now that my bowels were still, my stomach made never-ending calls.

"Will the court—the eight lords batab be accompanying us?"

"Only two of them—Imi Ex Loc and one other cousin of mine. When I go, they go too." He scowled.

In a moment he thought to ask me about Ghost. Had he been back to the House of Nuns?

I was offended. "I still do not think that was a joke. I could not understand why the blasphemy in the house of sacred virgins was allowed. Ex Loc did not think the people should be stopped. Do not nobles make these decisions?"

"In this my cousin was correct. We let them have freedom in celebrations and other small things as this, lest they press for freedom in the large things. And besides, I like the people."

Alone in my room I considered this. And, for the first time, I took out the amulet of the Seeing Eye, on its little lanyard where

I had put it with the tiny fish given me long ago by a girl at the Place of Rivers Meeting.

"I am keeping my eyes open, Hawk Eye. I pray that I may return to report to you, finally, what it is that I saw. If I can ever figure out what that is."

With that I lay on my wood slab bed, raised above the crawling roaches and spiders as big as a hand who inhabited the ground at night even in royal palaces and tried not to let the "perhaps" pageant start up and keep me awake all night.

Chapter 12

Litters, carried by slaves, bore the royal procession to the "taking of the breezes" spot the next morning. It made me uncomfortable to be carried like a baby or sick person in a sort of boat with a canvas cover over it, borne along by four stout, loping men, but Smoke Fox-god, Imi Ex Loc, the other cousin batab and his wife were all being carried along the road. Such was the custom.

I had left Ghost in his dwelling, tended by one of the nuns. His complexion seemed paler and his health poorer than when we came; he was being given figs and corn drink by a small, dark nun with a huge pile of hair on her head. I asked no questions, simply told him I would be gone for three days. Then I had attended to the palace business, checking in baskets of corn and being certain the cook could take care of the retainers with sufficient food while we were gone.

And the gardener—I had spent a half an hour with him, seeing to the planting of more slips of avocado. The new orchard was beginning to take shape; some of the plants were bushy, two-feet-tall plants, others just sticks sprouting leaves.

His name was Hoxek Yum. "Why are you not putting in seeds?" I wanted to know. "I have seen the seeds of this green fruit. They are large and in some of them the sprouts crack right through the nut. I say just throw them in, add a little water—in this warm climate, they will grow fast, yes?"

He did not answer instantly, but called me over to the square he had set off for the first slip. "Look at this soil," he said.

I peered down. "Where *IS* the soil?" I said.

"You are right. There are only small and large rocks. If there was soil, it would fall down between the rocks. Rain does not stay in the ground here, but runs off into the ocean or the underground cisterns."

"Then how—" I looked at the slip. It was a stem with one leaf at the top, growing out of the large seed.

"Something good takes time to grow." He showed me. "Let the seed soak fourteen suns, until a sprout makes a root. Make a small bed in your garden with rock walls with pointed stick. Put in leaf mold, so—" I nodded.

"Add water, gently, a few drops at a time. Then put in the avocado seed. Cover it with leaf mould and tiny rocks until—sun shines, rain falls, it roots in and grows! Time and patience for growth."

I looked behind me at the white buildings, thinking of not much at all except their beauty, which still made me catch my breath in awe, and the time they had taken to create. "And the city—it takes time and patience too."

"Time to be a real city," he said. "Like the avocado seeds, all things must be right." He stood up, putting a hand to the small of his back. He must have been sixty summers, and therefore, by the law of respect to elders, had the right to speak. "In the city, too, there must be rooting, Soil must be dug right—laws and gods must work. Ruler and nobles are like the sun and rain to nourish and husband from above. People are the humble soil to nourish and grow the corn. All make a tiny universe, mirror the universe of the gods. Make a real city."

"To make a real city?" "Are not the beautiful buildings of Zama, its ceremonies and riches real?"

"The real city is not the temples. Sure not to be the nobles, or even the people who grow the grain and live and worship. Not even the ruler. We do not build cities anymore for the Maya, no, not these two hundred summers. A building here or there—but the Old Ones built the cities, when all things in the universe spoke for growth." He had stopped working and was looking off beyond the gates, clearing his mouth and spitting on the rocky earth.

"What is wrong here do you say?" I asked. He did not look around at me, but his voice was a slow whisper.

"Too many wars. Foreigners from the north—and with them came change and—greed. Too much tribute. Too many rich, not listening. Too few voices who know what to say. Parts of the universe of the gods are out of joint. The harmony of all parts is needed, else no growth.

"What does it take, then?"

"All of them, parts of city. Trust each other. Ruler, gods, nobles—and the people. Together, working together, with time and patience they sprout and grow—" his hands reached out to a full-grown avocado, laden now, at this time of the year, with fine large fruit—"a fine city, where all are happy."

He knelt to pat the rocks and seed again, sprinkling a few more drops of water from a pot.

I wanted to be certain of what I had heard. "The Ruler is your Lord. You work for him."

"He is a good man. Too young, though. Supposed to be twenty-five, but the people wanted him when his father died. He—they all— go to the next city once a month, take nobles captive or slave, come back, cut out the heart—up there." He pointed up the temple hill." Now he rubs off the old god pictures—put up his own to prove he is the ruler. Out of joint."

I said nothing, watching him dig another hole with a pointed stick.

"How is your friend?" he whispered.

"The hunchback? He is—enjoying life."

"He was carried by the people to the Virgins' Nunnery."

"Yes—it was a joke, I think."

He snorted. "Desecration. The people are out of joint too. And as for the nobles—they talk, talk behind their hands about all of it. Nobody trusts nobody."

It had been an odd sendoff to our leisure party, but I was fast forgetting it now that we were on the road on this glorious day.

Then let me try to tell you, to let you really see for yourself, the splendid journeying procession that we made through the hot and sultry countryside in those days of my youth in the land of the Maya.

At the head of the procession were the guards, running, with protective armor of square-sewn cotton and heavy untanned deerskin boots. Just behind them were the warriors, an honor guard sent by Honacan, Captain of the Guard. The faces of the warriors were painted in red and black stripes, and they carried flint-tipped spears. (The flint were not nearly as good as those I had brought. My flint was probably being used at this moment by the savages, pardon, natives, up the beach, to skin some poor human alive.) The shafts of the guards' spears were covered with jaguar cat skin and were tasselled near the point. In the pierced ears of the guards were shafts of the green stone so valued here, jade, and for clothing they wore only the long, elegant loincloth and deer leather sandals.

Then came the young priest (not the one who had welcomed us the first night; this trip was too strenuous for him, I supposed) with bloody hair locks, wearing a strange, folded-back hat which was supposed to be the open mouth of the jaguar, and a long embroidered robe. He was blowing a conch shell and scattering copal incense to discourage the mischief of the gods along the road.

Following me and the three noble people's litters came the Great Ruler. His headdress was magnificent, made of the plumes of the green and gold quetzel bird, three feet in length and curving over. He wore the copper collar I had brought him, and on his wrists and ankles were priceless jade ornaments. Anyone seeing him from Cahokia would have been impressed. And anyone from Lake-of-the-Boulders—would have thought he was the Sun Lord himself, come down on the special Longest Day to journey on the roads of the south. They would have grovelled on the ground for an hour.

This was not the beach trail I had come in on, of course, and it was really the first time I viewed the stone road to Xel Ha which several had described to me. Eight feet wide it was, and constructed above the low swamp area like a causeway. The old steward had told me early this morning, as we were preparing for the trip, that it had been built by the great rulers of the Old Ones, who had indeed built all the roads. First these ancient Maya had built two walls opposite each other, running evenly above all the standing water and cane breaks, then they filled the area between the walls with loads of limestone and fine gravel. After that, a smooth water and sand cement was put over all, and it was allowed to dry and bake in the sun. I thought of the old gardener's words, "We do not build any more." Well, but they must repair— constantly. There was not a hole in this road, not a weed to take root and tear through the rock base.

"And the road to Xel Ha is not even the finest road," the steward had told me. "Outside Xel Ha is a road wider yet, and it leads to the Great Sacbe, or white road, fifteen feet wide."

Well, we would not see that on this trip. Trotting, our bearers would get us to Xel Ha in the late afternoon, after starting in the latter part of the morning.

We stopped for a meal: roasted fowl and fried tortilla cakes, filled with roasted beans and onions, warmed over the fire. I watched the animals in the underbrush and wondered at them. Flashes of fire—hummingbirds— darted into the mouths of many flowers. Green and purple dragonflies skimmed over the standing water. And now and then I caught sight of a long-armed animal the size of a newborn bear cub swinging through the trees.

"Good to eat," an officer of the guards told me with a smile, pointing at a tail twisting around a tree.

"What is its name? We do not have such things in the north," I said.

"Monkey. They are like little men." He was a strong-looking man of about thirty summers, and in his front teeth were shiny metal ornaments. He had his teeth pierced in the style of the large cities that all these people sometimes visited.

I tried to ask him more about the woods, but he seemed reluctant to speak, so I watched him carefully directing the little troop as it rose from its simple mess.

Both Smoke Fox-god and Ex Loc were strangely silent, standing off on opposite sides of the campground. The guard and warriors stood with hands near to their lances. Were we expecting an ambush? The savages did lurk near these beach areas, and feared neither god nor ruler, as I had seen. Or was it—something else. Surely the old man had been right when he had said, "There is no trust in the city."

Finally we came to the Meeting of the Waters—Xel Ha. A small village, with only a few stone shrines and noble dwelling places, stood back on the bay which the river mouth formed. We would be settling ourselves in two of the rather small royal villas on the bay.

"But there is time for bathing in the waters," Smoke Fox-god said, when our travelling baskets had been put into the villa and our beds set up. He seemed exhilarated, as if being away from the city and its cares had freed him to be the youth that he was. "You promised me I should go to the cenote, as I did when I was a child, and now you will lead me to the waters here. Just the two of us, with one guard."

Well, it did sound delightful. It had been a particularly hot day, and I wished to rid myself of the sweat and smells of the sweltering, breathless road.

"Is the water salt or fresh?" I asked Smoke Fox-god as we descended over black rock to the water.

"Both. The outgoing river and the incoming sea mix." Clumps of seagrape hid our bathing from the sight of the shore; still we wore a folded square of cloth to protect our privacy. The Maya were very modest people; even children went clothed. Smoke Fox-god glittered with jade and copper still though; the ruler would not surrender his jewels, his symbols of power, even in the bath.

We lowered ourselves into almost warm, clear water. I suppose because no one was near (the guard sat on a huge, black rock with his back to us) Smoke Fox-god began to relax completely. He was shedding his princehood as he had shed his garments, becoming the boy of eighteen summers that he was.

"Ahh," he breathed, in a long sigh of relief, or was it yearning? He stood in the waters, laughing as small, fat striped fish swam around his toes; we ducked down, keeping our eyes open pointing at bright blue fish and strange, batlike creatures that seemed to propel themselves with flapping fins like wings. The rocks were porous , although some rocks were flat and purple and fan-like. Or were those animals or plants? One could not tell; the whole world of the undersea was as wondrous as the kingdom of the dead.

I had never seen anything like it—do I keep saying that?

Finally, after many dips and laughing dives beneath the water, we arose to find cotton towels to dry ourselves, and walked—into the hands of hostile-looking guards with spears.

"Hold them." Ex Loc was pointing to us with a rudely arched finger. "As rightful ruler and the descendant of Smoke Second I remind you guards that you will be rewarded well." Ex Loc carried the scepter with his own family stamp-picture on it. He came to slap Smoke Fox-god on both cheeks, then ordered him, both of us, incarcerated until he could secure the entire premises for his cause. We had been ambushed, as I had feared, but it was not by the natives.

We were walked by the officer who had told me of the monkey to a small tower above the ocean. It was not clear whether we would die as soon as the nobleman returned, or on the morrow. Two guards stood outside the door opening, the obsidian points on their spears glinting in the full moon which arose over the sea.

"I—am sorry. I have involved you when I did not need to." Smoke Fox-god said. It was actually the first time I had heard him express concern about anyone but himself.

"Perhaps you will tell me why we have been seized. What is this of the rightful king? Smoke Second—that was the younger brother shown in the wall pictures?"

"Yes. In the time of the great-grandfather's great grandfa-thers—well, you heard the story from my cousin. What he did not tell you is that he is the direct descendent, the last one, of Smoke

Second, the younger twin who was born in those days of the Old Ones—the great Mayas who built the roads."

And who built no more, because the world was out of joint. "And you are descended from the first-born?"

"The first-born. But odd as it seems, though Smoke First was prophesied and judged to rule by the priests, he did not. He was physically weak, and his younger brother took the throne by right of merit, so it was said. And then that younger son's son and so on down—through the times when lineage was all that was heeded.

"But in the time of our grandfathers, mine and Imi Ex Loc's, my own grandfather took back the throne in a bitter war. And now..."

He was silent, looking grimly at the moon. "Exchel, help me," he muttered.

"Ex Loc has been working behind your back to gain support of the nobles—or part of the army."

"Yes. My father died young, and I was but sixteen summers when I came to rule. But I have proven myself in my own campaigns." Yes, of course. I had seen pictures in the Ruler's house of him taking sacrificial blood from captives, running a rod through their tongues and noses.

"I thought I had earned the respect of Honacan, Captain of the Guard, and most of the warriors—but I guess not all."

I was silent for a while, looking out the window hole at the two guards.

"We must act now," I said. "Can you trust me?" He looked up at me with wounded eyes. I had the feeling he did not really know the meaning of the word, brought up among people who told him comfortable lies, surrounded by intrigue and little else. But then neither, really, did I have more trust from my own wounded childhood. We had both best learn fast.

"Soon Ex Loc will be coming to sacrifice us on the spot," he answered, "to the god of war, Buluc Chabtan. At the latest tomorrow. We will have our hearts torn out and we will be thrown into the bay, I suppose." Moodily he stared at the moon. I could see those pimples—they made me feel the older of us.

"Listen. Great Lord, I will tell you true what we must do. Did you say that you believed the loyalty of the Captain of the Guard is yours?"

"I will stake my life on Lord Honacan."

"I think I can get us out of here," I told him. He looked at me with a small light of hope in his eye.

"If you could! Why, I would do whatever—"

"Yes, I know. Whatever my wish, you will stand ready to fulfill it. I am the Lord of Your Escape," I smiled, and put out my arm for the arm slap. Cautiously, with his head quizzically tilted to one side, he touched my arm with the inner part of his forearm and smiled a small smile. It might pass for trust in a tight situation. Then I outlined what I had in mind.

A still, cooling breeze blew from the northeast. I could hear the Ruler's voice, low, in the moonlight, persuasive. "—they are traitors who will be killed by the Royal Guard when we return. I can assure you of Lord Honacan's loyalty. He will never allow my cousin to rule, for he feels he is evil. We have spoken of it."

I stepped to his side, and it was at this point that I noticed that the taller guard was the one who had spoken to me of monkey stew. His eyes met mine. The Ruler spoke, his words enunciated, almost spat out in spite of the need to whisper. "I have among my possessions back home four of the longest obsidian blades you have ever seen, and a pearl that is as big as an avocado seed. I swear by the god Ek Chuah, my patron, that they are yours."

The monkey guard looked uncertain, but there was a flicker of interest in his eye. I had counted on the fact that this was a very new revolt, led by a man who was disliked because he "did things with men." The guards were not acting strongly loyal; well, at least they had not called others, or run us through.

"Here is what you must do," I told the monkey officer in an authoritative voice. "The Ruler and I will be going to the woods, to take our chances with the gods of the rainforest and the sea. You

295

will let us go, unnoticed. If the rainforest and sea smile on us with protection, you will know you have done the right thing. If we die, so be it. You can protect yourselves from the wrath of this interloper lord by leaving immediately. Flee to another city, where you have relatives, and await our return. When seven suns have passed, seek out the disposition of the gods, and if all is well, return to rejoin us and receive great rewards. The most you will have to do is live in exile for a while, short or long."

The monkey guard nodded slowly.

I plunged on. "There are times when a man has a chance to change his destiny if he chooses well. Will you take a risk for the chance of great riches for yourselves and your family? Choose the better man; you know who that is; the gods of justice will reward your choice, and the Ruler himself will reward loyalty with great liberality and advancement in the army."

The monkey officer was nodding vigorously now, and his companion was listening attentively.

Smoke Fox-god did not wait for further affirmation. "Here is promise of our word for your reward when we return to Zama." He took off the god earspools and ankle bracelets of finest jade and divided them between the guards.

"We will see you in seven suns," he said, and without further word we slipped into the darkness.

It was only afterwards I realized he had left on his neck the necklace I had given him.

"Curses on this moonlight," Smoke Fox-god muttered as our small dugout proceeded down the shoreline. "They can see us from Xel Ha if they chance to look hard enough."

"Pray to your moon goddess Exchel to hide her face," I said, paddling frantically with the short, broken paddles that had been with the dugout.

The wind, at least, continued and soon, by the fortune of the goddess or Whoever or just our own good paddling, we were around the bend and out of sight from Xel Ha. The barrier reef offered good protection from the rolling seas, and we stroked our way through only slightly rippling waters.

"I think Imi Ex Loc will have enough difficulty controlling the guards in that small group," the Ruler said. "By the time he secures his situation, makes his plans, and begins to follow us—it will be afternoon tomorrow. He will not trust the troops on the road tonight, even with the moon. But he will, of course, have traitors inside the walls of Zama tomorrow, waiting for him to return triumphantly with my head."

I did not turn to see his face, and his voice came hollowly out of the darkness. "We do not know how many are committed to him, do we?"

"I could count for sure only about twenty members of noble families. But if he is in possession of the temples and gets to the army—I do not know."

"What about the people? Are they with you or Ex Loc?"

"The people? Who would consider them?"

"Did they not do that in the cities of the Old Mayas?" something made me say.

"Yes," he said slowly. "But—he lay down his paddle and grew thoughtful. "They are for me. That I know. That is one of the bones of contention the batab and I argue over like dogs. I have given the people privileges, brought many into the precincts of the citadel city itself."

"Mostly to work, like your gardener."

"Yes, of course. But I like to see their faces, too. I came to power so young, with so few friends. It was easy to seek the people's favor, and then I found it satisfying. The priests stink with all that blood in their hair, and the nobles are doing abomination to the gods and showing filthy pictures." He made an obscene gesture and laughed and I did too. "The people speak to me and laugh with me when I wear my disguises. As to the older ones—I think they think of me as a son."

He said a few more slighting things about the batab and the nobles, and we began laughing and kept on for several minutes. There was a kind of comfortableness now between us. Shared danger creates such bonds, and they are stronger than the strongest hempen ropes.

It was at this time I told him why I had really come—not to trade, of course. And yet, I could not tell him of the full truth. I told him I was on a mission for my Female Sun to get a treasure for her—left earlier by my uncle the trader in one of the cities here. I spoke of the cave, of the quest I wanted him to authorize.

"It is forbidden to me," he said, in awe of the sacred taboos. "But should you ever find it—"

"Half will be rightfully yours," I promised.

He agreed to let me go when the time was proper and to take his share. We made good progress along the shoreline, pulling hard with the paddles. Clouds did come over the moon after He Is Halfway Through the Night, and I asked the Ruler if he knew the inlets of this coast well enough to let us pass under the searchlight of the city and land towards the south. "Probably. It is a difficult landing because the rocks come right up to the shore, but this is a slight canoe which can go anywhere. But why?"

"I will tell you when we pull into the shore."

He seemed content to let me plan, and I thanked fortune for that. There would soon be no time to argue details with an imperious ruler.

The north tower had a constant torch lit at night, to guide trading mariners off the dangerous shores to the small canoe beach at Zama. It was a beacon, but also a danger to us. We must not be seen. When we came in sight of it and the other buildings, flickering in sporadic light from the temple torches blowing flat in the wind and the moon coming in and out of the clouds, we silently brought the canoe onto the tiny length of beach. Then we picked it up with some effort, because small though it was, it was made of one of the hardwoods of the area., Hugging the cliffs, we carried it past the guards posted in the small temple of the god of merchants. We went further on, past the Temple of Itzamna high on the hill, on south and around the bend where we could again put the canoe in the water. Then we paddled silently a bit further, to where the common people housed. It was almost dawn.

"I must reach Lord Honacan, Captain of the Guard, and insure myself of his support," Smoke Fox-god insisted.

"Not yet. We must plot our strategy. There is a saying in my land: No one goes near the den of the bear in the spring unless he has found out how many, and how hungry, are the bears."

"Bears?" Smoke Fox-god looked puzzled.

I had used the word of Lakes-Like-a-Necklace, because I had not heard it in the tongue of the Maya. Maybe they had no bears. "Huge hairy beasts with big teeth—never mind. Follow me." We were on that beach in the first rays of dawn, and standing there, with only a short peasant's loincloth on, he gave me the haughty look of the Ruler of the City. It masked his uncertainty, possibly fear. "Remember, trust?" I chuckled, and he nodded.

An old woman was tending some tame rabbits in a pen in the first hut we reached. She was so startled she shrieked, but since no one else came out of the house, we did not have to face an entire family. She stood with her mouth open, obviously frightened at two men with the long, tied-back hair and lighter skin of noblemen. Did she recognize the Ruler? Was she simply overawed? Or was it possible she had never been inside the citadel city during his reign?

"Where is the house of the gardener to the Ruler?" I said. She shook her head. Then, after looking at me hard for a moment, Smoke Fox-god repeated what I had said in accents I did not understand. Finally, with her mouth still opened, the old woman pointed up a lane. Good! Hoxek did live nearby. I thought so—I had sent messages about work hours to the gardener in this village. Honacan, Captain of the Guard's signet was on stone signs along the lane, but I had not been sure until she told us. We had lit near the spot we needed.

Smoke Fox-god was angry now as we walked down the lane; his red-pimpled face hot. "What do you mean, the gardener. Are you crazy-headed? I am not going another pace. I shall simply return to the walls, call for Lord Honacan—" I grabbed him by the shoulders and spun him around.

"Now listen to me, fox cub. We are talking about your life—and mine too. You cannot walk into that hornet's nest now or they will sting you to death. You cannot name one single friend or enemy for sure."

"But I must return—" he was wriggling from my grasp. It was not easy, since I was larger by at least a head than he.

"You will go, but *in disguise*. We will get one at the gardener's house. I know he is your friend."

He shook me free but stood looking at me searchingly.

"How do you know?"

"Because he told me yesterday morning. He admires you. Now here we are. Third house up the lane, large corn patch just burnt off, she said."

Morning mist swirled about us. Through beautiful squared-off plantings of papaya, figs and flowers we made out way to the house of the gardener, Hoxek Yum. It was the hour of He Is Rising; the gardener had just gotten up from bed and was pouring a jar of water over himself, shaking his head like a dog. He did not see us, even when we had come just three feet from him. I cleared my throat.

As he looked up, and the knowledge of who we were sank into his thought, he fell to his knees. "Sirs—Great Ruler, steward—my humble yard is yours," and so forth. A dog came out and growled at us.

"Back, Ex Loc," Hoxek commanded.

"Ex Loc," the Ruler said, then roared with laughter.

I beckoned for Hoxek to rise. "We have—there is trouble between your dog's namesake and our ruler. We enlist your aid, Father. We would travel to the city shortly in disguise to determine who has taken traitorous steps, who remains loyal."

He nodded, then bent over to ruffle the dog's fur. "I thought it would come. Out of joint," he said.

Smoke Fox-god looked at him. "It could be dangerous for you to aid us, should things go wrong. But I have good reason to think we will soon be in the Ruler's house again, and at that time I will reward my friends."

"You always reward me. Treat me as a human being and remember my family with gifts," the old man said. "And your father before you." Then he smiled toothlessly. "But weddings should not be arranged, nor plans plotted without breakfast. My wife is cooking corn cakes today, for the old husband, and she has made many. And eggs, gathered yesterday by my grandson, and broiled fish steak. No rush—no one was being beheaded yet when I left last afternoon. You will have an hour or two yet. Will you eat?"

Would we! Smoke Fox and I set to at huge, round logs, and the woman brought out the hot, flat corn cakes and we filled them with fish and fried beans and ate till we could burst. And the honey—the marvelous honey, that he collected himself from hives he kept. We ate both comb and sweet together.

He wished to show us his house, his children and grandchildren. Two little boys with fat cheeks were running around, chewing the gum from some trees which shed it as sap. We stepped into the house, which was round, with thatching of the stickily-leaved trees that grew everywhere. Woven beds hung from the ceiling, one for every member of the household. Hoxek Yum's daughter-in-law was folding them up, hanging them on a peg against the wall.

A huge beam crossed over the whole span of the house. "The tree of stone. Strongest of all woods," said the old man. "It holds up this roof and brings it blessing. We call this beam the rat trail, because the rats love to run there at night."

"Rats at night? Do you not wish to rid yourself of them?" I wanted to know. At Cahokia young boys shot them with slingshots as a part of their daily duty. Rats ate the corn stores.

"Rats are good luck in a farmer's house," he told us. "We chase them out in the daytime." There was not much in the house except the corn pot, the cooking oven and griddle and the beds hanging against the wall. Yes, I thought, the ocean winds could blow freely through here since the underbrush was cut all the way to the beach. And with no stools or tables, the insects and snakes had nothing to hide under. It made sense.

In the yard were pots of honey. "It is part of my tribute. Honacan, who is our batab, will come this week to count our house, give us our fields, and take the honey. He will ask how many times I came to garden in the fields, and I will show him this tablet." There was the bark book he kept of his own work, with the ruler's sign at the bottom of each page, put their by the former steward, and lately by me.

"In the old days," he went on, indicating to us to squat in the yard on our haunches in farmer-style to talk, "when we had given the tribute, my grandfather and his grandfather would have gone to build monuments and worship houses, to lay new roads. But not now."

"We do not have the time to build," the Ruler said. "The wars keep all busy."

"Yes. The farmers must fight the other cities, and anyway, there is always a need to get more honey, or make more cloth, if that is the tribute portion."

"More?" Something about that sounded familiar. Cahokia. That was it. And being taken for the tribute wars.

"I do not call for more tribute," Smoke Fox-god said.

The old man looked directly at the ruler. Then he spat on the ground, as if embarrassed and looked away. "No, but your lords do. The batab, not all but most, take the tribute and enrich their own clans. Gamble, dissipate with the bad women, buy riches the traders offer and speculate in trade themselves. Outfit canoes to go far away to the gold cities of the south. With our tribute. Only part goes to you." He sighed. Bird of Thunder, Truth, I thought, you have spread your wings in the south, too.

The Ruler was silent, and we stayed for a moment, watching the dog scratch fleas while the little ones, Yum's grandbabies ran about pushing a ball of another kind of tree sap. It bounced all over the yard! Never had I—but my thoughts have strayed.

"You wish a disguise," the old one said.

"Can you give us clothes like yours?" I asked intently. "Sun hats of the farmers, coming down over the face? We will be gardeners, go to the gates and ask entrance to work—" I snapped my fingers in inspiration "—for the Ruler's steward, in the royal gardens."

"Yes," chuckled Hoxek Yum. "I could use two assistants." He looked at me. "You are tall enough to pick out, but there are also tall slaves, just in from a place north and west. They will think you are one of the new slaves. You may carry the avocado shoots, each in its little pot to the garden. He is rising higher, so we should go."

"We? You do not need, old one, to endanger yourself," said the Ruler.

"We have a saying in the countryside," Yum said, entering his house. "If a baby falls into the fire, and the crowd all stands around looking silly, he will die. Somebody has to go in to get him out, and now. I will help you, Ruler."

"How much time do we have to try to secure the city for you, do you think?" I asked after we had each put on old countryman's clothing and had headed up the road to the city.

"Several hours at least before Imi Ex Loc can bring the party to the gates. You saw how long the road trip took, and he could not have started before dawn." The ruler was strutting along in front of Yum and me, trying to look humble and lowly, and I had a little trouble restraining a smile.

"Another question is how far the conspiracy will have gone within the walls of the city," I asked.

"There is no way of knowing, but surely the few nobles in Ex Loc's party can't have taken over the whole city. I think they will be watching, awaiting his return to come into the open. They may have captured Lord Honacan." Hummingbirds, tiny hoverers with dark green feathers, darted across our road. The sun was climbing higher.

"There will be many people to talk to once we find out the where Captain of the Guard is," I said. "We must have him to secure your place. We have probably come in time. Ex Loc was counting on the fact that he could kill you, or bring you back as a penitent prisoner."

"Well, you can be sure he will be hurrying, because he knows I am at large. It is a tight ball game. My plan, once we're sure of where the playing court lies, is to just assert my power before he gets there. Be ready for him, declare him a traitor. You say no one had gone over, declared for Ex Loc, when you left the city last evening, Hoxek?"

"There was no stir at all, Lord Ruler," the gardener said.

We were silent as we approached the city walls.

"Some way these walls look high and forbidding, to one coming in from the country," Smoke Fox-god murmured as we approached the west entrance.

"Yes, well, there are no shell trumpets or incense priests this time, and perhaps that is all to the better," I said without looking at him. I was starting to be irritated again, my high spirits fraying like a shirt edge from lack of sleep.

"It is not likely that Lord Honacan will be at the guard station on this wall," the Ruler whispered. "But call up to whoever is there, Hoxek."

"I know," the gardener said a little crossly. "Guard of Zama," his old voice yelped like his dog's, "I Hoxek Yum have come with my helpers to finish the avocado orchard for the Great Ruler, Smoke Fox-god."

"Smoke Fox-god Three is no longer ruler here. He was deposed at midnight by orders from the military." We stood stock still; only Hoxek had the presence of mind to proceed.

"Well, whoever the ruler is, his garden must be cared for. May we enter?"

The gate was unbarred and with our hats pulled low and our pots of avocados held high, we entered. The guard had been relieved not long before, and a tired-looking warrior stood counting cacao beans in his hand.

"Bought out," Smoke Fox-god whispered. "But where is my Captain of the Guard?" But I put my finger to my lips; we had business to attend to with this man. I had told the others that I should not speak, for fear of my foreigner's tongue being recognized. So it fell to the Ruler, who was, of course, in mortal danger if his voice was recognized. Clever Smoke Fox-god put on the rough country accents. "Ah—we had not heard in the country about the change. You say the military ordered it?"

"So I was told," the man said, putting the cacao beans in a small deerskin packet. "Lord Honacan commanded our new loyalties himself when the guard came on. He said Smoke Fox's head would be brought back and the true lineage restored." I could see my friend's body tense. I thought, rather than spoke to him. "Control yourself in this bear cave. There is yet hope if we are cautious."

"Well, whether the Ruler comes or goes does not disturb my work. Things must be planted and watered and the road from the house to the great temple kept clear of weeds. We will go on with our work," Hoxek said casually. The guard turned his back on us and strode to the guard house.

"Go and dig in the garden of the Ruler's house," Hoxek told us. "Do't exactly as I told you yesterday. Do nothin' suspicious." We did what he said, kneeling with the avocado pots. Out of the corner of my eye I could see Hoxek drifting about with a sort of sledge, pulling weeds from the sides of the main road. He was also giving a casual word here and there to the workers of the city, who were all filing in through the gate to work in the cookeries and royal houses and temples and shrines and gardens of this citadel city. I had never really noticed how many of these workers there were: Smoke Fox-god had, indeed, increased their number, as he said: over two hundred, some slaves and some women, but most men tribute workers.

"What now?" Smoke Fox-god said to me as he poked at the ground with the pointed stick, only to have it break.

"Try again, and do not slam the stick against a rock," I said with what I imagined was a country accent.

Just then the great shell horns began to blow and all the guards ran from their standing positions at its inner limits and from the guardhouse to mount the walls. We stood, looking around the corner of flowering bushes to see the gate open again. The young priest, guards and the cousin batab and his wife filed in, followed by Imi Ex Loc, wearing Smoke Fox's great quetzal bird headdress of power and carrying his own family's scepter. I watched until the party was through and the gates were re-closed; the monkey guard and his friend were not there.

"How have they come so fast?" I asked.

"Must have—" he ran a few paces to the side of the hill and came back. "There are canoes on the beach. Why did I not think he could come by water if we could? I must go confront them— even if it means to die," the Ruler said. "My lineage is an ancient one, and I will defend it with honor."

"No," I whispered. "Your lineage is going to die out right now if you act rashly. Do you have another fine headdress in this ruler's house?"

"If they haven't moved it out," he said.

"He doesn't know you are here. Pick up a large flowering plant in a pot. Pull your sunhat down far and go into your house. Try to pick up the headdress of power and put it by the back door. And your scepter. Have it ready." He nodded and picked up an armful of pots for disguise.

Across the plaza I could see Lord Honacan, Captain of the Guards, in full dress and with a ferocious reptile headdress helmet on his head, being borne by his litter bearers to greet the new ruler—whom he had help to confirm. Traitor that he was!

I began to be frantic. Where in the world was Hoxek? He had been gone long now and—why, why were the servants, the country folk drifting about, their brooms and water pots and food trays in hand, whispering? Then, from my vantage point at the back of the city I began to see several things at once: Lord Ex Loc raising his hand in triumphant greeting to Lord Honacan as the Captain of the Guard majestically approached on his litter, a group of the servant men drifting like a quiet tide towards the guard house; the guards on the wall noticing the serving men, pointing and beginning to scramble down. At the very same moment, Lord Honacan's litter dropped and a knife was shoved through his throat by one of the litter bearers, as the group of men emerged from the empty guardhouse with spears and rushed at the wall guards.

306

"Quickly, Ruler," I shouted to my friend whose shadow I could see by the rear door of the Ruler's House. "The bears have come from the cave!"

With his full headdress of power and his scepter, and the long ceremonial loincloth, Smoke Fox-god advanced with me towards the battle going on between the servants with spears and the guard. It was being hard fought—the sides were about equal in numbers. But the people, pushing their spears and fighting with short knives had anger on their side enough to match the skill of the trained guards, who had been caught short of weapons anyway.

Quickly Smoke Fox-god set his headdress down, and we entered the fray. He picked up a spear that had been dropped; I fought a panting man for one and kicked him to the ground. My friend quickly worked his way to the head of the common people's force and, raising his spear, led them in a final rush.

Lord Imi Ex Loc had watched in horror as the Captain of the Guard was killed and decapitated. He had withdrawn with his fawning cousin to the center road and was heading for the high Temple Hill to join the priests and call to the gods and people for power, and from the height—

But he was never to make it. The rest of the common people who worked in the citadel city of Zama simply came quickly up, as hunters in the woodlands will gather around buffalo and encircle them silently. The angry mob surrounded the two pretenders to the throne of the city. The people had no weapons except for their brooms and water pots; yet grimly they stood, three and four deep, a human barrier between the prince they hated and the sacred Temple Hill.

Smoke Fox-god and his peasant force had won; the wall guards were either lying dead or wounded or held by their arms, captured. In a loud, panting voice Smoke Fox-god said, "Lord Imi Ex Loc has been surrounded and his false power is at an end. The judges of our city and the gods themselves will decide about him. I order the re-bellious guard unit dissolved. Your commander has been executed. I, your Lord and Ruler command it." He

307

ordered the citizen warriors to hold the defeated soldiers by the arms and stand with them in a row.

I carried forward his great headdress of power. He put it on and, his chest heaving with the exertion of battle, climbed the steps, straight on, so he could see the face of the god Itzamna face to face in the high temple, and there he met the priests.

All below watched him kneel, taking off his headdress and begging for purification. Then the priests threw incense on him and on the sacred braziers and came forward with knives—I instinctively began to leap towards the stairs, but he turned and raised his arms. Blood was pouring from his fingers. He turned and smeared the statues of Itzamna and the god of battle. And then he came to the edge of the temple platform and said one thing only. He held up his arms until there was complete silence, and he said, "The people have spoken."

You could not hear what else he might have said, because the roaring of the overjoyed crowd was continuous. The other batab and officials from outside the walls had now come through the gates and were joining in the cheering. Well they should; he would deal with them later. Ex Loc and his cousin had come to their knees and were begging for mercy; he ordered them hauled off and kept in ropes, heavily guarded, in the merchant's temple on the hill, the temple we had sneaked past only a few hours before.

We sat watching the stars in the courtyard of the Ruler's House that evening. A serving girl was whisking chocolate for us in a wide-mouthed pitcher on the chocolate stand in the corner of the house; her form, in the torchlight of the house, cast a long shimmering shadow out the door. Smoke Fox-god was rubbing the leg which had received a wound in the battle. The town healer had put balm on it, but it ached. But his mind was on the farm and on serving people, his people. "I do not see how they could have known so much, had so much power."

I had thought about this a good deal since the battle. "They have always had the power, though they may not have known it. It did take one good man—Hoxek Yum—who was not afraid, (I watched the shadow of the servant girl elongating as she came towards the door with our cups of chocolate) to whisk them into action.

"And weapons," I went on. "They needed to get weapons that were at least as good as those the guards had, so they went right to the guardhouse. The warriors hadn't even considered that the people might come in and it was left wide open."

"They must have been talking to each other for a long time," my friend said. "About my father, and I, and the new access they had to the citadel city. I and all the priests and nobles—we thought they were beneath talking of affairs of state—or had no minds, I guess."

I took a pottery mug of chocolate from a tray and waited for the serving girl to return inside. "You had no spies? There was no punishment for speaking against the royal houses?" I was thinking of Cahokia.

"There has been no punishment for that since the war of the nobles—when my grandfather took over the rule from the heirs of Smoke Second."

"A dangerous freedom, is it not?" I asked with a slight smile.

"Our house has had no heart for torturing peasants because they disagreed with something done at court. Besides, we had to call on them for fighting in the wars. And you cannot torture a man for speaking about the court one day and call on him to bear arms with real vigor the next."

"How true," I said, thinking of Hawk Eye back at Cahokia, and his hatred of the forced military service for rulers he did not respect.

"And yet, of course, it is dangerous to give the farmers freedom. To let them have knowledge, and any opinions at all on ruling. So most of the rulers of this land have said."

"Still, it saved our lives today."

"Yes, small good that it may do us."

"What do you mean?"

"We have no idea which of the batab are loyal, even now. They are a council—I need their support. And we have not dealt with Imi Ex Loc and my other disloyal cousin."

"Which I suppose will happen tomorrow."

"The council of nobles is to meet just after Sun Greeting ceremonies, outside the Great Temple of Itzamna."

Something occurred to me. "Do the priests go to those meetings?"

"They call, bless and officiate at them."

I was not sure why that did not reassure, but rather unsettled me.

It was almost He Is Halfway Home the next morning when Smoke Fox-god returned, wearily letting a servant take off the giant feather headdress and bring him water to wash his hands and face. Then, with a wave, he dismissed all the servants to return to their quarters.

"We have tied all up as best we can. Alton Ha, the high priest, will officiate at sunrise tomorrow."

"At what?"

"At the sacrifices." I looked at him questioningly, and he went on, a little irritated at my question. "Of Imi Ex Loc and my other cousin, of course. They deserve to die, and they can take my greetings to Itzamna, in his shining form as the sun god."

I snorted and turned away.

"I do not need your approval, you know."

"I do not believe in the sacrifice of human beings to the gods. Just call what you are going to do an execution. It is barbaric, wherever it is."

"We buy favor of the gods with blood. It insures the future good—"

I stood up and folded my arms. It had been a long day. "The gods, whoever they are, are good. They do not wish to have torture and pain inflicted on their children."

The ruler laughed, bitterly, I thought. "And so now you think you are Kukulcan."

"Who?"

"The plumed serpent—a god-man who ruled and taught in this land in the time of the great-grandfathers. He had come from the north, from the Toltecs, and he said to kill in sacrifice was beneath us as children of the gods."

"So? That is what I think, too." I still would not look at him, could not, because my own personal pain and fear for the two I loved more than anything ready to be sacrificed back in Cahokia, was like a sore tooth in my head. Still, I was curious. "But what happened to this Kukulcan?"

"He came from the north to set up the great city of Chichen Itza and he brought peace and harmony to the Maya."

"As you wish to do."

"Of a certainty. Possibly in his day, the sacrifice could be suspended. But for me—the priests wish it."

"And you are their tool."

"It is fate—in the great cycles of the Katun."

I shook my head, not quite understanding.

"The years circle around. When twenty of them are finished— it is a katun. And when they do, they repeat the good or ill of the former katuns in the cycle. The katun we live in now is ripe for human sacrifice. The gods wish it."

I could not answer, and so I left for my room. Dazed as I was with exhaustion, I slept until after the sun rose, and when I went out onto the plaza, it was to face the sacrifice and the crowds of people eager to see it.

At the top of the hill facing the temple of Itzamna, Imi Ex Loc was being held down by four elders, the "chac," old men especially chosen for the event and painted blue. The crowd made room for me and for Ghost, who came to stand by my side. And so I could see it all—the priest lunge at the lord, the scream of terror that emerged from the lord in spite of himself, the heart, pulled out still beating, being carried to the high priest of Zama, Alton Ha. Then, Alton Ha calmly walking to the sea and tossing the heart in, along with a strand of death bells.

311

And then the chac priest-assistants went to the altar, pulled off the body and kicked it down the stairs. It stopped halfway down; it was the job of the other "holders" to follow and kick it the rest of the way.

I saw one man skin the body, except for the hands and feet, and take the skin and wear it to dance with people in the crowd.

And my stomach, and heart as well turned, and I left Ghost and went out of the gates and along the road up a lane into the heavy woodbrush, to a half overgrown spot where a falling idol stood in an old shrine—god of death I am sure it was. I dumped leaves on the idol, and smashed colored berries on it, and then I made water on the brown, dumpy pile. I do not excuse myself; that is what I felt like doing. I held my head in my hands half the afternoon, with the scenes of "perhaps" at Cahokia becoming the scene I had just seen, and when I dragged myself home at He Is Setting, a swamp sickness had taken over my body as well as my spirit.

Three days I lay half in and half out of my mind, while sneering idols with their reptile faces hovered over me, singing loud chants with bells of death in them. I do remember some sort of feathered-serpent shaman rattling rattles around me and peering at me with his eyes behind a wild wolf (or was it dog) mask. "Get out of here," I said with a hoarse voice. And I remember Ghost saying, "Get well, Drum-of-the-Gods, so we can run home."

Finally, when I did awake, it was with the concerned face of Smoke Fox-god over me. I snapped open my eyes, tried to move my arms. I was weak as a newborn puppy.

"And so, have I slept into a new katun, oh Mighty One?"

"You should not mock sacred things. You are better, but you will need rest. I have asked the old steward to serve for a while."

"Good, I suppose." My head hurt fearfully, and my mouth felt as if it had the giant spiders in it, but I pulled myself up on my elbows. "What new violence have you done while I was asleep?"

I was surprised my mouth had actually said that; it was really beyond the point of friendship.

"I should have you tossed out of here," the ruler said harshly and turned from me. Then, more gently, he came and knelt by my side.

"Tunkel, your mind is yet dreaming. But since you have asked—I have spent time in the Great Temple on the hill. Altun Ha has been seeking omens and signs for me. He went into trance state—and came back with a message that informed me of what I was to do."

I struck my forehead to try to dislodge the pain. "What is it that Itzamna wishes you to do?"

"First, to set up a new Captain of the Guard."

"Well, that would make sense even if a god didn't say it."

"The guard who let us loose, the one you call 'Monkey Guard,' came to the gates by night. He had heard in the town he fled to of my restoration. I have inquired after his skill and found it good. He is to be the new Captain of the Guard. I have given him the name 'Monkey King' and many cacao beans as his reward."

"Good. What about the other guard?"

"He chose to stay in exile."

"So be it. We must all choose."

"The lords say they have all chosen me. I have replaced the two now dead with new batab—from different noble families. The old family signs have been rubbed out of the wall and prophecies, and I am having the wall painters brighten up my lineage pictures and symbol signs. Smoke Second's picture is being redrawn, much smaller than Smoke First."

"So things roll on and nothing changes in Turtle Island."

"What? I do not understand."

"Never mind. What else?"

"I am to take a bride. The high priest believes I need to secure the throne with a son."

I lay back down, slowly, so my head did not break apart.

"Some chocolate perhaps?" I muttered and Smoke Fox-god rang a bell for a servant. "Who is the fortunate maiden from a fortunate family in Zama?" I asked.

313

"Not in Zama, of course. We must find a bride for me from the first families in—well, in Chichen Itza, I guess.

"The famous city of your Kukulcan?"

"The most wonderful city of the Maya, and the one Zama owes tribute to. My bride is to be from the great noble Atza family."

"When will you go claim your bride? Will you give betrothal presents? Plan the wedding feast?"

"As soon as you are well."

"You do not need to wait for me to be well to go to Chizen Itza and make your betrothal vows."

"I am not going. You are. It would be beneath me. You will go, with your hunchback, Perahotan, if you wish—and make my arrangements. Be my marriage broker. And then—I will follow with my retinue for the wedding in seven passages of the sun."

I put both of my hands on the sides of my head to hold it together when it would split, any time now. "But—there will be dowry to arrange, love pledges to make, acceptance by the family. How can I do that for you?"

He smiled broadly and took my chocolate cup. "Trust, did you not say, Tunkel, trust. Was that not it?"

During the time of the bad dreams of my sickness, my quest for the treasure hidden in a cave in this land had rung in my head. I had seen a cave and a chest, huge and distorted, but it then reminded me of why I had come to these lands. I should have asked him them to honor his promise made when we were captured by Imi Ex Loc. "I will do anything for you if you help me get back my throne." Well, there would be time, I thought later, as I sat alone, staring at the sea. The tun roll on, just as the katun do, day follows day, an auspicious time for each. There would be time, later. I must go to Chichen Itza.

Chapter Thirteen

It is a good thing that we have rested and a few days passed. I now have stupendous things to tell you. Do not hold your hands up and say that I have already told you more stupendous things than you can imagine! I have told you nothing until I tell you of Chichen Itza, the city of the Feathered Serpent.

The trip was to take three days, two nights. Ghost and I made our way by a fine, broad road to the northwest. On the road we passed many fine sights. Along the ocean we saw men, working salt pits where the brackish water collected and dried. This salt was shipped, they said, all over the lands, so far south no man knew whether gods or demons ruled. As the road led inland, we saw roads branching off from the main one, every now and again, leading to other fine cities and villages and fields. As for the villages along our main road, all around them were fields held in common and weeded, with trees cut down, and some fallow. Then, further out, always holdings of farmers, with the trees being cut down with the big stone knives or burnt off in big piles, ready for the planting which would come in a few short months. In some of the fields they were digging in the ground, about a foot deep, to collect roots they had grown since fall. "Sweet potato," they called them, and there were many baskets of them sitting in the fields of the farmsteads.

We came to Coba, a fine large city set near shallow lakes, with all the buildings connected. We stayed in a visitors' house, where the hospitable people had provided rooms with beds or hammocks and a supply of corn and dried beans and spices. As soon as we made it known we would stay the night, a woman appeared, sent by the head steward, or Holpop, of the city, to make corn cakes and beans and other good things for us!

We walked around, observing the fine sights of this place, the market place, with its stalls with merchants putting away their wares for the evening, their earthenware pots, turtle shell containers and jewelry, their strings of the vanilla orchid which smelled sweet as their gods' breath, so they said, and with which they

315

flavored their chocolate, corn in sacks, the roots they loved and ate, the sweet potato, clothing.

We took one of the odd, long roots, bumpy and dark orange, back to the woman at the guest house and she boiled it for us. Its flesh was sweet and I vowed to get more of them, if I could. The sandfleas were bad in the guest house that night, but in some way I slept, and did not, for a change, dream of the horrible "perhaps" and the land far away.

Now I tell you what was interesting. Here at Coba, only the second city we had been in during our travels in the south, no one bowed at the presence of "Perahotan." Point they did and look with open mouths at him moving rather unevenly along, but they saw him as a strange wonder, a "marked one," not one of the gods. Why was this?

"Perahotan is a g-g-god of the shore cities," Ghost said, as we left the city, passing onto the great road. "Each area has some gods the same, some from very old times that are different. Perahotan is from the t-t-time of the Oldest Ones. So one of the priests told me."

"You are getting to be a sage," I said to him with a little scorn. I did not like it when Ghost acted like he was a chieftain instead of a servant. I considered him a man, had found that out, after all, while we were on the great river. He was also my friend, and yet he was not a chieftain or one of the nobility. People should keep their places, I thought.

Still, it was interesting that he had been talking to the priests. "And did Alton Ha tell you why it is they believe the gods walk among us sometimes? That seems odd."

"Why odd?" Ghost said coolly. "We believe Nan-nan—the Son of the West Wind—turns into a giant rabbit who walks the earth."

"Well, but who believes that? It is a story meant to teach us, to entertain on the long nights."

"They believe men can become gods and gods become men. The g-god of the great city we go to was once a man, and not so long ago."

We were passing markers along the road which told when the road had been built. I was getting good at reading the dots and bars which meant the time, but I could not read this one, so I asked a woman passing. She had a baby on her back, held in a head-bending cradleboard to make its forehead flat, so I knew she was noble.

She studied it a moment. "Over eight hundred summers ago the Old Ones built this high road," she said. I smiled and gave her thanks.

She wished to walk behind me in the custom of women of this country, but I had her come to my side. "Tell me more of Kukulcan," I said. "I want to be able to acknowledge him in the temples when we reach Chichen Itza." Not worship, just acknowledge.

"He was a man in the time of the great-grandfathers. He and his powerful clan came from the north, from the Toltec cities. He was a leader, greatest of all, so they say, though he was foreign, like the 'foreigners' they keep talking of. They fought and won and then Kukulcan married one of the Maya. He founded one city, then left to re-settle the old town we go to, Chichen Itza. It was deserted, its buildings not used. So he—they—built new, fine buildings. Greater than all in the land."

"There is a great temple on the hill," so Smoke Fox-god said, "called Kukulcan, Temple of the Feathered Serpent."

"Yes, he is worshipped there. For after this man-god built the city, he left it. He said he wished to go back to Mexico, the land of the north. He said he would return some day." I thanked her, and she returned to her spot walking behind us.

Down the road we walked, amidst drizzling rain. Wonderful here that the roads did not turn to mud! On we walked, for another day without reaching a large city. At night we camped. But the steward had prepared me. "Take the tent and pick ground as high as you can. Then hang the hammocks—the sand fleas and other vermin, not to mention the spiders, will not get you in your camp."

And so we did. And Ghost cooked fine stew, though it was not of monkeys, and talked of his life in the nun's house, his tongue less halting, I thought, than it used to be. In some way he was coming into his own down here, as if this whole trip were his moon-in-the-wild.

As we came nearer the City of All Cities, the crowds increased. We saw litters, carrying the "ones who have possessions," the fat merchants, eating figs and honey cakes as they rode along and others of various classes, with wares on their backs so heavy it did not seem two men could carry them. The loads, which were either in baskets all down the back, or carried in woven bags, were affixed with a strap to the carrier's head. We saw whole teams of men carrying the bags of salt on their backs—heavy load! And lighter back loads of woven goods, pottery (oh, Loon Feather I thought, when I saw them and remembered how she had learned the skill so cleverly) jugs and god images for the home and water pots sticking out of the woven carrying baskets which reached beneath their knees. And their women with carrying trays around their necks in front, full of pots of honey or chilies or salted fish or turtle meat. And we saw children eating nuts and sweets out of pouches and dogs dancing along. Litters, and even burden carriers, moved at a slow run: there were decrees that one could not occupy these royal roads to dally or slow the trade.

Then, across a slight rise, the towers of Chichen Itza could be seen afar off, gleaming like the halls of the gods all these people believed in. Truly, truly it was—but no more. Let me tell you of it. Pretend you are there. You can see the great stone temple hill rising ,across many lengths of land. It seemed to reach almost to the heavens, I tell you, and it gleamed in the sun of He Is Halfway

318

Home. It had terraces, at least ten of them, and steps between, leading up to a temple at the top. Along the sides were the narrow steps these people loved, going to the top, but it was tall, taller than anything I had ever seen, and because it was of white stone it surpassed the temple at Cahokia as a fair maid surpasses one of the Mayan monkeys. Other buildings stood out; we could see their towers in what seemed to be three sides of a square.

The first thing we came to were the white stone walls, like those of Zama. One had to have the best walls in the sacred area; if the warriors of other cities came, the gate had to stand fast. What a shock it must have been to see an enemy coming, their menacing god-animal helmets, their spears and spear throwers held high, their voices screaming insult—to kill the nobles of the city, to take their ruler into submission and offer tribute or revenge insult.

Or, to see these wild warriors descend suddenly to get the victims of the sacrifice and offer their blood to the voracious gods. These Mayan peoples could not take their own relatives—all in every city loved their own children and families and would be angry if the nobles or priests offered sacrifice too freely from the home people.

So the rulers had to look abroad to appease the gods' anger. The gods were angry often, very often lately, it seemed, and the rulers ranged afield to get the sacrifice victims—as well as the slaves that the merchants needed to carry goods and to fan them in their litters. The pain of the women and children carried to the slave market, the slaughter of the men stabbed for sacrifice—their bodies thrown into the pits or hurled off the temple walls—must have been awful. Small wonder Hawk Eye in Cahokia hated to see, or be, in the army when they took the defenseless. The Birds of Thunder must have frowned and hated this land, or any land, when they did that. Fighting only for just cause is what the Birds of Thunder taught.

Guards greeted us at the wall gate. We said we were from Zama and carried an inscribed bark book from the Ruler, telling we were his emissaries for the marriage. The guards touched earth for us and ushered us through the gate.

319

Inside it was as it had seemed from afar, a city built around a huge plaza two hundred man-strides on each side. We went to one side of the plaza, where were contained the homes of commanding noblemen. The Atza family's house, so the steward had said, would be there, near the old Star Watcher's Temple. We made our way, past a huge ball court, past that huge and wonderful temple hill dedicated to Kukulcan, past the town well, to the area of buildings from an earlier time and the houses of the ruling nobles.

Son of the Star Watchers that I was, I could not help but stop in awe at the star-watching temple, which stood not one hundred paces from the home of the noble family which was our destination. On a series of platforms stood the most wonderful round-roofed structure made like the roof of the heavens—it was obvious that it was aligned to view and honor the Sun Lord when he arose on that longest day of the year, on the day of Spring Equal Day and Night and perhaps, I thought, to see the limits of the moon's passage. There were windows for viewing from the height of that hill. How I wanted to know more!

Inside the door opening of the house we had been directed to, we heard a woman's voice that sounded like the bells of music. "They are here."

A tiny woman of about thirty-five summers stepped out to meet us. She wore the embroidered tunic of a merchant's family. A broken nose, plastered rather flat against her face, marred what would have been a roundly pleasant face. Let me tell you I was surprised to see that in this land a woman could be the steward of a huge and noble household! She—Comalca—would represent the family in the details of the wedding, as I would.

"But," she said, taking my walking staff to put in the corner of the large receiving room, "you have brought a companion." Ghost stood silent beside me.

"Yes," I told her. "This is my helper and friend of the road. In Zama they think to worship him as the god Perahotan, but he denies that he is quite a god yet."

"Here we revere the short and bent ones as wisest of all of the gods' children," she said, nodding seriously.

Ghost gave her one of his rare smiles, and we toured the house beyond the large receiving room, with its stone seats along the walls. Through a door and beyond a courtyard were smaller rooms for each member of the family, with beds covered with fine cotton spreads and hardwood clothing chests carved with gods' heads and household scenes.

In the back of the house were the granaries and cookeries, looking almost like Cahokia's, with corn grinding stones and huge pestles where young girls could grind corn, tubs for the kernels which were being softened, pots to store the wood ashes which would become corn softener, granaries on stilts, their sides covered with chains of peppers, baskets and bags of corn, pots of honey.

But the garden was a fragrant paradise. Up lanes made with small rocks, where one could walk with ease, were flowering bushes and trees of every sort. "One lane is for sweet smells. Lord Atza can take his chocolate here, on a stone bench of an afternoon. We call it fragrance lane," Comalca told us.

"Ahh," Ghost said, sniffing the vanilla and wild gardenia and red and yellow flowered plants.

"Do you love the flowers?" she asked, looking at him with her head on one side.

"I have always l-loved them most," Ghost answered. "My mother kept a rose hedge around our shelter—before she died." His eyes were far away.

"Ah, poor man, you were an orphan?"

"Raised by my village," I started to answer, but before I could get it out he was interrupting and pointing.

"Raised by his village in the far north." I smiled a little.

"But your name Ghost—in our tongue—means spirit of the dead one. That sounds frightening."

Ghost stumblingly told her the story of his naming and she looked at both of us wide-eyed, trying, I suppose, to visualize a place where it was not always summer and a spirit who spoke through the thunder and rain.

"Perhaps it is the rain god Chac," Comalca said, "in one of his forms."

"Whoever he is, he is my friend," said Ghost, smiling again. That was two smiles in one day, I thought with a smirk.

This enthusiastic, laughing, woman steward, with a slightly round middle which spoke of plenty to eat, took us all about the garden and then showed us domiciles at the back of it. "These are the guest houses and,—she averted her eyes humbly—"I have the honor to live permanently in one of them. Next to the one you occupy." She took us to it and we relaxed with slaves bringing us posol— hot corn meal in water, mixed with honey and vanilla, and salted nuts which we ate before the evening meal.

The Atzas met us in the receiving room, the handsome mother and father standing side by side, with a priest beside them (in a clean robe for once) blessing the occasion by throwing copal incense on a brazier which stood in the corner. I came forward, knelt and took up a small amount of dust from the stone floor and put it on my forehead, and then, in my halting speech saluted the lord and lady from my own lord.

They stood very still, and I wondered if I had said the right words. Even after three months of constant speaking of this tongue I faltered for words. Why had Smoke Fox-god decided to send someone to be his representative who could not even speak the tongue well?

But after a moment the wife of Lord Atza smiled. "We thank you, steward," she said. "But that is not your real name. I know you have the confidence of your young ruler, for so we have been informed. By what familiar name does he call you?"

"Well—I am—he calls me Tunkel."

"Drum?"

"Drum-of-the-Gods is my name. It was given me in my homeland of the far north. He has nicknamed me for the dance drum." A young woman, really no bigger than a child, was coming from an inner court. "Well, really, it is because I talk a lot. My words, he says, are as the drops of rain from the heavens."

They laughed.

"In a thunderstorm," I added, not knowing why I was blabbing on this way.

"This is Ela, Moon-path," the mother said, taking the beautiful girl by the hand to present her. Well! Smoke Fox-god would certainly have a beauty for a bride.

"How many summers has she?" I asked. Thoughts came of my own Loon Feather, at home, waiting, waiting, suffering with the agony of apprehension while I ate salted nuts and feasted my eyes—but I could not stop looking.

"Fifteen summers," the father said. He was dressed in a magnificent robe embroidered with some scene. I let my eyes stray to it, in spite of myself. It showed warriors, with odd-looking headdresses fighting with someone inferior—were they Maya?—and killing them.

Paintings on the walls showed the same things, and the decorations were intricate, with many serpent mouths and gods in the skies and odd, lined out animals—in the style of "the foreigners" from the north—those they called the Toltecs and Mexicas. All the architecture was of this foreign style. It was clear. Smoke Fox-god was marrying a "foreigner"—by design I suppose. These were the lords of Chichen Itza, and Zama was tributary to the city.

The father, mother and daughter knelt at the shrine as the priest scattered incense around them. "Is this for the wedding?" I asked in a whisper when they rose.

"No, it is the evening worship of the gods," the father said, with a serious face. He explained that they were a pious family; I had seen that myself on the tour we had taken; in every nook and room was a shrine to another god, effigies standing (as I thought) grotesquely about with their odd faces. Itzamna, king of the gods, Exchel, rainbow and moon deity, Chac, rain god, Ek Chuah, merchant god and the rest. The family was, as a matter of fact, in the god business. They manufactured the gods from stone and cement. The only one I liked, ever had liked, since I came was Yum Kax, the corn god. He had a fine shrine in the garden, and his

323

young face and the corn sprouting from his hat made me think of home.

Now the evening worship was over; the priest backed out the door, to return to read the signs tomorrow before we made the final plans for the wedding.

The girl, properly shy and retiring in the face of the event to come, bowed to her parents, and we were called to the evening meal. These noble people did not eat on their haunches around the fire, holding food, as almost everyone I knew ate even in these rich lands of the south—they gathered around a flat, carved thing made of boards held together. We all sat around its edges. Bowls of flowers sat on it; incense holders sent fine, good-smelling scents through the receiving room; torches in metal holders gleamed, illuminating the fine wood carvings on the beams and door opening and the gold inlaid tiles in the wall.

Slaves came in, bearing platters of delicious food in courses: there were clam or mussel things, small round fish objects which were gently fried in a little fat and herbs and were the best thing I have ever eaten in that line, served on their lovely, scalloped shells, all sorts of corn things, a roasted deer with its head at the end of the platter—and an odd, brewed drink. It was honey brew, fermented, and it was delicious. I must have thought I was Bear Belly again, because I ate and drank of the delicacies, especially drank, until I was satiated.

Musicians came in, playing love flutes. Ela, Moon-path, the fair bride-to-be we were honoring, sat with flowers in her pulled-back hair and listened dreamily, looking as if the spirits of love had enchanted her. Looking at her, longing for my own promised one, I felt enchanted too, and full of thoughts of love.

Ghost had not come to the festivity—he dined in the back quarters with the steward Comalca. As I left the festivity, I knew that Ghost was in our own guest shelter now; I could see his shadow in the torchlight coming out of the guest house. I felt unsteady as I came through the door opening.

"It was all fine—there was a drink fermented from honey."

"I know," he said. "I h-h-had some too." His speech was slurred worse than before. I sat down heavily, a little confused. Could this drink be good for people?

"And was your eating-time good?" I asked, looking at a spot on my merchant's tunic.

"She—Comalca—was a n-nun. I told her of my time in the nun's house in Zama. How they t-t-thought I was a god."

"Did you?" I was surprised at this boldness—to talk to a consecrated nun that way. The nuns—not the virgin ones reserved to the gods, but the concubines of the nobility—had initiated him into several types of love-making. Do not look surprised—those Mayan tribes approved of several things we do not think seemly. I have told you of the books with shocking pictures.

"She was a n-n-nun until a few moons ago. Promised to the god Chac, she was kept pure. Served the house of nuns as its steward, food buyer—the things you do."

"And so she came here?"

"In this c-c-city, by ancient custom of the foreigners who built it, the women are kept holy only until their thirty-fifth s-s-summer. But they do not have concubine nuns here in Chichen Itza for the rich. It is a p-p-pious city, so she says, and she came to serve a pious family."

I had taken off everything but my loincloth and lay on the bed. Sticks above it held a sort of fishnet tent, woven so closely it kept out insects, yet open enough to let in air. These rich ones had conquered even the mosquitoes!

Ghost's voice droned on. "Comalca is very pious. Visits each shrine each day and stays on her knees while the sun rises at dawn. Wishes for p-p-purity of soul."

"Umm," I answered, beginning to get drowsy.

"Says she wishes she could know the joys of the married women—the joys of joining."

"She said that to you?" I murmured, half-listening. "Surely she was opening her heart to a visitor. It is hardly seemly—"

"She said she was of an open nature, giving, made all of love. She feels no regret she was pledged to the g-g-god, but envies the women who now are married."

The last thing I heard before I drifted off was Ghost crawling under his net, lying down with a sigh. "Of course, I could hardly hope—"

I awoke with the moon shining full into my bed. My head half hurt and my thoughts tumbled. I knew only one thing—I was tormented by a burning, irresistible lust. (Are the children asleep again there on their pallets?)

My body of sixteen summers, for many months in the past used to constant exercise of its manly needs by a woman who wanted me, and stimulated by the rich food and brewed drink and talk of love, was out of hand. I was simply worse than any deer who ever rushed up when I rattled the antlers. My honorable quest—my vows to my beloved—all blew away like brown beech leaves in autumn before the wind. I was in the worst heat of my life.

Ghost was making snortling sounds under his net, deeply asleep, I thought. I crept out into the garden, smelling the overwhelming sweetness of night-blooming, white-star flowers.

I found myself at Comalca's door. I rustled the fabric covering a little, almost as a question. I heard her sigh in her bed, turn over.

I pulled the curtain back a little; the moon shone in on her form, beneath her net. Her body was covered with a thin sheet, but I could see. I thought I would die. "Comalca?" I whispered. The sounds of the love flute tootled in the back of my mind like a wheedling bird.

She opened her eyes and I stepped in the door. "I couldn't sleep and needed water," I said lamely, in a whisper. I was half afraid. If she should scream, call the noble family—my lord would put my head on the floor as he had the captives in the picture.

But no. She drew back her net, removed her sheet and sat on the edge of her bed, the garment falling away from her legs up to her thigh. "You are thirsty, are you?" she said and smiled. I took it as an invitation, and when I came near, she held up her arms. I

326

lay down at her side, but I did think to close the curtain. I did not wish to satiate my burning lust with bugs distracting me.

I am shamed to tell you (they are asleep?) that I deflowered that holy virgin in about twenty-five ways that night, forsaking every vow I had ever made in an orgy of pleasure. Every thing Soft Fur had ever taught me, many a thing in those pictures I did to Comalca, and what is more, she did them back to me.

The moon had moved away from our door. Perhaps it did not wish to see. The dark does mask a lot of sins, does it not? At great high moments I tried to keep my exultant voice down in the stillness of that garden; sometimes hers did sing out a little, a love flute of its own, newly whittled into life.

When I finally returned, dazed and ready to sleep, I stumbled off the path for an instant—knocked over something right by the door opening of the guest house. I looked down. I had tumbled the god Ek Chuah, patron of the merchants, off his pedestal. For a moment I felt dismay. Then I laughed a laugh. "We did it all for you," I whispered to the stone smirker. "We are cementing a new trading alliance, joining two great trading cities anew. You will be greatly honored." Then I lurched through the door opening and into bed.

The next day, with an aching head and eyes that avoided hers, I made lists with the steward of what would be needed for the wedding, who would be coming.

"The ruler has no family, except an aunt," I said. "She is unable to attend. But all of the batab noblemen and their wives have said they would attend—and in the old Captain of the Guard's district, the nobleman will bring three grown children and their families. Two of our priests will attend and three nuns to tend the sacred fires we will light. (Nuns!) There will have to be guest houses provided, meals arranged for." (And may they not include the rich creatures of the sea and the brewed honey drink.)

"We will provide lodging in the houses just built behind the Star Watching Temple," she answered gravely. "Food can be carried in—" We spoke of the feast to follow, the dishes the ruler would approve of, the guests to be invited, and then we went together to present the plan to the nobleman and his wife.

It is odd—we both seemed to have no more desire for one another; we were as distant as the stars. Perhaps it was her shame, as a devout woman, to have indulged in such decadence of the body. Perhaps it was mine—a pledged man on a mission for those he loves, to have lost the control of his manhood in such a way. "Bear Male Part," I called myself, now that I was no longer calling myself Bear Belly.

We walked single file along the paths, shame standing like a spirit between us, and would walk no more together in love during that visit.

But she did walk out, innocently, that evening with Ghost. She took him up the sacred walk to see the Cenote of Sacrifice. Past the great ball-playing field, past the Temple of Kukulcan, was the great well the Old Ones had used before the city had been abandoned the first time. It could not now be used for water, but it served another purpose. From its heights women were sent to be messengers to the gods at times of drought or other calamities. They were hurled from the high cliff into the well, drugged and with heavy jewelry on, and if they did happen to live, hours later they were picked out of the well to give their messages back from the gods. So Ghost told me when they returned.

"We prayed at the shrine there, and in the Temple of the Warriors too. She prayed for the city. Other powerful cities are jealous of it, have sent war parties and may send more. She is very d-d-devout. She seems to like me."

"Maybe she thinks you are Perahotan."

328

He waited a bit before he answered, then gave another of his rare smiles. "I don't care," he said.

Ghost was very helpful in preparing for the wedding visit, bringing firewood, standing up beds in the guest houses and doing the other bowlful of tasks that it takes to make a wedding work. And he worked in the garden in the late evening hours, with Comalca, cutting off dead branches, rooting shoots in pots, watering.

And I attended to the details of the dowry for the next two passages of the sun. I was too busy to think, calculating during the day and at night watching Ghost and Camalca. My servant, my friend, returned each night happy. "She sees me straight," he said, and there was real emotion in his voice.

I prayed it would not rain, that the vengeful spirits of the northern lakes might not have the opportunity to speak a shabby truth among the drops that fell to refresh the southern earth and tell my friend the truth about my wild night beneath the moon with the woman of his dreams.

I sent a message back that all was concluded for the wedding, and duly, in fourteen passages of the sun, our lord the Ruler came; duly the ceremonies were carried out between him and the shy, beautiful child of the nobleman. Both sets of priests arrived at the Atzas' house, looking suspicious of each other. Smoke Fox-god and Ela, Moon-path came and stood, both dressed in their finest garb. Standing behind the couple were the bridal party, their parents, I and three or four other of the nobility, led by Sky Many Deer, the lord who always smiled the large smile. In the back of the room stood those of lesser rank, in this case, Comalca and Ghost.

And so our priest asked Chak to send rain and Exchel to send children and Itzamna to watch over the home. And their priest, whose hair was bloodier than even Alton Ha's, with toenails even longer and stronger, like claws, asked Kukulcan, whom he called

Quexalcoatl, to bring peace and gentleness and goodness to the marriage.

Then Comalca and I were called on to talk of the details of the arrangement, and because her knowledge of the tongue was far better than mine, especially for figures, she read off the dowry and accounted for it (lengths of cloth to be taken by slaves home with the Ruler, the Ruler to settle so many lands outside Zama on his wife, to be held and farmed as one unit by the representatives of the Atza family and so forth).

Then the priests went through the house, both chanting, swinging the pots of incense until I thought I would choke, and then the couple knelt and were blessed by the priest and—it was over!

That part, I mean. The wedding celebration was to come, a week and a half of it. Tomorrow would be the music performances, with hundreds of dancers in a circle. Two special dancers would be dressed as hunter and hunted acting out a chase to music—the gourd rattles and tunkels and log drums and bells and flutes and trumpets—all would be lively. I would see little of it, of course, as it was performed on the flat stone Stage of the Evening Star, and I was required to stay at home this night and supervise the possessions of my lord.

"And so," I asked Smoke Fox-god when I was arranging for a litter to take him to the spot, "I see that the Stage of the Evening Star is also called Kukulcan."

"Yes. He is thought of as the evening star."

"Then mayhap he is another name for Nanaboozhoo?" I had told him a little of our lore.

"They seem to be alike, from what you told me. Both are called sons of the West Wind."

The litter bearers came to take the newly married couple to the Stage of the Evening Star, and I stayed to see to the cleaning of the royal quarters.

The next day I did get to see the drama plays in honor of the wedding. We went before He Is Halfway Home to see them at their beginning. All the actors wore masks—the plays were humorous on this day. Tomorrow would be the serious, religious ceremonies planned to appeal to the gods for the safety of the city in the face of the hostile enemies Comalca had spoken of.

A group of actors, robed like merchants and with signs of the god Ek Chuah in their hands, came shuffling in like lame rabbits. They had stuffed straw pillows under their robes, so they appeared fat, and the masks were of beasts of prey—jackals, wolves, vultures. One of the "merchants" had taken to gambling on the games to pay for a trip to "the south" to get gold. He bet everything he had, ended up betting his dog and his slaves and then his ranting, raving wife to pay for "southern gold." So the show went. The crowd roared, and I felt only a little uncomfortable as a merchant.

The litter bearers seemed to be ready to bring the Ruler and his bride home; I wandered over to the ball court. On my way I passed the wall of skulls—a solid wall put together with the skulls of those killed in the ball court and other sacrifices. I paused in fascination—the fatal fascination all of us have with inevitable death. This, I suppose, was the reason for all the sacrifices, partly at least. To somehow remind the living that beyond the bright sun of the day in which they lived and walked, lurked the darkness of the grim, gray moon, the darkness of cold clay and earth.

I studied the long court, lined with stone steps, with two temples on either side, empty now, but soon, on the morrow, to be filled with spectators to celebrate the wedding of my friend Smoke Fox-god and the noble daughter of one of their first families. And also to celebrate death in the middle of life, just as the wall of skulls did. The captain of the losing team of this contest tomorrow would be instantly killed at its completion on the altar platform I had just seen. He would be sent to bear a message to the gods and to buy pacification for the people of Chichen Itza and favor for the newly married couple.

Again, I drank a good deal of the honey liquor, and I could not sleep that night. I wandered through the garden, now lit only by starlight. I looked up, knowing that the Star Watchers were looking in the round-domed building behind me at the same constellations—the stars which Ghost always said looked like a big gourd dipper but which we call Monster Big Head. He has lost his head, my father always said, and is going around the pole star looking for it.

How long these Maya had watched the stars and how good they were at it! They had set the very city, the buildings, the windows, according to observations of the zenith and high and low days of the sun! And—I knew it was so because I had been told—on the days of Equal Day and Night, spring and fall, the feathered serpents that are at the edge of the north stair at the great temple of Kukulcan cast magic shadows which writhe like diamond-back rattlesnakes! It was so built, oh most wonderful of star-watching cities.

My eyes were cast so high that I almost bumped into someone who walked quietly among the flowering bushes.

"We watch them so much—but what do the Star Lords think of us, oh Drum-of-the-Gods?" Comalca asked in a soft voice.

I was in an odd mood, as I seemed to be after the drinking. "Oh, that we spend months growing a good corn stalk and then throw a whole ear of it into our stomach of an evening, only to have it pass out as waste and garbage. That we squabble over mates and fight over trifles and aren't really worth even looking at, I suppose. And that our passions, which are given to us as a treasure trove, to spend, a pearl at a time over years, we insist on dumping out by the bagful in an hour's time."

"Your words are harsh, but you are right." She came close to me. "I feel shame," she whispered.

"Do not," I said, feeling a guilt which came forth as irritation. "We harmed nobody. I see many things in this city worse than what we did."

"Yes. It is a city of shallowness, a time of uncleanness. Many blame the 'foreigners,' but I think—anyway, I was a nun, pledged to the gods, and I am now ashamed." She began to weep a little, and that irritated me.

"Ashamed, that we acted naturally? As animals do everyday with pleasure in every bush? As half of the good people, married and unmarried do any time they can in—" I gestured around "the city. I sometimes get tired of all this religion going on every day—and night."

332

Then I calmed down. "We have harmed nobody. The stars do not care."

"I wish I could be as distant and cold as they," she said, looking back over her shoulder at me with a meaningful look. She took a blossom and put it in her hair and went towards her door. Yet, I certainly did not think there was love for me in that soft voice, but instead regret, as if something had been lost that would never be regained.

The next morning the Atza family took litters to the ceremonial ball game and religious rite. Ghost and I went together, and since I have said a good deal about these matters already I shall tell you only that they played the game on the long court, each team member having his body protected by leather so the hard, bouncing ball would not hurt if it hit a knee or the chest. The crowd roared and screamed on the stone benches and hoped that the ball would not, as it did on rare occasions, go through the hoop, because then they would have to give the scorer all their jewelry. There was no one who actually got the ball through the stone hole at the side of the court, but many other scoring things happened, and finally the game was over. The captain of the losing team did, indeed, get carried by the priests to the altar of sacrifice right near the ball courts and did, indeed go through the horrid death rites— and did take whatever message he was supposed to, to the gods.

Although, after all of that cruelty, if it were I, I would simply walk away with my arms folded and my back turned when I got to the gods. Let them carry their own messages. If there were any gods that looked like turtle heads and did bad things. Which I doubted.

And then, after they had prayed many prayers for the help of the city in the face of war, they carried a few male captives to the deep, old sacred cenote and, all watching (except I, I had gone back by this time but Ghost told me,) threw them in with great force and they hurtled down and beneath the water, carrying the bells of death. And all the people went home and drank so much of the honey ale that they dimmed their senses. I too drank of it, again and again, because it made me forget.

That night I had troubled dreams. I dreamed of my distant mother, my worthless father, and I called to them to love me in my sleep, and yearned towards them, feeling pain in the heart even as I had felt it in my lifetime. But they did not love me. Finally, I saw a great bear, who stood before me with bright, sharp eyes. "Attend me," he said, and the voice was one of command, not as a dream voice, so that my spirit quelled within me. "You are lingering long in this land of shallow shadows, forgetting your quest," he said, and I knew the voice, though my mind would not tell me who it was.

I wanted to tell the dream bear that I was trying to build up the trust to go to the cave and get what I had promised, that it could not be done overnight. But my words were stuck in syrup or phlegm and would not come out.

"And, on a sacred quest, you are performing hurt." The voice, the voice, it pained me, yet I yearned towards it because I knew—

"Be off to your task. You are living among the mean-spirited, and their lowness has pulled you down, as quicksand pulls the body into death." Then the bear turned its back and walked away.

And I cried, "Uncle, Uncle, come back." But he would not even turn to listen to what I had to say.

The ruler and his bride left, then, and it took almost six days to see the dowry on the road and organize the maids and possessions of Ela, Moon-path, consort to the ruler of Zama for the trip back.

I chafed at the delay, because I knew the dream had been right. Ghost chafed too, but spent the time helping in the household with Comalca, whom he now seemed to adore. She for her part seemed to enjoy his company, looking into his face with real interest, as they tallied little god images delivered from the potters or took the statues of Ek Chuah, Yum Kax the corn god or Chac to the market for people to buy for family shrines. Perhaps she really did think Ghost should be revered as holy.

I for my part did try to follow the command of the dream bear by seeing if I could find a cure for the Female Sun in Cahokia, as I had promised. I did spend time consulting physicians, who were the best in the land there, to see what could be done for tumor in the womb.

But they all said the same thing: of this bad sort of tumor of the womb, which her own physicians had diagnosed, it would grow until it had reached all the organs, and she would die in great pain. There was nothing that could be done, they said. In places farther south, they did cutting on the head and some said on other parts of the body. If I could go south, perhaps I could find some sort of knowledge that would cure her.

The ball game was not going my way! No cure for the Female Sun. And so I would have to go back without what I had hinted— well, promised on that score. Would that I did not further lose points, or the entire game would be forfeit.

The night before we left I saw a shadow outside the door of our guest house just after dark had fallen. I stepped outside, and Comalca whispered, "Meet me at the small ball field behind the market soon."

I waited a few moments, then walked rapidly to the field. She stood behind a little temple and stepping out, grasped my arm. Her eyes were frightened. "I am with child," she said.

I stopped and stared at the hole the ball was supposed to go through without really seeing it. I felt as if I had fallen from a tree and landed on a rock. "How can you be certain of that?" I asked.

"Time enough has passed. I have tried all the herb women advise in such things—no."

I said nothing. I did not know what to say, but there was a tightness, a sickness inside me as if the Bird of Thunder were sitting on my chest.

The evening star arose, star of the Son of the West Wind—and the name of the platform of bloody sacrifice. "I will be killed," she said, looking at the star. "The pledged maidens may never know men."

"Not even after they have left the service of the gods?" There was beauty in her face, even dignity, in spite of the fear that was there.

"Unless some priest or holy man takes the maid after she has left the temple for his own in marriage."

Get off my chest, Bird of Thunder, I thought, an idea is thumping there. "A holy man?" I looked her full in the face.

She nodded, mutely.

"Would—would Perahotan do?"

"Perahotan?"

"Well, Perahotan in the image of man. A man upon whom the finger of the gods rests."

"Ah. Well—" She turned away.

"He cares for you. With only a little encouragement—"

She turned to me suddenly, as an animal wheels when the hunter has driven it into a corner. "I could not! To make him think—no, it would be deception."

"There is one path in the woods. I do not see a fork to choose." My voice was cold. This matter had to be resolved.

Silently tears came down her cheeks. Then they began to splash onto the ball court. In her agonized eyes I could see the years of her future flash by, made dull with a man she did not love.

"What would the arrangements be?" I asked rather insistently.

"He would—come to my house. Eat a meal I fix. It is the custom. Then go to the Lord Atza and propose a marriage."

"And they would agree?"

"I do not know. You are foreigners and the circumstances are odd. But—" she sighed and wiped away the tears with the corner of her mantle. "I suppose he could come to help me in the pottery

336

business. They would see that as gain, as he is a bright, clever worker. If they did not say yes for religion's sake, then for business."

"The business is the image of the gods." I laughed a little. "In the marketplace. Perahotan's sacred image shop."

"You are harsh and sharp as a sacrificial knife, for one who said we would hurt no one by what we did." Now, even through the darkness, I could feel the heat of her body and, curse me, I desired her even in spite of all of this.

"You are right. I do not wish to be so hard-hearted. What else would remain to be settled?"

"The man's portion for the marriage. My dowry would be the place I hold as security for the future and the house."

"How large should the man's portion be?" We began to walk back towards the noble district.

"It would have to be of good size in such a case."

"I will think on it."

I did think and realized that there was nothing for it except to do what had to be done myself to get her married to someone appropriate. Even if I could consider for one moment marrying her, I was not a priest or sacred person and so not eligible. But Ghost was, and he loved her! Still–the dowry; what to do about the man's portion of the dowry. Smoke Fox-god would certainly never help. He would probably kill me for corrupting a sacred virgin if he knew, and indeed he would be within the law and good common sense.

Inside my steward's deerskin pouch were the few trading treasures I had left. A very few fine obsidian blades—and three pearls. They were all the savages on the beach had left me. The largest pearl was the size of a large thumbnail and was of priceless value. I had saved it to trade for the medical knowledge I still hoped to get, the knowledge that would save my cousin and true love.

337

Still, we could not die just because we had broken the taboo. I showed the pearl to her, there at her door, and as I did, the mantle slipped from her shoulders and for a moment, before she straightened it I saw her firm, up- tilted breasts and yearned, beast that I was. She looked at the pearl and nodded.

"Which of us is going to be the one to bring the message of deception to our friend?" she said with scorn in her voice.

"I will," I muttered. She faded into the darkness of her doorway as the sweet perfume of flowers drifted about and large moths began to flutter around the garden torches.

And so, the next day I told my friend that if he wished, he could ask for the hand of Comalca, the steward of the noble family, because she had spoken to me hesitantly of her love, and I saw the light ignite in his eyes as if it were from a flint to tinder.

And, since lies begat other lies easily, as hundreds of maggots hatch out from one fly in the dead body of a dog, so I slipped into more untruths. "Since you are a good servant of my family's these many years, I will give a pearl for your marriage settlement. "

"For me?" the innocent joy in his eyes made me squirm.

"Well, you are my friend, too." That was not all made up.

"Can I h-hope for her? Can it be true?" He began to caper about, as if he were one of the dancers we had seen on the Stage of the Evening Star. "But then," he said, "I do not know if I wish to live here always, to be away from Lakes-Like-a-Necklace. I was born and bred—"

"Well," I said smooth as bear oil, "I will not be returning for a few more moons yet. If you find you do not like the role of husband, you can always divorce. It is easy enough here." But when you find you are going to be a father, you will not so easily leave. So the real truth went.

Truth—suddenly I recalled what should not have slipped my mind. Storm Spirit. True enough it was that it came to him in the rain, and if it should tell him of the child before the marriage contract was made, all would be lost.

I looked up for clouds. There were none. "Tomorrow. Tomorrow is the day we should make her yours. She has invited you for the noon meal."

"Well," he said a little hesitantly. I opened the pouch. Then I took out a smaller, but equally perfect pearl. I put it in his hand and closed the hand over it.

"A wedding present," I said. And then I went to the cooking stores and, opening the door, took out the honey liquor and drank until I was out of my head.

And so, after leaving alone that terrible town of Chichen Itza, with a full train of serving girls, dower gifts and warriors to guard us on the roads, I passed a series of stone pillars on the road. Each one told the tale of some fine conquest of some god-king who had put his enemies under his foot, let their blood, and tossed them to the gods in such and such a katun, repeating the good luck of the previous katun. And near them, twining around, were the faces of yowling beasts and the leering reptilian countenances of Ek Chuah the merchant god, Yum Cimil, the god of death, Chac the rain god.

"And so," I told myself morosely," they should raise a monument post to you, Drum-of-the-Gods. Only this one would tell the real truth. 'Came on a holy quest from the north, Drum-of-the-Gods.' (For they put the action first on their monuments.) Polluted it with his hot lust, drinking of fermented drinks, laying with a virgin nun, getting her with child, lying to his honest friend and bribing him to marry her.'" And my face, I thought, when I saw it in one of the obsidian mirrors a guard had hanging from his headdress, looked just as reptilian and aloof as the ones of the gods I had always despised.

For I tell you true that what I saw in that mirror was not my face but the truth, the reason the bear in my dream had upbraided me so. Appetite, appetite gone wild. It plagued me, threatened to destroy me. You have seen a flea. Once you dash it from your arm it waits a moment and then jumps onto your leg and begins to suck your life away again, and it is like false appetite, which can keep at you, biting in one way and then changing form if you aren't careful. In my case the craving had certainly changed form. I had gone from being a ravenous bear-belly glutton to being a ravenous bear male-part lecher. And it was impossible to tell which was worse, for they were two springs which flowed from the same source.

And the worst part was, whenever I thought of Loon Feather awaiting me at home in Cahokia, I no longer yearned for her. In my wild betrayal, I had lost the most precious thing of all—my love for my pure betrothed one.

The weather was particularly hot, and we stopped at a roadside rest station and worship shrine to let the maidens and baggage-bearers rest. In the clearing the birds had quit singing, and the lizards, large and small, were hiding by rocks, the little pouches under their chins throbbing. There was a sort of breathless oppression in that heat of He Is Halfway Home that made me pant, made my heart race.

I looked at the shrine, where worshippers of the rain god Chac could burn incense. He was not the only one represented here, though, for they had put out images of the thirteen deities of the upper world and the nine deities of the lower world, so that everywhere I turned there was an eagle-beaked, blind-eyed god.

The maidens and burden-carriers lounged about eating corn paste cakes baked in leaves and enclosing beans and meat. They ate separately, the young women with their backs to the men, as was seemly in their society. Some occasionally came and burnt incense for a brief moment and seemed to say a prayer.

I fixed my eyes on the shrines, stared at the faces of the Mayan gods. The smells of the baking rain forest, mixed with the pungent incense made me feel a wave of nausea, and when it did not pass after a moment but only grew worse, I had to pass into the clumps of odd trees and relieve my stomach. When I returned, I turned from the sight of those gods and sat beneath a tree. I desired, yearned with all my heart for the deep northern woods. For pine trees' sweet cool scent, for the darkness and refreshment of a bed of moss beneath an enormous oak tree, for rushing streams pouring over small rapids where one must carry the canoe, and the icy water chills your feet in the moccasins.

Lake-of-the-Boulders! With the honest spirits of the ancestors nearby and the devout and wondering worship of all nature and the power which made it. I longed for the goodness of it more than I had longed for the virgin woman in the mad moonlight, and I thought I could not stand my longing, that it would break my heart as too much pressure breaks an arm caught in a tree.

Now I could not look at the gods even if I had wanted to; I felt a revulsion, as when one has grown sick from food, and ever after in memory always associates the food that caused the nausea, or the house in which one sat, and cannot stand it. And as we went again onto the road I turned once more and saw the gods' small bodies on their stone stands there, and I spat over my shoulder at them all. "I scorn you, empty stones. All I can see that you bring to these people is bad luck and cruelty and ignorant bondage. Now I have said it, do your worst, if you do not like it. I cannot be in much worse trouble than I am anyway, for I am a worse enemy to myself than any god could ever be."

I wished my face to be set for home now. And yet, I did not see how that could be. My companion, it seemed, would not be coming home with me, I had little hope of finding a cure for the Female Sun, and I had not found the moon tablet I had promised her. And time was passing, passing. At Cahokia spring would be coming soon; dark-leaved skunk cabbages were forming the green tips they would soon push through the loam near the river, the first ducks and geese were winging in, looking down on ponds that would soon see thousands upon thousands of mallard, redheads, greens. A year, the physicians had said, and it would be a year at the end of the summer. Restlessness accompanied me as I came within the walls of Zama with the consort's train of servants.

Soon I was laughing sardonically to myself. Perhaps my sharp words, my revulsion with the gods, had humbled them and put them to work to speed my case and show they existed. For no sooner were the goods unloaded, the servants placed in housing and the litter bearers resting in servant guest houses than I received a message from Smoke Fox-god to take chocolate with him in the garden of the Ruler's House.

His wife, as was seemly, of course, was not there and the late afternoon sunlight filtered through the leaves of the large avocado tree. The little trees we had planted had grown two feet, I saw.

"I have a wife to insure the succession of my dynasty," the Ruler said, licking his lips with satisfaction over both the drink and the lovely garden. "Now it is time to think about the fabulous treasure of the Oldest Ones—the Olmec that you have told me of. It is time for you to go get it, Tunkel."

"Ah, Reverend One, you are eager, as a bridegroom should be in all he does." I stretched out on the stone bench and looked at him through half-closed eyes. "Why are you so willing to rush me away?"

"Because the more I think of what you said, the more I see it as an advantage to me. I am now confirmed by marriage as a chief tributary lord to the lord of Chichen Itza, and I wish to show him my power. Since I do not have any, I had better get some. Is that not correct?" He smiled brightly at me.

"Nothing more than good common sense."

"And I have yearly tribute, costing much to pay. These treasures—what do you recall they were exactly?"

"My uncle told me gold, jewelry of all sorts, many jade items and especially a foot-and-a-half tall jade god, very clear jade, very rare."

He absently stirred his chocolate with a ceremonial stirring stick topped by the god Ah Chicum Ek, god of the north star. Beams shot out of the small head at the top of the stick. "Such things would be wonderful to have." He stood up, setting the chocolate cup on the bench with vigor. "You will start in three days."

I stood too and positioned myself to stand above him. "Oh, Revered One, I beg to correct you. I will not start. We will start."

"We?" he seemed astonished.

I began to speak rapidly, lest he interrupt me. "Yes. I cannot go alone; my knowledge of the language is very limited, as you know. I cannot even make myself understood well in the language of this state; beyond I would be helpless. And I would not, could not go without the protection of the highest in this land. There are many dangerous peoples to pass through."

"I can send a guard of warriors."

"No, Ruler. With the recent uncertainties"—here I paused—"they could not be fully counted on. Besides, only you can represent your interest in this. You can trust no one but yourself with a treasure like this, if it is all I have been told."

"It had better be—" he looked at me with a threatening glower that was only half in jest. "Besides, it will be adventuresome. You will not have many more opportunities to live your youth free of responsibilities."

"You expect me to leave my beautiful, young, willing wife?"

"For the first and, I hope, only time. You will bring her back necklaces, pearls—I know not what."

He was silent, contemplating.

"We will need to go in excellent disguise. There is no doubt of that," I went on, temptingly.

He began to nod. I had him snared, like a rabbit in the woods.

That night was the first in many that I had not drunk the honey liquor. I slept well, and in the morning I vowed not to drink it again, even though the Ruler did sometimes. It was a pit to me as deep and dangerous as the cenotes, and if I continued, I thought no one would need to hurl me in; I would make the greatest sacrifice of all: myself.

Chapter Fourteen

"What I have," I said as we walked along the road to the outer villages, "is not a map like those I see merchants carrying here, showing the rivers as wavy lines and the position of towns the Maya hold."

"No? What do you have?"

"An ancient chant, passed from the Olmec Lords, the ones you call the Oldest Ones, to descendants in some town they held when they fell. It was given to my uncle when he came to the land of the Mayas some thirty years ago. He used it to somehow find the treasure the Olmecs had stashed away when they fled in haste."

We had come out of town so watching eyes and listening ears would not overhear what we needed to discuss. Besides, we wanted to talk again to Hoxek Yum; he had not come into the sacred precincts of the center town since we returned. I had been told when I asked that he was sick.

"Sing me the song, and perhaps I will know what it refers to. The old ones often had myths and stories that had meaning."

"Well, I cannot sing except to chant, but I will tell you the words," I said.

> Across the trail seen from the sky
> Through where there are no cities high
> To where the lords of land and water vie
> Past three great cats who never cry
> To the house at the foot which knows no day
> Where Star Lords never scatter
> There is found the Olmec hoard.

The ruler nodded, asked me to repeat it, repeated it once himself, then thought for a long while as we walked along in silence. And when we had reached the district of Hoxek Yum's house, he still had not said anything, so I knew nothing immediate had occurred to him.

Hoxek was in a corn field, burning it off to leave good ash to fertilize the crop he would be planting when the moon was next full.

He looked up as we walked across the plot, then fell on his face and rose again, putting dirt across his forehead, which since it contained much ash made him look like the god of death indeed.

"Ruler, steward, you are welcome to my humble corn patch," he said, then stared, as if wondering what we wished.

"We have missed you, Hoxek. The avocados are drooping; your helpers do not drip the water right," I said, smiling a little.

He started to say something, but then stopped. His mouth fell in dismay. "I was told you did not wish me to continue."

"What?"

"I am not allowed to be gardener any more."

"And who told you that?" the Ruler wanted to know.

Hoxek shifted his feet in his sandals, squirmed his toes.

"At the final tabulating of the tribute, my new lord, the one who replaced Lord Honacan said, "Do not garden at the Ruler's House any more."

"I did not issue that command. Do you know where it came from?" the Ruler wanted to know.

"I asked, but no one knew." He shrugged his thin shoulders. "Two Parrots, the new lord, said there were orders written on the bark book of tribute."

Smoke Fox-god's anger was growing; I beckoned him to the edge of the corn field. "Contain yourself. You must not show the rage you feel before him."

"It is obvious!" Smoke Fox-god said, spitting on the ground. "Someone observed him the day the nobles were defeated. Someone who is my enemy, and thought to quietly keep him from us. They had no idea we knew where he lived."

"Yes. Someone in the walled city does not wish his eyes around to serve your interests. But we will face that soon. Now let us reassure the old man that he and his family are in no danger."

To give the Ruler credit, he was gracious and cool when we crossed the field again. "There has been a mistake," he said to Hoxek. "I do wish you to be my gardener, and soon I hope that can happen. In the meantime, stay here. I will contact you when we can reinstate you." Hoxek nodded, I thought, gratefully. Being a lower-class political supporter of the Ruler was all very well and good except when it meant your cornfield and grandchildren were under threat.

"Tomorrow!" Smoke Fox-god said forcibly. "Give the order tomorrow and we will have the good old man back. This is not the only mischief that was wrought while we were away for the wedding. The army was changed in subtle ways, with a separate guard being pulled away by the priests for themselves. They seem not to know who gave that order, either. And the council met twice without me."

"Let us think about this, Great One. Who could do such things?"

"I do not know."

"Are there relatives of the other regime, Smoke Second's, still about?"

"You know there are none here."

"Elsewhere?" I asked a little surprised. I had understood him to say the ruler was now the last.

"Cousins of mine, indirect relatives of Smoke Second. But they are far away in the city of Mayapan."

"Mayapan?" I had heard it mentioned with disgust somewhere—was it in Chichen Itza?

"In the west. It is where my father and grandfather were born."

"I thought they ruled Zama."

"No. Zama is a fairly new town, at least as it now stands. It was settled by order of Mayapan, and the Smokes left the section of Mayapan they ruled to rule here. But the Smokes had come from other parts before they settled in Mayapan. Our ancient home is the city of Tikal." That city I had heard of. It was the greatest of all cities in the time of the Old Ones, hundreds of summers ago.

"So, could someone in, let me see, Mayapan wish still to be your enemy?"

"I do not believe so. I have never met the kin I have there. And the Cocom family, the great rulers of Mayapan have many other concerns. They are in disputes with Chichen Itza, grave disputes."

"But—let me keep this straight, I find your alliances so difficult to understand—Mayapan founded Zama, but Zama is now in alliance with Mayapan's enemy Chichen Itza?"

We were approaching the walls again. The ruler shrugged, then said in a low voice, "The katun cycles circle around and times change. What seemed auspicious in one katun is poison in another. But come, let us leave the road and worship the gods at the shrine of Yum Cimil."

That was the god I had made water on and knocked over on in my moment of outrage. I trusted someone had uncovered him and cleaned him up and that my blasphemy had not been discovered. Well, he did not look very good, it was true, I saw as we came into the clearing. Someone had tried to scrub him, but the purple berries I had heaped on him dyed him, and he was purple. The ruler muttered about "blasphemy," and "desecration," and knelt to say a prayer and I felt a little odd.

We sat on a log near the back of the clearing.

"Now let me say the chant to you again and tell you what I think. So far I do not have very much—"

The Ruler interrupted me. "Across the trail seen from the sky"—could mean east and west or north and south, any type of trip across the back of the giant turtle. We do not know what city your uncle was trader to?"

"No. He said a city near the tradeways, so I supposed it was the coast."

"Far from cities high–although there are many cities with tall buildings, there are also many places north, south east or west of the land of the Maya or Mexicas that are far from them."

I nodded. That was only about a thousand lengths of land in every direction but east.

"To where the lords of land and water vie. That confounds me. What does it mean? A war?"

I thought of something, a phenomenon I had noticed on the trip, but something he might not have thought of. "It may mean right near here, where the swamps and the dry lands are in constant battle. I have seen the raised roads and the raised fields, as the sea tries to come in everywhere."

"True enough," he murmured. "I'm sure that is it! So we have the part about lands and waters vying. But—" Then he stood, poking a stick around on the ground. "But what about 'past three cats who never cry.' The sacred jaguar cat never cries. That is all I can think of. And at the foot must mean a mountain. That just means that we really are speaking of a high mountain. "

"I think so too. I do know there is a cave, a large one, reached through a narrow passage at the top. That my uncle did describe to me."

The stick traced a picture of a jaguar cat. "What we are searching for, then, is a cave at the bottom of a mountain near the lowlands?" He placed a mountain near the picture of the cat, then swamp reeds nearby—and scratched them all out. "Such a place does not exist," he said. "It contradicts itself."

"Perhaps the lands and waters vie in a body of water. The ocean, or a lake. One stops and the other starts."

"Yes, that is clearly more logical. There are many old myths about the gods of the land and the water warring. But I do not think the chant speaks of the ocean. Mountains do not come down to the ocean. A lake, yes, I think that must be it. A large one."

"A lake near a mountain. It must be a mountain, because the trail to it was seen from the sky, and the only place one can see a trail from the sky is from a mountain top."

"Or high temple, perhaps. As at Chichen Itza."

"Yes, I suppose so."

"Well, this will take more thinking. Perhaps consultation. We need to know more about our Mayan cities. I have not travelled much."

"Who would know such things?"

"We will start with the priests. They have much knowledge, especially of the ancient places. Alton Ha, high priest of Zama, taught me."

"Will we be able to ask about the things we need to know without arousing suspicion?"

"I have already thought about that part of it. We will say we are going; in fact I have decided we will be going, on a trading trip, to establish new outlets for the salt and salt fish we take. The two of us. I will say I need to know of the towns, get more direct knowledge. And, as a matter of fact that is true. We can kill two turkeys with one stone on this trip."

"Good. But here is a thorn for you. While we are gone, who will insure the power stays in your hands? There is still restlessness."

"There is always restlessness it seems. But I have taken steps. My father-in-law, Lord Atza, is coming for a visit. I have made the arrangements. He will bring his wife, retainers and a large troop of guard."

"Excellent! He can see the sights, visit his daughter and, with a high lord of Chichen Itza and the alliance in the city, there can be no trouble."

"Yes. He comes in two days, I believe. Ela, Moon-path is expectant."

I looked at him. "She is expecting her father?"

"No," he smiled. "She is expecting the heir."

I pounded him on the back.

"Then we must be off on our travels soon." Smoke Fox-god knelt to prepare an incense offering, I touched my forehead to the forlorn and purple looking god of death and even gave him a sticky-sweet smile as we left the clearing. No sense in being bad-tempered as we started on the long and dangerous road.

"There are many cities you could visit to open trade, Ruler," Alton Ha said, slowly looking out to sea. We were sitting on the top of the temple hill, and the water beneath us danced in the bright sun of He is Halfway Home. Alton Ha had gone into the sacred repositories of the temple and brought out one of the bark maps. "Here are some of the major cities—well, you have seen this before."

"I have travelled but little," Smoke Fox-god said to him.

"I wish to know which are prosperous enough to make it worthwhile to go beyond the usual trading limits that Zama families usually visit. Extend our trade, that is the thing." He rubbed his hands together, looking every bit like a greedy trader.

"Well, you could go far west to the other ocean. There are great forests where the quetzel bird is sought for its feathers. Or to the land of the Oldest Ones, the Olmec, farther west."

"There are—tall mountains there?"

"Yes, some."

"Lakes?"

"There are lakes in the west, and large lakes and mountains are south, too. Why do you ask of mountains and lakes?" he wanted to know.

"I thought we might—visit a bit, see the fine vistas, appreciate the handiwork of Hunab Ku, the creator of earth. After all, I will not have the time or means to make such an extensive trip when I become a father. Since we live in these lowlands with no mountains and few lakes, my heart and royal wish is set on seeing them in my travels."

Did that sound odd? I did not think so, and Alton Ha did not bat an eye. We did not like to dissemble, but we trusted no one these days, even though the old priest was loyal to the family of Smoke Fox-god from his childhood, bound to them. He had, indeed, been the son of a slave, but raised as a special marked one to serve the gods, so Smoke Fox-god told me earlier.

It happened in this way. The orphan boy Alton Ha had a withered hand, and instead of sacrificing him, Smoke Fox-god's great-grandfather, an old man himself at the time, had been told to raise the orphan to the priesthood. He had followed the family and finally come with the youngest generation to Zama.

"You have been to the country around Chichen Itza. Most of our cities are now near it in this north part of our land. Some on the edges of the territory do not trade with Zama and could use the salt."

He put his finger on the bark drawing, on cities around Chichen Itza and, to its west, Mayapan.

"Well, but I have said—do none of them have lakes and mountains together?"

"None," the priest answered, "except of course the land of the Olmecs itself, to the west on the coast."

But we knew it wasn't to the land where the Olmecs had once lived that we needed to go. After all, they had left there to take their treasure away, far away to hide. And all the land in between us and their homeland in the west had no mountains and lakes—the site of the treasure could be nowhere in the northeast quadrant of the land of the Mayas. Alton Ha was being a little stubborn, or refusing to understand. "We will not go west," the Ruler affirmed.

"We live in the north," Alton Ha said, frowning. "East of us is—" he gestured across the blue water—"only the ocean. You do not wish to go west. And you wish as you trade to see the sights, mountains and lakes." He looked at us a little oddly, as if we were being too particular. Were we suspicious sounding?

"So there is the south, further into the rainforest. There are many lakes and mountains there. But the Old Ones' cities, now abandoned are there, too. It is forbidden to go there because of evil spirits. And of course there is no trade with dead cities."

"No, of course not," the Ruler said.

The priest stood up and looked far out to sea. "I have seen the dead cities of the south myself, and can tell you that you do not wish to go there. It was a sad day when, as a child with your grandfather's family, I had to leave Tikal."

I wondered if I could venture questions, and so I said, in a very reverent voice, "Why did you leave?"

"All left Tikal, had left years before. We were among the last to migrate." He returned to sit with us on a small stone wall. "Tikal was the greatest of all the cities of the Old Ones. Long before Chichen Itza, there was Tikal. All roads led to it. Some said it was founded by the Oldest Ones as a trading outpost to get goods not found in the west. Rivers ran nearby where in old days traders plied canoes loaded with goods. That was before the days of the ocean canoes and the foreigners who brought them to us." His voice was brittle.

352

"There are mountains and lakes near Tikal perhaps?" I asked hopefully.

"No, of course not. I said rivers," he said harshly. I knew he did not like me. He hated the "foreigners" and I was about as foreign as they came.

"The ruler's lineage left to go to Mayapan, where pure-blooded ones were pledged to preserve the heritage of Tikal, as foreigners took over everywhere else. They took me with them, and I served them as priest in Mayapan." Then the priest smiled, something I had never seen him do. "And then I came with the father of the Ruler here, to build the temple up in Zama and establish the worship of the gods to bring the city peace. It was my command from Itzamna, who came to this one's great-grandfather in the shape of a crane and commanded my service." I looked at his withered hand, holding the edge of the map and it did look like a crane's claw; he looked up at that moment and saw me staring.

"Prepare for us to worship inside the temple," Smoke Fox-god instructed, and Alton Ha went inside. "He does not have the knowledge that we need. I feared that," the Ruler said.

"How will we discover exactly where lakes and mountains are in combination and not far off from the land of the Olmecs? The treasure cannot be anywhere far south or to the western sea as he says. Those places would take many moons to get to," I said in a whisper.

"There is a way to seek more exact knowledge. I will tell you soon. Here comes the priest."

"We are in the north. But there is a farther north, is there not?" the Ruler asked.

"Of course, Mexica, where the foreigners come from."

"And there must be many fine sights to see along the way. I think I have heard that in Mexica are beautiful mountains and lakes to see."

Alton Ha nodded his head in acceptance. His eyes did not show whether or not he thought it fruitless to traverse among the infidels, the bringers of new, corrupt ways. Certainly he had not thought it proper to mention to us. Mexica–out of Mayan rule–

around the curve of this curving land and then north! Could that be the place?

We gave Alton Ha great thanks and worshipped with him while we were there and did not turn our backs on Itzamna, walking down the steps sideways, for the Ruler said he wished great blessings on this trip.

We were going to Cozumel, the island of traders, Smoke Fox-god said when we reached the Ruler's House, to seek more information, for, he told me, "They have a certain kind of wisdom." When he said that the words rang in my ears, and I recalled that it was the woman trader Ibix who had said that to me when I first came out to the land of the Maya. Five moons had passed since then, and days were flying by like crows in a row in the sky.

"Well, if we are to go, let it be now," I muttered a little darkly, and he looked at me curiously. Still, I did not tell him how worried I was about the lives of my loved ones and of my own.

He did not ask. I have said before that he was oddly uncurious. And I had not volunteered my anxieties, no no, not at all. It seemed to me that if I told him, he would have full power over me, in the way the peoples of the Great Lake, who believe that if an enemy gets too close to you, he will steal your courage and manhood. And so I, who preached trust, had none in the one man I should have trusted most.

The crossing was as good as it could ever be, said Smoke Fox-god Three as we came out of the ferry boat which had taken us to the island. We had properly fitted ourselves out for the trip, I in a new cape of fur to match my catch-your-eye loincloth; and prosperous did the Ruler look, too, in his new, embroidered, trading garments and hair worn long, pulled under a small but elegant dog headdress. He had new lip-hair, grown like some Mexicas we saw recently, and without any of his regalia, he looked every part the eager trader. We did not wish to draw attention to ourselves or this trip.

Before we donned our disguises, the Ruler said goodbye to the batab council, instructing them on their duties to command in his stead and giving special responsibilities to the lords Two Parrot, a distant cousin of his, and Sky Many Deer, the bumbling but smiling rich man.

Sky Many Deer fell on his face. "Ah, Ruler, may the god of the North Star guide you, and may the winds not blow so hard the water comes in and wets you and may the waves not rise so that the canoe swamps and throws you in the water—"

The Ruler interrupted him, raising him off his knees with a hand and a smile. "That is quite enough prayers, Sky Many Deer. They are not reassuring me."

We had been taken quietly up the coast a bit to embark, and after all left we put on the fine merchants' clothing, and if anyone knew us there or gave us a second look, I did not see it. I carried the several obsidians and the two pearls I had left after the "dowry" I gave to Ghost in their doeskin case in a sewn pocket in my cape. A fine wealth of cacao beans was sewn into the Ruler's. Mostly, though, we would be setting up contacts, meeting agents who would arrange the details for our salt and salt fish transactions when we came back. So we said.

And Cozumel when we arrived was as teeming with merchants and priests as the stone reefs of the ocean we had passed over were loaded with fish, and I pressed the Ruler to hurry and not linger among the many pleasures of the place, food merchants making honey-spice cakes, chocolate vendors with the finest of honeys and vanillas in their drinks, the ale-drinking houses, the places where one could buy a woman for an hour or a day.

And though he wished to worship in the shrines along the roads of the island, and to stop to admire the fine images of the gods, I nudged him along.

"This market is the best in the land for images," he protested. "Our road shrines near Zama are not well kept up, and I should look for some and order them delivered. They need not know it is the ruler who does this. See, here are the image makers of Chichen Itza, even."

And I looked up to see, behind a wooden trestle holding images, Ghost and Comalca. My heart leapt, then fell to think that my friend must hate me now, and I could not even meet his eyes.

But, to my surprise, Comalca cried out with joy, and my friend came out from behind the trestle and gave me the old arm slap of the woods.

"Perahotan," the Ruler said, surprised. I had of course, told him before this that the man-god was married to the steward of the Atza family back in Chichen Itza, but he was surprised to see them so far away without a city trading party.

"We were with the family household," Comalca said. "We journeyed with Ina Moon-path's father and came almost to Zama. But we did not come in, crossing over here instead." And, of course, no one in the royal party had told me my friends were near, considering the news of what stewards did to be not at all important to talk about.

The Ruler walked among the effigies, picking them up, examining, and I spoke privately to Ghost.

"I know your s-s-secret," he snorted. I stared at him. "The Lake Spirit came to me in a rainstorm. He said not to be alarmed. If I had my own son someday, we would have two lines from the north country here. Start our own l-l-lineage from Lakes-Like-a-Necklace."

Comalca came to me and smiled. Lord Atza was pleased with Ghost's work and had put him in charge of image-making and selling. The garden had never been so beautiful, with the loving attention it got every night from the two of them. She felt well and was becoming fond of her new husband. I was forgiven. My happiness was overflowing.

The Ruler returned. "I will buy this fine, tall image of Yum Cimil. The one in the small shrine near the town walls in Zama was desecrated recently, remember? This will be a fine replacement. It is hard to imagine who would commit such outrage." Hard indeed, I thought, trying not to smile in a wicked way. I must admit I did feel a little guilty about coming among a strange people, doing what I had done to statues they held sacred. But I added it to the bag of guilts I always carried about like a woman

356

with her washbag walking to the stream. Guilt over having made my father desert my mother, guilt over living when my uncle died, guilt over betraying my loved one not once but twice.

I spoke with Ghost about the affairs of Chichen Itza. The market was still busy in the great city of Kukulcan, though two traders from the northern Mexican highlands had come in and stayed long enough to cheat several of the local traders out of many goods. They had headed back north to their Toltec city with a long train of bearers and their own guard, loaded with the city's goods, and it was only after they had been on the road two days that it was discovered that the rare gold they left was some other metal, one never known in Chichen Itza but which turned brown on the skin. "If they could a-been c-c-caught, the official holpop would-a judged them and made them slaves or sacrifices, to buy favor for the city for all of us," Ghost said seriously. I smiled a little as I walked back. He sounded just like a Mayan city dweller already. Perhaps he could live here, never miss the woods the way I did.

That night, sitting on stone benches around the fire outside the guest house just after He Is Setting, we drank hot honey corn drink (at least I did, the others had the fermented juices I was staying away from) and talked to two traders who seemed to have been everywhere.

"What is your home city?" I asked, watching in awe the blaze of He Is Setting across the ocean and the far-off land of the coast. The colors of sunset seen from an island across the water are not to be compared.

"Mayapan, straight west of Chichen Itza."

"I am from afar," I said, and saw them smile. As if it was not obvious. With my height I stood out in any crowd. "Is Mayapan a great city?"

"Not yet, but we have hopes. Mayapan is a young city, like a child, squalling and growing but strong and full of promise. But it is the hope of the true Mayan people, free from foreigners. There our fathers came when other cities failed and they raised the flag of the Maya."

Mayapan? Odd that they should be from the home of the Smoke family. Had not the city of Mayapan sent the Smokes to rule Zama before Smoke Fox-god was born? I saw him move slightly into the shadows; perhaps he thought some family resemblance might come to the traders' minds. Still, he did not seem to fear it much. After all, he had never been there, and he spoke up boldly.

"I have been to the priests on this island to ask absolution from a grievous sin," Smoke Fox-god said, giving the story we had concocted, "and they tell me to gain forgiveness I must make a pilgrimage." The traders nodded, swatting at a few mosquitoes which had arrived to greet the sinking of the Sun Lord.

"Who are the gods you are appeasing?" asked an old one with wrinkles, whose eyes seemed to scrutinize us, intensely, eyebrows bunching together over his nose.

"Itzamna and Yum Cimil, Lord of Death," Smoke Fox-god muttered, and I looked up at him in mild surprise. That had not been in the story.

"What is the quest?" the other asked. He was of an age of my father, mild and easy looking, with folds of flesh hanging from his upper arms as they reclined on the bench. I wondered why he was still trading, sleeping in odd places, eating food that destroyed the stomach.

"I have to go to a place that has high mountains for access to the gods' thought and then that same day dip myself in a clear lake to cleanse myself of the impurity," the Ruler told them.

"And the sin to be expiated?" the wrinkled one wanted to know. He was not swatting. In fact, the mosquitoes did not seem to bother him.

"Unjust blood of a kinsman," the Ruler said, lowering his eyes. I continued to watch him, impressed with the sincerity he conveyed.

"Do you know of a place where high mountain combines with lovely lakes nearby?" I asked.

The relaxed-looking trader called the serving girl over, ordered more fermented corn drink. He sat silently for a while. "Well, perhaps to the west near the other ocean. Or, it could be in the south, especially far south." Just as the priest, Alton Ha had said. "There are some mountains a few weeks passage by sea to the south, some good ones where land narrows to a fine strip and lakes are right nearby. I go there now and then, though the rainforest is thick. And beyond, in the far south in the land of the Golden Ruler, are the highest mountains in the world with cool, clear lakes. Few have been there, but I have heard."

"Well, I do not think—" what I was going to say was that I didn't think my uncle's trip was anything like that long to get there from the north, where he was. In his story, though for the life of me I couldn't remember that part, I got the idea that it took a few weeks, not months. "Do you travel much around your own region?" I asked the younger trader.

"Around Mayapan? Yes, for it is as good as anyplace for trading. All roads connect in the north of the land of the Mayas where we are. Our roads lead easily to all the great roads of the Old Ones, where for hundreds, possibly thousands of summers traders have gone east and south. The Great road. But more importantly now, we connect to the lands of the north. Though we hate the Mexicas, their goods are important to us, as to all."

"So you go north?"

"All the time," said the easy trader. "And it is there, young travelers, that I think you could find your place of holy pilgrimage. There, in the north, in the sky-high city, where a great lake sits in the mountains is a spot such as you describe. I will tell you of it." And so he described the land of the Toltecs and other "peoples of blood" as they were called by the Mayans, whose sacrifices were a regular and brutal cult, whose cities were as high as the Mayans and much wider, and whose skilled warriors brought terror to all around. There, near the highest of mountain ranges, was a lake of great beauty. There the gods would listen, of all places, to the quest for purity. So said the traders.

"Are there caves there?" I asked the wrinkled, scrutinizing one.

"I suppose so. There are caves everywhere," he said.

"And are any of these lakes far from cities high?"

He laughed at the way I said it. "Most are near cities very high," he said. "You will have to go, young upstart, and see them for yourselves." We picked up our cups and went indoors to escape the mosquitoes as best we could. But I seemed to feel the old man's eyes following us through the night, and I told myself that he might have noticed something about Smoke Fox-god that reminded him of the family of his city, Mayapan.

We spoke of the cities of the Mexica at night, alone in the small guest house we had taken and paid for with cacao beans. "It sounds like the likeliest place of all," said Smoke Fox-god. "We know your uncle was in the north. And since all roads lead easily to Mexica and have for many, many katun, and you think it was but a few weeks' trip—"

"There are cities high through the area, but the merchant said there were also areas in those mountains far from cities. Surely there is a large cave, where both the Oldest Ones, Olmec, and my uncle could have hidden the treasure. The local people will know of such a cave. But—what about the cats?"

"I do not know," he said, "but I believe this may be the place. I do not know where else to look. We will seek the cats when we get there."

So, the next day, we started out to take ship for this place of the Mexicas. "As Kukulcan did," said Smoke Fox-god, "for he left the people of the Mayan lands by boat to return to Mexica, the land where he had come from. He is worshipped there as Quexalcoatl."

We spoke once more to the traders of Mayapan, and they arranged for trade for us with the smaller cities west of them. So we were doing the trading we had committed to with Alton Ha. We would have salt and saltfish from Zama brought to the traders' house in Mayapan when we returned.

On the way to the harbor, the Ruler wanted to stop by again to check delivery of his new god-image with the sellers of Chichen Itza. As he went over the details with Comalca, I had a last word with Ghost. I told him to send messages to me with the family servants who passed back and forth, telling me of Comalca's health.

He asked me–generously, I thought in the face of what I had practiced on him–to be the naming-day uncle of the child. I told him with real regret I would be gone by then. And we said goodbye with the arm slap and wondered if we would ever meet again on Turtle's Island.

But as I left he called after me, and came along to tell me something. "I f-f-forgot. The same time the Lake Spirit told me of the child, it said something. I think it is for you, perhaps. The voice said, `Tell Stupid Head he must be careful to avoid a mistake. Though the snake may sting, it can also help.'" I looked at him blankly, and he shrugged. He waved goodbye as he turned and left.

I thought about it on the boat to Mexica as we sat in the midst of pilgrims and poor vendors who sold fruit and woven cloth at the stands of Cozumel.

"Stupid Head? So even the spirit world calls me Bear Belly," I snorted to myself a little and turned around, trying to keep the spray off with my fur cape. But snake—what in the world was all that about? And I had to be careful about a mistake? A mistake about going back to Cahokia? Was I too late? Had the worst happened? Maker of Stars say not so. Or was the mistake something else?

We got off the boat further up the coast and stayed in a small, poor town. As we lay in the bug-infested guest house, I tossed and turned. Serpent, serpent. Why should I believe what Ghost said anyway? I was long past reliance on that sort of thing. But it had been right in the past. Snake. Well, surely he did sting us, no doubt about that, as we landed on the shore near Zama and the savages—pardon, natives, nearly roasted and ate us. They carried the banner of the serpent. And there, at the town of the feathered serpent, Chichen Itza, I had been possessed of a lust which flung me and my friends into a—well, a snake pit of trouble. But help?

I rose and went to the door of the hut and lifted the ragged covering to see the stars and moon, a half moon of great beauty. I looked for the traveling unblinking stars —the ones the star priests charted in the round tower in Chichen Itza. There all the windows of the tower on its high platform allowed the priests to chart the passing through the seasons of the evening star—the star of Ku-kulcan, and the red star, and the less bright unblinking stars. How much wisdom the Mayas had to chart them all. And they tried to chart the moon, too, Smoke Fox-god said. But they did not know all its movements.

The evening star was still bright. Nanaboozhoo, my uncle's patron spirit, the Son of man, who came to him to help and heal, here was the plumed serpent. Did the peoples of Chichen Itza believe their plumed serpent who lived in the star helped them too? Suddenly my mind shot into a slot, as an arrow shot from a bow goes into a hole in a tree. Help. Serpent. In my mind's eye I saw the Serpent Mound above the great Ohio back in my own land, laid out across the earth to please and honor the one who saw it, the serpent god. Where was he? Up in the sky. That was why they built the mound–for him to see. Click. Another slot.

I went to the swinging bed of Smoke Fox-god and shook him. "Wake up, Ruler. We may not need mountains. I have thought of something important. Could the Oldest Ones have built roads to be seen by the gods? To honor them in some way and let the gods see the sacred tribute from their home in the sky?"

He turned over and opened his eyes. Then he sat up, no easy thing in one of the swinging beds. He looked very young, with his hair undone and eyes sleepy. "I—think so. In the old books there are ceremonies for the opening of roads. Each road is dedicated to a certain god who is the correct one for the calendar date. The Road to Chichen Itza is still the provence of Chac."

"And so it follows that the greatest of all roads, the one the traders talked of as being the widest, most sacred and ancient, even for a thousand summers, would be dedicated to the most high god."

"The Great Sacbe is that road," he murmured, beginning to fully come awake. He knew what I was after, the real answer to the riddle. Both of us did not feel we had found it yet, had simply been going as if in a trance because we knew not what else to do. "The Great Sacbe--dedicated to the Feathered Serpent himself," Smoke Fox-God murmured, considering it.

"I thought he came in the near past and was a king."

"In human form. Some scoffers say Kukulcan was a human king who took the name of the god of the past. But whoever that leader was, the feather serpent has been worshipped as long as there have been people in these lands."

"And the road is still used?"

"The Great Sacbe is still there, running east and west, with a northern branch to our cities near Mayapan, but it is falling into disrepair because no one trades that way any more and no city will fix its stones. The coastal canoes take all by water and have for hundreds of summers. What are you thinking?"

"That the road seen from the sky is the Great Sacbe, created by the Oldest Ones not only to trade but also to honor the Feathered Serpent as he saw it in the heavens as the Evening Star."

"Yes."

"So," I said slowly, ideas coming to me, "if the Oldest Ones, the Olmecs, had a treasure to deposit, the key chant would refer to the place the treasure was hid. Out of their area, we have to suppose, so it would not be found. So in the future they could go and get it again."

"I suppose so."

"And it cannot be in the north. The greatest cities of all are in the north, in Mexica, is that not really so? "

The ruler nodded. "Though the merchants said there were some areas far from huge cities."

"But in a chant meant to find a treasure, meant to give clues, they would not send us to the very place where cities were high, I think. It would throw everyone too far off the track."

"Perhaps. So, as you say, they were sending them in another direction than north."

"Well, then, if the road seen from the sky was a god-road, and if we don't have to look for a mountain—" I scratched the animal bites, kept my feet off the floor, and thought. "We can wait to think about the lake until later. What we want is someplace out of the Olmec territory, far from the cities. How far did Olmec territory reach?"

"The farthest east was my people's city Tikal. In olden times it was the Olmec outpost, to protect the traders who would be journeying on further south yet, to the lands of the rainforests."

"And if they were going on a road seen from the sky, far from cities high to where the land and water vie—they could have only been going one way—east from their homelands."

"Well, or south. Yet your uncle found the treasure in a few weeks. The far south would have taken much too long to get to."

"Does the Great Sacbe go south?"

"It goes, well used to go south from the lands of the northern Mexica, then west to east as the land turns in our land, shaped like a dog's leg, and then far south again to where the land grows very narrow and both seas almost meet, as the traders said. At least in one form or another."

"So they would have to have been passing from the west to the east if they were going someplace with no tall cities to pass in those days. Their destination was somewhere east of Olmec lands, a town, and it was in a place where Lords of lands and waters vie. Is that a lake?"

"Or it could be someplace in the lowlands. Except that there were no towns.

"Except for one small one. An outpost."

He jumped out of his swinging bed. "Tikal!" he shouted.

"Yes," I said, my eyes flashing excitement in the darkness. "It must be Tikal. It was the only city you could take on the Sacbe within walking distance of my uncle in our populated north that existed for the Olmecs too."

"Now I am confused," Smoke Fox-god said. "I had thought your uncle followed the chant to get to the treasure. And if the Olmec chant was ancient, meant for Olmecs to use to get to the east—how could someone in a city in the north follow it?"

"But then, my friend, he must have known the destination when he was sent to look for the treasure. The old lustful ruler must have told him he was going to Tikal, outpost of the Olmecs. That much the ruler suspected. The rest was unknown." Smoke Fox-god nodded, and I went on, growing ever more excited.

"Yes, and of course, many cities lead from the Sacbe's northern arm south, so he could have found the Sacbe and travelled south until he came to Tikal, then tried to act upon the rest of the chant. After all, he did not knowof the cave and the other things, but found them after great troubles, so he said. That was the part that had been unknown, that interested him. He knew where he was going."

The Ruler sighed. "Of course. It did not matter where he started from in the north."

"No," I agreed. "It does not matter where he started in the north. We may never know it. But—does the rest of the chant fit?"

"Where lands and waters vie? I do not know. Tikal is not on the seacoast, or near a great lake. It is near a river. Perhaps there is some part of it that would fit the chant. And the cats?"

"Did I not hear you say, at some time in the past, that the jaguar was the sacred animal of the Oldest Ones? That they worshipped it and used it everywhere as an emblem? If this was an Olmec outpost in ancient days—cats that do not cry must be somewhere."

"How soon till dawn?"

"Hours yet. The night is still young."

"Curse it!" the Ruler said, adding a few other choice pieces of profanity I had come to recognize in the language.

"Well, of course we must wait until dawn so we can get a boat back south to start on the road to Tikal—"

"I did not mean that, although it is true enough." He threw a stone at me. "I am cursing you because you awakened me to feel the bites of these sandfleas and mosquitoes and other vermin for five more hours. I hope a scorpion bites your toe." His voice grew calmer as he settled his cape around him in the swinging bed. "A small one of course. I will need you to help find this treasure." He laughed a little. "Now that I have discovered where it is for my friend."

In spite of the blustering language, the term was not lost on me.

Back down the coast by boat we went. We were near to Zama and yet did not go to it, wishing to encounter no one and raise no questions about our trading mission. And yet we did see someone. There across the coast from Cozumel where ships came in we came across one of the batab of Zama, Sky Many Deer, the sleek, pleasant lord with oiled hair, "Ruler!" he shouted, seeming to be pleased.

He would have knelt, but Smoke Fox-god grabbed him by the arms, looking about to see who had heard or seen.

"Remember, Lord Batab, that we are travelling modestly, as traders, not in retinue. It will be better that way, so we can get the truth not always told to those on high."

"Of course, of course, Exalted One."

"Is my wife and her family in health?" Smoke Fox-god wanted to know.

"They are enjoying the good weather we have had," the lord said, showing the large smile. "You go to cities North? West? South? he asked politely.

"North," the Ruler lied through tight lips. We nodded farewell; it was time to go on the road.

"Take care and return in health and fortune to your subjects who love you!" Lord Sky Many Deer said, backing away, touching his forehead over and over until he stumbled on a root.

On we went—across the road seen from the sky, less and less wide and white as we went south—past cities high and many of them ruined, with trees growing around the temples and through the roofs, as spring came in a little and then a lot and the countryside bloomed with new rain and bright sun.

We shared all, and my friend learned much of the ways of the land he had not known. We spoke of our yearnings and our flaws and finally he said, "I have told you all I know of the Smoke Fox lineage. I have told you how it goes back to one of the queens of the underworld, Beast with Two Snout, in the First Creation of the world. I have told you how in this final, Fourth Creation, the Maya rose and we were of them. I told you how we were nobility in the city of Tikal when the Old Ones made it the greatest city of the Mayan world. And I have told you how we stayed as long as we could when the city died, longer by far than anyone else, and then went to Mayapan and thence to Zama."

I nodded. I felt as if I knew the lineage as well as I knew my grandfather's. Better, probably. How they loved to tie in their lineage with the gods' decrees, warrior heroes, ancient myths, buildings they built, magic numbers, the sacred calendar and the meaning of life. It was as if the entire cosmos had labored with all its energy, spirit and physical meaning to produce their one family of noblemen.

He went on. "But you have told me only little of your lineage. You are noble, you came from the city Cahokia on the Longest River North where wood temples sit on dirt. You are of a trading clan, your uncle travelled here as a trader to an unknown city and was sent to find the Olmec treasure, which he did but left in a cave. That is all I know. There must be more, for I do not think you would come so far for jade figurines and god images sacred and valuable only to our people. You love wisdom and truth too much."

I thanked him, truly glad that a different self was appearing and old ways were being left behind, at least a little. Then I looked at him hard for a moment. I had felt, as I told you, that to open myself fully to him would be to have him steal my manhood, my soul, even.

But he did not feel that way, it seemed now, and had opened his life to me. Truly, with the laws of hospitality and the true friendship I did feel for him, I could do no less. What a risk! I cleared my throat and told him the whole story that night, how I had been born the Sun Watcher's child but abandoned by both father and mother, how my people were people of peace under the command of the Bird of Thunder, how my uncle, a worldly man who had become a shaman, became the dearest one on earth to me and his child, White Wings, as loved by me as my own child. How our village at Boulder Lake had been crushed by the Dune Devils, our people enslaved, my uncle tortured and killed and how I had been saved and come to give my captors grudging respect. How I had lived with Loon Feather's grandmother and been taken by the nephew to build the moose drum, how the gift of chanting and drumming had been given to me.

Then I told him how when the Dune Devils were themselves attacked by the tribute seekers of Cahokia, I went to the city itself, how I served the Female Sun as willing slave of her lust, how I knew and met good souls in the villages outside the walls and found my true love. And then, how the Female Sun grew ill, so that her death was near, and as her death came, so would the sacrifice of the two dearest now to me on Turtle Island. And how I had promised to go to find the treasure I knew about, returning the stone of the moon to the evil prince and bringing any cure I could find home to the Female Sun. And some of the treasure too, of course.

"And so," I said to finish, "we re-trace my uncle's trip, not knowing from where he started. It does not matter. His was a spiritual trip. In the cave Nanaboozhoo appeared as the Evening Star and washed him clean of sin, sending him forth into the earth to do good. That—spiritual cleansing was the object of his trip to the Maya, though he did not know it.

"As it is mine," said Smoke Fox-god in a low voice.

I watched his eyes glow in the darkness, and I wanted to pursue the sadness in his tone. "You said to the traders from Mayapan that you were seeking a mountain to climb and a lake to wash in."

"And it seems we will not find those, but I need to be purified nevertheless."

"Because—"

"Because I sought the death of my kinsman not for the gods' purposes but because I wished him eliminated from the lineage so I could rule without opposition."

"The priests told you he should be sacrificed."

"I did nothing to stop them. I wanted him dead because he opposed me."

"Many other rulers do the same every time the moon comes round."

"Yes. We have no time for anything else in Mayalands. So said Hoxek Yum, the man of the people."

"Your cousin sought your death."

"All the more reason for me to win him over to kindness and reconciliation. So say the best teachers. So said Kukulcan."

Kukulcan again. The serpent helps and heals.

"But you have not been this way. You have painted pictures on the wall, erased others to keep your power."

"It is true."

I looked beyond him, into the trees. The air was stirring a little. The odd, musty smell that was usually present everywhere in these lands was missing tonight.

"I feared greatly, so I would do anything to keep the power. But that was before you came. You bothered me, with your sacrilegious talk, your scoffing. It made me consider. And the rebellion—I stood so near to death that life seemed to me more dear, each day a necklace with beads which could be cut with a knife and spilled at any moment. And I did not wish the days that had been miraculously given to me to be filled with blood and fear. I have listened to priests too long. I must be different from the rest now. My heart tells me so."

For a moment the sadnesses and losses of my own life came and stood by me so that I could feel their pain and count them, like the chain of beads he mentioned. I had made a good many of the beads on the chain myself, I now saw, with my own rotten appetites. Then I said, "It is the heart which rules, and if it is right, the body shines with light. If it goes in wrong directions, there is darkness."

"Yes."

"We will look for our lake and mountain—together."

We did much camping as we reached sparsely settled areas, and stayed with farmstead families, whom we paid well. They did not speak the language of the lowlands, exactly, but we made ourselves understood by using a few words they seemed to know, gesturing, and pointing at foods. Always there were flat corncakes stretched out thin and baked on the griddle and good black beans and, when our money bought them, tapirs or boars roasted over coals in the yard, basted with good spices and honey.

"Why did the cities die?" I asked as we left the place on what would be the last day of our journey. "Why did your people leave the oldest of cities, Tikal? Was it not rich enough, were there not temples enough to worship, trade enough to pay for fine houses, and armies enough to get tribute?"

"The answer to your question lies back at the farmstead we have just left."

"What do you mean?"

"What did we do there, last night and this morning?"

"We—well, we ate. Richly, I might add," I smiled and patted my stomach, which though still lean was well-satisfied.

"There is abundance in these plots in the trees. These wise farmers cut, they let lie fallow, they grow corn and beans and squash and sweet potatoes and orchards of fine fruits and hives of honey. A man can be a ruler, here in the woods as far as food goes. Is it not true?"

"It is true. But surely a man can be a ruler in the city, too, with fine food. You have many hundreds even at Zama. They eat well." The sun was growing hot along the road, which was weedy and not well kept. Shrines, old temples and even noble houses were slumping into the hillsides, disintegrating like children's snow houses in the spring. Markers by the side of the roads had the

370

picture sign for "Tikal" interspersed with their usual picture-writing of dates back to when the Mayan world began

"How many people do you think live in Chichen Itza?" the Ruler asked.

"Well—Lord Atza said thousands."

"How much corn do you think it takes to feed one child for one complete trip of the sun, morning to night? How much in a katun? Then think of feeding a man. Think of the thousands of bushels of corn. How many fields, how much land does that take? Sweet potatos? Meat now and then? Sixty thousand people lived in Tikal. It spreads for miles—what we have been seeing, for two passages of the sun, is only the outer sections of the town."

"Cahokia has many souls too. There is food enough there—"

"For now. We have food enough in Zama too, now, this year. We do not depend on the garden plots around the town. You have seen the terraces, the large fields, and the way the communal, raised fields through the marshlands raised above the level of the water."

"Yes. So,—" it made me uncomfortable to think of it "the fields end up not producing enough."

"Their fertility dies, though we let them lie fallow and burn them off to increase fertility. When there is plenty, near the city, more babies are born. More people come to the cities to eat more, and finally—" He shrugged.

"There is not enough food to feed them." We came around a bend in the overgrown road and there before our eyes, was the city, spread out as far as the eye could see, with fine plazas, many, and high temples of the gods, and great ball fields and dwellings for the nobles. And even though the vines were creeping over the outer buildings and the stones, and the woods was claiming its own there in many places, there was a grandeur I have never seen elsewhere, no, not in Chichen Itza or Cahokia or any of the other cities I visited. Truly, it was a time of greatness when this city had been built. The people who built it knew who they were, and their blood ran pure with the virtue and strength of manhood. That I could see as I looked at their buildings.

371

"But that is not the end of the story, because as the fields grow lame, the rulers send far to get the food the people need, and they make war to get tribute of corn, and more fertile fields. And the sons of the rich, and then finally the poor, must go to be in the army. And without good food in variety, the babies grow up lame and sick. And if foreigners come, as they do, with strong armies, they can conquer. And the rulers grow cruel, and break the backs of the people with more toil and tribute and army service."

It all sounded familiar. Oh, Hawk Eye, how I wish you could hear this, I thought.

"And finally, then, they cannot support the city even then and the people must go scattering, in their kinship bands, and leave behind the fine towers and the dancing and performing plazas and the marketplaces and the temples which reach to the sky." We stopped and looked at Tikal, spread out there before us, as we stood on a higher place above it. And it seemed sad to me, saddest of almost all the things that I had seen, that man who made such grandeur and glory of spirit as this city could not learn to rule and manage it well enough to make it endure. Oh Cahokia! Would it happen to you, too? Man seemed very small to me at that moment, and without meaning in the face of a glowering, menacing world.

We sought shade among the ruins, inside one of the lesser shrines. People did live here, it seemed; cooking fires rose out of the roofs, out of partial roofs of some of the buildings.

"They have come here because there are shelters already built," said Smoke Fox-god.

"Where was your family home?"

"I do not know," he said. "It has been three katun since the last one of my family left." Sixty summers. And they were one of the last to leave. Sad, sad, when a city decays.

At He Is Halfway Home we ate food which the homesteader's wife had sent with us, cold turkey and flat bread. And then we slept, on rocks we hoped were high enough above the ground to keep huge spiders and scorpions away. Finally, as the afternoon sun slanted low, we walked around and came upon an old orchard. There we picked fruit from the trees, ripe and luscious in deserted gardens that owners had proudly planted before the new Zama was even thought of. Or Cahokia, for that matter.

As we ate the orange fruit of many seeds, a boy of about ten summers came out from behind a tall pillar with writing pictures on it. "Stop that," he said. "These gardens are the territory of my family." That was the sense of it; Smoke Fox-god understood the tongue and responded.

"We are sorry," smiled the Ruler. "Perhaps you will accept some payment for what we have taken. And help us to find more food." He took out a cacao bean and gave it to the boy. Immediately the young whelp began to test it to see if it was filled with meal or real chocolate meat.

"You had better be careful, strangers," he said. "This city is not always safe for traders with coats of fine fur and dog head-dresses." I could catch a little, and he gestured at our fine garb with a mocking smile.

"Why, I should cuff you," I said, stepping forward. But I was secretly amused, and he knew it. He took us to his house, if you could call it that. Crumbling steps, with trees growing out of them, led to a building which had once been a headquarters for the Holpop judge.

It did have a roof, and the ceremonial braziers were now being used for holding cooking coals. A slightly-built woman, who seemed too young to be the boy's mother, turned her head from cooking to see us. She was startled.

"We have paid the young one and he says you will give us food," the Ruler said. "We are traders travelling. My friend and I wish to make a pilgrimage visit to the ancient shrines of his ancestors and worship the old gods." The boy had come up and stood beside the woman, almost defiantly.

"Is he your—son?" the Ruler asked.

"My brother," she said. "Our mother was carried away in a raid   when a northern city came to get slaves and sacrifice victims."

"I am sorry. And your father?"

"He had already died—of a fever the year the small one was born."

373

"What is your name?" I respectfully asked the woman. She told us it was Elan-Ya.

"And what is your name, Bear Cub?" I asked, seeking a word or two first from the Ruler.

He told me in the dialect of these southern parts, and I could not even pronounce it. "I will call you Bear Cub," I said.

"What is a bear?" he wanted to know.

Smoke Fox-god answered for me. "A big hairy monster of the north lands where my friend's home is. It lives in caves and kills men if it can get paws on them." He gestured as he described.

"Well, then, I will be a bear. I defend my sister," the upstart boy said proudly.

"There is a room here in the back. I keep it clean and there are extra beds. The few travelers who come here sometimes stay with us," Elan-Ya said.

We supped with her nicely on more cold turkey and bread. "Do you have cornfields?" I said, beginning to pick it up. It used an old-fashioned language form the scribe who taught me had acquainted me with a bit.

"No, but my kin in the country bring us baskets of corn. I tend the shrines of the ancient gods of the Old Ones. We all must take care of each other here, for there is no ruler."

"What a pity," Smoke Fox-god said.

"You think so?" she said, bending to pick up the serving dishes we had eaten on. "I do not. There was a batab here when I was a child, reporting tribute to some far away city, I forget which. He was cruel and intolerant. I served in his house when I was only six, and his wife slapped me each day across the mouth. My teeth did not come in right." She pointed at her teeth and I understood. It was true; her smile was odd, with the front teeth crooked. Somehow, though, it only seemed to make her more delightful.

"Well, rulers can be good," Smoke Fox-god said with a weak smile.

"There is an old saying here. 'It takes a hundred good men in the valley to support one bad man on the hill.' We were glad when that batab thought we were too small to care about and left."

I had been studying her as she spoke. Her breasts were visible through her summer shawl, and the curve of her thigh through the high cut skirt. I tried not to stare, but I could not help it. And at night again, I had my old trouble when I was too close to womankind with soft curving bodies. But this time I clenched my fist and beat the wall gently and tossed and turned and finally, it did pass about He Is Halfway Through the Night.

I knew Smoke Fox-god was awake there in the dark, too.

"It is hard not to be married and feel the hot urges of the body," I said.

"I can tell you truth, my friend," said a voice from the other side of the room. "It is harder yet to be married and feel those same hot urges when the wife is on the other side of the land. Let us finish our pilgrimage soon."

"Here is what we need to know, Bear Cub," I said to the boy as we walked about the empty streets of the town.

"We are on a pilgrimage from priests to gain our purity. We need to find a cave and pray there. Do you understand?"

The Ruler filled in some of the gaps.

"You know of a cave, a large one?" I asked.

"Perhaps," he said, slowly, eyeing us. "There may be more than one."

"And will you guide us?" Smoke Fox-god asked.

"If there are enough cacao beans and"—he leered at us through the fingers of his hand— "you are good enough."

"At what?" the Ruler demanded to know.

"Just good enough. I will think about it."

We wanted to find the nearby waterways, and we did find a rather sluggish one nearby. But it had no canoes on it, only litter and debris.

"This was once a trading center?" I asked Smoke Fox-god.

"The portage for small canoes carrying goods between rivers. The beginning of the roads, as we saw, north and west from areas further south."

"But trade died?"

"It went to the great ocean-going canoes. Even in earliest times there were both kinds of trade, though, by river and by land centered here, so my father told me when he spoke of his homeland. Then there were trading wars between the rich merchants. So—" He stopped himself. "Where the Lords of land and water vie," he said softly.

We went to seek Cub, and when he saw us, he came up and pounded me on the arm. "I have decided. You are good enough. You can hire me to take you to try to find the cave you wish."

"And why is it you think we are good enough, Cub?" Smoke Fox-god wanted to know.

"You are two young men like buck deers and you stay in the house with my sister for two nights without offering affront. You are good."

"You know too much for a man of ten summers," I said.

We sat in the old shrine in the heat of the morning, planning our trip to the caves. "Dog Head and Cat Cape, there are many caves in these parts. Which one do you need to pray in?"

I thought a moment; after all, we had to be careful in what we revealed. A priceless and sacred treasure of the ancestors was involved. Smoke Fox-god had told me it was not the precious quality of the jewel stones that made the treasure valuable, but the sacred, ancient quality and power of the images, the power of great magic they would convey from oldest times. No one in his land would have anything like them. The moon tablet and jade I would take to the prince; and the Ruler would take what was left with a share for me. So we had said the first night we planned.

"We need to find a special cave. It will have an entrance that goes far in, then will be blocked by stones so one can go no further. Near it will be—a stone, perhaps, a monument to—jaguar cats." It sounded a little foolish, but that was what I thought it must be.

"The rich people of the north are silly," he said to the Ruler, and the Ruler helped me understand. "To come so far to worship in our cave to gain forgiveness of the gods. But then to wear shiny bracelets on the arm, kill so many cats to get a cape, sew fine riches in it as if thieves could not find the pockets if they wished—" He held up one of the fine obsidian knives which had been sewn in the cape.

I headed towards him. "Why, you small robber rat . . ."

He smiled and shrugged. "I know the ways of surviving. But you are my friend." He tossed me the knife; I took it to him and closed his fist around the hilt. "I know the cave," he added.

Excitedly I grabbed his arm. I had not expected such good fortune. "Take us to it."

"A moment, Cat Cape," he said pulling his arm away and then began speaking to the Ruler. "It is far, half a day into the deep woods. We will need someone to cut the path for you, rope and torches for you to take into the cave, food, someone to cook it, even the things to camp."

"Let us hire some bearers," the Ruler said. "But where will we find any in this deserted city?"

Cub put his fingers in his mouth and gave a loud whistle, which startled us. Then, we saw heads pop up from behind rocks all around us and soon six boys scrambled down over falling temple stones to sit at the feet of the cub.

"These are the Order of the Broken Heads," Cub said. They looked broken enough. Sawed-off teeth, tattered loincloths, long, unkempt hair, round foreheads. No loving mother from a noble family had bound these heads to the cradle board in a fine house.

"We meet at the cave once each moon, to carry on the old rites. The cave was once a shrine for the Oldest Ones."

The Ruler translated the word he used for the Oldest Ones.

"And how do you carry on the rites?" the Ruler wanted to know, looking with some amusement at the group sitting at his feet.

Cub answered for the group. "My sister Elan-Ya tends the shrines of the gods in the city, as much as she can, for there are many shrines. She burns copal, sweeps leaves out and does the

377

rites of the ancient gods as our father taught her before he died. But we, the Order of the Broken Heads, we tend the woodland shrines of the oldest ones—the Olmec, so they say."

When the Ruler explained what he had said, I was confused. "But I thought no one went to the Oldest Ones' shrines. That they are forbidden for fear of spirits."

"No one else goes. We are the only ones who will visit the shrine and since most of these are orphans who have escaped the slave masters and sacrifice parties until now we have little fear of the spirits, anyway." A general laugh rang out, and the boys put their hands in their mouths and whistled.

"And what is this of the broken heads?" the Ruler asked.

"You will see, Dog Head. It is not to be spoken of here," Cub said, avoiding our eyes.

The troop of boys scrambled all over the roads and old temples collecting the things we needed, strong hatchets with flint and obsidian blades (where had they gotten them?) charcoal stoves and food and camping beds and even fabric tents with woven screens to keep the bugs out. Then with each of the boys bearing a basket on his back with a strap that went around the head, and with ourselves carrying other things, we left that afternoon to go into the deepest woods.

"The road is long since lost, though sometimes you can see a stone," said Cub. "But we cut the vines away from the standing stones along it." Then, as we cut our way through the overhang of wild gardenia and palm, he pointed now and then to a standing stone, with odd pictures, looking a little like the Mayan's but not much.

"One last thing remains to be solved," the Ruler said over his shoulder to me as we strode along after the boys. "At the foot. What could that mean? At first we thought it must mean the foot of the mountain we were looking for, but now there is no mountain. The foot of what?"

"We will have to see," I said, puffing a little at the exertion of the trail.

Shadows were falling on the path as the boys in the front began to cry back that we were nearing the spot. Then, in a sort of reverent tone, they whistled and pointed. At the side of the road, with a shaft of sunlight falling on it, was a standing stone with the giant, grimacing face of a cat surrounded by its tail, or perhaps it was a serpent. Writing and other faces and twisting things were on the stone beneath it. But then, oddest of all, a giant head with fat lips and wide brow lay beside the pillar. It had, I suppose, sat on the top and then toppled off. The top of its skull was shattered.

On, for a few moments more, as the path twisted and then, another pillar, another, larger cat and another head, this time split in half.

Finally, we heard water, and we came to a gorge, with a stream at its bottom.

"The cave is down there. The hole you go in by the stream."

"Let us go," urged the Ruler, but Cub was firm, a man in charge. He pointed at the sun.

"It is too late in the day. We will go in the cool of the morning, when light is bright."

The boys ran about setting up camp and preparing for the evening meal. Three disappeared into the rain forest, two set up the beds and insect tents with sticks over them. The last built a fire for us.

In a few minutes the boys came out of the rain forest bringing three rather large, brightly colored birds. "Have you trapped those?" I asked, surprised at the ease they showed in hunting. I did not see bows and arrows.

"See—these blowpipes," one confessed, holding it up and smiling triumphantly. He had a reed pipe with hard, round pellets. The boys whistled and placed the pipes to their cheeks, aiming at trees. Pings and thuds were heard all around, and two unfortunate lizards soon were carried in to be cut up and added to the dinner pot.

"Boys in Zama have these in the outer villages," the Ruler said, looking at the blowpipe, "but I have never seen such skill."

"We are never without small game, or large," Cub told us. I wondered what he meant by that.

The birds were plucked and roasted with the lizard meat in no time, and we ate a fine supper in the middle of the rain forest. But it was not long until we all retired beneath the tents, Cub going out from time to time to keep up the fire so wild animals would stay away.

Right after He Is Halfway Through the Night there was a scramble, a youthful curse, and a yowl. I quickly got out of my tent to see a large jackal lying by the fire, dying, I supposed. His breath was coming in heavy gasps which wrenched his body until finally, all breath stopped and he lay still. Cub stood looking into the gorge and behind us to a hill.

"There may be more," he said.

But when no more came, and we all prepared to get into the tents again, I called Cub over and pointed at the dead animal. "That jackal did not die from a pellet," I said. "And I did not see a spear." I had looked at his body; there was no wound on it.

"Many things are in the woods and in the city which threaten harm or death," the boy said. "We have had to learn to live in the midst of viciousness. We have our ways." What did that mean? I wondered, but could not give it much consideration.

I heard the Ruler stirring in his tent a few feet away from mine.

"Are you awake?" I asked.

"Yes. I am nervous and excited by what we will do tomorrow."

"There is one part of my story about Cahokia that I did not tell you, because I did not know how to say it."

"And so?"

"You have said you were my friend, so I will tell true all, as if you are not a ruler."

"Say on." It was odd not seeing his face, speaking to a disembodied voice in the blackness of the night.

"The ruler in Cahokia is hideous—a servant of the powers of darkness. He is dissolute, uncaring of people, making war on the helpless. There is also a group unknown, I think, to those on Temple Hill. It is called "Those Who Say The Things That Are Not Said." Their amulet, which you have seen around my neck is the Eye of the World. They record injustices."

"Our foreigners—the traders--do that for all the people here," the Ruler said ruefully.

380

"The common folk's burden is almost too much to be borne and they are my friends." I listed for him the injustices of the Prince at Cahokia. "I dread returning to share their lot."

The voice from the other tent was silent for a while. Finally the Ruler spoke. 'A ruler must be good. That is why I seek to purify my life now that I rule and have a child to carry on my line. For if the ruler is malignant, then the people—" He paused.

"The people?"

His voice was hollow against the sound of the rushing stream. "The people can rise up and throw off their bonds. They have that ability—that right, perhaps. At least they take it."

I had never heard or thought of such a thing. "Rise up?"

"You saw the power the people had on the day we came back from the rebellion at Xel Ha. They simply refused to do what their evil superiors wanted."

I really was stunned. It did not seem possible that the people could throw out rulers, like old pot-washing water. "Why then, do they not do this all the time? Why have the people of Cahokia never even considered such a thing?"

"Because we—the kings and the priests—hold the keys to sacred mysteries. There is power in religion when it is practiced in a group—access to the gods and blessing for the afterlife. The priest can kill your soul and the group in the city reaffirms what he says."

My heart recognized it as true. The priests! They controlled the kings, and the kings controlled the power. Groups, controlled by corrupt priests, worshipping odd cruel gods who demanded more, ever more, from priests and people alike.

The Ruler went on, his voice calm but insistent. "You saw the cat stone?"

"Yes."

"And on the ground? A split head. How do you think it got there?"

"Perhaps through time it fell down when the earth shook? It was poorly joined to the cat part of the pillar."

"The heads are likenesses of rulers of the Olmec. They were thrown down in a farmers' revolt."

I was incredulous. Rulers of such power. "How do you know that?"

"It is known in my family." The stream roared; a boyish, jerking snore came out of one of the boys' tents. "I will tell you something that I would not say to another human being. My father told me. This vast city we have left, this most wonderful of all the cities of the Maya, did not die because the ground wore out and people left, although that did happen. But it really died when the peasants, dissatisfied, rose up and threw out the rulers. They tried to rule themselves and solve the problems themselves, but could not. It is never, never spoken of by those outside the ruling families who left."

"Why do you tell me, then?"

"Because the knowledge is the finest thing I can give you. You can use it someday. You are my friend."

It was almost dawn before I drifted off to sleep among the loud cadences of the insects of that dark and green forest.

Chapter Fifteen

Morning came too early for me, but the boys were up fixing food, whistling, jostling each other. They packed up quickly; we all were interested in getting to the cave as fast as possible, and we scrambled, slid and fell over roots to get down the hill.

There, at the bottom of the hill, by the mouth of the cave, we found the largest cat of all. The jaguar—the cat that does not cry— his mouth most of the sculpture and his body curving around so it fit into the square shape of the pillar, was as tall as I and thick as the tallest tree's trunk. And, as we had seen before, the statue was cut off just above the cat. The human head which had sat above the cat stand, this hugest of all heads we had seen, with heavy lidded, expressionless eyes and huge lips, lay in three pieces beside the cat. Had it shattered as it fell? Or had whoever destroyed the statue decided to further mutilate the head?

"How did they do this?" Smoke Fox-god asked wonderingly. "To get stone to shatter? Axes would not work—they must have used a stone batterer with many people carrying it. Or built a dirt mound and climbed it to push the head over. How they must have hated the ruling house to overcome their fear in this way." He was fascinated by this deed of sacrilege against an ancient ruler who must have had almost the status of a god.

The boys were clambering in and out of the cave mouth, calling to each other excitedly. "Who? Who did it?" I asked, but the Ruler was silent, somber.

"Perhaps the rival royal families who took over power?" I murmured, thinking of the erasing of the old names and the putting in of the new.

But the Ruler was still silent, looking around amidst the rubble on the ground. He pawed among a clump of small trees which grew over something, began pulling at them, then called the boys to chop and dig dirt away. What was he doing? I wondered impatiently. Why were we not proceeding to the cave after we had come so far to reach it?

A shape was emerging from the mound of dirt, made of crudely sculptured stone. "I wondered what this was," the Ruler said. We stood back to look. It was, rather clearly, a huge foot. The boys were digging out the toes.

They were murmuring to each other. Cub seemed excited. "In old stories, the name of this place is Foot Cave. We have never known why."

"Foot?" I was completely bewildered.

"Remember what our friend Yum said about the ruler?" Smoke Fox-god asked me softly.

"He said—let's see. That the ruler was the—I don't remember."

"He said that on the body of the city, the ruler is the head."

"Yes, now I recall."

"And the people—are?" He shrugged his shoulders and pointed to the giant foot.

Smoke Fox-god walked towards the mouth of the cave. "The people overturned these god-kings. When they had had enough, they simply took over the power and pushed over the monuments. And put up their own. A foot, to represent what really stands under kings." I was surprised to see him smiling.

"At the foot! That's what the chant said! But the foot had been buried; my uncle may never have known of it, except for the local name." The power of the foot! To go against the nobility of thousands of generations all the way back to the two-headed boar or dragon gods, against hundreds of generations of priests who controlled the very sun and the afterlife! The people pushed over the god kings and put in their own symbol.

"And what happened to the rulers of the Olmec?"

"They were probably killed, or exiled. New families were put in power, maybe even from the people, to rule more justly."

"And did they?"

"After some generations of power and wealth, probably not. But it is a good lesson to those of us who rule."

"I think you know it already," I said.

"Thank you, my friend, for seeing that," he said, and he came and gave me the armclasp, as he had seen me do so often with Ghost. I was truly honored.

"Dog Head will go into the cave with one of you for the first stage of what he must do for his cleansing," I said to the boys. So we had arranged it, so it would seem to be real to them, that the Ruler would go into the cave a certain distance, set up his idol and say his prayers, sprinkle incense and then come out. Then we would tell them that we had a second ritual obligation, to descend like the descending god into the cave itself from above.

We did all that. The boys went a short way in, then after a while, I saw them emerge, and we informed them we would need to search for an upper opening.

They did not know of one; that did relieve me, because it meant no one had probably come to search for the treasure.

"Fifty feet high, the chamber was," I murmured to the Ruler. "And my uncle had gone—which direction was the passage inward?" I asked.

The Ruler gestured in an easterly direction, reminding me it did twist and turn. We climbed the cave hill, looking ever for signs of some sort of declivity, a sunken-in spot perhaps. Finally Cub called, "Dog Head, here it is, a small opening. We never saw this in all our play!"

We ran towards him, as they pulled branches and leaves of many years off the mouth of a hole about three feet wide. And there, sure enough, I saw as I peered down through its opening, were rocks, but not all the way up to the mouth. "How in the world did Uncle get out of this thing?" I asked. "The rocks do not reach the opening. He would have been stuck two manspans from the top. And of course, the rocks blocked his path back through the cave." I spoke softly to the Ruler, who was looking after me. The boys with their sweaty bodies were hovering behind us, panting.

"The rocks have probably shifted, slid down in. Did he not say there was a quaking of the earth that opened up the hole and sent the rocks into the cave? Perhaps there was a later quake. After-quakes do come, so the wise ones know. Or the rocks could have settled."

Yes, that must have been it. But it would mean we could climb neither down nor up, but must be lowered by a rope. And how would that work? The Ruler and I walked away to talk alone.

"One of us must stay outside to lower the rope. We cannot leave our lives and fortunes to these boys, good as they have been to us."

But which would stay, which go inside to the treasure? I looked at him, then looked away, old distrusts and doubts rising in my mind. How well did I really know him? After all, I had come only a few moons ago, to a place where customs were strange, loyalties shifting. I had seen him execute his relative with few qualms, after all; though he said now he regretted it, did I really know?

"I will stay; you will go." Not friendship, but a royal command. Had I expected anything else?

So, down, down I went, with a torch in one hand on a rope securely fastened to a tree and held by two boys. To the rocks, where still hanging onto the rope, I bounced myself on and off as they let out more rope, because climbing down those rocks, made slippery by moss and trickling rain, was too slippery and uncertain and long a process.

Finally I arrived at the bottom, with, thankfully, the torch still burning strong in the odd, musty air. I could see the head of the Ruler up there, small as an idol's, looking down. "What do you see?" he demanded.

"Odd long needles of rock dripping a little water, a path of some sort that men have used—" I turned my head and walked a little—"and the blocked entrance, laden with rock." I sat down. Suddenly my uncle's presence was with me, as he must have felt, laden with his own pride and many sins, here in the cave of his death, black as the underworld. Except for—I looked up. "Where Star Lords do not flee." There were none, now. The ruler's head was in the way; no stars, of course, were visible this daytime; the torch's light well illumined the chamber.

"And, let me see—" I walked around, saw old animal bones from long ages past when the passage was still open, even a few ancient leaves, drifted down from above, I supposed and—there it was. The woven chest, black now with age and mold and the tar that had been used to preserve it—but not disintegrated, and embellished with some sort of a crest—a jaguar! The Oldest Ones.

I did not speak further, and, setting down the torch between some of the broken fragments of long needles and rocks so it would stand up, I opened the lid.

There inside were wondrous things, I tell you, and I knew that I had not come in vain through these awful trials and troubles to get to the Olmec treasure. Necklaces there were in plenty, of fine shells and bright stones, and ear ornaments, carefully separated in fine, light bark boxes, some now rotting away. And jade, beautiful jade carved more exquisitely than I had seen, idols, small worship pots with cat heads and snake heads. Most wondrous was a tall idol of pure jade with red stone eyes, a foot and a half tall on his knees. Truly he must have been meant to represent the king of the gods, for this was the king of all idols. I set him out carefully on flat ground with no bumps.

Then I examined the great wonder my uncle himself had left in the cave—the flat, stone device that told the times of the moon's hiding. I examined, in the dim light of the torch. Many holes were dug in a circle, with slight depressions in them, so that a stick, still in the device, could rotate. And beyond them, on the outside, another circle with markers of some sort placed in other places. Then a circle in the middle with a few, large, key notches dug in. I did not understand it, but I felt that truly, it must be a thing of great medicine. It had the sign of the new moon on the bottom, in the right hand corner.

Then I searched through the treasure again. In the midst of the jewels and idols was the oddest thing of all—the crystal skull head my uncle had mentioned. I put the other things aside and, transfixed, looked at the beautiful, hideous thing. Odd, but I had never thought to mention it to the Ruler.

The torch cast shadows that shot across the cave floor, making it as eerie as a tent with a shaman in it. The flame was blowing. Truly there was a draft from somewhere that kept the air fresh.

But I could see things in the skull—oh yes, it seemed alive! I could see into that skull. Things were drifting and swirling around, like the mists off the Twin Lakes near my home.

I heard Smoke Fox-god's voice above me, commandingly. "What have you found? Call up the things you are seeing."

But I could not—the skull was binding my eyes. Suddenly I was irritated at all the heads and voices up above. "I have found many fine things and our search is rewarded. I will call up in a wink of the sun's eye. But go from the hole; let me be with the spirits alone down here for a brief time." And then the hole was empty, quiet.

I looked deeply into the skull. And what I saw I tell you was more wondrous than anything I have heard described when the holy person climbs the tree of life in a vision. Or stranger yet than when a marked one dreams a holy dream at night. Three things I saw, and the first was this. It was near dawn in a land like that of Cahokia with large forest trees. In the middle stood a stockade also like that of the greatest cities of the north, except the guards upon the wall had light faces, lightest brown or white faces and eyes of blue. Somehow I knew they had eyes of blue. The Blue Eyes my ancestors had spoken of, who came to the land of the Beautiful River! Then came the woodland tribal people towards this stockade, and I saw a man who looked like he was of my people, tall and strong, but he carried a magic stick of power. The dawn came; the tribal people shot the sticks of power, which blazed like lightning; the white-skinned people in the stockade ran around and shot fire sticks back, but not enough, and finally the tribal people entered through the stockade doors triumphant, and took as captives the Blue Eyes there. But there was the tribal man I saw outside the gate; he had been shot and looked up into my eyes before he died. Through the skull of power! I swear to you he saw me. And I knew he had the blood of all my people in his veins and he was my kin. Somehow I knew.

The second thing I saw there, on the damp cave floor as the torchlight shot around the cavern, was a woman, like the Blue Eyes, white in skin, but her eyes, odd to say were brown. She wore a dress of finest cotton and she stood upon a hill, over a dry creekbed just as leaves were falling in the month of burning grass. And she watched, as in a dream, while Blue Eyes in long leggings and many, many sticks of power shot them like bows and arrows at each other. All of these Blue Eyes seemed to be warriors fighting for the water in the creek.

And the woman mourned, mourned and feared. And she too turned and startled me because her eyes were near, near in the crystal skull of medicine.

But the last thing I saw was the finest and most startling, because I saw a boat, a boat like a house, and on it was—a man with hair upon his face, wearing a short, odd skirt like a woman's and thin cotton leggings. And he looked, he looked I tell you, at the towers of Zama. He seemed to look into my eyes, and his skin was as white as the rest.

And then the sight went away and the torch blew out. I was left there in the dark, the pitch black, and for a moment I was frightened, with a pure, bear belly fright at the vastness of the cavern and my aloneness.

But there I could see up, now, up to "where Star Lords never scatter." My eyes grew accustomed to the dark, and sure enough, through the hole, I could see the stars. I sat down, fascinated by the sight as my uncle had been. And I begin to think, surely I too will feel the power of the stars, and Nanaboozhoo will come to me as he did in the form of the evening star and take away my sins and I will know him as Lord. I yearned for it, for truly, as I have told, my sins were many, and I have not told them all, and my sorrows stretched back to my birth, with each guilty sorrow a stone on a string. Lately what I had done, especially to my friends, weighed heavily on me. And, to tell the truth, it had been in my mind for a long time, that when I was in the cave, something wonderful would cleanse me of my heaviness of spirit.

And I also tell you true that as I sat and waited for my spiritual transformation, for the sign my uncle had, for the proof that the Maker of Stars does exist, I saw—nothing but the stars. It had been enough, I suppose, to see the sights of the skull of power.

Then, finally, I saw the head of Smoke Fox-god peering down the hole.

"What is in there?" he asked.

"Many fine necklaces and bracelets. Incense pots of rarest forms and beauty. An idol, a foot and a half tall, like one you have never seen. And the odd moon token made of hard clay."

I saw him go away a moment from the hole. And that was not all. I saw the rope being hauled quickly up. "What are you doing?" I screamed up, and there was a kind of an echo.

The head was there again, helping to draw the rope.

"My friend. I will bring you up in a moment, but I must have your promise on something important," the voice of the Ruler came down.

"Say on." I was angry—and I was afraid.

"You cannot take the treasures home, not the jade god, or the moon token, or any of the rest, to your Cahokia."

"And why not? I promised it to the Female Sun, and with it I must buy the freedom of my loved ones."

"Because it is not destined to go away from the lands of the Maya. The treasure was born here, all of it, hidden here for the people to come, and here it must stay, where the gods will be honored and the spirits of the Oldest Ones appeased."

"I cannot think you are saying this. I shared the secret of the treasure with you, and you are betraying me."

"If I sent the things with you, I would be betraying myself and my people. For the treasure is mine. I am Olmec, just as I am Mayan. In my blood runs the blood of the Oldest Ones, for I did not tell you that my house was the noble one of the outpost—ancient, ancient tale. We could have been the ones overthrown or even the ones which overthrew. But we are also the ones destined to bring the treasure home. Hear me and accept."

I heard him, but I did not accept. "I must take these things, at least some of them, to the city of the Female Sun. It means life and death to me. Besides, the moon token is legitimately mine. It was brought here by my uncle." If he was in the cave at this moment, I might have strangled him, ruler or not. It wasn't just that I was being deprived of the very thing I needed to buy life for the people I cared about, and myself too, for that matter—it was that in the long chain of beads of betrayal and abandonment in my life, my mother, my father, the heads of the village who had not respected me, the beautiful women who had tormented me as a bear belly—this man I counted as friend was betraying me. One more bead in the chain.

390

"Send up the treasure first," the voice commanded.

"First?" I yelled. "I must come out with it. Send down two ropes."

"No. I must be sure you understand me and comply with my wishes."

My heart was almost stopped; my throat closed with pain and fear. Thoughts of the empty darkness, the stairway of slippery rocks that led two manspan from the top but not further, that made this place a hopeless tomb, took my breath from me. He would take the treasure and leave me here, as the rest had. "There is another thing," the Ruler's voice shouted down finally. "You have told me of the corruptness of this prince of yours. If he rules with these things of great power, he will use the sacred things for destruction. Is that not so?"

I was silent. Of course that part was true.

"You should not have promised to help this evil one in the first place."

"What will I do to gain my loved ones' freedom? What can I bring to the city?"

"I think you have the answer to that yourself."

"How can I know that you will haul me up after the treasure comes up?"

There was a short silence, then the words, "Your heart knows I have told truth. Remember when you said 'only a true friend will tell ugly truth.' I have done that. Trust me."

"No. You may be right, but there is one more thing. I will not put the treasure up until you give me a promise, fair exchange for fair. There is one more thing I did not mention. It is an ancient skull of great power. It seems to work for me, and it must not stay here. I must take it home."

"Why?" the voice wanted to know.

"Because it is dangerous to the Maya. If your priest Alton Ha, or any of his kind should learn to use it, they could do great evil to the throne and to the people. I know because I am a drummer of power, and these things are ill omens for all but the one they have been sent to. It was you who told me last night that the priests buy power and submission from the people with their sacred toys, as parents throw sweets to children who cry too loud, to silence them. You must learn to rule without the priest, if you would be great. The skull should go out of the land. I will bury it in the north."

"How do I know you will dispose of the skull? That you do not want this power for yourself, to gain your own riches and city?"

I too was silent, then said. "How often truth is ugly; how painful it is to share. We have lanced our boils together. Trust me as friend."

Then the rope came down, and I tied it firmly all around the basket, taking special care because it was so old and I did not wish it to drop.

Holding my breath, I waited for the rope to come back down, and it did. I put my foot into a loop on the bottom, and climbed onto it like a vine, and all of them above hauled me up a little at a time.

We walked the trail home, passing the broken-off cats and the huge heads. We brought the treasure between the two of us, and we watched our boys carefully.

"What did you tell them?" I asked Smoke Fox-god in a whisper. He had sent me off with them to break camp while he had counted and assessed the treasure. It was very great indeed, he told me, then looked me in the eye, "but it is great only to our people. "I had grudgingly nodded. Of course he was right. But I carried the skull of power in my own doeskin bag. It would have been a thing of great evil for the priests of the Maya, and in this he knew I was right.

About halfway back to the city, a boy I had not seen before came running around a bend in the trail. Cub went out to meet him. The boy, whose face was shining with sweat, was winded from running.

"Strangers in town—asking if there have been other strangers," he panted. Immediately we were alert.

"How many?" Cub wanted to know.

"I—saw but two," the boy told him. "And a bearer for their traveling goods."

"Have we been followed?" I asked the Ruler.

"I do not know. We saw Sky Many Deer as we got off the boat at the seacoast. If there are enemies in Zama—"

"But your father-in-law and the Chichen Itza guards are there."

"Perhaps they left for some reason. Or a secret plot is afoot they know nothing of."

The boy who had come from town held a bark writing in his hand. "On all the things the bearer carried, the cases and baskets, was a city stamp. I drew a picture of it."

"Ah," said the Ruler, smiling a little. "We shall see which of the families of Zama identify themselves as our enemies." He stepped forward to look at the bark drawing, then returned with a stone face, giving orders for the troop to proceed up the trail again.

Burning with curiosity, I asked, "Which of the batab? Who is seeking you and me?"

"None. The city stamp was not of Zama. It was the royal crest of another city entirely."

"Which one?"

"I will tell you soon," he said in a low voice, then began to stride up the trail.

In the outer precincts of the center city we stopped to rest and speak together before we entered to meet whatever dangers faced us there. We sat on stones in the outer courtyard of what must have been a fine batab's villa, with many outbuildings and guest houses, kitchens, shrines and workshops. Huge stone pictures of the lord's family, in war dress with feather headdresses, were carved across the front of the main palace building.

"Perhaps this was the home of the Smokes while they were in Tikal," I said.

"Perhaps. But now I do not care. Our lives, and my city's future, are in danger."

"But what can these men want? If they are not from our city, how could they have known and why would they care that we are here?"

"There is only one answer," the Ruler said, drinking water from a gourd one of the boys had brought. "When we read the chant and solved our puzzle, we overlooked one thing."

He offered me the gourd. I drank deeply. "And what is that?" I asked.

"We did not think it important where your uncle had been, what had been his place of origin when he went to seek the treasure."

"That is so."

"But it may have been important to those in the city that sent him. He did not return those thirty years ago, did he?"

"No. Without the treasure, and a man changed by what he had seen in the cave, he came back north to take up the quest the Son of the West Wind had given him."

"He travelled alone?"

"I believe so, at least that is what I think he said. There was no time for details; he was being tortured and knew he would die."

"I think no ruler would have trusted anyone to accompany your uncle to discover the whereabouts of the treasure. The lecherous ruler, as you called him, would have wondered, though, what happened to the slave he sent on the important mission."

"Since the treasure was there, I guess we can think that lecherous ruler did not find out its exact whereabouts."

"Yes. But he—or his descendants, told the great secret—wondered all these years what had happened to it."

"Why would they not have gone to seek it themselves? Or sent another?"

"Because of the great taboo. Only one from far away can enter the groves and caves of the Oldest Ones. There is great, deep medicine and danger here. That is why they were waiting for the promised outsider to go and do the quest. None of them could do it, and none would go back now to find out what happened to your uncle's quest. The taboo is far too great."

I set the gourd down. "You came here."

"Yes. But these are my own people, all the way back to the Two-Headed boar god. Even so, I took great risk. That is one of the reasons I needed to purify myself."

"Have you yet?"

"No, but in the gods' good time. Now we must act, and soon."

The boys were beginning to mill about, eager to get on the trail and back to their homes.

"But you have not yet told me—which is the city from which my uncle started. You have read its royal city seal."

"There is only one place which could have sent your uncle, where he could have come from, and I should have known it before. The seal was from Mayapan. He came south from Mayapan on the trading routes, from the new home of the Smokes and others too ancient who had left Tikal. That is how the ruler knew the most ancient of legends about the Old Ones' treasure."

"Ah, I see," I said, understanding. "So they have come to protect the treasure. But how, how would they know we were following the ancient chant to treasure? No one, not one soul in Zama knew. "

"That I do not know now. But in some way they had information. And Mayapan is not our friend."

Cub stood before us. "May we go on, Dog Head and Cat Cape? We are hungry for the corn cakes and honey fruit of our evening meal."

"Bring the boys together. I have something to say," Smoke Fox-god told him.

We looked at the small group of bright-eyed boys. "Boys, you have done a fine task for us," the Ruler said. "I think you may know we are of royal blood, and I can say to you now that we are of the Old Ones of Tikal, the ones who loved and built this city." Well, at least he was. They gasped and smiled with pleasure.

"I am impressed with the way you care for the shrines of the Oldest and Old Ones. Someone must do homage to the ancient gods, remember the great age of Tikal." They nodded proudly.

"I have come to return the sacred objects of the Oldest Ones who lived and worshipped here a thousand summers ago or more to one of the royal families of the city." He opened the basket and held up several small but wonderful effigies. "When we leave, taking the treasure to care for it, I will leave these here with you, as the present lords of the town. The gods give you the special privilege of guarding them always, and passing them down to your children, that their ceremonies might not be forgotten."

The boys smiled broadly and looked with interest as Smoke Fox-god put the gods back in their basket.

"But first, I must tell you true, because I know you are my friends, that Cat Cape and I must overcome our enemy in the town. The men who have come are evil. They wish to take the gods from the people who have found them in the sacred quest." Cub and the boy who had met us on the trail nodded vigorously, understanding.

"My friend and I must go into town. We do not know what awaits. We hope that we can speak to these men; certainly we cannot avoid them. We do not know what they wish, and it may be grave harm to us." He put his hand to his forehead in the sign of death.

The boys began to dance up and down. "What can we do? We will help! Dog Head and Cat Cape forever!" they called out until finally Smoke Fox-god raised his hand.

Now I touched his arm, letting him know I wished to speak. I stood before them, and when my tongue faltered, the Ruler translated. "Young cubs, I come from the lands of the north. There we have a warriors' society that joins all men of courage in loyalty to a cause. I ask that you let blood and pledge with us to be brothers. We will not forget the greatness of this town. We will not let its sacred places fall to ruin. Some will remember. Will you let blood in pledge?"

The boys held back, silent. The Ruler whispered to me, "What do you have in mind, Tunkel? They are no doubt thinking of the kinds of blood-letting some rulers do on themselves to petition the gods—women put stingray spines through their tongues and men—well, these warriors do not wish to put a spine through the foreskin of their male part." The boys heard and shook their heads, seriously.

"No, no, I do not mean that." I said to all of them. "What I intend is blood from the arm." I opened the secret pouch I had carried since Cahokia and looked at the few bright obsidian knives, and took one to cut a small place on my forearm. Then I passed out the other knives to the boys.

"Keep these, pledge of our faith to you. All who wish to make the Society of Broken Heads one of sworn blood brothers, come to me and share blood of life."

One by one, starting with Cub, the boys made a small cut on their arm and came to touch my forearm. Then, with ceremony, I went to the Ruler and handed him a knife. He seemed to hesitate. All his years of noble Mayahood must have told him that to surrender his blood to commoners from far away was to pledge something very grave and serious indeed. But, nodding slowly, he cut his arm deeper than any of us had, and touched with the boys. Then, finally, he came to me. Looking in my eyes he placed our forearms together, then held them both for a moment with his strong hand. "Kin," he said.

I knew that whatever we faced, it would be as twins.

Then we hid our treasure, with Cub alone knowing where it was. And I realized, as we came towards the city what I had not known in the cave. Surely, the greatest of all treasures is friendship itself.

As we came over the final mile of the trail, the Ruler and I plotted. We decided on boldness. We would coolly enter bearing ourselves as if we had all the right in the world to it, as indeed we did. Then we would trust to circumstances.

One boy, running ahead to scout, announced that the men were informed we were returning. "They are there," he said, pointing to the huge temple. Then the boys all scattered.

So, they were at the foot of the Great Temple of the Jaguar, magnificent crowning jewel of the city. We walked to it, as the sun sank low, and my eyes swept up its sides. There up the steepest of steps was a fine and tall temple which seemed to shout at the gods themselves. Of course the steps were crumbling; bits of rocks had been chipped off and plant roots stuck out of them. At the foot of the last step men—not two but three—noblemen stood. One was a man of high nobility and large ceremonial headdress; the second was the old trader we had met on sacred Cozumel Island; the third was Zama's priest Alton Ha!

"Ruler, we come to claim what is rightfully ours," Alton Ha said in a voice as smooth as turtle oil.

"I have come on a sacred quest to bring the items of power from the ancient ones my family served a thousand summers ago to Zama," the Ruler said. "There the sacred gods of the old ones can be worshipped."

"You come to stucco your power to the people of the city by impressing them with this great, sacred cache of the gods," the priest said scornfully.

"If that happens, all the better for Zama," the Ruler answered, and then pointed at the others behind the priest. "Who are these men and what right do they have to interfere in the happenings of another town?"

"This is Lord Cocom of Mayapan. He has come to claim the treasure in the name of his father Lord Cocom. And of his mother, cousin of Smoke Second." Ah, so that was it.

I spoke up for the first time. "And how did he happen to know we were on a quest for the treasure of the Oldest Ones?" I looked at the Cozumel trader. Someway, somehow, we must have given it away when we were asking about the lake and the mountains.

Alton Ha glared at me. "Silence, lowly steward of the royal household. What gives you the right to speak?"

"I am the personal protector of the Ruler. Answer my questions, old land rat." I looked directly at the old trader.

"Well you may look at me, tall one with the big mouth. I knew on the sacred island that I had seen you, and your face haunted me so I could look at little else the night we talked." So it was I he stared at! I had thought it was the Ruler.

"Land rat I am not," the old man said, "because I am of a noble family of the hope of Maya purity in Mayapan. But old I am, old enough to have seen the face before, when I was a young man at the court. The trader from the north, who gained the confidence of the ruler's old father—you are his image. I and a few others knew of the quest, knew that it had failed when he did not come back, and spies told us the tall, northern trader had shipped out with the foreign boat captains to the Land of the Longest River North. Left without anything in his hands, or baggage even. We knew the treasure was unrecovered, that the gods had denied the quest."

I continued to stare at him. "And so, you went to Mayapan and told them that someone had come to seek the treasure the northern trader had gone for."

"But I think the priest, Alton Ha had a hand in this too," the Ruler said with cold eyes. The priest said nothing. "Do you not serve the city of Zama? What kind of treachery are you involved with?" he demanded, walking forward to reach for the priest's throat.

Suddenly, three armed guards rushed forward from behind the temple. The sharp lances they carried and stuck right beneath our noses bore the city sign of Mayapan.

"I serve Mayapan," Alton Ha shouted in a harsh voice. "That was the city of my boyhood and of my allegiance. It is there that the ancient gods will be worshipped, not the city where the strangers have come, the foreigners of Chichen Itza!"

I could stand it no longer. When a bear corners you in the forest and you cannot run, you had best stare him in the eyes and aim for his heart—you can at least go down quickly. I broke through the circle of armed guards and rushed Alton Ha with the sharpest of the obsidian blades I carried. "Surprise," I yelled. I held back his head and cut his throat.

Old man that he was, I had a slight twinge of guilt, but not much. The Ruler jumped the old trader and the guards tried to pull him off as the prince of Mayapan bellowed at them, "Take him alive for sacrifice to Chac."

I ran to the guards who held the Ruler as he struggled to free his arms and finally he broke free; one guard turned and aimed the most awful looking short sword at my heart. It was then that the Ruler turned away from his own man-to-man conflict to deflect the blow, taking it deeply in his own arm. Blood splashed around on my chest. "Kin," he murmured, burying his knife deeply in the gut of the guard, who fell, writhing in agony.

I was engaged in knife combat with the guard who had pursued me in the first place. The prince of Mayapan stood by, shouting instructions, refusing to sully himself in political warfare, though his stone carvings might show him with angry face leading the troops. Other guards appeared over the rise in back of the temple; were there five or eight? I could not tell.

"The end is near," the Ruler panted out at me. "Let us die as noble people in close combat. Honor the god of war!"

"The honor is ours," I screamed; suddenly the man I was struggling with, who had wounded me in the side and whom I was slashing in the face, dropped at my feet. At the same moment, so did the old merchant, and the last two guards. What in the name of the Maker of Stars?

I stood stock still, panting as deeply as a half-dead dog, and the ruler and I looked back towards the Temple of the Jaguar. The reinforcement guards were lying on the ground. From behind us a troop of boys advanced, whistling, stepping over the bodies, none of which seemed to have an ounce of life left in them, as if they were frozen in death in an instant.

Cub advanced, waving his blowpipe.

"Last night you asked me a question. Now I will answer it." I stared at him open mouthed. He pulled out a tiny, straw-like arrow, and told the Ruler, "My family has had a secret poison–a secret they got from some far-away trader in the long-ago past. Put on the end of a sharp and tiny arrow and shot from the blowpipe, it kills instantly. It is for large and threatening animals." He kicked the body of one of the guards, then knelt to strip it of valuables from the belt and helmet.

"You have saved us, blood brothers," I cried, but then saw that the Ruler was slumped on the ground. I turned him over. The arm wound was not the only one he had received saving me from the guard. His side was bleeding profusely. I listened for his heart; it beat, faintly. I grabbed an ornamental tassel from the loincloth of the dead guard, wadded it up and stuffed it in the wound. Then, weary as I was, I picked up the Ruler's body and carried it over my shoulder, as the boys shouted and ran in front of us all the way to the temple where Elan-Ya and Cub lived.

All that night and the next, I bore night vigil. The wounds, deep and serious, sent the ruler out of his head at times. Elan-Ya tended him, bringing to him the traditional herbs to cleanse the wounds, binding up his side and arm cleanly.

Once or twice he awoke to himself. The second time he beckoned me over and said, "Do the things of the woods for me. Climb the tree of life you have talked of and speak to your spirits."

I thought for a moment, then took his hand. "I cannot. I am not called. The spirits, if they are out there, would not listen to me." He tossed and turned, and seemed to grow worse, and called to me for help.

"Is there a drum in the town?, I asked. "A tunkel from the olden times or new?"

Elan-Ya thought there was. It was under the floor in one of the secondary temples; she had left it there when she had found it once looking for incense pots. Quickly she sent Cub for it. When he returned, I saw that it would do. It was well strung, and while not of heavy animal hide, I could reach the creator with it. I did not intend to talk to anybody else but the top chief.

There was a problem; the deerskin sticks I would need could not be found; long lost under the debris of the ages or rotted away.

"Get me tanned deerskin," I said. "And a proper stick." I showed him what I needed. "And hurry. The Ruler is growing weaker."

He returned; as I cut the deerskin I told him to get the Broken Heads together quickly and bring them here.

They came as the sun was setting; we knelt around the Ruler's bed.

"We are lifting our friend to the sight of the Creator of the Universe," I told them. "We are making a prayer in song for his life. I will tell you a word to chant when I tell you it is time."

And then I sang my song, and this time, instead of singing of the goodness and power of Nanaboozhoo, son of the West Wind and Son of man, I sang of the goodness and power of the man Kukulcan, son of the West Wind and Son of man. And all I knew of his legend that the Ruler had told me I put into the song, of his coming from the Mexica people, of his founding his own city, Chichen Itza rising from the ruins of a former city, his teaching of different doctrines, laws of love and kindness and the respect of each being for each. His going to found Mayapan and then leaving from the coast, where he built a small temple so the people of the upper coast could remember him. His promise to return someday to bless his people. And I sang of the wonder of the Maker of Stars, who had created such a messenger and the stars and bodies of the heavens, and then—

Then I sang of my friend. All the love I felt for him, from the time he had made me learn the language, to the trip where we grew to be friends first at Xel Ha, when they would have killed us but we escaped together, to the trip here, where as twins we overcame all the trials we had. Finally, I sang that he saved my life, stepping between the spears and my own body to take the blows on his. Truly a friend joins the gods in grandeur when he will give up his own life for yours. And I sang the name of friend, friend, dear friend and told the boys to sing the word, and I felt the love the powers above have sent us all in friendship until my own tears fell. When I opened my eyes, I saw the boys were crying too.

We all went away in the soft darkness, and when I returned from a walk, the Ruler had opened his eyes. I do not know whether it was by our drumming and chant or not, but I knew I was overjoyed as never in my life to see his eyes had sense.

Later, he said, "I heard the throbbing of the drum, and a chant, great and deep. What was it—something in your own language?"

"Yes. I sang in my own tongue, for it is the voice of the woods and the simple powers there, and I love it best."

"The same word over and over. It seemed to rouse me, and I wished to swim to the surface as a man beneath the waters."

"Ni-ka. Ni-ka. That is what we sang." I looked at his bright eyes in the darkness and smiled. "Friend. It is the word for friend in my language."

"Ni-ka," he whispered, his voice hoarse. "Now I see."

He rested much, and I went out to walk in the starlight the shattered streets of the City of Magnificence, Tikal the Grand. I wandered to the foot of the Temple of the Jaguar. My eyes went up the steep steps to the temple at the top, where, Elan-Ya had said, a famous king of the great days of the Maya was buried, deep in the foundation. Gone they all were, these ones of such great power and strength and beauty.

Had they failed their birthright, their gods, and were so punished? Partly. But I thought as I stared at the temple that it was not so much that they had failed their gods as that their gods had failed them. Weak gods to give and withdraw favor, to support one city over another. It could not be so. I had given the god of death the treatment he deserved. All the rest of them deserved that too.

I sighed and sat down, staring at the stars instead of the temple. I had rejected many gods, but I had never given up thinking true power was there in the spirit world. I had asked so often to know who I should worship and adore, had thought the answer would come in a dream, or in a trance, or from some priest or miracle in the cave where Star Lords showed themselves, miraculously to illumine my thought. I had seen in the skull, but that was not of gods but of men.

No, what I had found was a simple answer. The powers of the universe spoke through man. The true gods or god lived, yes lived! and I had found their nature—in the face of a friend.

We needed to pick up our pieces and depart as soon as we could from Tikal. The line of days, like crows, grew ever longer until now it covered the horizon. Spring had come and gone and early summer bloomed with rich fruits and fields of tasseling corn across the land of theMaya. Two, almost three more moons and it would be a year since I had left Cahokia. Was she there, had she survived, my link to life and love, the Female Sun? Or had her corrupted body, ridden with rottenness and pain, sunk into the earth, taking with it beauty and light?

The day after the fight we had buried the dead from Mayapan and the priest Alton Ha in the common gravesite at the edge of town. I had sent for the father of the messenger boy, the one with a strong hank of hair cut short on his head and a pudgy body, as I had had when I was young. He was, second to Cub, the best and brightest of the lot of boys.

"Where is your father, young one?" I wanted to know.

"We have a field outside of the citadel precints. Not far."

"Bring him to me. I have need of a good, smart man."

And so the farmer, looking like his son, with hair sticking up, ever surprised and on the alert, came to see me carrying still his planting stick. He had been putting in late pumpkins between the hills of corn.

"Farmer, I need to send a messenger to our home city and I will pay well with cacao beans," I told him. The man nodded.

"Your son is bright and responsible. Can you take him with you and take the northern Sacbe road to the eastern sea? A father and son would arouse less notice than a man hurrying down the road." The farmer, though, shook his head in bewilderment.

404

"I have never been far from Tikal. We have learned to be independent of other cities here, now that we are on our own. Still—I can try."

"I will draw a bark drawing for you and my finger will stand for lengths to walk," I told him. "Then, as you get nearer, you must stop and ask the way to Zama. Zama. That is not a hard name to recall."

And so we talked, and he agreed to go to get help. I gave him beans to buy his way along the road.

"One more thing," I said. "Haste is everything. You must go at the trot as often as you can, and you must go armed. There may be dangerous parties on the road."

He went to get short swords and knives. Bird Beak, his son, stayed behind. I turned to see him talking to Cub, who had hidden behind a standing stone while I had spoken to the farmer.

"Bear Cub! Come here! You lap up conversations not meant for you like a dog stealing from the soup pot."

Bird Beak answered stoutly for his friend. "You should have had him here to talk with my father. He is our leader."

"And?"

Cub spoke for himself. "I am giving him blowpipes and many rations of serpent venom. These will serve him better than the sword on the road."

"If they are not caught unawares. But, take me, Young Cub, to the place you make these blowpipes."

"No one has ever seen the place or method."

I smiled. "We are sworn blood brothers." He did not move. Did he understand me? I was getting better at this variant of the tongue, it is true. But I had something better than talk; I held up a cacao bean. The smile lit up his face and he beckoned me to follow, as Bird Beak hastened to join his father, stowing his blowpipes and venom bag in a belt around his waist.

There were twin triangle plazas built high up in Tikal. Beneath one was a cave-like entrance where rocks had tumbled from the structure and been dragged away. Inside was a little workshop. I ducked down to go into its dark interior.

"We spend many days seeking the deadliest serpents. There are two, and one will paralyze in an instant. It is his venom we wish the most."

"But that is dangerous. Are you not struck yourself when you go for him?"

Cub nodded. "Two have died."

"Then why?" It did not make much sense to me. They were such young boys.

"There is a saying. Where there is no ruler in the forest, the fox is king. When there is no governor, no batab, no army, no ruler, we of clever wit must be all in all. And since we must protect those in our homes and we are small men, we must make up for our small size with big weapons."

I looked at the snake heads, the gutted lengths of snake, the venom glands. "We must not touch them directly," Cub went on, staring at the ugly things, "but handle with a rubber stick. We crush the glands, then make a deadly potion. This we put into the small pots, with tight lids, that we carry." He showed me tiny pottery pieces, obviously made especially to hold the venom. These were put into deerskin bags, closed tightly with a string.

"And the blowpipes?"

"These have been made for years in many families. The best branches are chosen, hard outside but with soft pith inside. This is bored out so the branch is hollow. The end is made just the size of the dart by covering it with a bored seashell. Then, put the dart in, being sure not to touch the point and—puff! Well, you have seen."

Yes, I had seen! And I marvelled at their cleverness. That was before the ruler awakened, before I had played the drum. I was apprehensive about our situation still, but the farmer and his son Bird Beak had been on the road several days now.

And now the Ruler was recovering, and I had the pleasure of seeing him better. He sat about a good deal in the warm sun and was slowly regaining his strength, fed good duck broth by Elan-Ya, who clucked about like a pigeon herself worrying about us. Would that he could take the road home now! It was true that each day we waited we risked reprisal from Mayapan. The roads, even here, had eyes, and someone must have reported that the noble-man and the old trader had not been seen, or even that they had been killed by upstart visitors. Would anyone else but the men who had been here know of the treasure?

Every hour brought uncertainty for me. It had taken my uncle weeks to get here and find the treasure, but then he did not know the roads and was traveling in secret. If the noble enemies, with their army guard wished to hasten double time—well, I could not rest with the situation as it stood. The Ruler's treasure was safe. Each night either Cub or I went to the dry well on the villa outside town and checked. It was best, I thought, to leave it there—here it would be prey to thieves from the town—blowguns or not. We were as open to danger as a mother dog lying on the path with her just-born babies.

But the message for help—the message was on its way. It would take several passages of the sun, but I had pressed them hard to hurry.

Many days of anxiety passed and then, finally, Cub and his boys charged into the city to say that strangers, a whole troop of them, were approaching on the ceremonial road from the north. Maker of Stars! Were they from Mayapan or from Zama? "Quick. Note the emblem picture on their baggage. But stay out of the way! This could mean your life if you blunder."

Soon Cub was back. He could not see the round stamp on the baggage and dare not go closer. But—the leaders of the very well-equipped guard bore the banners of the feathered serpent! And a man with an open mouth was marching eagerly at the head. The troops of Chichen Itza! Lord Sky Many Deer of Zama leading! Relief as sweet as liquor or gentle sleep flooded me.

I welcomed the troops with real appreciation. Not only had the Ruler's father-in-law sent the troops of Chichen Itza, Sky Many Deer said, but a contingent of our own guard had come too. The two allies joined as one against the powers of Mayapan. Yes, there was Monkey Captain himself, waving his spear arm.

"We should have come sooner, but Lord Atza had to send for more troops from Chichen Itza and it took them a few days forced march to come to us."

407

"Never mind, you are here now. And the best part of courage is to depart and leave our memory only in the dust of the city for any enemies to find. We will rest the night, and the Ruler can be borne by litter home."

And thus it was, that on the day following, we bade goodbye to the boys of the Broken Heads. The Ruler put his hand out to Cub, leaving a signet amulet with him. "When you have eighteen summers on you, Cub, I expect you to come to the court at Zama. There you will learn the ways of ruling. The remnant people of Tikal should have the dignity of a government and will be under the protection of the lords of the north. And I thank you. May Chac and all the gods bring you fortune and health."

So, we were on our way. I looked back only once at the towers of Tikal before we went around a bend of the road, imprinting them in my memory. Grandest of all cities! They stay in my mind as clearly tonight as they were on that day so long ago, and I wonder, often wonder, about the Maya and their gods and fields and splendor.

On the way as the litter passed through slow places I thought often of my return to the North, now imminent. I knew now what I must do, and the Bird of Truth would help me. I had purged myself when I fought with my Ruler, had climbed the tree of my life to ask for the life of my friend, and somehow when that happened, I had climbed the mountain and bathed in the lake of my purification. Friendship had shown me the face of God, and I would no longer be afraid, ever, I thought. I had the strength of the tree of life itself. There are some times in life when you have reached a plateau of knowledge on the climbing road of life, and you cannot, do not go back.

408

But as I thought of my return to Cahokia, though I was not afraid and knew I would face the trials of freeing my loved ones come what may, I was puzzled. It was because now the quest had dimmed, I think. I had not lost sight of my cousin's face, the last of my clan along with me. No, I could still see her in my mind, still hear her baby syllables, feel her arms around my neck. So I was clear in my vision of why I had come in her case.

But in the case of my love, Loon Feather, it was different. Whether it was that I had sinned so deeply with Comalca, betraying my friend at the same time, or whether time had done its work, I know not how but I did not love her in the same way. I saw her but dimly in my mind, as an orphan who has lost his mother early can remember but one faint thing of her, the shadow of an instant, far away in the past.

The fervor of love had dimmed, and I was troubled over it. "You have changed through all you have endured," I said to myself sometimes. "Grown strong, as burl does in the woods when it is wounded. But she is dependent on you. The only reason she loved you is because you were her old friend of the former time; she is dependent on you. She is weak, not woman enough for the man you have become." So my thoughts went, and they troubled me sometimes worse than the bites of bugs, there on the road to Zama and the future.

I spoke to the Ruler, too. I knew there would not be much time when I arrived at Zama, because I intended to find the first trading ship I could to go to the land of the Father of Waters.

I carried my crystal skull, carefully wrapped in softest deerskin, in a bag in my cape. Not much longer would I be able to wear the royal jaguar skin around my shoulders! In the land beyond the sea I must trade it for leggings and jacket again. But not at once—I must gain the power I would need for the trip northward in a hostile land, and I would use the garb and symbols of the Mayans to do so.

I told Smoke Fox-god of the vision in the cave. "I saw Blue Eyes, many of them, with fire sticks. One was on a huge house on the water, taller by far than any canoe I have ever seen. What can it mean?"

409

"Kukulcan come again to his southern homeland," said the Ruler nodding in affirmation.

"But the clothing in the vision was odd—not Mayan. Short bulky leggings on the legs they had on, but above the legging they wore a skirt like a woman's. And a headdress close to the hair, made of metal like a soldier's helmet. And a beast—ah, what a beast. Behind the man in a ship was a flour-footed beast larger than a deer with wide, intelligent eyes. They rode on it."

"I do not know, but there are prophecies. They say that in the repetition of 2 Ahua, 8 Zac, there will be men of danger come from the sea. They will, so it is said, bring us destruction. They have, some of them, blue eyes."

"Ah, the Blue Eyes." I told him of the Blue Eyes who had come to our shores in the time of the grandfathers, had known my people, had wonderful things of hard metal to use for every purpose. How they had not stayed with the people, but had gone west—who knows where? To the Stony Mountains, perhaps.

"And it is they who have brought this—" I reached behind in the treasure chest which travelled everywhere just behind us, "this stone of the hidings of the moon's face."

We had not really looked at it, because the treasure had been out of sight from us, hidden at the old estate outside of Tikal. He picked up the tablet as big as a man's face but light, with carvings made in it. Wondrous they were, as I have said, a circle of many markings and another circle within it, exact counts and notches at certain points and notches on the edges of the stone.

"I do not know the meanings of these carvings," he said, "but the Star Watcher at the temple of the evening star in Chichen Itza may if he can study them."

"Great power is there," I said, looking longingly at the stone. "And it is not to be mine?"

"It is not safe with the brutal power-chiefs of your people," he said without smiling. I nodded. It was, in a way, a relief not to have to take that stone of power into the domain of the evil prince of Cahokia. It would be trouble enough to have the skull of magic with me. But as much as I could, I memorized the markings and took them with me in my mind. I could make a good likeness if I had to.

Finally, with great relief, we did come to the walls of Zama, and the ruler kissed the ground. I took the dirt upon my forehead, but I did not kiss it, for it was not home, and home I must go with the first trade canoe that set its prow towards the rising sun.

I stood that night above the sea. Still it was, with a rippling breeze, and the flowers blew their night-time perfume at me, and the strange birds sang their evening songs, and I thought of my child, soon to be born.

I would not see it, would never know whether I had left a man or woman in Chichen Itza, the city of Kukulcan. It was my destiny to leave a part of me and my line, the brave, tall folk of the forest amidst the short-statured, large-nosed Mayan people. The blood of the Great Star Watcher, my great grandfather and the Grand Shaman, my uncle Bo Jo, would flow into countless of these beautiful people in the land of the rain forests and bright, calling birds. And sad punishment for my many sins, I would never know my child, never see his growth, never hear his laugh and see his strong adulthood. Or hers. Like the priests on this high hill at the sacrifice, I must throw part of my heart into the sea, where it must sink into the depths, never to surface. Sad among men are those who have a child of their own blood and must part from it forever, never to know it in all the length of life.

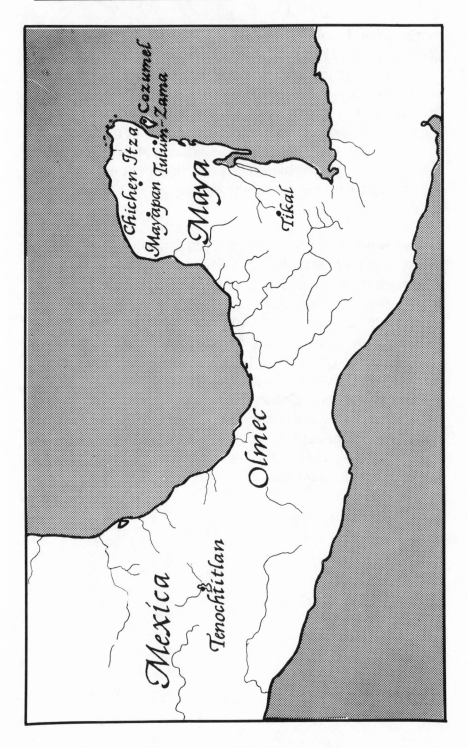

Chapter Sixteen

The wind that I had felt freshening as I stood on the temple hill picked up all that night, and on the morrow a good fair southwest breeze blew. A trade canoe bound for the lands of the widest river prepared to hoist its sail.

"You are favored," the Ruler said as he stood in full headdress and mace of power to bid me farewell. "It is surely because Yum Cimil's desecrated image has been replaced with the fine new one from the island we visited."

"That must be it," I smiled though tight lips. I was not looking at him. We had said our goodbyes last night, and it was odd that we did not speak our hearts even then, but stood aloof from each other a bit. There are times, partings, which are too strong for words, and it is then the heart pulls back into itself, fearful of being wounded, like a hand that draws back from fire. But before we went to bed, he to his beautiful wife, I to my last lonely bed in the land, he brought to me a necklace of rare gold, finest of all the treasures I had ever seen in all my travels, and put it in my trader's bag sewn inside the lining of my cape. Oddest of all, I tell you as I placed it there, I saw that one of the symbols made of gold that hung from its circlet was the eye of the sun, seeing all things it beheld each day, great symbol of wisdom in the world.

And the necklace of gold and a few other things I had in my ample bag to take with me, gave me the knowledge that I would have chips to gamble in the great games which would await me when I returned to the city on the river. And so, if I did not have what I came for, leaving the sacred treasure in the temple of Zama that looked across the sea, I had others, mostly inside myself, which could be even more valuable than those I had sought.

Thus it is in life, when we enter the dark forest seeking some fine thing in the hunt, when we have emerged from its trials we may come out not with that thing, but with a better animal we never sought. And so the Maker of the Stars instructs and blesses us.

413

How can I tell you of the trip? Well, in a short way I think. A long tale is not good dragging along for either a dog or a man. Some who started this tale have crept away to other lodges long ago and put aside the story never to take it up, some have turned their backs in weariness and are at the far side of the lodge, dozing. So I shall hasten.

After a trip of moderate trials and having travelled several days on the Great Sea, we came to land, and I found the city near the mouth of the Father of Waters. And staying only overnight, I found and paid a guide to take me north along a land trail. Behind me called the voices of the crows, "Hurry, hurry. The days slip by. It is the time of the Sun Lord's longest day on earth; north, north you must fly."

I was tired of the crows. "Hoot, hoot," I shouted in my mind, like the owl they hate when he approaches their babies' nests. "Go from me. I am hurrying as fast as I can."

And I was.

I took out my amulet, which had never left my presence in one form or another, and put it around my neck, and I saw the eye of wisdom. Yes, my friends, in the land of the Maya I had imbibed a certain kind of wisdom, like the bee honey drink which had saturated my pores from time to time. I knew I would need wisdom on this trip, for many were the dangers lurking along the way.

My guide was a taciturn man of middle age who was returning to the Natchez peoples that Ghost and I had avoided on the hill above the river. "Why do you dress strangely?" he asked, eying my jaguar cape and ceremonial loincloth curiously the first day out.

"I am wearing the garb of the Mayan merchant."

"They do not often come north, and we never see them at Natchez. But you are tall and the Maya are short." He was speaking in the tongue of the middle part of the Father of Waters, and I was glad to realize I could recall some of the words, if they

414

spoke them slowly. It was odd to hear, but it was vaguely similar to Cahokia speech.

"I am tall, but nevertheless a Mayan merchant. And I will be trading with your people."

"Do you not fear, as the others do, the—ritual feast?"

"Well—I have a few things your ruler—"

"Sun—"

"Your Sun will value. And I have negotiations for him. Do you sense danger?"

"I do not think he will kill and eat the trader of the Mayans."

And so you have answered your own question, I thought. And so I have used wisdom piece number one of the Mayans, do not be afraid to play the part of deceit. But if you choose to play, play it well. That I could do. I knew the language now, of course, as if I had been born to it, and I was as haughty and ruler-like as anybody in these scraggly dog villages along the river. I intended to keep my customs, to bow to the earth, to pull out the jade images of Chac and the rest, to let a few drops of blood from my—fingertip, of course.

And so I marched right into town, as if I were the prince himself. In fact, I had brought a headdress, compressed, of folded quetzal feathers, and I put it on. The miserable little town, for so it seemed to me now, (though if I had seen it when I lived in Lake-of-the-Boulders I would have thought it was grand indeed) was high on a bluff overlooking the river.

The guide grudgingly guided me to the log shack of the Sun on a sort of temple bump. "Request the Sun to come out and meet the envoy of the City of Zama," I said.

Their eyes were frightened. "Give him this," I said, taking out a small jade statue of Ek Chuah I had brought. It had tiny gold eyes.

There was arguing and fluttering around inside the "palace," and finally an old man came out, wobbling on shaking knees. Two fanners ran around trying to fan flies away from him. There were flies everywhere in this filthy city. The fanners placed mats on the ground, and he stepped onto them and peered into my face.

"Kneel before the Sun," he said.

"I am not allowed by the Ruler of the City of Zama, in alliance with Chichen Itza to kneel. But I can offer you the slap of equal friendship." I think that is what I said, at least I tried to say that. I put out my arm. What difference did it make? If these people were going to kill me and take what I had, they would do it, I suppose.

Hesitating, the Sun watched me. Then he gestured for his minister, standing by, to come to me and receive the slap. "He cannot touch mortals," said my guide in a whisper as they retreated.

I put out my hand, with some small offertory statues made of jade in it. I waited, then presented two obsidian mirrors, which I believe they had never seen the likes of. "I come to offer you alliance with the cities of gold in the South. Call forth your best feast and bring the dancers and singers. Great days have come for the town."

It wouldn't take much to be greater than it was. The charnel house stank, the people stank, the stinks stank. Yet I bragged and praised and fawned until I almost made myself sick, but it had to be done. The Sun was taken with it all, and I described in rather halting words and slow speech the cities of the South, making their gods seem the strongest, their rulers the richest, their women the most seductive. I did not have to lie much there.

Then came the best feast, by the light of the moon and the buzz of ten million mosquitoes. Roasted chunks of meat turned on the spit. I looked warily at them, thinking of the serpent people on the beaches near Zama who would have turned us into stew.

Women with wooden bowls served the meat and corn porridge they ate with two fingers put together. The Sun sat on a high chair, with a back of wood made of crudely carved skull heads.

"The meat," I said, through a rank-tasting bite. "It is—enemy thigh flesh?"

"No," the old ruler sighed. "Bobcat." Bobcat. Bah! Any self-respecting person in the poorest tribe knew you could not eat a cat.

We watched brightly-painted men and then women do their ritual dances, rather like the dancers long ago I had seen at the Place of Rivers Meeting, Tippecanoe in the northern land. I thought of the drum, hidden at Cahokia. Would it still be mine?

Would there be anyone I cared about to hear it? Crows cawed in my mind, and I mentally aimed a bow and arrow at them to shut them up.

"You spoke of an alliance?" the old man whined.

"Yes. We will start trade with you, offer new weapon lore from the Mexicas." I described the fine spear throwers, the leather armor, the flags flying.

"Yes, yes," the old man said eagerly. "When can it start? We have heard of the fine places south, but no one has ever come."

Of course not, I thought. If they hadn't heard about the enemy thigh flesh or fresh cat meat, the odor alone would have kept them five lengths away.

"Here is what the Ruler has said." I stood, letting my quetzal feathers flop about. "I must go up the trail as an emissary to the north when I leave you. You will send an honor guard of your best soldiers with me. They will walk the Natchez Trail with me, guarding against the many evils of ambush, to the river I will take."

"And when will the trade start? The weapons come?"

This was important, because he must know he was accountable to others for my safety. "In a month a small group of highly-armed Mexicas will arrive—with trading goods. They will seal the compact with pipes. You will have ready your trading goods at that time for them to take and show in Zama and Chichen Itza." Certainly. All your possum fur hats and turtle shell nose pieces. And stink balm. Plenty of that.

The ruler stood and had his minister slap my arm again. "Done. We are partners with the fabled south. And now—" he clapped his hand. "Bring forth the parade of maidens so that our visitor can choose—"

"Ah, well, yes. You see—" I thought fast as the slovenly charmers came forward. I bent and whispered into the old ear of the minister, telling him delicately of a slight condition of the private parts—he nodded and bade them leave.

I passed the night in the guest house, near where the tame raccoons of the village scuttled about in a pen. Towards dawn I heard voices coming from the bench near the front of the guest shack. Without moving from my bunk I listened to the noises of what seemed to be two men rummaging in the small packet that I had put in the lining of my large cloak. To breach the laws of hospitality so! Where else but here? I had the skull and necklace in pockets within my breechclout but the rest—.

They stood outside, but I could hear, faintly, their voices. " I saw little there. A few blades, obsidian, a couple of pearls, and— something else? Small and larger sticks in a bundle—to start fires easily I suppose—some sort of unguents and perfumes in pots— nothing really."

"What shall we tell the Sun?"

"Report he speaks as a rich man, travels as a poor one."

"What will the Sun do?"

"That we shall see. But his anger if he is foiled is as that of the wildcat we ate tonight."

And that, I knew must be bad because the wildcat was certainly bad.

They left, and light came. I rose as if nothing had happened, went to wash in the river, a thing which drew the entire village to the hill to observe. Obviously, it was a thing not often done. I kept my breechclout on.

Then, as I finished my climb up steep steps and walked the street to prepare to go, I found myself surrounded by men with spears. The Sun came out of his shack. "It is not enough, what you have given. If you represent the rich cities of the South, you must give more."

"And if I do not?"

He said something I did not understand, and then one of them ran up to me and put his hand on my upper leg. Thigh meat. I pushed him off.

"I will give you one more chance," I said. "When the Mexica guard and my traders come north, they will be enraged if I have been ill-treated." The ruler and his men stood still, but they did not offer to let me go.

"Still," I said, pulling the last arrow out of the quiver, "I have a handsome gift for you. Display the personal guard you plan for me, equip them well with weapons, and I will present you a gift

worth all that you now own in this village. I had planned it for the
Ruler of the North, but now that I see your power—" That part
was true.

We were playing a game of chungky. He was throwing his
pole out, I would throw mine. We would measure to see who
was the better thrower.

I went behind a tree and took out the necklace, the one to buy
my dear ones' freedom in Cahokia. Must it go? Soldiers' heads
appeared behind the tree. It appeared it must. Oh, Smoke Fox-
god, I regret the loss of your great gift.

The guard was lined up. I gave the necklace to the minister,
who put the circlet around the ruler's head and there it gleamed,
beauteous glowing reflection of the Sun Lord's fire and heat. The
people who stood by were stupefied.

"I will reward the guard with treasure when I get to the City
Of The North," I said, "but they must stay with me now. And no
evil must befall me. I am the blood brother of the Prince of Zama.
He would seek highest revenge."

I certainly had taken the name of Smoke Fox-god Three in
highest blasphemy, committing him to things he had never heard
of, had no idea of doing, and could not possibly fulfil. But they did
not know that. And I had lied, but oddly enough, I did not feel
I had breached the Bird of Thunder's vow of truth on me.
Perhaps sometimes telling untruth in the service of truth is
acceptable. I knew I had to have a guard of tough and brutal
soldiers, or I would not survive the trail north. It was notorious.

"I have special protection of Quexalcoatl," I said. "Have you
heard his name?" There was murmuring. Word of the Mexica son
of the Evening Star must have come even into this coon pen.

And so, with my quiver of ideas to save myself absolutely
empty, the Sun let me go north with the honor guard, who were
about as honorable as a pack of jackals. Still, they would do. They
and their ruler believed two things: that I would possibly reward
them when I got to wherever it was that I was going, and second,
that if they didn't do well by me the entire city of Chichen Itza and
Quexalcoatl himself would descend for revenge.

We proceeded north, I in the middle of the warriors. We went up the trail which was sometimes low and soggy and damp, sometimes loaded with big bugs which flew at us in blinding clouds, sometimes dry and high with hills. At all times it was very, very hot, but I, having lived through heat in Maya land, did not complain.

We did meet bands of rovers and warriors, but they eyed us warily for the most part. Only one time were we chased, and we mounted a hill and hurled arrows at them, whoever they were.

I had for night companioning my own thoughts, and they were dark but determined. Often I dreamed, and my dreams showed all the things I had gone through, from the horrors of the devastated village at Lakes-Like-a-Necklace to my uncle's torturing, to the fighting at Tikal, to the fending off of death at Natchez. Never did I dream of what I would meet at Cahokia. The land of "perhaps" that I had lived through had become too real, too much the land of possibility. Almost a year had passed, and the Female Sun might be, could be—dying, dead. And my trip would have been in vain. Sometimes, as I lay there, awake because never could I fully trust my guards and slept only when I could no longer fight exhaustion, I had that small and nagging fear like a gnat, that I did not love my dear one Loon Feather any more, that she was a dependent, weak woman, and that even if I should overcome the fate decreed for her, I would be married to a wife I could not be soul-mate to. For all of life—that was the worst.

Finally after many trail days, we came to the Land of the Fighting, the Dark and Bloody Land, where the peoples north of the beautiful Ohio river seem always to meet the peoples south of it in bloody contests. A lovely country it was, like the Cahokia lands rich with oak trees and other hardwoods and rolling hills. Some of the guards said odd things I had never heard, that there were castles here, that the Blue Eyes had built them before going to Ohio, and then on west. Madoc, they said, was the leader of the Blue Eyes, who had at one time fought a battle with the people of the middle river country and been defeated. The Blue Eyes were smart, very, very smart, the guard said.

Being tired of the foods of the hunt, we moved near to a small river, so we could fish and get mussels. It had been my suggestion; I knew we were near home and we had travelled speedily and well on the trail and I was hungry. Does that not sound like me? Or perhaps it was another lesson of the Mayans—eat well, above all else. Other things will follow when you first appease the god of the stomach. Of all people I ever visited, they ate the best.

We gorged on fine fish caught in a weir that had been left by some other tribe and that we could put in the water; we steamed open the river mussels and ate them steamed in the shell.

Afterwards, as we dozed by the campfire, I planned this, my last part of the trip. I would of course not be taking them with me to Cahokia. We would soon be to the Beautiful Ohio; there I would leave them. I would slip away at night, cross the river into territory I knew, find the Buffalo Road and—

Did they know? Could they read minds? That night I awoke to see eyes around me, short spears glowing in the dying embers of the campfire.

"We know you have treasure," the tough, thick-set man who was the captain of this guard said. "You keep something closely guarded on your person, carried in your breechclout. Out! We will have it!"

I stood quickly and knew that of all times in my life I must think. To give them nothing was to lose my life. And nothing, was all I had. Almost nothing—well, I had the skull.

And then I used the last lesson of the Mayans I had learned: wits are better than swords to win the war. Thus had Smoke Fox-god and I escaped from Xel Ha, by cleverness. Thus had the lords of Chichen Itza often overcome their neighbors. I unclasped the skull of crystal from where it had rested, uncomfortable to me but well- cushioned during the journey in a large side pocket under the flap of my breechclout.

I hoped to whisk the skull out for best effect to make them grovel, but as events always work, it took a while to get it out of the carrying pocket while they stared and mumbled amongst themselves. But then, stepping near the fire, I brought it forth and held it up high in the light of the campfire. "Oh, whoever it is that makes this skull work, make it work now if ever!" I prayed.

My voice was deep and hollow. "I am a drummer-shaman of great power," I intoned. "This is my deepest medicine, my mirror of the spirit world."

They hesitated, then the one of tough sinews pressed forward. "And of what value is this?"

"None to you. It is a curse to those who do not own its medicine. It is mine, but I can give you a year of special blessing if I wish by having you touch this. Should you harm me in any way, it will be as many moons of special cursing."

There was silence.

"How do we know this is a token of power? That it can work the magic?"

"I will show you. Build up the fire so we can see into its sacred depths."

Now I tell you true and you will find it hard to believe, but I had not looked directly into the skull's eyes in all the time since I had brought it out of the cave. No, not in the city of Tikal, not on the road to Zama with my Ruler nor any other time since. I had disciplined myself as a warrior does on the trail, abstaining from it, because I did not know its power or my destiny in that power, and I feared it as somehow able to do me harm. I had promised to bring it to the Dark and Bloody Land, Caintuck, where magic is greatest in all our northern lands, and there to bury it, and I had no reason to doubt my promise and choice.

Still, the thing did seem to have some sort of love for me, some affinity, because I had seen in it before great things of my own line. And so, as the fire leaped higher and flames lighted the clearing, I looked inside, gesturing the others to stay back. And yes! To save my life it came to life. And there were not the same things I had seen in the cave, the attack on the fort, the lady with white skin watching whiteskins battle. No, now I saw the same Natchez-on-the-Hill, but in another time, for the old man was not there, but instead a Female Sun was being fanned and mats put out for her. But as I stared I saw some, many warriors in the odd headpieces made of shiny metal, and the skirts with metal armor over them and the fire sticks too, and these warriors were standing beside the Female Sun. And one was scratching in a book of white bark.

The Blue Eyes! Always the Blue Eyes! Well, I called the warriors over and, wonder of wonders, all of them looked in but only one could see what I saw. He was a young boy, son of one of the older ones and on his first warrior's journey.

"Our town," he cried, looking in. "But it is not now, because there is a woman, looking like Madame Two Bones of the noble Bones family but younger, and she seems to be the Sun."

He told them what he saw, of the Blue Eyes, of the man writing and of many gifts given by the Blue Eyes, which even I had not seen in the skull.

Finally he turned to us. "It has gone. The skull is dark." The warriors fell on their knees, murmuring oblations.

Now was the time for me to speak. "Tomorrow I take my leave. Your reward, which I promised you, is a year of blessing. Tell your ruler he will not see me. Tell him, though, that I have sent the vision of the skull to tell him what is to come." I looked at them, gave them a solemn arm clasp, as fire shadows danced around us. "Each of you will have different good fortune, but the boy most of all. Come all, and touch the skull."

"Flies-Towards-the-Dawn has second sight," said his father with pride as he came forward. "He once saw an entire flock of wild turkeys, and they came on their own into the town the next day."

None of us slept the rest of the night. The next morning I left and buried the skull as deep as I could in a hole dug by an animal, on a high bluff overlooking the Beautiful River. It was raining. I wrapped my jaguar cape around it carefully, that it be not hurt through the years until, who knows when it could be dug up by the one whose destiny it was.

It was time for me to put on deerskin garments, given me by the boy's father as thanks for the gift of blessing. I had given him my ceremonial loincloth and merchant's belt. It was, after all, time for me to return to the garb of my northern self. With little else but the few small things in my pack, I was returning to plead for life for my cousin and my love in Cahokia, where someone very important had hatred for me as big as a hill. All I carried with me to combat him was the few inconsequential trifles in my bag, and the wisdom of the Mayas in my heart. Whether they would be enough was in the hands of the Maker of Stars.

Chapter Seventeen

It was early evening when I finally approached Cahokia from the water side. It was hot, sweltering, a night without air even on the river, and it was the same time again, half-moon at the time of Elk's Moon, a year since I had left the place to which I was secretly returning.

I looked up and saw again with comfort that the stars were in the familiar places of my childhood. There were A-tci-ka, Monster with the Big Head, a-la-kwi mi-tch-lang-wa, evening star of Nanaboozhoo. And there, also were the Owl constellation and the path of souls across the sky, white like milk. It comforted me, some way, to think that these same groups were seen by my uncle, seen by his father and constantly charted by the Great Star Watcher my great-grandfather.

By morning they would have moved, and all here in Cahokia would think they had fled in fright before the arrival of the Great Lord of the Sky. But I did not, for I had seen the stars bright while the Sun Lord strode the roof of the world. "Where Star Lords do not flee." The Land of the Maya seemed so far away, and yet at times I yearned for it, I do not know why. It was comfortable there and beautiful, with breezes carrying scent of eternal flowers and birds so bright they dazzle the eye in great trees. And I could have lived in great comfort as my Ruler's right hand man basking in his friendship and love.

But in life why is it that we cannot walk the easy path of flowers and birds? It seems it would have been just as easy for the Maker of Stars to strew flowers at our feet rather than hindering boulders for us to trip on. But He did not; and I think it is because we do not grow when we walk through blossoms, but only when we blister our feet and must climb over the rocks. As my uncle Bo Jo did, as I had to do, there in the depths of my life in the cave of my changes. And now the boulders would be largest of all—in the city where my blood enemy lived and I must act against all the people. I walked towards my destiny.

Little had changed here at Cahokia, that was sure. There was the stockade wall, there the great temple and the Ruler's House on

425

the hill. But oh, stars, you have not told me—are they alive or is she dead? Am I here in time or—not?

I dare not go into the stockade, into the citadel city of course. If Soft Fur was alive, she must be very ill, and I did not have any herb or chant to cure her sickness. I would be seen an enemy by one and all, because all now knew I had made a bargain with death, and when I broke that bargain, I would be as one shunned and hated at the top.

No, my approach must be another way. I crept along the trails through the woods to the outer villages. Through the branches I could glimpse the campfires of the shell-crafters' homes. I walked on, and soon I saw the fires of the marl potters glinting through the maples and the hickory trees.

I crept closer, glad for the shirt I wore in this forest, though, oddly, there were no insects. It must have been dry lately, I thought in passing.

There it was—the smoke rising from the hearth inside the house of Hawk Eye and All Joy. My heart did leap, I tell you; old friends are fine friends indeed. Like pearls it has taken a long time to grow inside a shell, they are precious.

A thin woven sheet was over the door of the shelter. I could hear the measured breaths of folk asleep, and the child came from the back of the shelter. So the little one was with them and in health! There were so many things to take the little ones down the path of the stars, I thought, and my heart felt a pang for one I would never know back in the land of pink birds and high temples.

I lifted the door covering. "Hawk Eye, All Joy, it is I, returned." There was a slight stirring on one of the bunks. "I, Drum-of-the-Gods. Wake up." I had almost said "Tunkel."

There was a low sigh, and soon out of the darkness emerged the face of my friend Hawk Eye. "In the name of the gods, have you come? Or are you a spirit?" My friend's hair was touselled with sleep.

"Not a spirit, though many times I thought I would be," I said with a slight smile, looking into his eyes. He laughed, looked closely at me, then pounded my back, murmuring in wonder the news that I had, indeed returned, against all hope. He came outside and we walked to a log at the edge of the woods behind the house, that we might not awake others. And that we might not be overheard.

"One thing I must know right away," I said, placing my hand on his arm. "Is she—the Female Sun—alive or dead?"

"She lives, barely. She has not ruled for four moons now. The growth in her womb has swollen faster than any could have thought and sapped her strength and wasted her body until—now. Many days she has lingered, holding onto life as to a frayed thread. Watch was being kept by her family and the physicians when the sun set yesterday. But it will be soon, perhaps now is. You may have returned on the day of her death."

How could that be? On the very day? Things do not happen that way. Blessings to you, Maker of Stars and spirits of this place. I have come almost too late, but not quite.

"And the prince?"

"Ruling in her place. He has grown in riotousness and warfare, as you would suspect. Each family must supply its sons from the age of manhood rites up. The cities around us are in revolt. They refuse to send the tribute corn. And the tribute here in the city—it has increased threefold."

A meteor came across the skies. There had been many in the last few nights as I had been out, watching. A sign?

"But he has also grown in cruelty," my friend continued. "Many are called to build the mound for the tomb, and the palace guard calls those who are on sickbeds, old men too and even women, to work building. Noble families must supervise the draft of people."

"In haste for the coming death? They could inter the bones, later."

"No, for the Prince's own coronation. He wishes the greatest in the memory of man. His power grows on him apace. He was not born to rule in any way, and the revolt of the cities has made him fear. Corrupt, ignorant, afraid—he quenches his fears about himself with our sweat and blood."

"Blood?"

"He executed two lords of the council who opposed him in the matter of the wars last week."

"But custom says all the lords must agree in matters of war."

"He says he will say what custom is. His Father the Sun tells him what is right and what wrong."

"The Powers beyond earth do not support injustice. Of that I am convinced."

He did not answer. He knew I said blasphemous things beyond consideration."I learned a lot in the land of the Maya," I told him.

"Maya? I do not know of them."

"No, but you will. I will tell you much you will want to hear, but not now. Your father has stayed out of the charnel house?"

"Yes, and in health, thanks to you. We owe you much." He bowed low, and I raised him up. Friends do not bow to each other. That was what I had taught the Ruler in Mayaland.

"Now I must save my White Wings and Loon Feather. You have said that the Female Sun was not dead yet. They are safe, then?"

"No. They are held in the citadel city, in a house at the top of the hill, preparing for purification." My heart fell. Gone up there already. Bad omen crows, you may have done this. After all, though, I wanted to shoot you. Well, I must act on my own, some way. But what?

"Purification! For ones without spot," I said, then spat on the ground.

"Yes, they feed them clear juices, fine breads and meat of turkey and pigeon. They are waited on hand and foot by the nuns of the prince's nunnery."

"What—was it like—when they came to get Loon Feather?" I was torturing myself as surely as the Mayan princes did when they let blood.

"She went with her head held high."

"Had anyone—had you told her I was going to try to help?"

"Yes. But we had all given you up for dead. The cities of the south—they are so far, so many to kill or keep you. So short a time." He looked at me hard. "I still do not know how you did this. Did you bring the charm to heal? The prince's treasure?"

"I will answer that soon. Now tell me more of my love. She was taken by soldiers?"

"The old herb woman begged on her knees for them not to take her. Shamefully, so they said. The guards were so angered at this breach of reverence to the gods that they took the old woman with Loon Feather. They have determined to make her a servant to the Female Sun, too, in the Land of the Shining Place."

I roused myself a little at this odd news. "I thought they only took young virgins, perfect in all ways, and children."

"Mostly. But there must be someone to empty the slops in the kingdom of the Sun. There will be many going with our ruler when she goes."

"How many?"

"Thirty now."

"And the families like me? Whose children go?"

"Some are honored, as in the days of her grandfather. But many are bitter and unhappy. This rule has been a rule of misery and burden on the people. They feel little joy in the coming ceremonies."

"Have they spoken?"

"Who would speak to the Daughter of the Sun? Or the Son of the Sun? It would endanger immortal life for ourselves and loved ones."

"Still, there are Those Who Say The Things That Are Not Said," I muttered. Even here, out on this dimly lit night, we found ourselves looking around constantly. The darkness in that town seemed always to have ears, and with this increased danger no one could be secure. If they ever were.

We rose and stepped even further into the trees, and finally my friend spoke. "We still meet, even more than before, and our numbers have grown to real strength. And real risk."

"What do you mean?"

"With so many, trust cannot be guaranteed. There is always the chance of an odd duck in the flock who will fly the other way. They are suspicious on the hill."

"The prince knows?"

"I think so. As discontent has grown, as the ranks of those owning the secret amulet has grown, so has the group of spies. I sense they are everywhere."

"Have they acted against any of the order of Those Who Say The Thing That Is Not Said?"

"Not yet. But they have arrested the prince Fire-on-the-Plains."

I was surprised. The cynical, sharp-minded prince who had often spoken to me as friend when I went to the top of the hill? I had thought him only an observer when I left. The river was rushing down an odd and bending channel since I had left. "Fire-on-the-Plains is of royal blood. Was he of our secret order?"

"No. But he was of the group that opposed. Two, as I have said, were killed—the nobles who had stood in council against the prince. And he had spoken to some of the army who have been discontented, asking them of their objections to the prince. So it is said. He is to be executed at the crowning time."

I shook my head, almost not believing. "Why not with the other two? They are keeping him?"

"The prince dares not move in that way against the family of Fire-on-the-Plains. Their ancestor was the brother of the Great Ruler. They are the prince's cousins. But the crowning, with all the people there, will be the occasion of great celebration. The princes yet loyal, soon to join in more warfare, will be present. The prince will act with all the force of ritual and the priests to back him up."

It sounded like something Alton Ha would have done in the land of the Maya. We sat for a moment, considering.

"And White Wings? My little cousin?" For whom I had risked so much, travelled the world.

"She is in health, as I said, and at the top of the hill. Walks-Up-the-Steps is with her as her handmaid."

A sudden sharp thought hit me. "She—she is not—"

"Yes. She is to go to the Shining Place beyond this world too."

The first streaks of dawn were appearing in the east. Bugs began stirring, as they do at first light, hungry and rested, so we stepped out of the woods.

I began considering something, something that was coming to me. "The river-clay potters' oldest aunt—the one who adopted Loon Feather. She is to carry slops when all the sacrificed ones go on into the world of the Shining Place."

"I said that as a sad joke, but something like that."

"And the tall ones, captured ones of my race, still carry the slops, really, for the lords of Cahokia."

"Of course." He looked at me curiously. It was an odd question.

"One of the things I learned with the Mayas was the art of disguise. Going among the people in other form to learn what you must know, be where you must be."

We stood looking at the sky as it lightened. "And yet," Hawk Eye whispered, "it would be a little difficult for you to be in disguise, as you are known on the hill and you are tall when the nobles are shorter."

"There are tall ones I've just asked you about. Ones whose faces are not seen."

He was silent for a moment. "You will be a slopgatherer?"

"Those are my people, of the lakelands, who are doing it. I will wrap my face about with scarves, as they do, against the odors and the shame of the job."

We walked back to the door. "Come inside," he said. "You should not be seen even here. Your story is known and the prince is apprehensive against your return."

"I know he would have wished me dead, but if he awaits the treasure, he should be waiting."

"Well, he would have taken your treasure rightly enough. But he considers you an enemy. He has put the mark of death on your head, should you return. Something about your being a sworn enemy of his family."

So someone, surely Soft Fur, must have told him of my uncle and his insult to his father, the Corn Clout. It was no worse, really, than I had expected. I had come home with a death price on my head, with none of the things I had promised to bargain with, and with an impossible task—to free the two I cared about with almost no time left. Why, oh why, I asked myself were the rocks one had to crawl over to get out always so huge?

All Joy had awakened and was smiling at me in disbelief. The baby was awake, playing with its toes and talking in baby words in its little bed. The sun slanted through the door opening, but not directly, as it would at this late summer time of the year, the house having been carefully planned to honor the Lord of the Sky in summer. Suddenly there was a din, a wailing and crying that reached even these outer parts of town. It was coming from just south, from within the walls.

"Keening, the sacred wail for the dead in highest places. I must act at once," I said. "The crows have flown over the hill."

"What?" Hawk Eye asked, going to pick up his son.

"Never mind. The Female Sun is surely dead. I need the rags of a slop-bearer. Can you help me?"

All Joy was already up, evidently aware that something portentous was about to occur. To be out of the way she took the babe outside to watch it toddle about in the light of the rising sun.

I slipped my small back pack into the corner. Then I threw logs on the hearth pit. I was hungry, hungrier than I had been for many a day or year. And I was full of energy, the energy of someone who knows he must do an impossible task with odds against him large, but who knows that what he is doing is right. "If I die, it will be with honesty in my eye, and that is more than I can say for most of those people on that hill." And, because the sun was rising and there was thanks to give for the beauty of the day and my safe return to the city of my destiny, I took a sacred pipe from the medicine stand in the corner and put tobacco on it and went out and blew smoke in the four directions, both as thanksgiving, and as invocation, a prayer for the day, and days to come.

Then I took out of my pack a little cup made of wood on a stick. Attached to it on a string was a ball of the odd, bouncing rubber.

I took it to the little one, now taking a few steps and ready to walk. "I promised you something when I left, little one. Keep this to know who your teaching uncle is," I said, and left.

"I had best avoid the other slop-carriers," I thought as I climbed the last step to the top of the hill, "for they may see me as a stranger, and raise questions." I had slipped in the gates with others coming in from the outside to serve the palace hill, and now I was headed for the royal residence.

I knew the routine well enough; sometimes I had lingered on the furs in the royal bed chamber until after the sun-welcoming ceremony, and had seen these silent people slip inside the sleeping places of the rich and powerful to remove their night waste in huge pots. Lowest of the low, their faces were covered so they would not contaminate with their glances the privileged ones of the hill. And these were my people, at least had been, the fine tall people of the ancestors' time, who had lived at the serpent mound.

They were related to us who had filtered into the land of Lakes-Like-a-Necklace. I had never given them a thought before because they were slaves, but that was in a different time. I was awake and alive now, and I saw much more, as if my eyes had been opened. Truly, like my friend and Ruler, I had been up my mountain and had swam in my own lake, and when I had learned what one true friend was, I learned that all on earth are really friends. Now my eyes and heart were opened to the people of Turtle's Island, and I now saw the humble who crawled around to serve the rich. Truly, as the Cub's sister had said in Tikal, "It takes a whole city of poor people to support the lords on the hill."

I went into the back door I had so often departed from during my time in the royal residence. Yes, there was mourning, wailing. The body of the Female Sun had been removed to the burial ceremony house. The servant girls were weeping, laying out Soft

433

Fur's jewelry, her weaving spindles, her ointment pots—all for burial after the three ritual days were accomplished. I tugged at my face rags a little; it was here I was in most danger. But they were preoccupied; they did not pay me notice as I went into the royal bedroom, then the servant quarters to get the night waste pots. I took my time going from room to room, setting the pots by the back door until I could complete my task. I needed to hear what I could.

"The small one was crying last night," I heard one of the youngest of the maids say as she combined ointments from several pots into one. "Perhaps she knows now what is coming for her. So small. . ."

"Well, she is a foreigner, come from the land of lakes in the north," said the older, more thoughtful one. "We are of this place and the royal household, and we have been taught what is correct behavior. And yet, soon, before He Is Halfway Home we too shall know which of us will go on the long journey to the Shining Place beyond this world."

"I will not mind if I am chosen," said the youngest maid. "It will be a day of complete honor. Finest clothes. The meat of stag and turkey breast. Then—the royal procession to the new burial spot before the sun begins to lower. They say it will not hurt. The priest is quick, with a scarf around the back of the neck. And then, to have the Star Lords welcome you, guide you to the shining palace, where bright stones glint and the Sun Lord rests with all of his lustrous children."

"I do not feel much honor," said the older woman. She was thin but tough-looking, like a grape vine. "I have a child at home and no close relative. I would rather wait to join the Sun Lord in the Land of the Shining when my time comes of Nature."

"Shame!" said the young one. "We must follow the priests' sayings with complete adoration. Adoration is the word they preach. And that means even giving up our lives for him and his children, hard as it is."

"Still, you are my cousin, and I tell my heart to you, knowing you will not disgrace yourself and your kin by revealing it."

So much I heard, and also that the great ceremony would begin at He Is Halfway Home today. The Prince had ordered it speeded up, and even now his guard was calling people to complete the digging and mounding in the grave hill, so that all would be in readiness. The stewards would organize the funeral parade, the priests would perform the sacrificial rites, the funeral lords would bury the Female Sun. Then all in the city would feast and celebrate the coronation of the Prince for two days.

The conch shell was wailing and hoo-ah-ing at the wooden sun-watching circle. The first of the ceremonies would be held there, and they were practicing marching in carrying standards, the procession of noble families, such as that of Fire-on-the-Plains—but where was the prisosner anyway? And where were my two darlings?

I walked to the far edge of the hilltop, to three outbuildings. Could they be in here? I opened back entrances discreetly, poking my swathed head in as if in great search for the chamber pots. Yes! There in the darkness was somebody, and at his or her feet somebody else. I picked up the pot and my eyes grew accustomed to the darkness. It was the Lord Fire-on-the-Plains, with a guard, sitting beside him with a spear. So much for that.

So, perhaps, next door. The one thing I dare not risk was letting Walks-Up-the-Steps see me, indeed, know I was there. She was a noblewoman of Cahokia and much as she liked me, when I had left, she was in full accord with the sun rites which would prescribe that her little adopted daughter must go as handmaid to the fallen Female Sun. Even though she was going too, and I did not know what her feelings were now, she could not keep a secret. She would uncover us all and doom the small hope I had of somehow getting them out of here alive.

And what was the plan to realize that hope? At that moment nothing more than a few ideas and a great deal of bravado. And, of course, the wisdom of the Maya. I could not forget that, shrewdest of warriors and plotters on all of Turtle's Island, at least as far as I had seen. The Mexicas, they said, were worse but then I had not seen them.

Still, I must satisfy myself that the two I loved were here at the top of the hill, safe and well until the midpoint of the day. Then— I poked around at the back of the other two houses on the edge of the hill. Inside I could hear a voice, a little voice, the voice of a child!

"But Mama, when are they coming to fit the new dress? And bring the candy? You said they would be here a long time before He Is Halfway Home."

My cousin. And she could speak in sentences now, so beautifully. Oh, no, they were not going to kill such precocious cleverness. Not while I walked the earth.

There were murmured answers, as Walks-Up-the-Steps described the final fitting and sewing of the fine garments that would take place soon.

"No! No! I want the candy now. I want the pretty necklace. Make them come or I will hit you." Then there was a kind of grunting and tiny slaps and mild reproaches.

Well, if I had any doubts before that it was White Wings, now I knew for sure.

And Loon Feather? Puttering around by the back door, I raised my eyes to see her coming in from the path, a serving woman following close behind her. She was coming my way! Luck of the gods! Could I speak to her without blowing the chances for our lives away like cottonwood seeds to the winds? Would she be startled enough to cry out if I did speak?

Suddenly the form of the mean old man of the Dune Devils flashed into my thought. Bright-Coals-in-the-River and his kin did not cry out. They were made of stone harder than any I had seen in Mayaland.

"Pardon me, oh Noble Miss," I said. "Do you know if the pots have been emptied in here?" She was three feet from me, looking up with a little irritation that such a question should be asked. The serving woman was lingering, looking at a plot of morning glories that were being cultivated to colorful splendor, to adorn the bodies of those going to meet the Glory of the Morning, the Sun.

"I say, do you know—" I stepped up to her and dropped the bandages so she could see my eyes, my mouth. Her mouth dropped open, but she did not cry out. Thanks to the Maker of Stars!

"I must speak fast," I said very rapidly. "I am working to free you and White Wings. Under no circumstances should anyone know, not even Walks-Up-the-Steps. She will betray me. Await events and I will come to you soon to take you to freedom."

I turned to scamper away, but not before her mouth formed the words, "I love you."

I could hardly contain myself. She was even more beautiful than ever, and so strong! So strong as not to cause an outcry even after giving up hope of seeing me this long year! I had forgotten her, turned from her in my thought and now I remembered. I must, I would find a way.

But now I must take these pots and leave, because the real emptiers would be—ah, there they were. I was a bit late. If they should they see me, raise questions.

It was too late. A man just under my height had come to me, walking authoritatively.

"And so you do my job? I do not know you, shit-eater," he said in the blunt way these people had of speaking to each other.

"Still, I am your kin. My height and eyes show me so," I said. "And I am your friend."

"Am I to believe so?" the man said. He was a person perhaps ten summers older than I, but his eyes had a keen, intelligent look behind the rag scarf he wore.

"Do you like what you do for these noblemen?" I asked.

"It is not our portion to ask whether I like, or do not like— what I do. I am a slave."

"And did you walk free once? Free as the Birds of Thunder? Know the wind and hunt for yourself seeNanaboozhoo in the sky shine for you alone? Where was your home?"

"Fool that you are I will tell you as we walk a little here," he said, helping me set my pots down. "I lived in a land of great joy by a small lake two hours north of a lake called Lake-of-the-Boulders."

"Lake of Bass," I said. "Shallow, warm and pleasant place. I have been to it to fish myself, for I am from Lake-of-the-Boulders."

He took down his rag scarf a bit and looked at me. "Then kin we may be. But that is all gone now; we are all slaves. It is the will of the spirits."

"I do not think so. The powers of the heavens made man to be free, and our good race most of all, I think."

"Odd thoughts, those. You have come in late to our slavery, but I think you will not last long in it. "

"What is your name?"

"My vision quest name, given so long ago when I walked free, was Wolf Ribs." A brief silence, then, "I have a wife and two children living in squalor in a miserable hut by the river. And you?"

"I have come but lately, but I will not forget you. Do not forget the woods. Or the man you are." Then I turned on my heel and walked to the edge of the hill, conscious of his eyes following me with deep curiosity. I did not think he would betray me.

Two hours. One, two. That was all I thought I had before the ceremonies would begin. Quickly, still dressed in the garb of the waste-collectors, I went to the house of Walks-Up-the-Steps. It was unusual, but not unheard of, to see a slave of such low status near the houses of the well-to-do, but I could not risk the discovery of my real identity—yet.

In the outbuilding behind the house, there, there it was. My drum. I took it and the sticks to the hill and, going as quickly as possible, carried it up the steps to the first terrace and hid it by a rock. There was so much bustle, now, as the processional was beginning to assemble, as the corpse of the Female Sun, swathed in burial wrap, was being taken reverently by litter to the high temple, as the participants in the ceremony were being assembled, that nobody noticed me or cared.

But I had a contact to make while I was still on the hill. Earlier I had not been able to find the steward, the old one who had surprised me by wearing the eye amulet before I left. I believed he would be in only one place—the palace. He would not, could not involve himself in these ceremonies knowing what he did and being who he was. He would be at the royal home.

And, sure enough, the domicile was empty of all but the serving maids and others being readied to go within the hour to the grand processional to death, soon to begin in front of the temple. The prince and others of his loyal nobility, I had heard as I circulated, were even at this very moment sending a group of soldiers off to re-take the rebellious city up the Beautiful river, the City of the Island. But how many more were there? All in my plan depended on knowing the size and location of the troops.

The steward stood in the food preparation house at the back of the royal residence. He was doing what I had done in the land of the Mayan, I recognized it now, totaling the stores, seeing how much corn there was in the hominy pots, how much in the vats, how many of the first squash were heaped in their gathering baskets, and so forth.

"The great eye sees much today that he will not forget," I said, coming up behind him.

Quickly he turned; I pulled down my face scarf so he could see my slightly mocking smile.

"You! I thought you had been swallowed by the great ocean."

"He burped me up again," I said. "And I am returned to a city in mourning."

"Yes, but not for the dead queen. For the loss of justice in the face of the gods."

"So I see." We looked at each other for a moment, unsure where this discussion was going.

"Have you brought the prince his prizes? The dying queen raved and my ears caught the details," the older man said.

"I have brought nothing, except perhaps," my voice was so low he had to lean towards me to hear it, "the opportunity to throw off the hempen chains that bind."

There. I had said it. Bird of Thunder, truth is out.

439

"And what—how will you do that? It is as impossible as to slow the sun in his march across the sky or to stop your loved ones from joining the Lord today."

"What does the word impossible mean? I have been to many lands in this year, and I have seen many things happen to some, that others would consider impossible. For instance, some places I have been, men choose who they wish to rule. And if the ruler is bad, I have seen them throw down the evil ruler."

The steward stared at me hard. "That is an idea which is—impossible. The ruler here is put in place by the Sun Lord himself."

"And yet in those places people began to say that a god would not wish to leave in place a man of great evil. So they came to feel they had been lied to."

"Can such a thing be?" the steward murmured. "And yet I have wondered. If it were so, and we had only been told by priests and rulers—such an idea, turned loose could—"

"Yes. But I do not have time for meditation and quandaries about the gods' ultimate purposes. I need information and at once. Then I will let my idea loose, and we shall see. How many troops are in the city?"

"Perhaps two hundred of the royal guard. All the rest are—"

"I know. And where are the troops?"

"Here, at the garrison beyond the sun circle. Some are preparing to participate in the entombment ceremony. Already they will be marching from the garrison. The prince is at this moment sending off the last of the regulars along the trail to the east."

"I know, and I will act." I raised my amulet from my neck, flashed it in the morning light, and nodded to him. Then I went down the back steps.

I raced out the stockade and along the back paths through the villages. I dare not take off the rags, and yet the folk were all curious, as they thronged the streets to come to the burial ceremony, why a disposer of waste from the palace should be hurrying with such precipitate speed in the wrong direction.

440

It was clear that Hawk Eye would not be heading inside the sacred precincts. He would be where he always was–in the river-potters' village, treating this as any other day. Except that he would have contacted the rest of the inner circle of Those Who Say The Things That Are Not Said, and they would be close, perhaps in the woods nearby. This was a time of apprehension and disgust for them. The Prince, detested by them all, would soon be officially in place for a rule of malign repression.

I found Hawk Eye, as I knew I would, spoke with him in the house for perhaps ten of the precious remaining minutes, and sent him off into the woods. "I taught you to hunt," I said. "Now find your fellow hunters and let us go to rattle the deer." He and whoever of the others who were willing to risk all to stalk the most dangerous game would follow me immediately back inside the sacred precincts of the city of Cahokia.

"And what of betrayal?" he said, as he left the house.

"The time is short, and there will be little time for betrayal. Still, there is risk of it with so many knowing. We must bear the risk. There is no other course."

By the time I returned, the sound of drums and flutes had begun. Huge crowds of townspeople, thousands, I thought, had gathered at the foot of Temple Hill. I wandered among them, provoking their curiosity, looking for a moment, listening to their voices. They were grumbling, hostile, watching the ceremonial group assembling on the top of the first terrace, pointing at the bier which carried the dead queen under its richly embroidered shroud and its four blue-clad royal bearers, the Sun Priests with their sunburst headdresses and their long, golden robes, followed by the lower priests with masks of deers, cats, snakes, dragons. And around them, lounging now but soon to get in line, the royal guard with their armor of leather, their leathern boots, their spears.

And then—I began to go up the back steps to the terrace—the chosen sacrifice victims. My heart wanted to freeze as I looked there: in beautiful garments, silent and stone-faced stood Walks-Up-the-Steps; beside her and holding her hand, fascinated by the

441

display and silent for once, my own White Wings, and at the far edge, staying as far from the scene as she dared, my own love, Loon Feather, with the river-clay potters' herb woman by her side. Other maids, some trying not to weep, eight young men, oiled and tattooed and wearing golden-painted loincloths. All were being placed in line by—the steward. Music had begun in front of the temple above; they were waiting for something—surely the prince, coming from his emergency troop dispatching.

This I could see before I started for the back steps, as I all but raced up them and reached the top. I headed for the captive hut where Fire-on-the-Plains was being kept. Was he still there or had he been taken away? No, he was still alone. But two of the guards were climbing the front steps—was it to get the most important sacrifice of all?

I must hurry. I spoke through a back window opening in the small hut. "Nobleman. We must hurry. I am Drum-of-the-Gods returned to help you escape death." He turned his head, looking at my face in disbelief.

"The people of Cahokia need you. It is time to act to free the city from this despicable royal house. There are many involved. Will you join and agree to rule if we succeed?"

I had never seen him at a loss for words, but now his mouth flew open. "What will you do?"

"While I was in the lands of the south I discovered the greatest weapon of all against the cause of tyranny and enslavement." His eyes were a question. "It is the people. They have the right to do as they wish. They are upset enough to change, if someone gives them the idea."

"And you are the someone?"

"I. And a group called—"

He interrupted me. "Those Who Say The Things That Are Not Said." I have had knowledge of it, and contacts in it, these past two moons. But how will you—"

"No time to tell you. The risks are great. But we will die anyway, and now is the moment, ripe as a pumpkin in the fall."

"Now or never, I suppose. As you say, we can only die anyway. What shall I do?"

"Be ready for events, then seize them. I see your guard almost at the door."

I doubled over and slipped down the hill. There would only be a few more moments, then the prince would arrive to take his place at the beginning of the processional. Now was the moment. Bird of Thunder and all you Whoevers, I need you now. Now.

I got my drum from the space under the small juniper. Beside it lay the robe of a Cahokia nobleman I had found in my former house. I stripped off my rags, put it on in an instant. There, behind me, I could see filtering among the crowd, like water through moss, the members of Those Who Say The Things That Are Not Said. There was Hawk Eye, there even Winter Bird, whom I had not known was in the group. Earlier in the crowd I had caught the eye of No Corn, his mother. I had thought she might know, sense who was under the rag disguise.

People were beginning to look at me, at the drum, instead of up the hill. Thank you, Powers, for keeping the prince for these last, long-stretched moments. The funeral line on the terrace above us was well formed. My eyes searched it for the ones I cared for—Walks-Up-the-Steps, White Wings, now growing restless and pulling on her foster mother's hand, Fire-on-the-Plains, looking down towards us on the lower terraces, the royal guard, now in ranks. And Loon Feather, looking down also. I turned full face to her, and I knew she saw me. I knew it.

There was a fruit seller's stand nearby. I jumped onto it and began to play my drum. First I began by chanting of the sun, of his glory, of his brightness. That was easy. People began to gather around, eager for diversion until the festivities began. "I will sing a song to honor the departed Female Sun," I said, then began to beat and chant. In my short chant I called forth appreciation for the Female Sun's qualities of motherliness and beauty. That was not hard to do.

Many, many were listening now, indeed they had stopped talking and chatting. I looked at their faces. Some women and children, relatives of the forced sacrifice victims, were crying, trying not to show it. Men, many of them thin and gaunt and old. All the young men were gone to the conquests.

I stopped the drumming. "People, do you know me? I am Drum-of-the-Gods, the foreign nobleman. I went to the lands of the South, where I tried to find a cure for the Female Sun." Some nodded in affirmation; they had heard the story. Others remembered me vaguely or not at all, but still gave attention.

"When I was there, in the lands of the south, in the realm of the Maya and the Mexica, I learned that there is good and bad rule. I know you know of that."

The people's eyes filled with apprehension, their eyes grew evasive. I was speaking the Things That Are Not Said.

"In those lands, the Sun himself shines all the time and is an even greater Lord than he is here. I went into his temples, on hills twice as tall as this, overlooking the great sea. In his greatest temple I came to learn that he does not like bad rulers."

Now there was silence. I had better be good. This was it. "He told me that the priests here have lied to us. They told us that the Sun Lord put these people on the throne of Cahokia for always, better or worse. But the Sun Lord in his greatest temple cannot want bad. He is good. He did not put these people on the throne. They took it themselves."

Now there was real murmuring, filled with great fear. Above, the officials began to realize something was going on. The high priest peered down, then gestured for two of the lower priests to come down the steps. They did not even bother to go down sideways.

My words came rushing out. "How many of you have had sons sent to die for the conquests of Cahokia?" There was a murmured affirmation, slow at first, then growing.

"How many of you have had daughters violated by the lust of this house? I should know. I was a part of it, until I prayed for purification and paid my penance." More murmurs, growing like the murmur of the sea.

"And now we are told the prince has foul part disease and will spread it through all of our households as he picks and chooses those he demands to lie with.

"Now is the time, oh people, to choose. By corruption and poor management the corn supply fails. Your tribute is so much this month that your old ones beg for gruel and go hungry. There will be more wars, more waste, more deaths from treason if there is opposition. This cannot be the gods' will. Our own hearts tell us this. It is time to act, and I am giving you a choice. We may bury this queen and at that moment crown the new Sun. Or we may ask another. It is in our power. We support the throne as the foot supports the head."

The two priests were heading rapidly towards me. Now, behind them, scrambled five of the royal guardsmen. Now. Now, Hawk Eye if you are there.

On the hill, conch shells blew. The prince was approaching, finally. But as I stood firm on my table, as all music stopped, the two priests approaching me stopped, clutched their hearts, dropped.

Then the soldiers raising spears to send me out of this world dropped the spears, standing stock still, their faces frozen, then tumbling into the crowds. Other soldiers came down the hill, followed by the prince, the soldiers, one by one were picked off and toppled.

The people gasped in awe. What—what could be the power which was stopping the army in its tracks? "Cub, back there in Tikal, do you know what gift you gave me?" my thought flashed. "The serpent does, indeed sting, but for me he has helped! Thank you, thank you, for twenty-four blowpipes carried north and enough venom to kill the snakes who live here."

Then the crowd began to surge forward. Most, cheering, welcoming the dispatch of the hated soldiers, some fearing the prince's wrath as he, with the last ten soldiers in back of him advanced on us,

Some people, supporting loyal noble houses or just angry at the stoppage of the sacrifices (brutal natures that they were) demanded that I be seized or die—all was confusion, and I did not see how it would end.

The secret group of the Seeing Eye, Those Who Say The Things That Are Not Said, were being surrounded too by the surging mob and could not aim the blowpipes—soon I would be seized.

445

But no, the crowd pulls back, points upward, past people spilling down the sacred front steps, past the breaking up of the royal procession to—smoke! Smoke, then flames, coming from the royal residence. And there—there on the hill, at the top, triumphantly holding a torch with none to stay her, was my love, my Loon Feather, child of the fierce Dune People, who had shouted defiance at Cahokia and its corruption long ago in their woodland shelters. Loon Feather! She had fired the palace! And I had thought her weak. Our opponents fell back; the people stood gaping, then silence fell.

But that did not stop the prince from reaching me. He stood, with two of the remaining guardsman at the foot of my table and shook it until I lost my balance, and my drum and sticks and I fell into his hands. He was shorter than I but consumed with absolute rage, and he had two soldiers to help him dispatch me.

"You lowest of all scum, you will—disrupt—the royal funeral—" He was strangling me, and the power of his hatred was great. And who was this, who beside him? It was Winter Bird, helping hold me.

"Sire, I told you we know this man. He is opposed to the rule and all our old traditions," he panted, trying to hold my arms. Curse him! I had thought him my friend.

But at that moment, also, several members of Those Who Say The Things That Are Not Said reached us and began pulling on the soldiers, scuffling with them, fighting with knives, and a blood battle was underway, with the people all the while milling about, screaming, pushing and so forth. Somewhere, near my feet Winter Bird was down on the ground, severely wounded. So be it.

And I was left with the prince. Exhausted from all the events, I looked into his puffy face. His eyes were slits, and his breath was terrible. He couldn't even fight; he put up his fists and pounded like a girl. Suddenly I felt exhilarated. This was a bad man. I was telling truth, as I'd thought.

Since I was three inches taller than he and a good deal stronger, I pulled him up onto the table of logs. The people stopped milling a moment, noticing something new was going to happen. "This is your prince," I shouted. I picked him up by his ceremonial shirt, leaving his legs dangling, running little races in the air. The people stopped talking and shouting and listened to me. "Look at these cheeks, bloated from too much evil indulgence. Look at these eyes, ready to send your sons off to conquer innocent people for his own house's enrichment. Does this man represent you at your best? Will he care about whether you live or die?"

Shouts came out, for the first time. "No, no, he does not care." "The prince is evil."

"Do you think the soldiers will support him? Not unless he kills a few as examples. Ask your sons and brothers! Do you want to pay your corn and meat to support this bloated pleasure-seeker?" There were more shouts.

Then, there was Hawk Eye beside me, clambering up on the table. I still held the prince, binding his arms now behind him.

"People of Cahokia," Hawk Eye said. "We have earned the right, with our sweat and blood and courage in battle to live in peace and plenty. You all know I quit the army because we slaughtered the innocent for evil gain, breaking the commands of the ancient laws of all our people and the Bird of Thunder that our grandfathers revered. We should be making friends with trade and alliances, not always fighting to the death to bring the necks of our own kind under our feet."

Then the prince began to try to speak to the people. His voice came out squeaky as a mouse's. I looked at him, then I punched him in the nose and blood came out a nostril. The people were almost silent, watching us. Then, I began to laugh. I could not help it. What a duck pizzle he was!

I laughed and laughed some more. "Son of the Sun," I said. "The Sun would have to be a duck pizzle indeed to have such a son," I roared. The people began to laugh, too, and hooted, and yelled, and finally coming through the crowd, parting it, I saw Fire-on-the-Plains.

"There will be no sacrifices today," I said, looking firmly at him. He raised his hand and nodded in solemn affirmation. Then he turned towards the crowd and began to speak and truly I cannot remember what he said, except that it was about proper and just rule and his own house's interests. I dropped the prince and some members of the amulet society came forward and took him away, a prisoner, along with the rest of the soldiers. I could no longer worry about this; my heart was yearning to be with the sacrifice victims. I leapt towards the stairs, the assembled people parting as I went.

There on the second terrace was Walks-Up-the-Steps, still holding the hand of White Wings. "Drum-of-the-Gods!" my little cousin shouted. Walks-Up-the-Steps seemed in a daze, not knowing which way to turn. The Female Sun was dead, the prince was in captivity. The base of the house of her security was crumbling, as a flood takes off foundation stones and hearth and all, leaving only a few posts behind.

"There will be no sacrifices at the sacred funeral. The Sun Lord does not wish sacrifices today." Or ever, at least as far as I was concerned. A slow smile began to break on her face. Life is, after all, better than death, even for religious martyrs.

White Wings came to my arms, and hugged me hard, kissing my cheeks. She did remember! For a moment anyway. Then she began kicking my stomach. "When is the parade beginning? I want the parade to begin! Have you spoiled the procession? Where is my toy?" Well, some things never change.

The huge palace was now a charred and smoldering ruin. Beside it, cool and collected, stood my Loon Feather. I came to her, went to her arms. I took the time to kiss her, a long time there, to feel her sweet cool lips that promised much for the future. "I would have fired the temple, too," she said, finally, "but I did not think the people were ready for that. Yet."

There was a gigantic shout of affirmation down below us, and we looked down at the crowd of people. There, on the table, was Fire-on-the-Plains and beside him, the high priest, giving him the mace of power.

And I stopped, and stared into the sky, where my old enemy had hid his face beneath a cloud. I gestured at him and nodded and smiled to myself. "Long live the Sun," I shouted, descending the front steps from that first terrace, head-on like a true man of the woods ought to, my loved one close behind. "May his rays bless his people and his house enjoy the fruits of peace and plenty. And may the free people of the great town all tear down the house of nuns, and bring back the soldiers to farm the lands in new ways. May they develop trade, yes, as far as the fabulous lands of the South and worship the true Grand Father of the Universe, Father of the Stars, by whatever name he is called with all their children around them. And free the tall slop bearers to go back to Lakes-Like-a-Necklace and repopulate it so all, all can live in peace, even for generations to come."

And then I turned around and said, only for the ears of my beloved one,

"If only they can."

Epilogue

And, having gained so much, I finally gave it up. Fire-on-the-Plains asked me to stay and celebrate my marriage and live with my cousin as an honored nobleman of Cahokia forever, but I did not do it.

Celebrate my marriage I did, with Hawk Eye and All Joy and our other friends looking on, to the daughter of the people of the far-away Falls of Great Magic which had moved my uncle so long ago. But I did not, could not stay at Cahokia. My heart was sundered from the life of the city and had been ever since a time in a sweltering glen in the rainforest of the Mayalands, when I had yearned for the pure life of the woodlands and pledged myself to them if ever I should return.

Still, I could not go back to Lakes-Like-a-Necklace. My tall friends of the woodlands, who had been the slop slaves in Cahokia, were freed to return to the woods, and some did. But for me too much had been lost there, and the ghosts of the past would mourn round the scattered campfires for a whole generation before those beautiful lands would be cleansed. Sometimes you cannot go back, for in a certain spot the reality of the past looms large and brings pain, and will not let you live the life of the present there.

And, as I have always said, I was above all else curious. And so I would go on, away, to a new adventure, rather than search the embers of past cooking fires to blow them back to life.

Somewhere, somewhere across the Father of Waters was a whole new land, the West, with unknown hills and plains and woods that few saw. The cities did not stand in the Northwest, but animals roamed, fish jumped in rivers and the wind blew free.

More, my people were out there, challenging the spirits of the unknown wilderness, living as free as the wind. The tall, broad-faced people who had come into the valley of the Ohio and built the Serpent Mound, some of them, my kin and clansmen of the time of my great-grandfather, had gone west with the Blue Eyes.

I did not know where they were, but I had travelled far, learned many tongues, grown skilled in travelling, conquered both fear and the stars. We, Loon Feather and I, could go and we would find the people with the blue eyes. For what I had seen in the skull that last night, just before the vision faded and as I looked over the shoulder of the young son of the guard in Caintuck, had made me know destiny.

The white-skinned woman I had seen earlier at the battle looked out at me for one instant, and her eyes met mine. She had two hands in the air, bent at the elbows and the first fingers raised. Slowly she brought the two hands together till the fingers touched, then she disappeared.

Change, great change was coming, just as Uncle had said, just as the Old Dream-Singer at the Serpent Mound had prophesied. We had seen the great sign, the Snake Snout as large as a wall, and now Winter Bird and others were dead because they could not live the destiny that the signs of change meant. We must all change or we will die. Change, and it is really growth, is at the heart of the meaning of the stars.

More Blue Eyes would come, led by Kukulcan or not, to these shores, and there would be trouble, that I had seen, terrible thunder sticks and killing and hatred. But that would pass, would have to pass, as winter passes into spring, and the two races, Blue Eyes and Black Eyes but all men, would, must learn to live together. The fingers had joined. It was destined. What a lot would have to happen before this came to pass! I would start now, go west, and join the group of blue and black eyes who were already living the prophecy.

Change is the law of the stars.

I told myself that as, sadly, I left my cousin behind in Cahokia. White Wings could not, should not come on such a momentous and magic journey. She had had enough change, and last (with me) of our clan that she was, she must stay here with her new mama. Perhaps some day her children, or grandchildren, would come out of the walled city with all of its pomp and pride and problems and return to the woods. Thus would the circle be fulfilled. Who knows? They might come again sometime to Lakes-Like-a-Necklace, even to Lake-of-the-Boulders, and build the campfires up on the scattered stones of the past. Things do go in circles, even as the stars do.

You know of our journey, that we wandered far across the branching river and asked, and escaped death not a few times, and finally did find the tribe of Madoc, the Mandan, my people and the Blue Eyes. And they accepted us and you my children and grandchildren were born, here, where two groups live, mixing customs of the far-away land east of the ocean and of the serpent builders, my ancestors. My dear mate of the soul lived in happiness with plenty of meat in the pot and many children to make her days blessed, until she went along the path of the stars.

But oddest of all, as if some old dull or ugly god like Chac or Yum Cimil was finally having revenge, when I drew my magic chart of the moon hidings for the Star Watcher of the tribe of these followers of Madoc, he said they had indeed lost the knowledge of the stars of the other place in the long journey they had made and yes, they were glad to see the scratchings on the tablet that I had memorized.

But, he said, that was of another sky, of one certain monument far, far away across the ocean. The sacred stone I left for my friend as greatest of all wisdom totems was worthless here in our skies.

And so my tale is over, as the campfire has burned low on this last night of my telling. We have held Old Man Winter back now these several days, and are one step closer to the end of the test Nanaboozhoo has set for us, so I have succeeded in my purpose.

And, I have liked this vast expanse here, where the lands themselves are seas such as I used to sail, where the buffalo gives us all we need, and the wind, the wind blows cool and free on my face. The stinks of the city, both those you see and those in the hearts of men, are far away.

Still, sometimes of a cold and lonely night, as I lie on my bed of warm furs, and wispy smoke filters upward from the dying campfire, my mind returns to Mayaland as if in a dream. I sniff the fragrant breezes fresh off the sea, hear the odd, bright birds. And I see before me my friend and the great towers glinting in the sun, the towers of the city. I do not think of Zama, or even Chichen Itza. No, I stand again on the hill above the city of Tikal the Great, with its lengths of shining streets and temples and buildings so bright they dazzle the eye. Sixty thousand souls lived there in joy and plenty once. Their only enemy finally, was themselves. And I tell myself the city did not have to die, and I murmur into the rising wind, "Someday, someday, perhaps we may do it right."